A Special Agent Dylan Kane Thriller

By J. Robert Kennedy

James Acton Thrillers

The Protocol

Brass Monkey

Broken Dove

The Templar's Relic

Flags of Sin

The Arab Fall

The Circle of Eight

The Venice Code

Pompeii's Ghosts

Amazon Burning

The Riddle

Blood Relics

Sins of the Titanic

Saint Peter's Soldiers

The Thirteenth Legion

Raging Sun

Wages of Sin

Wrath of the Gods

Special Agent Dylan Kane Thrillers

Rogue Operator

Containment Failure

Cold Warriors

Death to America

Black Widow

The Agenda

Delta Force Unleashed Thrillers

Payback

Infidels

The Lazarus Moment

Kill Chain

Forgotten

Detective Shakespeare Mysteries

Depraved Difference

Tick Tock

The Redeemer

Zander Varga, Vampire Detective

The Turned

THE AGENDA

A Special Agent Dylan Kane Thriller

J. ROBERT KENNEDY

ISBN-10: 1545563462

ISBN-13: 978-1545563465

First Edition

10 9 8 7 6 5 4 3 2 1

For Police Constable Keith Palmer of the Parliamentary and Diplomatic Protection command, who stood his ground, unarmed, and paid the ultimate price, as well as the other victims of March 22, 2017.

THE AGENDA

A Special Agent Dylan Kane Thriller

"We may get to the point where the only way of saving the world will be for industrial civilization to collapse."

Maurice Strong
September 1st, 1997

"It is hardly possible to maintain seriously that the evil done by science is not altogether outweighed by the good. For example, if ten million lives were lost in every war, the net effect of science would still have been to increase the average length of life."

G. H. Hardy
A Mathematician's Apology, 1940

PREFACE

The technologies described in this book are real, and the hacks described are technically possible, many having already occurred, a recent minor example the hacking of Dallas' emergency sirens. The perfect storm described in this novel has yet to occur, but the rapid collapse of urban society is a near certainty should it.

As of 2010, over 80% of Americans lived in urban centers. In these massive cities, there is nearly zero food production—all food and water are transported in. Should a nation's transportation system be compromised, and its fresh water systems threatened, those within the cities could find themselves thirsty and starving within days.

Leaving a simple, devastating question that demands to be answered by all law-abiding citizens.

When your child is starving, when your significant other runs out of their medication, and when your government appears powerless to stop those responsible, how long would it be before you took matters into your own hands, and acted to save your family?

Bronx, New York

Larissa Williams tightly gripped the package under her jacket, trying to look as inconspicuous as possible, a difficult task with so few people on the streets. Hundreds of thousands, perhaps millions, had already fled New York City in the aftermath of the attacks, yet millions still remained, huddled in their homes, terrified to go out. Under a dusk to dawn curfew, most voluntarily extended it to the daylight hours for their own protection.

The city was shut down.

Businesses were closed, transit was at a near standstill, and tens of thousands of cars were abandoned in the streets, paths cleared along major routes by the National Guard using bulldozers. During the first 48 hours, there had been rioting and looting, but the Guard now had orders to shoot looters on sight, returning a frightening calm to the city.

Her stomach rumbled.

As a nurse, she had been deemed essential personnel, so was first in line for rations if she showed up for work. Which she did. It was the right thing to do, but she didn't do it for the food. In fact, she had passed on the rations. She had plenty of food at home.

Or rather, she did.

Her apartment had been looted, all their food and water taken, and the babysitter murdered, leaving her three kids alone until she could reach them. It had been hours since she had received the desperate call from her young son, and had heard nothing since, not even from her brother who had promised to help.

And yet that wasn't what preoccupied her thoughts.

Before leaving the hospital, she had done something she felt horrible for doing, something she had never thought she *could* do.

She had become a thief. One of the very looters she had urged shot just yesterday.

All the food she had to feed her three kids was now gone, and they would be starving by tomorrow. She was racked with guilt, though felt justified, albeit only slightly. She was, after all, feeding children, not herself.

But what if she were caught?

Would the National Guard accept her reasoning? She doubted it. She'd probably be arrested, for she had taken food from the mouths of the sick and dying.

Yet she had no choice. Weren't the lives of her three young children worth as much as the patients this food had been earmarked for? And many of those people were certain to die. Didn't it make more sense to feed those who could live through this crisis?

The government kept promising relief, yet it never arrived. It could come tomorrow, or next month. Those responsible for the catastrophe promised it never would, and right now, she believed them more than Washington.

A glass bottle rolling on pavement had her head swiveling toward the alleyway she was passing.

"What you got there, lady?"

Her heart slammed as footfalls echoed.

She ran.

Part of her didn't want to look behind her, the prospect of seeing whoever was chasing her more terrifying than not knowing. She spotted a National Guard unit ahead at the next intersection, at least a dozen armed men that were there to protect her.

Yet she was a thief, breaking the law.

Would they shoot her for looting? And if they did, who would take care of her children? She glanced behind her, finding herself alone. One of the soldiers walked toward her, tapping his watch. "Five minutes, ma'am!"

"I-I'm almost home."

He nodded at her, returning to his post. She dared not get any closer, the bulge in her jacket too obvious.

She took a chance.

She dashed down an alleyway, a foolish venture, yet she had little choice. Somebody grumbled from between two dumpsters, yet she pressed on as fast as she could. She could see the street just ahead, her apartment building on the other side, when two men stepped in front of her, blocking her path.

"What's the hurry?"

She cried out, trying to push through, but it was useless. They grabbed her arms and the food she had managed to conceal for so long fell to the ground.

"Holy shit!" The two men scrambled for the loot, and she took advantage. She raced past them, bursting out onto the street, tears streaking her face as she rushed for the doors of her building, a siren wailing a warning of the impending curfew, and she left to wonder where the next meal for her children would come from.

Tonight, she had failed her family, her helpless children, and soon they'd be sick enough to join those in the hospitals, too weak to go on.

If they were still alive.

She unlocked the door to her apartment building, stepping inside and pulling it shut, feeling safer, though not safe. For in today's America, friends and neighbors were no more. No one could be trusted. The country was collapsing, and the government was powerless to stop it. She had stolen food from the dying, then had it stolen from her.

And tomorrow, God willing, she would do it all over.

For there was no one left to help her.

She was on her own.

Philadelphia, Pennsylvania
Three days earlier

CIA Special Agent Dylan Kane sprinted as hard as he could, a grin on his face, the hormones pulsing through his system giving him a natural high that only vigorous sex with a beautiful woman could provide.

Though that was frowned upon on the streets of Philadelphia.

He glanced over his shoulder to see the only woman he had ever loved keeping pace, less than ten feet behind him, taking advantage of the slight delays he encountered as he threaded his way through the crowds of pedestrians.

Lee Fang had changed his life in ways he could never have thought possible. He was madly in love with the former Chinese Special Forces soldier, the brave woman having chosen what was right over what was safe, forced to betray her country in order to save it. She now lived her life in exile in the United States, a grateful American government providing her with a pension and strict conditions that were driving her crazy.

She was a doer, a woman of action, with skills that would make most men envious, yet she was forbidden from using any of them, lest it attract attention. The Chinese had been quiet so far, no sabers rattled, insisting she be returned. And if she kept a low profile, along with a shut mouth, they'd probably leave it that way, though it meant never returning home, never holding down a fulfilling job, and lying to any friends she might make.

But with him, it was different.

He had been the one who had extracted her, who had saved her life, so she knew exactly who he was and what he did, and he her. It meant they could be completely open with each other, no secrets beyond operational.

They could be themselves.

Like right now.

Two highly competitive athletes, sprinting all-out in the streets of Philly, without, for a moment, a care in the world. His career as a spy, a member of the CIA's Special Activities Division of the Special Operations Group, had been one of quiet distinction, a solitary life with few friends, and a family left in the dark, his relationship with his father estranged because of it.

His cover story as an insurance investigator for Shaws of London had never sat well with his father, especially after blindsiding him with the announcement he had left the military, a profession for which his father had tremendous respect. It had been a betrayal, never forgiven, and a sore spot at almost every rare family gathering, no matter how desperately his mother tried to keep the peace.

But that lonely life had changed when he had met Fang, though not immediately. She was a job, a package to deliver. Yet he had felt sorry for her, understanding her isolation, and that had led to an unexpected friendship that had quickly blossomed into much more.

He loved her.

He had even told her so.

He had told plenty of women he loved them over the years, his marks sometimes needing to hear those words before they spilled their secrets or offered up their bodies for clandestinely taken compromising photos.

But this had been the first time he had actually meant it.

Yet he was tormented, tormented by a secret eating away at him, a secret he could never share without shattering the heart of the woman he loved.

Somebody dropped on the sidewalk ahead of them, a crowd quickly gathering. Kane eased up and pushed through the crowd, an Asian man gripping his chest.

"I think he's having a heart attack!"

Kane looked about. "Is there a doctor here?"

Two black SUVs skidded to a halt only feet away, Asian men—Chinese—pouring out.

Ahh, Christ!

He stepped back when the man on the ground suddenly grabbed him by the leg. Kane delivered several quick blows to the man's throat, leaving him choking for air when Fang cried out. He glanced over his shoulder to see two men hauling her toward the open door of one of the vehicles. Kane reached for his gun, finding none.

He had left it at Fang's apartment.

This was supposed to be a jog, one she took every day alone, one he took every day with her when visiting.

He frowned.

That's how they knew where we'd be.

Apparently, the Chinese had been searching for her the entire time, and now they had her.

Not if I can help it.

He spotted a shoulder holster on the decoy and yanked the weapon, rolling to his side then popping up on a knee. He squeezed off two quick rounds, dropping one of the men holding Fang, then fired two more, eliminating the other. Fang grabbed their weapons, blasting double-barreled at the targets to her right as Kane continued to fire at

8

those on her left. Six were down, another six remaining, when something hit him and every muscle in his body seized. He dropped to his knees, the sensation overwhelming, a sensation he had experienced in training and real life.

Somebody had tased him.

He collapsed to the ground, his entire body shaking, his muscles tensed to the point of exhaustion, and out of the corner of his eye, he saw the decoy holding the device with one hand, his heavily bruised throat with the other.

Fang cried out, rushing toward him when she too was tased from within one of the vehicles. She tumbled forward, smacking her head hard on the pavement. Kane tried to reach for her but couldn't, completely incapacitated by the 50,000 volts coursing through his body. The surviving attackers grabbed her and hauled her inside the lead vehicle, its tires chirping as it sped away, the other quickly following.

Kane felt hands on him as onlookers, cowering moments ago, rushed to his aid. "Get me up," he moaned, and he was hauled to his feet. He stumbled into the roadway, staring after the vehicles as he tried to regain control of his muscles. He heard the whine of a motorcycle engine behind him and turned, sticking out an arm and clotheslining the unfortunate rider. His shoulder almost dislocated as the Kawasaki careened out of control before falling on its side and skidding fifty feet.

"Sorry, buddy."

He stumbled over and picked up the bike, climbing on and restarting it. He glanced in his side mirror and saw the crowds that had helped him, now help the new "victim."

He'll live.

He gunned it, the front tire popping off the pavement for a few seconds as he tried to close the gap, when his eyes narrowed at the sight before him. He could see the SUVs in the distance, blasting through every intersection, the lights green the entire way ahead of them, and as they cleared, turning red.

This is way too well coordinated.

He pulled his phone from his armband and speed-dialed one of the few friends he had in the world, and the only person he could think of that might be able to help.

Leroux-White Residence, Fairfax Towers
Falls Church, Virginia

CIA Analyst Supervisor Chris Leroux moaned in ecstasy as he leaned back in the tub, hot water enveloping his body, bubbles up past his nose. But all of that had been forgotten as his girlfriend, CIA Agent Sherrie White, sitting at the opposite end of the tub, worked her magic with her toes. It was exquisitely dirty, and as his eyes rolled back, he gasped out a warning that only encouraged her further.

His phone rang.

"Oh, God, don't stop."

She didn't, though she did offer commentary. "That's Dylan's ringtone, isn't it? Tomorrow I'm bringing some equipment from the office to sweep this place. There's no way it's just a coincidence every time we get in this tub together, he calls."

"Oh, God, yes!"

"Is that a yes to sweeping the apartment, or something else?"

He sighed, his tension relieved, then gave her a look. "Yes to both." He reached for his phone and swiped a wet thumb across the screen. "Hello?"

"Hey buddy, it's me. I need your help."

Leroux recognized the urgency in his friend's voice and immediately began his one-handed struggle from the slippery tub, Sherrie becoming all business, her lithe, highly trained form leaping clear and offering a hand.

"Somebody just kidnapped Fang. I need eyes and I need them now."

"Just a sec." He put the call on speaker. "I'm at home with Sherrie. You're on speaker." He glanced at her as she quickly toweled his hands and arms dry, then her own. "Fang has been kidnapped. Call my team," he whispered, then raised his voice as he headed naked for the living room, a trail of bubble bath and water behind him. Sherrie dialed her phone as he logged into his laptop. "Where are you?"

"I'm in Philly. I've lost sight of them, but I think they're hacking the traffic signals. They were getting greens, and I kept getting reds." Kane's voice was strained, occasionally punctuated with the loud whine of what sounded like a motorcycle engine.

Sherrie stepped away slightly. "Hi Sonya, it's Agent Sherrie White. Hold for Chris." She sat beside him and pressed the phone to his ear.

"Sonya, it's me. Assemble the team. I need access to the traffic cameras in Philly. Lock on to Special Agent Kane's cellphone and look for a hack of the system, and—wait." He leaned toward his phone, sitting on the living room table beside his laptop. "Dylan, what are we looking for?"

"Two black SUVs, Ford Expeditions. I've got a plate on the second vehicle."

Sherrie held her phone close to Leroux's as Kane read off the plate, then pressed it back against his ear. "Sonya, did you get that?"

"Yes, sir. Just a second."

The voice of Randy Child, one of his young hot-shot analysts, jacked in. "Sir, it's Randy. I'm seeing your hack. Looks like they're just taking a straight shot east."

"Can you give him some help on the lights?"

"Just a sec."

Leroux heard keys tapping then Kane laughed. "Awesome. I've got greens!"

Child cut in. "He's got green lights, but I can't stop the hostiles. He might be able to catch up, though."

Leroux frowned. "You can't give them reds?"

"No, they're in the system deeper than I am, but they seem to be just setting and forgetting them once they're past. They're heading somewhere in a hurry, and they seem to just want to get there first."

Leroux exhaled loudly. "Any guesses?"

Tong replied. "They're heading for the Delaware by the looks of it."

Child cursed. "If they get there, they can put her on a boat, and we'll never find her."

Leroux exchanged a concerned look with Sherrie. "We need eyes in the sky."

Tong was way ahead of him. "Sir, I've got someone on a motorcycle, and two black SUVs on camera. Patching the feeds to you now."

Leroux watched his screen change to show a map with three pulsing dots. He smiled. "Dylan, you're gaining fast. You should be on them any second now."

"I see them."

"Sonya, send local PD and notify the local FBI office. He's going to need backup."

"Copy that, already on with local PD now. They're dispatching units."

Child cut in. "FBI has been notified."

"Good. Dylan, are you armed?"

"Affirmative."

Leroux pointed at Sherrie. "Get me the Director."

Sherrie grabbed the landline and quickly dialed. "This is Agent Sherrie White for Director Morrison. We've got an urgent situation.

Authentication code Niner-Alpha-Charlie-Echo-Four." She waited, her finger tapping her naked thigh, when Kane cursed.

"Make sure you keep those locals out of my way!"

Leroux saw the problem, local police cruisers now chasing Kane, two cutting in front of him from side streets. "Sonya, deal with it."

"Yes, sir."

Leroux watched Kane gun his motorcycle and thread it between the two cruisers.

"I've got the Director." Sherrie pressed the handset against Leroux's free ear.

"Sir, this is Leroux. I've got Dylan on the other line. Someone has just kidnapped Lee Fang, and he's in pursuit. I need clearance for him to take action."

"Where is he?"

"Philadelphia. He's in pursuit of two black SUVs, one with Lee aboard."

"Locals?"

"Also in pursuit, though at the moment they think Kane is a suspect."

"Let the locals handle it. We can't have an agent killing people on the streets of Philadelphia."

Leroux frowned. "Umm, sir…"

"Tell him that's an order, directly from me."

Leroux closed his eyes. "Umm, okay. Dylan, the Director says to stand down and let the locals handle it."

"You tell him to go fu—" There was a burst of static as the motorcycle engine overwhelmed Kane's voice. "—himself."

Morrison's voice rose slightly. "What did he say?"

Leroux wasn't sure what to do. He didn't agree with Morrison's order, yet the Director was right—technically. The problem was he was ignoring who Kane was. There was no way he'd stand down, not when Fang was involved. "I, umm, don't think he heard me, sir. He's on a motorcycle doing over sixty on city streets."

Sherrie pointed at the screen, the three dots almost converging.

"Sir, he's about to engage them. I need a go or no go."

Morrison cursed. "Tell him he's cleared to engage. Have him identify himself as a Homeland agent without his ID. I'll get the identity live by the time they run it."

Leroux grinned. "Thank you, sir!" He leaned toward his cellphone. "Dylan, you're cleared! You're now Homeland if asked."

"Copy that. Engaging now."

Philadelphia, Pennsylvania

Kane drew the liberated Type 92 5.8mm semi-automatic pistol from his belt and took aim, squeezing off two rounds into the front tire of the second vehicle. It swerved hard to the right, hitting the curb and flipping on its side before sliding into a gas station. He ducked as it erupted into a fireball, cringing as he silently prayed any civilians were able to get clear. A quick glance in his rearview mirror showed the road behind him cut off, the police in pursuit now blocked.

He was alone.

Which was the way he liked it.

He closed the gap on the remaining vehicle Fang had been hauled into. Somebody leaned out the passenger side window, a JS 9mm submachine gun belching lead at him. He leaned to the left, the bullets tearing at the asphalt, then fired two rounds into the rear tire, allowing the driver at least some control. The vehicle careened to a halt and Kane braked hard, coming up directly behind it, the vehicle itself providing him with cover. He leaned to the right, squeezing off a single round, nailing the passenger in the side of the head as he foolishly stepped out.

Kane surged forward, the passenger door now open, and put two in the driver. He stepped up and aimed into the rear, finding only Fang, bound and gagged. He leaned forward and snapped the zip ties with a jerk of the blade hidden in his keychain, then yanked the gag free.

"You okay?"

"Yes."

"Then let's get the hell out of here."

16

Fang hopped out the rear door and Kane stepped down, quickly surveying the area for new arrivals. Flashing lights were quickly approaching, the police having made it past the fireball roadblock.

He turned to Fang. "I'm with Homeland Security if anyone asks. Special Agent Dylan Kane. I don't have my ID, it's back at the apartment."

"What if they ask to see it?"

"It'll be there by the time we get back. Don't worry."

A chopper thundered overhead and he looked up, shielding his eyes from the sunlight behind the silhouette.

Police?

It finally came into focus, a black civilian chopper with a large dome mounted on the side, aimed directly at them. A crushing, earsplitting screeching sound erupted, overwhelming his senses. He squeezed his eyes shut, grabbing at his ears as the air sucked out of his lungs. Fang cried out beside him, dropping to the ground in agony. He raised the weapon to fire, but it meant uncovering an ear, the excruciating pain too much, forcing him to drop the gun and press as hard as he could against his ears as he collapsed to his knees.

The chopper landed, and between forced blinks, he saw several men with ear protection jump out. They grabbed Fang and hauled her inside, another man walking over to him and bending down. He shouted something at him, but between clenching shut his eyes and jamming his palms into his ears, he could hear nothing, and only lip-read the last word.

Eternal.

The man rose and climbed into the chopper. It lifted off, the incredible din finally subsiding as it banked away. Kane picked up the gun, but it was no use. They were gone. She was gone.

And he had failed.

Leroux-White Residence, Fairfax Towers
Falls Church, Virginia

"What the hell was that?" Chris Leroux stared at his laptop screen, watching as the helicopter took off, the camera feeds returning after momentarily experiencing major interference.

"I don't know," replied Sonya Tong.

"Where's that chopper heading?"

"East."

"Okay, track it. I'm coming in."

"Yes, sir."

Sherrie hung up the landline, the Director apparently ending the conversation. She disappeared into the bedroom.

"Dylan, can you hear me?" There was no reply, but he could see from the footage that Kane was alive. He finally responded.

"Hey, buddy. They got her." There was a burst of static. "The bastards got her. Please tell me you're tracking that chopper."

"We are. It's heading east. I'll have a destination for you shortly."

"Okay, I'll wait for your call."

"I'm heading to Langley now. Remember your cover."

"Yeah, looks like I'm about to use it. I'll call you back in a few."

Kane's voice was replaced by shouts as Leroux watched local police surround his friend, dozens of weapons pointed at him. The call went dead as Sherrie reemerged, clothed, carrying an armful for him.

"I'll come in with you, just in case there's something I can do."

Leroux nodded, turning his attention to the last call he was connected to. "Sonya, I'll be in shortly. Keep me posted if anything happens."

"Will do."

He ended the call then quickly toweled off before slipping on his underwear. He sat, awkwardly catching the pair of rolled up socks Sherrie tossed at him, batting them about several times before finally snagging them.

I'm definitely not a sports guy.

"It's gotta be the Chinese." Sherrie handed him a shirt. "They were after her, not him. He wasn't even a target, otherwise they would have shot him when they took her."

Leroux agreed. "They've clearly been looking for her since she defected, so it makes sense. They don't like loose ends, especially loose ends that know state secrets." He stepped into the bathroom, applied antiperspirant, then a spray of Yves Saint Laurent cologne.

Sherrie leaned in and inhaled deeply. "Mmm, love that stuff."

He eyed her in the mirror as he buttoned up his shirt. "Don't get any ideas."

She patted his package. "I know, I know. Business time."

Leroux pulled his pants on and stuffed his shirttails inside. "Belt?" Sherrie disappeared then returned a moment later with one as he zipped his pants. He quickly fed the belt through the loops as his phone rang. Sherrie put it on speaker for him.

"Sir, it's Sonya. We've got a destination on the chopper. It landed on the roof of Temple University Hospital."

Leroux's eyebrows rose as he buckled his belt. "Okay, send the locals to that address immediately, and make sure Kane knows."

"They're already on their way, sir, and I've texted the destination to Special Agent Kane's phone."

Leroux headed for the door to their apartment. "Good work. I'm about to leave. ETA twenty minutes." He stuffed his feet into his shoes, leaning over to pull them on, the laces still tied from last night.

Sherrie opened the door and gasped as two men stepped inside, one holding a gun, the other something in his hand. A spraying sound was followed by a fine mist, aimed at Sherrie's face. She collapsed without a sound, the spray turned on Leroux. He spun but felt himself fading, the world closing in around him as whatever he had inhaled took effect. Someone stepped beside him and a voice said something in his ear, though what it was, he had no clue.

He was already done.

Operations Center 2, CIA Headquarters
Langley, Virginia

Sonya Tong pressed her finger against her earpiece. "What did he say?"

Randy Child shook his head. "Something is eternal?" He leaned back in his chair. "What the hell does that mean?"

Tong stared at him, puzzled, then gasped. "Wait a minute! The *Assembly* is eternal! Holy shit! We need to tell the Director, now!" Tong pointed at Child. "Do it!" She reactivated her headset. "Sir, can you hear me? Sir!" No response. "Chris!" The desperation in her voice had probably just revealed to everyone in the room her true feelings for her boss. She was infatuated with him, yet it was never to be. His heart belonged to the beautiful, sexy, stylish, intelligent, exciting, Sherrie White.

And what was she?

Just a dorky mid-level analyst with no fashion sense, that had a hard time looking anyone in the eye, let alone making conversation. She would forever be a wallflower, while women like Sherrie would dominate the dating pool. She was definitely intensely jealous of her, though she'd never wish her any harm.

Did she want them to break up?

Every damned day.

But she'd never want their relationship to end like this, with her death. It would hurt her dear Chris too much, and she'd never want to see that. Though if she played her cards right, and were there to console him—she stopped the thought.

You're terrible!

She held up a finger, silencing the room as she heard footsteps then a door close, the call still open, but no one responding. She turned to Randy Child. "Get me footage of their lobby, now." Fingers flew and Leroux's lobby camera appeared on the main screen of the operations center. Four men exited the elevator, one pushing a large box on a dolly. "That has to be them. I need external cameras. And notify the locals about a possible assault and kidnapping."

Child shoved a thumb up in the air, covering his mouthpiece. "The Director just dispatched a team by chopper. Patching you in now. You're Control."

Tong caught her breath. She had never been Control before—that was Leroux's job. She was just an analyst, and she was compromised due to her emotional connection to the subject, yet she couldn't exactly tell the room that and cede operational control to someone even more junior than her.

She squared her shoulders and drew a deep breath, imagining what Leroux would do in this situation. She heard a burst of static.

"Control, this is Echo Leader. Status on the hostiles?"

Tong gulped, then snapped her fingers like she had seen Leroux do a hundred times before, pointing at the screen. Child brought up cameras showing the four men climbing into a vehicle after loading the crate in the back.

"Echo Leader, this is Control. Four hostiles in a black SUV, leaving Pimmit Drive, turning north onto Leesburg Pike. They loaded a large crate into the back that we believe contains either Analyst Supervisor Chris Leroux, or Agent Sherrie White, perhaps both, over." She stunned herself with her confident delivery, though her hands trembled.

"Copy that. ETA five minutes. Keep us posted of any changes, over."

"Roger that, Echo Leader, Control out." She tapped a key at her station, muting her end of the conversation, her heart racing with the excitement and pressure of being in charge as she dropped into her chair, about to close her eyes. The door to the operations center burst open and National Clandestine Service Chief Leif Morrison entered.

"Status!"

Tong leaped to her feet, stepping to the center of the room as Leroux would have. She pointed at the screen, traffic camera footage actively tracking the hostiles. "Director, sir, Rapid Reaction Force is en route via chopper. We believe four hostiles have taken either Leroux and-or White, and are headed…"—she glanced at Child—"Still northbound on Leesburg?" Child nodded as Morrison's eyes narrowed.

"Believe? You're not sure they've been taken?"

She shook her head. "They exited the apartment building with a crate large enough to hold at least one person, but we have no confirmation on whether or not anyone was actually taken."

"Their cellphones?"

Tong glanced at Child.

"Both are still showing at their apartment, and Leroux's is still connected to us."

Tong turned to Morrison, explaining. "I was on with him when the attack occurred. I heard someone say 'The Assembly is eternal.'"

Morrison froze then his eyes widened slightly. "You're sure someone said, 'The Assembly is eternal?'"

She glanced around the room, everyone nodding. "Yes, sir. That's the consensus."

Morrison tossed his head back and cursed. "We knew they'd eventually come back, but not like this. When we named a few during

24

that Titanic business, we thought that would be enough to warn them off. But to try and kidnap our people? That's ballsy!"

"But they didn't just target our people."

Morrison's eyes narrowed. "What do you mean?"

"I mean, they kidnapped Fang."

"Do we know that?"

Tong paused. "Umm, well, no, but I can't believe it's a coincidence. Two abductions, minutes apart?"

Morrison pursed his lips then nodded. "Agreed. Let's go under the assumption it wasn't the Chinese but the Assembly. You were saying?"

"They didn't just target our people. Fang's not one of us. It was as if they didn't care about Dylan at all."

Child spun in his chair, his head tilted back. "Not entirely accurate."

Tong tensed slightly at the cockiness of the youngest member of the team. "Excuse me?"

Child dropped a foot on the floor, halting his spin. "If they didn't care about him, they would have just killed him, but they didn't. I think we're looking at this all wrong."

Morrison eyed him. "Explain."

"They took Fang because she's important to Kane. I'm willing to bet they took Agent White because she's important to Leroux. Who are the biggest thorns in the side of the Assembly? Kane and Leroux."

Tong's eyes popped wide as she realized what Child was getting at. "They're leverage! They're going to use them as leverage over Kane and Chris!"

Morrison's head bobbed slowly as he folded his arms, a finger tapping his chin. "Makes sense and fits the facts, *if* Agent White was the one who was kidnapped. And if you're right—"

"Then they must be planning something big, and they don't want any interference from us meddling kids!" Child spun in his chair.

Morrison chuckled as Tong shook her head.

Kids!

"Scooby-Doo references aside, we need to know what happened at Chris'—I mean Mr. Leroux's—apartment." Tong turned to Child. "Have the locals arrived yet?"

"ETA less than five."

"And our Rapid Reaction Team?"

"About to overtake the vehicle."

Fairfax Blvd, Fairfax, Virginia

CIA Special Agent Brooklyn Tanner, officially on loan to Homeland Security so she and her team could operate legally on American soil, leaned out the side of the Bell 412EP helicopter, her FN P90 strapped to her chest, gripped loosely as she eyed the road ahead. The latest update was that the target SUV was still heading north with no deviation in course, and was obeying all traffic laws, likely trying to draw as little attention to themselves as possible.

Which was idiocy.

What made anyone think they could kidnap CIA personnel only miles from Langley, and not trigger a rapid, unforgiving response?

You don't mess with our agents. Especially on our soil.

The chopper roared up beside the SUV, about fifty feet overhead on the driver side.

"Signal them to stop!"

The pilot nodded, activating the loudspeaker. "Driver of the black SUV. Stop your vehicle immediately. I say again, stop your vehicle immediately!"

The SUV continued with traffic, though the traffic was thinning, those that had spotted the helicopter, backing off, leaving a wide gap behind the vehicle.

"Tell them we'll open fire."

"Driver of the black SUV. Stop your vehicle immediately, or we will open fire! I say again, stop your vehicle immediately, or we will open fire!"

Again nothing.

Tanner shrugged at her team. "Oh well, they were warned." She leaned out and took aim at the rear driver side tire and squeezed the trigger, pumping three rounds into the rubber. The vehicle swerved slightly then rapidly slowed to a stop. The chopper blew past, the pilot banking hard. She let herself drop out the side of the helicopter, her feet on the skid as the harness held her in place, her weapon trained on the windshield where the driver should be.

Where the driver *should* be.

"There's nobody driving! Get us down, now!"

The pilot complied, pulling up and dropping them fast and hard. One of her men unclipped her from the harness as they hit and she jumped out, sprinting to the side of the vehicle as her team followed, quickly surrounding the black SUV, the tinted windows giving no hint as to what they were facing. The vehicle's engine was turned off and its flashers were on, traffic on both sides of the boulevard slowing to a halt as the chopper's rotors continued to thump at the pavement.

"Lower your windows, now!"

Nothing.

"Lower your windows, or we will treat you as hostile and kill you!"

Again, nothing.

She motioned to two of her men and they surged forward as the others covered them. The first smacked a window breaker against the large rear window and it shattered, the second tossing a flash-bang inside. Tanner turned her head away slightly, her Sonic Defender earplugs protecting her from the overwhelming explosion, her sunglasses muting the flash.

And again, nothing.

She stepped forward and yanked on the driver's door. It was locked. She smashed the window with the butt of her weapon then stepped back as smoke billowed out, her P90 trained on what was an empty seat. The others did the same, smashing all the windows, the smoke from the grenade quickly dissipating, revealing an empty vehicle. She activated her comm.

"Control, Echo Leader. We've got an empty vehicle here. Did you see anyone leave when we stopped it, over?"

"Negative, Echo Leader. Nobody left the vehicle."

Tanner shook her head. "Then, Control, either they were never in this thing, or there's a ghost in the machine."

"Hey Brooklyn, check this out."

Tanner leaned into the vehicle, one of her men, Agent Michael Lyons, pointing at the navigation display, a warning message flashing.

Tire pressure reduced. Emergency override engaged.

"What the hell is that?"

She checked where Lyons was pointing, a device sitting on the dash with wires extending through the sunroof. She stepped out and looked at a small black dome sitting on the roof. "Umm, Control, we're going to need some techs out here. I think this thing has been customized so it can either drive itself, or be driven remotely."

"Copy that, Echo Leader. Is there any sign of our agents?"

Tanner leaned back inside, finding no crate or anything else to suggest it had ever been there. "Negative, Control. The vehicle is completely empty. Retrace the route and see where they got out, over."

"Retracing the route now, Echo Leader. Stand by."

Tanner headed for the chopper as local police vehicles began to arrive, her heavily armed team causing some hesitation in how to respond. She pointed at Lyons. "Go settle them down before they start shooting."

He grinned. "Yes, ma'am!" He jogged over, holding up his Homeland ID, weapons lowering, tensions eased.

She leaned into the chopper. "Let's get airborne just in case we get lucky."

Operations Center 2, CIA Headquarters
Langley, Virginia

Sonya Tong stood in the center of the room, the pressure of an operation gone bad weighing heavily on her shoulders, and now she realized the pressure her boss and fantasy, Chris Leroux, must feel every time he was in command. She didn't envy him, and understood why he had been reluctant to take on the role.

She glanced at Director Morrison, the man who had forced him into the job, still standing at her side, watching as the chopper powered back up. "I'm sorry, sir. I screwed up."

He continued to stare at the display. "Screw-ups happen. It's what you do next that matters."

She nodded, then turned to the team. "Okay, let's retrace the route. Look for any gaps. We need to see when they were out of our sight, then see if they took longer than they should have to get to the next point."

"You got it." Child hammered away at his keyboard, the screens rapidly following all the shots they had of the SUV, a simulated route running beside it, as the gaps in the cameras were too many for a complete picture. "Okay, here they went under this bridge. We don't have any footage of them, but when they do appear, they're about 40 seconds later than they should be."

Tong shot a smile at Morrison, who responded with a frown.

And he was right.

It meant she really had screwed up. She should have caught the discrepancy earlier, but hadn't, and now Chris and Agent White might be lost.

She activated her comm. "Echo Leader, Control. We've got a new location for you. Relaying coordinates now." She snapped her fingers and Child tapped at his keyboard then gave a thumbs up. "Confirm receipt, over."

"Confirmed, en route now. ETA two minutes."

Tong turned to the team. "They won't be there. Let's analyze all the footage of the vehicles in the area at the time the exchange must have happened. See if we can spot them. Look for vehicles that head under the bridge, but don't come out. This was well-planned and well-coordinated. They wouldn't sit around for too long because they wouldn't want to risk detection, so let's start about five minutes before the phone call from Chris."

Heads bobbed and the screen filled with time-segmented views of the two traffic cameras showing the bridge underpass, the analysts splitting up the work by timecode. She itched to return to her station to help, but that wasn't her job. She was Control. And it shouldn't take long to spot an anomaly, regardless, then hopefully they'd trace where the second vehicle had gone.

Child held up a hand, as if still in school. "Umm, Sonya, locals are entering Leroux's apartment now."

She sucked in a deep breath and closed her eyes, saying a silent prayer.

Please God, let him be okay!

Leroux-White Residence, Fairfax Towers
Falls Church, Virginia

"Hey, buddy, you okay?"

Chris Leroux groaned, then grunted when someone smacked his face, too firmly for his liking.

"You good?"

He opened his eyes, blinking them rapidly, then raised a hand to block the next friendly smack. "Yeah. What happened?"

"Not sure, you were out cold when we got here."

He pushed up on his elbows and moaned, his head throbbing. He grabbed his temples with one hand and massaged them as he closed his eyes. "What the hell was in that?"

"In what?"

"They sprayed me with something. They sprayed both of—" He sat up, spinning his head back and forth, searching for Sherrie, his head pounding in protest. "Where is she?"

"Who?"

"My girlfriend. They sprayed her, too!"

"There's no one else in the apartment." The cop stood and extended a hand. Leroux took it and he was hauled to his feet, the world spinning. He reached out for a wall, finding empty space instead. The cop grabbed him and held him steady. "Woah, buddy, let's get you onto that couch."

Leroux nodded, regretting the movement, and carefully made his way to the couch, helped by two officers. He sat, and someone brought him a bottle of water from his fridge.

33

"Drink this."

Leroux took the bottle and downed almost half of it, his mouth parched. "How long was I out?"

"We've been here about five minutes. Dispatch says they received the call five minutes before that, so I guess ten minutes?"

Leroux's eyes widened. "Shit! That's an eternity. We've gotta start tracking her. Any leads?"

The cop chuckled. "I think you've been watching too many cop shows. Why don't you leave the investigation to us?"

Leroux pushed to his feet. "I'm CIA." He looked about. "Where's my phone?"

Another cop held up a plastic bag. "Is this it?"

"Yeah. I need that."

"It's evidence."

"It's mine, not theirs."

"Are you sure? It was connected to a call when we got here. The woman refused to identify herself, only demanded to talk to Chris Leroux. Is that you?"

"Yes."

"Who's she?"

"One of my staff. I was talking to her when we were attacked."

The cop's eyes narrowed. "You've got staff at the CIA? Aren't you a little young?"

Leroux stepped forward, grabbing the plastic bag with his phone. "Apparently not." He pulled it out and redialed.

"Tong."

"Sonya, it's me. They took Sherrie!"

"Oh, thank God you're okay! I was so worried about you! When I didn't—"

34

"No time for that, Sonya. What's the status?"

"A Rapid Response Team took down the SUV that had Sherrie, but it was empty—driven by some sort of autonomous set-up. We've got a tech-team heading there. We found where they did the switch and are analyzing footage now."

"Do we know who's behind it?"

"You didn't hear what he said?"

"No, they sprayed us with something and I passed out." His eyes narrowed. "What did he say?"

"Just before I guess you passed out, we heard a voice say, 'The Assembly is eternal.'"

Leroux closed his eyes as his heart pounded. If the Assembly was back, and were indeed behind the kidnapping of Sherrie, and possibly the too coincidental kidnapping of Lee Fang, then they were up to something, and it had to be big. "What's the status on Lee Fang?"

"Still missing. They're converging on the last known location now."

"Okay, I'll be there in twenty." He turned to the officer who appeared in charge. "I have to get to Langley, now. Am I free to go?"

The cop shrugged. "You're the victim, so I guess so. I'll need to take a statement, though, otherwise this investigation is going nowhere, fast."

Leroux strode toward the door. "Trust me, with the people they pissed off today, they're not getting away with this."

"Who's they?"

Leroux chuckled. "If I told you, I'd have to have you killed."

Temple University Hospital
Philadelphia, Pennsylvania

Dylan Kane jumped out of the police vehicle the moment it stopped, though with no badge to flash, he had to wait for his escort, who seemed far less committed to the urgency of the matter. Kane finally strode toward the command center set up in the parking structure across from the main entrance of the hospital, a heavy police presence in evidence surrounding the building. "Who's in charge here?"

A grizzled but vibrant fifty-something officer, pouring over a map laid out on a table, stood straight. "I am. Chief Inspector Scott Meinke. Who the hell are you?"

"Special Agent Kane, Homeland. That's my partner that was kidnapped. What's your status?"

Meinke glanced at Kane's assigned escort, who gave him a slight nod. "We've got the entire building surrounded as of five minutes ago, but the chopper landed ten minutes before we could secure all the exits."

Kane frowned, the update as he had feared.

She's long gone.

"Perimeter?"

Meinke shook his head. "I can't authorize that. This is Philadelphia, not Poughkeepsie. The perimeter I'd have to set up is just too big. If they're not in the building, then they're already gone."

Kane drew a deep breath, biting his tongue. The man was right. If they had made it out, which he had no doubt they had, then they would be nowhere near here. "Okay, we'll need to review footage. See if there's anything—"

"We know how to do our job, Special Agent. If we need Homeland's help, we'll let you know."

Kane spun on his heel before he crushed the man's larynx. Meinke was right. This was his city, and these were trained professionals.

And he didn't need them, regardless.

He had no doubt Langley was already reviewing the footage, though their attention would be split if the update he had received before arriving were true.

Sherrie White had been kidnapped, his only friend besides Fang in the world had been assaulted, and the Assembly was back.

The thunder of chopper blades pounded the area as a black, unmarked helicopter landed nearby, two men in dark suits and sunglasses hopping out. He gave them a wave and nods were returned. He turned to his escort. "That's my ride. Thanks for the lift."

The officer stared at the chopper. "You're not Homeland, are you?"

Kane grinned. "You don't want me to answer that."

Around him, all of the police radios squawked. "Code Thirteen-Delta, repeat, Code Thirteen-Delta."

Kane paused, the reaction from the police on the scene immediate. Concern.

He turned to his escort. "What's Thirteen-Delta?"

"It means the entire 9-1-1 system just went down."

9-1-1 Emergency Call Center
Brooklyn, New York

Christine Toohey stood near the back of the 9-1-1 emergency call center, watching for any problems, signaled by the displays arcing around the front of the technology-laden room, or the low-tech raising of a hand. It was a typical, busy night, and she wouldn't have it any other way.

She loved her work.

Despite over 25 years on the job, she was still excited about coming in each day, and couldn't see herself ever tiring of it.

She loved helping people.

And that's what they did here. They helped people. People having perhaps the worst moment of their lives, victims of a crime, a horrible accident, or a medical emergency for a loved one. Each one was unique in that it was some new individual, who had probably never before called, and who had probably never before experienced what they were now going through.

It demanded compassion and patience, and every one of her people were saints as far as she was concerned, especially with some of the abuse they had to put up with.

You don't call 9-1-1 because McDonald's shorted you a McNugget, or your boyfriend cheated on you.

A chart showing incoming call trends abruptly spiked, the green line turning yellow then red. Every station's call status indicator went red, indicating all of her people were on calls.

Oh no!

Some disaster had to have just struck the city she loved. There could be no other explanation. The call origin map showed the spike spread across the city, which could only mean one thing.

Another 9-11 type disaster.

Hands started to shoot up and supervisors rushed forward. But Toohey couldn't wait for their reports. She stepped down toward the sea of operators and tapped the nearest with her hand up. "What's wrong?"

"They're just hanging up, ma'am."

Toohey's eyes narrowed. "What?"

"I've taken five calls in a row. As soon as I answer, they hang up."

"Me too," said the operator at the next station. More nods from the others, the supervisors rushing over to confirm the same.

"What the hell is going on?" She stared at the displays, the call volume continuing to skyrocket, the average time per call plunging, and more concerning, the number of calls the phone company was reporting couldn't get through, was shooting through the roof.

Whatever was happening was dangerous, and people could die. Reliable access to the 9-1-1 system was essential in a big city like New York, and whatever was going on had to be stopped.

"Christine! It's the VoIP lines!"

She spun toward one of her techs, rushing into the room, waving a tablet computer. "What?"

"All the calls that are hang-ups are from Voice over Internet Protocol lines. Internet phones."

"So no landlines or cellphones?"

He shook his head. "Those volumes are the same, it's only the VoIP calls that have spiked."

She looked back at the screens, the dropped calls continuing to climb rapidly. "What's causing it?"

He shrugged. "Dunno. If I had to hazard a guess, somebody's system's been hacked."

Toohey cursed, pointing at one of her people. "Get me the Commissioner, now!" She turned to the tech as the call was placed. "Is there anything we can do?"

He pursed his lips, staring at the screens for a moment before replying. "I could set the system to automatically block any incoming calls from VoIP lines."

Toohey didn't like the sounds of that. Blocking any legitimate call went against everything she had been trained to do. "How many people would be affected?"

"Dunno. Maybe ten percent of the city?"

She sighed. "So, if we do it, almost a million people won't be able to dial 9-1-1."

He nodded then pointed at the displays. "But if we don't, nobody will."

She turned to face the screens, the call volumes continuing to rise, the dropped calls spiking, and her operators' frustration growing.

People are going to die!

She turned to the tech. "Do it."

Leesburg Pike, Falls Church, Virginia

Special Agent Brooklyn Tanner sat in the chopper, the doors closed, the sense of urgency gone. Whoever had executed this kidnapping was good. Damned good. Foreign government good.

"Chinese?"

She glanced over at Michael Lyons. "Good guess. North Koreans, perhaps."

"Russians. Iranians."

She shrugged. "Could be anyone or no one. Agent White was clearly targeted. This wasn't random."

Lyons nodded. "I've seen her at the Farm. She's pretty hot. Maybe that's why she was taken."

Tanner shook her head. "Sex-based kidnappings are never four guys."

Lyons raised a finger. "Unless it was for the sex *trade*. Maybe someone placed an order, and she fit the bill?"

Tanner grunted. "Perhaps, though why anyone would target a CIA agent for sex is beyond me. They're just asking for trouble."

"Well, wouldn't that be the thrill of it? I mean, fruit from the forbidden tree?"

Tanner sighed. "Maybe, but I hope not. I know if I were in her position, I'd rather be kidnapped and tortured by the North Koreans than be some pig's plaything."

Lyons frowned. "Yeah, me too."

Tanner gave him a look. "Who are you kidding, Lyons? You're the horniest mimbo on the team."

The others laughed as Lyons grinned. "This is true." He held up a hand cutting the others off. "But my luck, it would be the same *guy* that would be my new master, and that just doesn't float my boat."

"ETA sixty seconds."

Tanner repositioned her mike to acknowledge the pilot's message. "Copy that." She shifted toward the door and slid it open as the helicopter rapidly approached the parking garage that HQ had tracked a white Chevy SUV to, the suspect vehicle having spent a little too much time under a bridge overpass. There was no way the hostiles were still there, but the hope was that there might be some clue left behind. At this point, they were desperate.

And that meant mistakes could be made.

She turned to her team. "Watch for hostiles and booby traps. Just because they haven't killed yet doesn't mean they won't start now."

The helicopter bounced to a stop on the roof of the garage and Tanner stepped down, her team spreading out as the chopper lifted off to provide air support. A few cars were parked on the top level, none the white Chevy they were searching for.

"Let's go!" She headed for the down ramp, at the head of a wedge formation, her Glock held out in front of her, prepared for anything. As they entered the third level, the sun was blocked, and she removed her glasses, scanning from left to right and back, as she first looked for movement, then for the SUV. They quickly cleared the level, finding nothing, and advanced to the second.

"There it is, on the right," said Lyons.

She took a quick glance, confirming a white Chevy, then continued to survey the area, watching for any movement, anything out of the ordinary. She motioned for her men to take up covering positions around the vehicle, and they rushed forward as she continued to search for anything odd, unusual video cameras, lights, installations, or idling vehicles.

A chime sounded then there were voices, a woman and children. A door opened and a family stepped into view.

Tanner spun toward them, holding out her hand. "Go back downstairs! This is a police operation!"

The woman froze, staring at her, then grabbed her children as her eyes bulged. She yanked them back into the elevator room and Tanner heard the chime again, the doors opening then closing, one of the small children beginning to cry.

"Area is secure." She turned her attention to the SUV, its plates matching what they had been given. There was no doubt this was it. She slowly approached the vehicle, and again could see nothing inside, though this time there was no dome on the roof suggesting it might have been computer driven.

They should ban tinted windows.

"Check for—wait!" She held up a fist, stopping her team. She leaned closer, a red flash having caught her eye for a split second.

Lyons froze. "What is it?"

"I don't know. I thought I saw something red, like a beam of light or something."

"Sensor?"

"Could be. Everybody step back."

Her team edged away from the Chevy, and she caught the beam out of the corner of her eye. "Lyons, no!"

His head swiveled toward her as he finished his last step, but it was too late. The beam she had spotted, coming from something mounted on a nearby pillar, was interrupted.

"Ev—" She never got a chance to finish her warning as the vehicle erupted into a fireball, sending her flying backward. She smacked the concrete hard and continued to skid before slamming into the wall near the elevators and blacking out.

Operations Center 2, CIA Headquarters
Langley, Virginia

Sonya Tong gasped as the footage from the helicopter overhead suddenly showed the parking garage erupt in a fireball, flames and smoke billowing out of the openings in the second floor. She spun toward Randy Child. "Get local fire and ambulance, now!" Child made the call as Tong activated her comm. "Echo Leader, this is Control, do you copy?"

Nothing.

"This is Control to anyone on Echo team. Do you copy?"

Again nothing.

She turned to Child. "Are we getting any type of signal?"

He nodded. "They're all receiving, but no one is transmitting."

She turned back as she watched the footage change, the chopper dropping to the second story. "Control to pilot, do you see anything?"

"Negative. Let me reposition, I can't see anything through the smoke."

The angle changed as he moved back toward the front of the building. His light turned on and sliced through the darkness of the garage, the lights on the level all out, the smoke beginning to thin.

"There!" She stepped toward the display, pointing at something on the garage floor. It could just be a piece of debris, but it was big enough to be a body.

It sat up.

"Echo Team, this is Control, can anyone hear me?"

"Control, Echo Leader. Stand by."

Tong's heart slammed as sweat trickled down her back, her eyes filling with tears. She had never sent a team on a mission in her life, and she had no clue how she would react if one of them were now dead because of orders she had given.

I wish Chris were here. He'd know what to do.

"Control, Echo Leader. We're shaken and stirred, but we're all okay."

Cheers erupted from those in the operations center and Tong wiped away the tears threatening to pour down her face.

"You'll want to send a forensics team here, Control, but I don't think they're going to find much."

"Copy that, Echo Leader. I assume no sign of our agent?"

There was a pause. "Negative, Control, let's just pray she wasn't still in there, over."

Chris Leroux cleared security and rushed toward the elevators that would take him to the operations center his team was in. As he rounded the corner, Randy Child flagged him down.

"Hey there, I'm supposed to take you directly to the Chief's office."

Leroux nodded, skipping the elevators and heading deeper into the complex. "What's the latest?"

"Nothing good. The second vehicle was booby trapped—nearly took out our team."

Leroux's heart skipped a beat. "Are they okay?"

"Yeah, bumps and bruises, but they'll be fine."

Leroux was afraid to ask the next question. "We're sure Sherrie—I mean Agent White—wasn't in it?"

Child glanced back at him, and Leroux could see the empathy in the young man's eyes, the first time he could recall him ever expressing an

46

adult emotion. "No. A forensic team is on the way, but our Rapid Response Team says it looks like the vehicle was empty. No evidence of remains, or the crate that we think was used to take her out of your apartment."

Leroux breathed a sigh of relief as they passed through another set of security doors. "Any word on Lee Fang?"

Another headshake. "Nothing beyond that she's still missing. The police cordon around the hospital where the chopper landed got there too late. We're going through footage now, but even if we find anything, she'll be long gone."

"Hey, buddy!" Leroux spun to see Dylan Kane jogging down the hall to join them. Kane gave him a thumping hug, Leroux returning it awkwardly.

"I-I'm sorry about Fang."

"And I'm sorry about Sherrie."

"Sirs?" Child held out a hand, urging them forward, Director Morrison apparently having given him orders to deliver them quickly. Kane put a hand on Leroux's back, gently propelling him forward as he walked beside him. The touch was at once uncomfortable and comforting. He wasn't a touchy-feely person, though Sherrie had mostly cured him of that, at least when it came to her. Having a guy touch him in this manner was something he was yet to become accustomed to, and he wasn't sure if he ever would. His family had never been a hugging family, he had never played team sports, and his experiences in a locker room had always been ones of awkwardness and humiliation as the jocks teased those who didn't perform well during gym class.

He remembered once in high school when there was a points competition, a dozen different exercises set up, each worth various points, that you were supposed to do a circuit of, and the pair that earned the most points, won. He and another awkward kid named Sean paired up and quickly ran down the rules. Each exercise had to be done at least once, but nothing said you couldn't do another exercise over and over. Sit ups were worth two points each, and could be done rapidly. He and Sean quickly did the circuit, then just did sit ups for the rest of the class.

They won.

And the jocks were pissed.

He and Sean had used their superior intellect to find the weakness in the strength and endurance challenge, designed by a jock—the teacher—and won.

Handily.

It wasn't worth it.

The teasing and insults lasted for days, the pain of the names that were never supposed to hurt, lasted for years. He glanced over at Kane, his best friend from high school, the man—boy—who had protected him for his sophomore and junior years, who had made those years at least bearable, and found himself suddenly yearning for those simpler days.

But it was foolish to do so.

He had put over ten years between him and high school, enough time for much of the horrible experiences to fade away, replaced by the past couple of years of an incredible life with Sherrie, success at work, and the respect of his peers. He was looked up to now, by team members both younger and older than him, by his supervisors and fellow analyst supervisors far more senior than him, and by agents like Kane, or Delta operators like Bravo Team. He spoke with confidence

48

now when dealing with situations that could mean life or death, though he still quaked on the inside at times.

And much of this newfound confidence was because of Kane's faith in him, of his friend's efforts in getting Sherrie back into his life, and of Director Morrison taking a chance on him.

"You okay?"

He glanced at Kane. "Not really."

"I hear ya. Let's get our women back, then kill these bastards once and for all."

The Director's aide saw them approach and lifted her phone, whispering for a moment before hanging up. "Go right in, gentlemen."

Child opened the door and Kane gently pushed Leroux through.

"Chris!" Sonya Tong erupted from her chair, racing toward him and hugging him hard, her head buried in his chest. "Thank God you're okay!" She let go of him, stepping back quickly, staring at the floor as she clasped her hands in front of her. "Umm, sorry. I shouldn't—" She sighed, then snapped her mouth shut, returning to her chair.

Kane grinned at Leroux, his eyebrows climbing suggestively, Tong clearly crushing on her boss.

"It's okay. I'm lucky to be alive, I guess."

Morrison, sitting behind his desk, motioned toward two empty chairs. "Thanks, Randy."

Child nodded and left the room, closing the door behind him.

"Glad to see you're okay, Chris, but I don't think luck had anything to do with it."

Leroux's eyes narrowed. "What do you mean?"

"You two were targeted, not your better halves. If they were the targets, then you two would most likely be dead. Especially you, Dylan, since you took out so many of them. They want you two alive, with leverage over you."

Kane frowned. "Fang and Sherrie."

"Exactly. They know you two won't do anything to risk their lives."

Kane growled. "So there's no doubt it's the Assembly?"

"We heard the recording. One of the team that took Agent White was heard saying, 'The Assembly is eternal.' That's not a coincidence. Nobody knows about the Assembly, and that's the only link you two have beyond high school. They're up to something, and they don't want you two involved, and by extension, the CIA."

Leroux frowned, hating to say what needed saying. "We can't let this influence the CIA's reaction."

Morrison smiled. "And it won't, trust me. As heartless as it sounds, two lives are not going to stop us from confronting the Assembly."

Kane grunted. "Just give me the nod, and I'll find them myself."

Morrison delivered. "Consider yourself unleashed."

Kane's knuckles whitened as he gripped the arms of his chair, as if containing himself, forcing himself to remain in the room rather than sprint for the door to begin a killing spree until he found the woman he loved. "Do we know what they're up to?"

Morrison shook his head. "No, but there is a nationwide incident occurring right now."

Leroux leaned forward, his eyes widening. "What?"

"All 9-1-1 systems across the country are being flooded with fake calls, overwhelming the systems. There isn't a major city that hasn't been affected."

Leroux's eyes narrowed. "Why the hell would they do that? How could disrupting the 9-1-1 system possibly help them?"

Morrison shrugged. "No idea." He leaned forward in his chair. "That's what I want you and your team to find out."

Leroux caught Tong staring at him. She looked away, her cheeks flushed. "What are our parameters?"

Morrison leaned forward. "What do you mean?"

"We have some intel that we're not allowed to legally use. Can we use it now?"

Morrison's fingers steepled in front of his face, the tips bouncing off his chin as he pursed his lips. "I think it's time we eliminated this problem once and for all. When we're done, this won't see the inside of a courtroom. Find the Assembly, find out what they're up to, and feed the intel to Dylan." He turned to Kane. "And you do what you do best."

Harlem Hospital Center
Manhattan, New York

Larissa Williams groaned as she massaged her feet. "I need to lose weight. The human body was never designed to carry this much fabulousness around for this many hours."

Her friend and fellow nurse, Nina, laughed. "I hear you, girl, but today was something special. I've never seen anything like it. So many walking wounded!" She waved a hand at the television. "What the hell is going on, anyway? The entire 9-1-1 system goes haywire, and nobody can get through? It's crazy!"

Larissa agreed. "Yeah, and it wasn't just here. Apparently, dozens of cities were affected."

"Well, I hope they catch the bastards responsible."

Larissa grunted. "They should line them up against a wall and shoot them."

"I'll second that! No judge, no jury, just execute the sonsabitches. Maybe then, these hackers will think twice before messing with people's lives. How many people died today because of it?"

Larissa frowned as she slipped her shoe back on. "The news is saying dozens died just here. A lot of people couldn't call ambulances, and once the criminals realized what was going on, there was some looting and a few people were shot."

Nina shook her head. "What is it about situations like this that make people think they need a new TV?"

Larissa chuckled. "I don't know, but I know I could sure use one."

Nina gave her a look. "You *definitely* could use one. You do know that they have flat screens now, right?"

Larissa smiled. "Hey, I know, but I also have mouths to feed, and that no-good loser of an ex-husband of mine hasn't paid child support in over a year."

"Shoot his ass too!"

"Damn right!" Larissa pushed to her feet. "Okay, I'm outta here. If you need me, you know where *not* to find me."

"You go on home to those boys of yours before they get up to no good."

Larissa tossed her head back and growled. "Argh! Don't get me started on them. You know that yesterday I caught Michael holding a gun outside the apartment? The older kids were showing it to him. What is it with kids today? I pray every day that my boys grow up like their Uncle Leon. Join the Army and keep out of trouble. But you can't join if you're dead or in jail!"

"Well, with everything going on today, you better get home to them. Oh, look!" Nina pointed at the screen, a local news anchor, Aynslee Kai, replaced by the head of Homeland Security.

"Today's disruption of the 9-1-1 systems in multiple jurisdictions was caused by the hacking of eTALK's servers, the nation's largest Voice over Internet Protocol provider. This allowed the hackers to send calls from these phones through the E-911 system that links your home's VoIP system to your local 9-1-1 system. The result was a massive influx of calls that stayed connected long enough to prevent legitimate calls from getting through, thus overwhelming the system. The security breach has been plugged, and Croft Technologies' SecuraVault Anti-Intrusion System installed to protect from further breaches. At this time, we have no suspects, however the investigation has just begun—"

Nina batted a hand at the screen. "Blah blah. What else is new? It'll be the Russians or the Chinese, and we'll do nothing about it."

Larissa frowned, her friend right. "I'm going home. See you tomorrow." She stepped out of the change room and headed for the elevators, waving goodbye to the night shift. She shivered as she exited the building and headed for the subway. She stopped at the curb, waiting for the light to change, mentally preparing a grocery list. The pedestrian light turned and she stepped onto the street when somebody grabbed her from behind and hauled her back. She cried out, not sure what was going on, when a city bus whipped past her, missing her by inches.

"Oh my God!" she cried as she turned to see who had saved her life. A man in a business suit stared at her wide-eyed as he eased his grip on her arm. "I could have been killed!"

"Did he run a red light?" asked a bystander.

"No, I'm sure…" She turned and stared at the light, definitely indicating it was their turn to cross.

"Look!"

She turned to see her savior pointing up at the opposing traffic's signal. It was green.

"What the hell?"

"Something's wrong with the lights. Look!"

She stared in the direction of his finger and saw every traffic light, for as far as she could see, was green.

This can't be!

The businessman shook his head. "I don't think those hackers are done with us."

Tires screeched and someone screamed, a heart-wrenching crunch heard to their left.

Oh no!

Operations Center 2, CIA Headquarters
Langley, Virginia

Chris Leroux stepped inside Operations Center 2, his team already manning their stations. All rose to their feet, concern written on their faces. He waved them down. "I'm okay, everyone. Thanks for your concern." He gave a special look to Sonya Tong as she took her seat. "I understand Sonya filled my shoes quite capably. A special thanks to her."

Kane patted her on the shoulder and she flushed as clapping and a few cheers erupted.

Leroux silenced them with a slightly raised hand. "Okay, here's the situation. The Director has given us carte blanche to deal with the situation. We're not worried about due process here, we're worried about results. The Assembly has been on our radar before, and despite our warnings to them, they are back. For those of you in the room who are new, what I'm about to tell you is about as Top Secret as you can get. Repeat it outside of this room, and somebody downstairs will be reprinting your yearbook with your photo not in it. Understood?"

Heads bobbed around the room, some eyes wide with fear.

"Okay, here's what we know. We know they have been around for at least a century, perhaps longer, perhaps *much* longer. We believe they are a cabal of about one dozen people, very well-connected, mostly industrialists. We were able to trace several of them a little over a year ago due to some sloppy email security by one of their new members. When we reached out to the Assembly, warning them off from their attempts to target myself and Kane, as well as our families, they did

56

back off, but all of the members we had identified were later found dead. We now have no idea who they are, or where they are, beyond a single opening in the dark web."

Randy Child raised a hand slightly. "What's their purpose?"

"From what we can tell, they try to influence world events to their benefit. Whether that's influencing foreign and domestic policies, industrial espionage, or whatever, they have been manipulating things for over a century. To be honest, we really don't know that much about them. All we know is that they are dangerous, powerful, and have their fingers in everything. We know they were involved in trying to trigger a war with China, so we assume they are heavily involved in industries that would benefit from that. Bringing them down will be difficult, perhaps even impossible, but we need to try."

Child spun in his chair. "Where do we start?"

"The only place we can. The dark web. Let's see what we can find. Also, we know they must be up to something big. This 9-1-1 outage could be a coincidence, but it might not be. Remember, to them the world is a chessboard. Moving a pawn might seem insignificant to us, but tomorrow or next year, it could have significant consequences. We can't let them succeed in whatever it is they're up to, because for them to do what they did today, it must be big. And that can't be good for our country, or the world."

Port of Baltimore
Baltimore, Maryland

Nadja Katz stared at the laptop screen, a hint of a frown on her lips, something her subconscious told her was the typical human response to what she was watching.

Yet she felt nothing.

Almost nothing.

There were emotions behind the façade she presented the world, but they were muted, subdued. The car accident that had killed her parents and injured her brain when she was younger, had left her...different. The years of abuse in the foster care system in Germany had led her to run away and fend for herself.

It hadn't been an emotional reaction, it was a logical one. Why would you stay where you were abused, physically, mentally, and sexually?

That was when she had met Dietrich, an ex-East German Stasi spy, who despite reunification, was still busy. He had taught her the trade, taught her to kill, and she had excelled. When you don't have emotions to get in the way, it's easy to remain calm when about to make the kill—it reduced the mistakes caused by unchecked adrenaline or a cluttered mind.

When Dietrich had died, she had taken over his business, and eventually found herself employed by the Assembly as he had been, one of their go-to problem solvers. That was until they had betrayed her, deciding she knew too much. She had witnessed the purge triggered by the CIA identifying some of their members, but had survived the Assembly's attempt on her life.

And had vowed revenge.

It was an odd emotion, one she had actually taken some pleasure in—another odd emotion. But it was also a logical reaction. The Assembly wanted her dead, and with the power they had, they would eventually succeed.

Unless she could eliminate them first—a tall order considering they had been around for generations, their rank of twelve ruling members replenished as needed, none knowing who those who came before them were. They rarely if ever met together, almost always meeting by video conference, the system configured so each could only see the faces of those they helped recruit.

When she had been privy to these conversations, where she would never see any of the faces as she wasn't an Assembly Council member, it always made her wonder who Number One was. He was the oldest recruit, though not necessarily the oldest in age. He may have been recruited when he was thirty or forty, others in their sixties. She hadn't known who they were, except that they were powerful men, all controlling vast amounts of wealth, whether through corporations they owned or inherited, or positions they occupied.

She did know they felt their role was altruistic. They were there to better humankind over the long term, so they placed little value on the individual. From what she had gathered, the Assembly's current goal was one of renewal.

They wanted a war.

A global war.

They wanted to shatter a system they considered broken, and from its ashes, create a stronger, more sustainable one. It was evident from overheard conversations that they felt Western governments had become weak, unable to deal with the threats Islam, the Chinese, and a resurgent Russia posed. Their belief was that if they could trigger the next war, the United States and her allies would be forced to make the decisions they refused to make today, and in the end, they would be victorious, triumphing over their enemies, with a form of government that would necessarily be more firm in its dealings with groups that were only concerned with themselves, and not the greater good. A government that would stamp out nuisances before they became problems. A government that would lead the world forward for generations allowing humankind to achieve a new golden age.

All laudable goals, in her damaged mind, but how many had to die to achieve them? Today, surprisingly, that number had been low, and those that had died, had not been innocent. One of the mistakes the Assembly had made in failing to kill her, was not scrapping their entire communications network and intelligence infrastructure. She had intimate knowledge of everything, and changing passwords and IP addresses wasn't enough.

She knew where they kept the bodies.

Literally.

She knew where the safe houses were, where the holding cells were, where their secret communication sites were. And the Assembly had kept most of them, only closing down those they thought she knew about. What they hadn't known was that she had been privy to far more than they realized, her mentor, Dietrich, having kept an extensive file on them, his dealings spanning decades.

They hadn't known this.

This had allowed her to regain access to their communications, and when she had heard what they planned yesterday, she took action.

Their ultimate goal wasn't her concern. If they wiped out half the planet to save the other half, she didn't care, though she'd prefer to be on the half that wasn't wiped out. She had a sense she'd excel in a future that relied on the strength of the individual, at least for the short term.

The goals of the Assembly weren't her concern, though they would be to the governments they hoped to reshape, and with their help, she'd perhaps achieve her own selfish goal—the elimination of the Assembly, once and for all. It was a goal she couldn't achieve alone, but with the help of the Americans, she just might succeed.

Unfortunately, she was a wanted murderer, her work for the Assembly costing far too many lives on American soil to be forgiven, so she needed leverage that could assure her freedom.

The corners of her mouth hinted at a smile as she watched the video feed on her laptop, her leverage arriving.

Lee Fang struggled to control her breathing, this the first action she had seen in a while, her training lapsed. They had drugged her once they had reached the rooftop in the chopper, a large H and red cross on the landing pad suggesting it was a hospital. The spray that had hit her face had been pungent, and she recognized it as an aerosolized carfentanil, something she had used herself in her previous life. She had held her breath, avoiding the initial inhalation, but a swift punch to the gut had caused her to gasp in the second spray, and she had been out within seconds.

She had no idea how long she had been asleep, but judging from the overwhelming bladder pressure and the taste in her mouth, it had been awhile, perhaps even a day.

They must have kept me drugged.

She was now in some sort of road vehicle, a hood over her head, her hands and feet bound with what she sensed were zip ties. They'd be easy enough to get out of if given the opportunity, though that was probably unlikely. Kane had put up one hell of a fight, eliminating the entire ground operation, but who could have expected a chopper with a sonic weapon? Without the proper gear, there was no way to defeat it, especially when taken by surprise. The only defense was to leave the area, not an option for the man she loved.

I hope he's okay.

He had still been alive when the chopper took off, and she had no reason to believe there were any more hostiles on the ground to pose a challenge, which was an interesting bit of information she had only now begun to ponder. Why had they taken her, and why had they left him alive?

The initial group that had kidnapped her had been Chinese. She had at first assumed her government had come to reclaim their asset, and didn't want to kill any Americans in the process. But they were *too* Chinese. Chinese decoy, Chinese team members, Chinese weapons. If her government were after her, they wouldn't have made it so obvious.

Or so public.

And those who had arrived in the chopper were white, and everything she had heard since her capture had been in Russian, a language she happened to be fluent in, though she wouldn't let them know that tidbit yet. It wouldn't be unheard of for her government to hire an outside team, yet if they had, why was the initial team all Chinese?

It didn't make sense. Something else was going on here, and for the moment, she had no clue what it was. For now, it appeared they wanted her alive, either to extract information from her, or to deliver her to someone who would later kill her. Her government would torture her for weeks or months, then either make a public spectacle of her, or more likely, as she had come under American protection, kill her quietly.

Yet she still wasn't convinced they were behind this. If they knew where she was, they could have grabbed her at any time. Why would they have done it during one of the rare occasions a trained-CIA operator was with her? Surely, the wiser, safer move would have been to wait until he was back on assignment. She'd have been one against a dozen with no hope of winning. Instead, they had taken her while with Kane, and left him alive. It suggested the team sent to abduct her had been waiting for a go-no go order, and it had arrived at a time not of their choosing.

The fact nothing had been said to her since her abduction had her wondering if perhaps she wasn't the real target at all. Perhaps Kane was the target, and she was merely leverage to hold over him. The thought had her chest tightening. If she could talk to him now, she'd tell him to let her die. She didn't want to be anyone's pawn, and she didn't want anyone hurt because of her. She let out a long, slow breath.

If it comes down to it, I'll kill myself.

"We're here. Is our guy on the gate?"

"Yeah, just flash your lights twice as you approach, he'll wave us through."

The vehicle slowed slightly then sped back up.

"That was easy. Gotta love port security."

There was a round of chuckles. Four of them. All men.

"Do you have the container number?"

"Yeah. Just keep going, it's ready to be loaded. The other target is already there."

Other target?

She wasn't the only one? If that was the case, then it almost definitely wasn't the Chinese government, unless they were repatriating two former citizens at the same time. It was possible, though she doubted it. These types of operations didn't have budgets. They wouldn't take two of their people at once just to save money—it doubled the risk, and it doubled the chances of the operation failing.

And it could put two highly trained operatives together, who might just figure out a way to escape.

No, something else was definitely going on here. A Chinese crew and a Russian crew, a broad daylight takedown with Kane present and left alive, and a second target.

"There it is."

They turned then came to a stop, three doors opening. The vehicle rocked then the door beside her opened.

"Get out," said someone in English, the accent thick.

She swung her legs out and felt a tug on them as the bindings were cut. A firm grip on her arm helped her down to the ground, the drop suggesting an SUV. She was led about thirty paces, the sounds of what was clearly a shipping port, surrounding her. Then she was in an echo chamber.

"Enjoy your trip."

She was shoved hard and stumbled forward, falling on her knees. Metal clanged, probably doors, followed by muffled silence. She reached up and yanked the hood off her head, finding total darkness. Though that wasn't entirely accurate. There were a few slivers of light near the door, and a red light at the far end of whatever she was in. By the metallic, rusted smell, she guessed a shipping container.

"Hello?"

She flinched, the voice echoing around her. She rolled on her back, stretching out her arms and curling her legs up. She pushed her feet through her arms, her bound hands now behind her. She pushed to her feet then pulled her hands apart as hard as she could before thrusting them up and her bum down.

The ties snapped.

"Who are you?" she asked, her eyes slowly adjusting, though not enough to see anyone.

"You first."

Fang grunted. "I don't think so. Tell me your first name, and I'll tell you mine."

"Sherrie."

Fang's eyes narrowed. "Fang."

"Lee Fang?"

Fang smiled slightly. "Sherrie White?"

"Oh my God, yes! They took you too?"

"It would appear so. Do you know—"

She was tossed off her feet as the floor shifted, the entire room creaking as they were picked up into the air.

Definitely a shipping container.

Which meant they were about to be put on a ship and sent to God knows where.

"I don't think we're getting out of this anytime soon."

Nadja Katz stood on the shipping container, holding onto one of the cables as she swung the mass of metal using the remote control for the crane system. The container with the two hostages was lifting toward a massive cargo ship to her right. She had one chance at this, but she wasn't worried.

Worrying was pointless.

In fact, the only reason her heart rate was up a few points was the physical aspect of what she was doing. She pushed the joystick with her thumb and the boom swung her toward her target. She killed the motion, the container arcing high and to the right as she tossed the controller aside. She bent her knees and shoved off, sailing through the air, landing on the target container with ease, tumbling forward then onto her knees.

She pulled a suction cup speaker from her belt then stuck it to the metal container and activated her headset. "Move away from the door. Now." She scurried to the front as someone below noticed what was going on, gunshots pinging off the thick metal skin of the container.

They had no angle on her.

She rushed forward and flipped over the side, one hand gripping the rim of the door, the other pulling a brick of plastic explosives from her belt. She slapped it on the lock in mid-swing then continued, flipping her legs back up on the side.

"Final warning, move to the back. Blowing in three... two... one..." She activated the trigger, a small blast rippling through the metal, the doors flying open. She swung inside, pulling her flashlight out and shining it at the two occupants. She didn't know the Chinese woman beyond what she had read in her file, but she knew the American.

Katz had shot her a little over a year ago.

Fortunately, the woman couldn't see her face, Katz making a point of keeping the light shining in her eyes. She tossed the Chinese woman a knife. "Cut her loose."

Fang wisely didn't ask any questions, instead freeing Sherrie White of her bonds while Katz secured a rope to a tie-down anchor on the floor. She handed two Glocks over. "Everything below is hostile. Understood?"

Sherrie nodded. "Yes. Who the hell are you?"

"A friend." Katz jumped over the side, letting the rope slide through her gloved hands, firing at the Russian team sent by the Assembly, two dropping immediately, the other two running for cover. Gunfire from above tore through the air and another dropped, causing the final man to hesitate, and, unwisely, make a stand. He opened fire on them, spraying the air with unaimed lead.

Someone cried out above her.

Katz took aim and silenced the weapon as her feet hit the ground. She stepped away and Fang landed beside her with a thud, Sherrie following a moment later, her descent controlled. Fang was gripping her side, blood oozing through her fingers.

Katz pointed at her, keeping her face turned away. "Pick her up and follow me." She sprinted between the stacks of containers, toward her vehicle. Rounding the corner, she held out the fob, the lights flashing as the doors unlocked. She opened up the rear and urged the two women inside.

"She's going to need a doctor," said Sherrie as she helped roll Fang into the back of the van.

"Just keep pressure on the wound for now."

"Wait a minute, I know—"

Katz spun, shoving the heel of her hand into Sherrie's chest, sending her tumbling into the back of the van, then slammed the doors shut. She pressed the fob to lock the doors, then held it in. An indicator on the fob flashed then a hissing sound could be heard as knockout gas filled the rear of the van.

Katz climbed into the front cab as the two women in the back struggled to get out, their attempts waning as the gas took hold. There was a thud, then another, as both lost consciousness. Katz started the vehicle and pulled away, heading for the front gate and flashing her lights, the guard, on the Assembly payroll, waving her through.

Now for Phase Two.

Fayetteville, North Carolina

Command Sergeant Major Burt "Big Dog" Dawson sat in his prized 1964½ Mustang convertible in original poppy red, the engine purring as he slowed for traffic ahead. He looked up at the cloth roof. "Too bad it's so friggin' cold today. It's a sacrilege to drive with the top up in this car."

Sergeant Leon "Atlas" James nodded, his impossibly deep voice vibrating through the vehicle. "It's not that cold. I'm game if you are."

Dawson saw the light ahead change to red and he eased off the gas as he approached a railroad crossing. "Not worth it. We're almost there." He crossed the tracks with enough room for him to clear, but out of habit checked his rearview mirror to make sure he hadn't misjudged his ass-end.

He hadn't.

Something caught his eye to his left and he turned his head, a train in the distance rapidly approaching. His eyes narrowed slightly and he inched forward a little more, just in case. He checked his rearview mirror again, the car behind him on his bumper. "Look at this idiot! He's on the tracks!"

Atlas leaned over and peered out the rear window then toward the train. "Shouldn't the gates be coming down?"

Dawson cursed. "Something's wrong." Traffic passed in the opposite direction, oblivious to the oncoming danger, the light ahead now green. The car in front of him moved as he spotted a school bus coming toward him.

"He's not stopping! Jesus Christ, BD!"

Dawson cranked the wheel and hammered on the gas, blocking the bus as the high-pitched squeal of the train's brakes threatened to overwhelm his senses, its horn blasting as the engineer tried to warn the vehicles still on the tracks.

Atlas, twisted in his seat, stared at the locomotive. "It's gonna hurt!"

The train slammed into the car behind them, tearing it in half, the wreckage tossed into a nearby parking lot, slamming into several parked cars. Dawson jumped out with Atlas and they rushed toward the school bus, the driver sitting stunned, her eyes wide as the children behind her screamed in horror as the train continued to lumber past, the massive force a juggernaut that wouldn't be stopped before it had finished wreaking its havoc.

Dawson pounded on the door and the driver finally noticed him. She opened it.

"Is everyone okay?"

She glanced back at the kids. "I-I think so."

"You got a phone?"

She nodded.

"Call 9-1-1. Tell them what happened."

"O-okay."

Dawson sprinted after Atlas, the big man already halfway toward the shredded car. Dawson arrived to find the driver bloodied but alive. He began checking for broken bones and other wounds. The woman moaned. "Just stay still. Help's on the way."

The woman stared straight ahead in shock, saying nothing, as he continued assessing her. Her eyes shot wide open. "My baby!"

Dawson paused, his chest tightening. "What?"

"My baby! Where's my baby?"

Dawson glanced behind her, nothing left of the rear seat. He almost dared not ask the question. "Where was your baby?"

The woman turned slightly, wincing, then screamed as she stared in the rearview mirror. "My baby! Oh my God! Where's my baby!"

Dawson didn't know what to say, instead falling back on his haunches as he turned away from the horror and sorrow on the young mother's face.

A paramedic rushed over, gently pushing him aside. "I'll take over, sir."

Atlas rounded the car as Dawson rose.

"Anything?"

Atlas shook his head. "It might be on the other side, but I'm guessing it was shredded by the impact."

Dawson sighed and closed his burning eyes.

"BD."

He opened his eyes and looked to where Atlas was pointing.

"What the hell is going on? Those gates are still up!"

Dawson shook his head. "I don't know, but with everything that's happened over the past two days, I can't believe it's a coincidence."

Operations Center 2, CIA Headquarters
Langley, Virginia

"So, we've got a 9-1-1 system overwhelmed from a VoIP network hack, the traffic signals are being messed with in most major cities causing gridlock, and now the railroad gates are all stuck in the up position, wherever they're centrally controlled."

Chris Leroux listened to Director Morrison's summary as he struggled to keep his eyes open. He hadn't slept since Sherrie had been kidnapped yesterday, the trail cold. They had no idea where she or Fang were, and there had been no word from the Assembly on what was needed to get them back. It was frustrating.

And terrifying.

He sighed, saying nothing.

"Chris?"

He looked up. "Huh?" He realized he had nodded off for a split second. "Oh God, sorry, sir. I haven't had any sleep and, well, you know how Sherrie feels about energy drinks."

Morrison chuckled. "I'm not one to interfere with a man's love life, so I suggest you get some sleep before you start making mistakes."

"Yes, sir." Leroux straightened in his chair, remembering what Morrison had said. "With respect to what you said, you're right. Those are the hacks we know of. Who knows what others are happening that we don't know about yet?"

Morrison stood, pacing back and forth in the operations center as he squeezed his chin. "And no claims of responsibility yet."

"No, which suggests they're not done."

"Anything we can do to stop them?"

Leroux frowned. "Find them, that's about it."

Morrison paused. "Are *we* safe?"

Leroux nodded. "Our systems are protected and isolated. We're mostly Intranet-based as opposed to Internet-based."

Morrison gave him a look. "What the hell does that mean?"

"It means we're wired internally, with no links to the outside. Our systems that *are* connected, are isolated from the internal network. There's no way anyone can hack us."

"Unless they do it from the inside," said Randy Child.

Leroux nodded. "True."

"But even then, they'd still be stuck on the internal network, wouldn't they?"

Leroux shook his head. "Not necessarily. If we actually had a mole, and they were skilled enough, they could tap our network internally with a transmitter that would allow communication with the outside world. We've got all kinds of sensors to detect that type of stuff, but just like we can hack pretty much anyone in the world, we have to assume someone out there can hack us."

Morrison frowned. "Not very comforting." He motioned toward the displays, several news feeds showing the chaos in the cities, and the aftermath of several railroad incidents. "If these are all related, which we have to assume they are, what the hell's their endgame? What do they hope to possibly achieve by messing with traffic lights and the 9-1-1 system?"

Leroux shrugged. "No idea. This is big. A lot of resources are going into this, and this is a significant, coordinated undertaking."

"So government?"

Leroux nodded. "It's definitely not Anonymous or some other White Hat hacker group trying to send a message, even a Black Hat group can't pull something like this off. To hit every major city in America takes money and resources."

"So definitely a foreign power."

"Or the Assembly."

Morrison sucked in a deep breath. "Are they capable of something like this?"

Leroux chewed his cheek a moment then let out a loud sigh. "I don't know. They would definitely have the funding for it, and if they've been around for as long as we think they have, they could have people on their payroll everywhere. We already know the former Secretary of Defense was compromised. And BlackTide had thousands of personnel before it was shut down. I think this is them, and they've taken Sherrie and Fang to try and keep us from looking too hard."

Child spun in his chair. "Well, we're not going to let that stop us, right?"

Leroux tensed, but he nodded. "Right. The best way to save them is to figure out what's going on and stop it."

The door to the operations center burst open and Morrison's aide rushed in. "Sir, there's a situation!"

Morrison stood, the aide whispering something in his ear. His eyebrows jumped. "Are you sure?"

A quick nod.

"We'll be right there." He turned to Leroux. "You'll never guess who just cleared the front gates."

Nadja Katz drove through the outer gates of Langley with ease, the forged ID a leftover from her previous life, created several years ago by an Assembly mole within the CIA. As far as the Agency knew, she was an employee named Catherine Ingels. Fortunately, the Assembly hadn't canceled the ID, probably because doing so might bring attention to the dozens of others created by the same person over the years. Her pass would be allowed to expire, and no one would be the wiser.

Fortunately for her, that wasn't for another six months.

She parked in the employee garage and tucked the rental's car keys behind the rear tire, brushing off an imaginary scuff from her black leather pants. She strode confidently toward the employee entrance, mingling with the others, getting some looks, no one saying what they must be thinking—that she was an operator.

Staff didn't dress like she did, nor typically looked like she did.

She had long ago learned that her body had an effect on men and women alike, and used that to her advantage. She dressed the part, sexy, sensual, dangerously seductive, enough to throw most men off to the point they couldn't properly concentrate, leaving them easily manipulated, and to make enough women self-conscious about their own inadequacies, that they wanted her out of their presence quickly, especially if their sexual partner was with them.

It was something she would never completely understand.

She had sex, the act somewhat enjoyable for her, at least physically. The mental aspect was never really there, just a dull sensation in the background. It made truly satisfying sex difficult, that easier to achieve on her own than with a partner. For her, sex with a partner usually needed pain, her own pain, to trigger a genuinely physical and mental response that was completely orgasmic. A tingling sensation rushed through her body.

Curious.

The thought of being punished actually excited her. She'd experiment with that when this was all over. When that would be, she wasn't sure. She was taking a gamble. What could be the ultimate gamble. She had Sherrie White and a severely wounded Lee Fang in her custody, safely ensconced in a facility the government had no idea existed.

If she wasn't freed, they'd never be found, but just in case, she had set a little surprise for the ladies in the event she didn't return within 24 hours of their initial incarceration. The CIA might shoot her on sight, though she doubted it. They would more likely interrogate her, which would be a waste of time.

She wasn't here to help them.

She was here to help herself.

That meant certain information would be imparted, and then they would have a choice. Help her, and save their people, or not help her, and either let her go, or hold her. Either of those latter options meant her prisoners died. She was curious to see what their choice would be, though only one of those outcomes was the preferred one.

And to ensure it, she could talk to only one person.

She walked up to the security desk with a seductive smile.

The guard adjusted his tie. "Yes, ma'am, may I help you?"

"Yes, you can. Contact Director Morrison and tell him you have a walk-in. I want to speak to Special Agent Dylan Kane at once."

Third Avenue, Manhattan, New York

Larissa Williams sat in the back of her Uber taxi with her eyes closed. The past twenty-four hours had been hell. Emergency Rooms across the city were slammed, the traffic light hack of last night resulting in hundreds of pedestrian casualties, with far too many of those fatalities.

The lights were working again for the moment, so she had taken a taxi rather than risk walking the streets to get to the subway, as the traffic control system had randomly failed all day. Traffic was at a crawl, but at least it was moving, albeit slowly.

She sighed as she watched the pedestrians, double and triple-checking before crossing the road. She had provided first aid to the woman who had been hit last night, but it had been of no use. She had died before paramedics could arrive.

"There go the lights again."

She opened her eyes and looked to where the driver was pointing. All the traffic lights, for as far as she could see, were now flashing red. She didn't drive, so had to try and remember what that meant. "That means you treat it like a four-way stop, right?"

"Yup. Doesn't work too well though when you've got five lanes."

She frowned. "That's different than before, isn't it?"

"Yup. Before, everything went green, which was worse. I'm betting the city finally pulled the plug on the system. Too many dying."

She nodded and leaned back to close her eyes when she realized something. She glanced about to confirm her suspicions. "Why are you on Third? Shouldn't you be on First?"

"I am on First." He pointed at the navigation system attached to the dash. It was centered inside a building, from what she could tell.

"That says we're inside a building."

"Well, they can be off sometimes." He pointed at a road running an inch to the right of the dot indicating the car. "That's First right there."

Larissa shook her head. "You're new to the city, aren't you?"

The man turned and grinned. "I arrived from Sierra Leone three months ago. I love America!"

"Uh huh, well, you're on Third, not First."

"No, ma'am." He tapped the display. "First."

She leaned forward and pointed at a street sign. "Third." The driver looked and his eyes shot wide. He slammed his hand down on the GPS.

They were still in the middle of a building.

"I'm not sure what's wrong."

Larissa gathered up her stuff. "Listen, we're not going anywhere now, so I'm just going to try and take the subway."

The driver shrugged. "Your choice. You prepaid."

"Uh huh." She climbed out and shut the door, weaving between two lanes of traffic before reaching the sidewalk. A large group was gathered in front of an electronics shop, watching a newscast, the audio piped outside. "What's going on?" she asked as she joined the throng.

A young man glanced at her then back at the TV showing the aftermath of a transport truck versus locomotive competition. "They just shut down the entire rail system."

Pacific Coast, California

Vincenzo Anastas peered through the thick fog, unable to see the bow of his ship, the MV Caliente, a supertanker carrying almost two million barrels of oil. Yet he wasn't worried. A few decades ago, he'd be anchored offshore, waiting for the fog to clear, but not in the 21st century with satellite navigation. As long as everyone obeyed the rules, radar and GPS satellites would keep them on course and away from the navigation hazards present off most shores.

He stared at the computer display showing their location, the shore to the east off their port bow. He peered out the window, seeing nothing but fog.

Or was it?

He could have sworn he saw something, just a glimpse. He stepped out onto the weather deck and leaned over the rail, peering hard into the fog. He could hear horns from other ships and the sounds of birds. Nothing out of the ordinary. He turned to go back inside when he heard something he shouldn't.

Sea lions.

Very close sea lions.

He rushed back to the railing and looked over the side at the water below, and not fifty feet from their hull was a large rock jutting from the water, dozens of sea lions spread out over its surface. "We're off course!" He rushed back inside. "All stop! All stop!"

"Aye, Captain, all stop!" His helmsman killed their speed, the massive propellers slowly winding down, stopping a behemoth like this a long process.

"Sound collision alarm."

"Sounding collision alarm, aye!"

A wail no mariner wanted to hear tore through the air.

"What is it, Captain?"

He ignored his First Officer, instead examining the map. He pointed to the port side. "There. That should be three hundred meters off our bow."

"Yes, sir. It isn't?"

"No, it's right there!" He jabbed a finger toward the sea lions' perch, through the deck. His jaw dropped as he continued to examine the map. "Oh no!" Another hazard was indicated, and if he estimated their actual position, they were about to run straight into it. "All engines astern!"

"All engines a—"

The ship jerked, tossing them all forward before his order could be fully acknowledged. He slammed into the helm, his ribs protesting as he swore he heard a series of cracks. He gasped in a breath, the pain sharp and overwhelming as the din of tearing metal screeched through the ship.

Then he heard the engines building up power as his last order was executed.

"Stop the engines! All stop!"

But no one was at the helm. His helmsman pulled himself to his feet, reaching for the controls, yet it took several seconds before he could kill the engines.

And it was too late.

He could feel them drifting off the shoal, the damage already done.

"Captain, we have a breach of the forward hold!"

He clasped his ribs and limped over to where his First Officer stood, the displays indicating the integrity of the holds storing their precious cargo showing the forward hold losing pressure.

And that meant only one thing.

They were spilling oil off of Long Beach, California.

The Oval Office, The White House
Washington, DC

President Jacob Starling sat in the corner of one of the couches in the Oval Office, half a dozen of his most trusted advisors seated around him, another dozen aides lining the walls. The door closed as the last to arrive stepped inside—Director Leif Morrison from the CIA.

What's he doing here? Isn't he special ops?

Starling looked around the room. "Okay, ladies and gentlemen, what's going on?"

His Chief of Staff, Andrea Krige, spoke. "Sir, yesterday evening the 9-1-1 systems of our nation's cities were compromised by a hack to eTALK's Voice over IP system. They've shut down their service and are patching it now, as well as installing Croft Technologies' SecuraVault system. That particular crisis is now over, and 9-1-1 operations are returning to normal."

Starling's head bobbed with the first bit of good news in over 24 hours.

Krige continued. "The traffic light systems have been intermittently hacked in dozens of major cities. New York City has just shut down the system entirely—too many casualties every time the system was turned back on. That solves the immediate danger, but will cause unprecedented gridlock—"

Starling held up a finger, sensing something his government might help with, at least with manpower. "Can we provide them with personnel to help?"

FBI Director Fitzgerald cleared his throat. "We're trying to identify the source of the hacks, but until we do, we have to leave everything essentially on a flashing red. The cities are putting police at every major intersection to try and get traffic moving, but they're going to need help. States of emergency are being declared, and the National Guard is being sent in to assist."

"How long?"

Fitzgerald frowned. "We're hoping to have traffic moving again in a few hours, but it will be brutally slow, Mr. President. The automated systems are vital to smooth traffic flow in a modern city. Police and Guardsmen standing in the middle of intersections aren't going to be coordinated. But worse, people are abandoning their vehicles. It's going to be a nightmare, Mr. President."

Starling frowned, his idea of throwing Federal employees at the intersections apparently not a good one. "And the railways?"

Krige shook her head. "The system has been fried. Anything connected to a central control has been wiped. Each gate is going to have to be manually reinstalled. It's going to take days, if not longer."

Starling sighed, shaking his head. "Anything we can do *there*?"

Fitzgerald threw up his hands briefly. "Again, we need to find the source of the hack, otherwise they'll just do it again like we saw with the traffic signals. Police and National Guard units are rolling out to the crossings, so we should be able to get rail traffic moving by midnight, but they have to slow at every crossing. That's going to delay shipping times dramatically."

There was a knock at the door then it swung open, one of the Joint Chief's aides rushing in. He handed him a piece of paper then left the room.

"What is it, Fred?"

The Chairman of the Joint Chiefs of Staff, General Fred Parsons, flicked the piece of paper. "Thirty-eight minutes ago a patch was uploaded to the entire satellite GPS system. This patch reset the system so that all readings are now off by two hundred meters."

Starling's eyes widened. "What the hell? Was it a software bug?"

General Parsons shook his head. "No, Mr. President. This was an unauthorized upload."

Starling's pulse quickened and he took a slow, deep breath.

This isn't the time to panic.

"Two hundred meters. What does that mean? What does that gain anybody?"

"Mr. President, it essentially means every navigation system in the world just became useless. Sir, this is a coordinated attack on our transportation infrastructure, it has to be. They've turned our roads into parking lots, slowed our rail system to a crawl, and now with this, they can affect our shipping systems. Every modern ship relies on GPS to dock at our ports and navigate our waterways. That system is now useless."

"Do we have any idea who's behind this?"

Director Morrison cleared his throat. "Mr. President, we do, but I'll have to ask that the room be cleared."

Starling's eyebrows shot up. "I think we can trust everyone here, Leif."

Morrison shook his head. "I'm sorry, Mr. President, but we can't."

Indignant protests erupted, but Morrison stood his ground, ignoring them, instead keeping his focus on Starling. Starling stared back, assessing the man, then nodded. "Clear the room."

General Parsons rose. "Yes, Mr. President."

The room slowly emptied, the protests subdued, though annoyed glares were tossed in Morrison's direction. Vice President Harold Vance remained seated.

"Him too."

Vance gave Morrison a look. "Are you kidding me?"

"No, sir."

"Harry, please." Starling motioned toward the door and Vance let out a heavy sigh as he rose.

"You'd think it was goddamned aliens or something." He stepped outside and the door closed, leaving the two men alone.

Starling motioned to the other end of the couch. "Have a seat, Leif."

"Thank you, Mr. President." Morrison sat, crossing his legs.

"So, what is it that you can't say in front of my top advisors?"

"Mr. President, do you remember the briefing I gave you on the Assembly?"

Starling's jaw dropped slightly. "You...you think they're behind this?"

Morrison nodded, sending Starling's heart racing. "Yes, Mr. President, I do."

Observation Room 8C, CIA Headquarters
Langley, Virginia

Chris Leroux peered through the glass of the interrogation room at Nadja Katz, the woman who had killed so many a little over a year ago, and nearly killed his girlfriend, Sherrie White. The cold-blooded assassin sat calmly, staring back at him, despite there no way she could know he was there. A glass of water remained untouched, and the handcuffs she had been placed in, sat neatly, unlocked, to her left.

He had smiled when he saw the ostentatious display, and instructed the guards to leave her be. If she could defeat the handcuffs that easily, the restraints that would be necessary would probably kill any chance they had of getting her to cooperate. She had turned herself in, asked for Kane, then refused to say anything else beyond her name, and the fact she was the one who had shot Sherrie a year ago.

That fact alone made him want to raid the armory and shoot the bitch a dozen times in every part of the body except the chest and head, allowing her to feel every single shot before she died a horrible, painful, slow death.

Though judging from her leather and latex outfit, skin-tight with a set of ta-tas that could float the Titanic, she might get off on the pain. Her emotionless, sculpted face, certainly suggested she was cold-hearted, and if he didn't know Sherrie and Kane so well, he would have thought all people trained to kill would be like this.

Yet they weren't.

She was a special breed, someone he hoped to never run into outside of the safety of this building, though with what she had done at the police station in Annapolis, perhaps he wasn't as safe as he presumed.

The door opened and his heart skipped a beat before seeing who it was. "Dylan!"

"Hey, buddy." His friend, who had been on his way to Philly to continue looking for Fang, whistled at the sight on the other side of the glass. "Man, she's built."

"Sonya was in here earlier and had to leave. I think she was getting jealous."

"That girl has a thing for you."

"Yeah, when it rains it pours. A few years ago, I couldn't get a woman to look at me. Now I live with one, and work with another that's having trouble concentrating at times."

Kane slapped him on the back. "You're a lucky man." He held up a finger. "Just don't act on it, or you lose it all."

Leroux grunted. "No worries there. I can barely handle one woman, let alone two." He motioned toward Katz. "She insisted on talking to you and you alone."

Kane nodded. "Okay, let's see if I can charm those leather pants off her."

"Hey, remember, you've got a significant other too."

Kane's face clouded, as if guilty about something, his eyes growing distant, the joy of a moment before wiped clear. "Yeah. Balancing that with this job is sometimes difficult."

Leroux turned, staring at his friend. "You mean…" He couldn't finish the sentence, though the shame on Kane's face told him everything he needed to know. His friend had strayed, but not willingly.

Kane looked away.

"Was it the job?"

"Of course it was the job. You know how I feel about her."

"Then she'd understand."

Kane huffed. "I don't think any woman would understand. Hell, I don't even know if *I'd* understand."

Leroux stepped closer. "You love her?"

"You know it."

"And she loves you. The fact you feel so guilty about it proves that. Your job is important. That means you do what's necessary, and then you don't talk about it with your friends and family, because it's *classified*. She knows the job, she was in the business. She knows if you have to do something, you're not betraying her, you're just following orders. She'd forgive you if she ever found out."

Kane frowned at his friend. "Look who's giving relationship advice now."

Leroux flushed. "Yeah, I guess I'm not the best guy to be advising you."

Kane grabbed him by the shoulder. "Bullshit. You're the best man I know. You're like a brother to me, and I respect you." He nodded toward Katz. "Now, let's see what this woman wants, so we can get back to finding our far better halves."

Leroux smiled, not trusting himself to respond without his voice cracking.

A brother.

He turned away and Kane headed out of the room, the door to the interrogation room opening. Katz looked up at him, her face remaining expressionless as Kane sat across from her. "Nadja Katz. Why shouldn't I just shoot you right now?"

Unknown Location

Sherrie White woke with a groan. Her head pounded like the day after St. Paddy's Day, and her mouth was as dry. She blinked her eyes clear then gasped. "Fang!"

Lee Fang lay beside her, gripping her side, her breath shallow and rapid, a pool of blood beside her from the gunshot wound she had received during their escape.

"Oh my God, are you okay?"

It was a stupid, instinctual question, and Fang gave her a look, rather than waste energy replying. Sherrie pressed her left hand on the wound, Fang wincing with a sharp breath. She checked their surroundings, a windowless room, and saw a large duffel bag sitting nearby. She stretched to reach it, not wanting to take her hand off Fang's wound. She snagged it and pulled it closer, unzipping it.

And breathed a sigh of relief.

"Medical supplies." She quickly began yanking the contents out, spreading them around her, making a quick inventory as she planned on how to treat the wound. She smiled when she spotted the XStat applicators, an injectable combat field dressing that would seal the wound and stop her from bleeding out.

The bullet!

She frowned, eying the basic surgical equipment, enough here for her to go in and get the bullet before it caused an infection or did further damage.

Remember your training!

She mentally head slapped herself and pulled Fang's shirt up. Fang winced.

"Sorry." She sighed with relief when she saw an exit wound, the bullet a through-and-through. She took Fang's hand and put it over the wound. "I'm going to seal it, just give me a second."

She opened the XStat package and quickly read the instructions before moving Fang's hand away. "This might hurt, sorry."

She shoved the applicator into the wound then squeezed the plunger, the tiny sponges filling the hole, eventually oozing out the other side. She tossed the applicator aside and watched as the sponges expanded, the free-flowing blood easing to a trickle, then stopping.

Now let's just hope that holds.

"You'll have to stay as still as possible, okay? I don't know exactly how stable that stuff is, so moving might reopen the wound."

Fang nodded, her face covered with sweat, her breath still rapid and shallow. Several bags of IV solution were Sherrie's next test at remembering her training. She opened the IV kit, and after a few attempts and even more apologies, she had an IV in place.

"This should help, but you've lost a lot of blood."

Fang didn't respond, instead just nodding as she tried to relax and conserve her energy.

Sherrie examined their surroundings, deciding to occupy Fang's thoughts with something other than her current medical situation. "We're in a rectangular room, maybe ten by twelve. There are no windows, and a single door just behind you. It has no door knob or any other type of locking device, and it appears metal." She stared up at the ceiling and grunted. "There's a dome camera right above us, so someone is watching, or can watch us, and we've got four sets of fluorescent lights with no obvious light switch." She glanced over her shoulder at the far corner. "There's a half-height wall there with a toilet and sink, and nothing else."

"Who-who?"

She looked down at Fang. "That was Nadja Katz. She shot me a little over a year ago. She works for the Assembly, or at least she used to. Hell, I don't know what's going on. Why would she rescue us? And rescue us from who? And why would they take *us*?"

Fang was about to say something when Sherrie held out a hand.

"Don't answer that. You need your strength." She grabbed some gauze and wiped up some of the blood from the floor.

Damn, she really lost a lot.

She reexamined her supplies. There was no blood plasma here for a transfusion, but she was a universal donor. Type O. If she could figure out a way, she could transfuse her own blood into Fang and quite possibly save the woman's life. She chewed her cheek as she examined the supplies. She could use the needle from the second IV kit on herself, and the tube from it. That would allow her to get the blood out of her, though it could be slow.

But where to hold it?

She needed to hold the blood somewhere before she could give it to Fang. Her eyes popped wide and she stared at the IV already set up.

Skip the middleman?

Would that work? She had no idea. It hadn't been covered in her training. If she put a needle in both their arms, with a tube between, how could she be sure it would be her blood going into Fang's, and not the other way around? She had always seen the bottle or bag of blood hung high during a transfusion, at least in the movies, so gravity must have something to do with it.

Could it be that simple? She just had to make sure her arm was higher than Fang's? And if she were to do this, it would mean unhooking the IV bag. Was blood more important than fluids? It had to be, otherwise during surgery they'd be pumping sugar water into the patient, not blood.

She looked at Fang. "Do you trust me?"

Fang nodded, and Sherrie believed her, the two of them having fought side-by-side in Baltimore a year ago.

"We're going to try an experiment."

Interrogation Room 8C, CIA Headquarters
Langley, Virginia

Nadja Katz regarded Dylan Kane as he sat across from her. It was an interesting question he had posed. Why *shouldn't* he just shoot her? She was, after all, the enemy. She had tried to kill his friend, had killed countless members of law enforcement, and she had worked for an organization that had sought to start a war. If the roles were reversed, she'd probably have put two bullets in his head and been done with it.

But he was constrained by rules, and she wasn't.

Though from what she knew about him, few rules applied, at least when on assignment, out of the country. In here, in this room, in this building, she suspected his options were extremely limited.

"I have your women."

If Kane had a reaction, he hid it well. "So you *do* work for the Assembly."

She shook her head. "No. They took your women from you, then I took them back."

"Why?"

"To give you an incentive to work with me."

"And why would I want to do that?"

"Because we want the same thing."

"Which is?"

"To destroy the Assembly once and for all." She leaned back, folding her arms, her breasts squeezing together. Kane's eyes remaining glued to hers.

He's got willpower.

"You damaged them a year ago, but they've replaced those who died already, and now have decided the time is right to implement their endgame. They took your women to keep you off balance, to disincentivize you from interfering." She leaned forward slightly. "Now I've eliminated that leverage they had over you. Now you're free to act."

Kane continued to stare at her, emotionless. "Hand over our people, and I'll listen."

"No."

Kane rose. "Then I'll arrange transport to one of our black sites. The Constitution doesn't get in the way there."

A hint of a smile crept up the side of her face. "One of them was wounded."

A quick breath that would probably have been missed by most, betrayed Kane. "Who?"

"Does it matter? Isn't one your girlfriend, the other the girlfriend of your best friend? Shouldn't you care about both?"

Kane didn't respond. Even her emotionless nature knew it wasn't a fair question. Of course he'd care about Fang more, though he was moral enough to at least struggle with his preferences.

"Who?"

"Not your concern. Just know that one of them will die without medical assistance, and both will die if I don't send a coded signal within"—she checked her watch—"twenty-two hours."

Kane returned to his seat. "What do you want?"

"I want your cooperation. I can help you bring down the Assembly, but I need access to your resources. Help me, and I'll set your women free."

"Why? Why do you want to bring them down?"

Katz leaned forward, staring deep into his eyes. "Because they tried to kill me. And I don't like it when people try to kill me."

Kane pursed his lips then nodded. "I can understand that." He leaned back and she mirrored his moves. "What are they up to?"

"The implementation of their ultimate agenda."

"Which is?"

"A war that will fundamentally change society for the betterment of mankind. Every great war triggers a surge in technological advances, a unification of society against a common enemy that sets their petty differences aside, then an economic boom that lasts decades. The Assembly stands to profit from all this, as well as use it as an opportunity to reshape the democracies of the Western world to more suit their vision of what's best for mankind over the long term."

"Which is?"

"Think elected authoritarian rulers, providing the illusion of peace and freedom within the borders, and zero-tolerance for any dissent, or threats, from outside."

"So dictatorship. I presume military."

"Of a sort. Closer to the modern Chinese model, I would guess. Can you imagine how great a country the United States would be if it weren't constrained by the laws that currently hamper its leaders? You could rule the world, unchallenged. Problems like ISIS, Russia, North Korea, even China, could be dealt with swiftly and brutally. Do you think in World War Two, that your leaders worried about how things would play out on CNN? They leveled cities, destroyed factories with civilians inside—they did what needed to be done to win.

"Do you think today, the public would let them drop two nuclear bombs on Japanese cities, despite the fact it saved millions of lives? Of course they wouldn't. Your society has become too moral for its own good, and those who don't share those values, *will* drop those bombs, *will* kill those innocents, and in the end, they *will* win the war you refuse to fight. The Assembly has seen this, and wants to prevent it the only way they know how. By triggering the next great war, by forcing America and her allies to choose life or death. By eliminating the gray areas in between, they know you will choose life. And once the choice is made, you will prevail.

"The price will be high, but they think in the long term. Eventually what will emerge will be stronger and more advanced than ever before. Mankind will rid itself of the problems that plague it today due to indecision and political correctness, and thrive. This is what the Assembly offers, this is what their agenda is." She leaned forward. "The question is, does this excite you, or terrify you?"

Kane said nothing, though his eyes spoke volumes, the laser-like focus of moments ago gone, his eyes distant, as if imagining what the world she described would be like. She guessed it would appeal to him. He killed for a living, and rules got in his way. If he were given free rein, he might get his job done a little easier, a little more effectively.

It was people like him the Assembly counted on to achieve their goals. Those who had lost their faith in the government, lost faith in the pillars of democracy like freedom of the press and freedom of speech. In a world where the news media continually reported opinion as fact, and lied through falsehoods or omission, where speaking your mind labeled you as a racist or fascist or some sort of "phobe" if you didn't agree with the Social Justice Warriors, in a world like that, it was the people who recognized these problems that would say "Hell, yeah!" to a government that would promise to end the insanity.

And if that meant giving up some freedoms, it would be embraced.

The proof was 9/11.

More than fifteen years later, few complained about taking off their shoes at airports, about not being able to bring a bottle of water or shampoo on a plane, of being subjected to random searches despite not being in the target demographic responsible for 99% of terrorist attacks, or the countless other forms of security and surveillance that Western societies now took for granted.

The Patriot Act had been embraced by most, and though parts had expired, most were renewed with the USA Freedom Act, with few now questioning it.

And it would be the same when the Assembly had their way. Things would change, a promise made that it would be short term, then eventually the public would forget what it used to be like, the generation that had fought for the freedoms they enjoyed would be gone, and the youth, so quick to take offense at anything that didn't meet their narrow worldview, would never have experienced the nation that once was.

A prime example was today's Russia, where too many of the youth cheered on a leader mired in the Soviet past, a past none had ever experienced. They wanted strength and respect, yet didn't understand the oppression and atrocities committed to maintain those desires.

Were Western democracies that vulnerable?

She felt they absolutely were, as did the Assembly. Would the world that came out the other end of the Assembly's plans be better? Perhaps, though she didn't care.

They had tried to kill her.

She was going to kill them.

That was all she cared about. Mankind had done nothing for her, so why should she care what happened to it? She wasn't here to stop the Assembly's plans. She was here to stop the Assembly.

Somebody rapped on the glass behind Kane then the television mounted on the wall to her right flicked on, a series of images showing the chaos around the country played—tankers spilling oil, derailed trains, traffic chaos.

And terrified people.

A computerized voice spoke. *"We are the Utopians. We are responsible for bringing your cities to a standstill. We have poisoned the reservoirs of ten cities in the continental United States with an undetectable poison. Anyone who drinks this water will become violently ill within five to seven days, then die as your hospitals are overrun and unable to treat the infected.*

"We have the antidote, and are willing to share it, if your leaders are willing to meet our demands. You will hear from us again soon, but know this: Your leaders are no longer in control, you are no longer safe, and your cities are no longer habitable. Return to the country, return to your origins, and never let what will happen over the coming days happen again."

The screen went blank then the broadcast repeated. Katz stared at the images, the human suffering of no interest, though the carefully chosen script had her curious. The screen turned off and Kane looked back to her.

"So, if the Assembly is behind this, then who the hell are the Utopians?"

Moore Residence, Abbotts Park Apartments
Fayetteville, North Carolina

"Leon, come here!"

Atlas glanced toward the bedroom door as he dried his hair. He and Dawson had been covered in dirt and blood by the time they left the accident scene, and he had been called up as he reached his girlfriend Vanessa's apartment. "What is it?"

"An Emergency Broadcast Alert. You've gotta see this!"

Atlas rushed into the living room and watched the brief broadcast, his eyes widening the entire time. It repeated, and he turned it off.

"What does it mean?"

He looked at Vanessa. "It means we've got big problems."

"Is this why you were called up?"

"I'm guessing." He pointed at the phone as he rushed back into the bedroom to finish dressing. "Call my sister."

Vanessa dialed as he quickly pulled on some pants then stuffed his undershirt into them. She entered the room, holding out the phone. "It's ringing."

Atlas took the phone and Vanessa pushed him onto the bed, grabbing his shoes from the corner.

"Hello?"

"Hey, Larissa, it's me. You okay?"

"Oh, Leon, what a day! It's been crazy here! First—"

"No time. Did you hear the Emergency Broadcast?"

"No, what—"

"Just listen. Can you leave the city?"

"No way, it's gridlock out there. Nothing's moving."

"Okay, here's what I need you to do. Go to your nearest store as soon as you hang up. Buy as much water and canned goods as you can carry, then bring them home. As soon as you've done that, go do it again. Keep doing it until there's nothing left, understand me?"

"Leon, what's going on? You're sounding crazy."

"Listen, Sis, they're choking off the cities, okay? That's what's going on here. If things go south, you'll need food and water." Vanessa finished tying his shoes and he flashed her a smile. "Wait, do you have any prescriptions?"

"Yes, but I just refilled them a few days ago."

Atlas breathed a sigh of relief. "Good, then that should last. When things get bad, stay inside. Do you have a gun?"

"You know I'll never have one of those things in the house!"

Atlas frowned. "You live in the Bronx and you don't have a gun? You're a very trusting person."

"Don't you start—"

"You're right, I'm sorry. Now, what are you going to do as soon as you hang up?"

"Get as much food and water as I can."

"Exactly. And keep doing it until it's no longer safe."

His sister's voice finally sounded as scared as he felt she should. "Leon, is it really going to get that bad?"

He closed his eyes, picturing his sister and her kids, all alone thanks to that deadbeat bastard of an ex she had. "It could. Just get yourself stocked up, don't tell anyone you have supplies, keep the door locked, and if it truly hits the fan, I'll come get you, understood?"

"They'll let you?"

He stood. "They might not have a choice."

The Oval Office, The White House
Washington, DC

President Starling watched the broadcast, shaking his head. Morrison had said it was the Assembly behind the hack attacks, and now these Utopians were claiming responsibility. At first, he had thought it might be one group claiming credit for another's work, but he was assured that was unlikely. Which meant Morrison was wrong. "Do we have any intel on these guys?"

FBI Director Fitzgerald held up a tablet computer. "Yes, sir, but not a lot. They're a fringe group, eco-nuts. They've been linked to several protests surrounding pipelines and logging operations over the years, but nothing like this. Certainly nothing technical. No hacking." He looked up from the tablet. "Frankly, Mr. President, this just doesn't match their MO."

Starling nodded, rereading the script broadcast through the hack of the Emergency Broadcast System. "Clearly they've gone to computer camp." He sighed. "Do we know who they are? I mean, names?"

"We have a few, but they haven't really been on our radar. If we monitored every environmentalist organization, we'd have nobody left to investigate the real crimes."

Starling grunted, motioning at the television, now on a news channel, the talking heads delighting in the chaos. "Look like real crimes to me."

Fitzgerald bowed slightly. "Of course, Mr. President. I didn't mean to imply otherwise."

Starling raised his hand. "No need to apologize, Cliff, I know what you meant. Find them, round them up, and I'm going to have to address the nation. Let the networks know." He frowned, tapping the transcript of the broadcast. "Do we know what ten cities they're talking about? Have we detected any poison?"

Fitzgerald shook his head. "No idea, sir, though every city with a population over one million is performing testing now and advising their communities to not drink the water."

Starling sighed. "God help us all." He looked out the windows at Washington, DC, now secure under the blanket of darkness, the capital of their great nation for some reason left untouched. "How long can a city like New York hold out?"

"Days at most. And that's the problem, that's what they're talking about in their message. They're targeting our cities, our modern way of life. There're no farms in cities. All of the food is brought *to* the cities. They've disrupted our shipping systems, rail and road traffic, and now our water supply, which is also transported in through aqueducts and tunnels. The human body can last weeks without food, but only days without water. People will become desperate for water within a few days, and they'll drink from the taps unless we shut down the supplies. If we don't, and these Utopians have indeed poisoned the water, then people will begin to get sick. Millions will be dying in our biggest cities, and there won't be anything we can do about it."

"Can we be sure there's a poison?"

"No, that's the beauty of what they've done. Because they created havoc through these hacks, our citizens have no reason to doubt their claim about the poison. There doesn't need to be a poison to create panic. I guarantee you, Mr. President, before this week is through, we will have people killing for the last bottle of water in their local supermarket."

Starling closed his eyes and drew a deep breath. He looked at Fitzgerald. "Arrest every member of that group, now. Do whatever it takes. I don't give a shit if it stands up in court next year, our country needs saving today."

Williams Residence

Bronx, New York

Larissa Williams rode down the elevator with her three children, her heart pounding as she replayed the conversation with her brother. Immediately after getting off the phone, she had turned on the television to make sure he wasn't crazy, and had heard the emergency broadcast.

It had terrified her.

Something bad was happening, of that there was no doubt. That wasn't a government broadcast, that was some terrorist organization, though like none she had ever heard of. The typical terrorists usually demanded death to America and Israel, the killing of Jews and Christians, and various other hateful things. And they usually shot or blew up people.

But mass poisoning?

She had never heard of that. It didn't fit the pattern she thought of as terrorism. Islamists preferred martyrs to the cause. Poisoning water supplies didn't produce martyrs.

Perhaps it's not Islamists.

Just because 99% of the terrorist attacks around the world were committed by Muslims, didn't mean this one was. This had to be related to the hacking she had already encountered herself. The 9-1-1 system, the traffic signals, the trains, the GPS. That sounded more like the Chinese or Russians. But the message at the end of the broadcast is what had her puzzled.

Your cities are no longer habitable. Return to the country...

They weren't calling for death, they were demanding a *return to the country*. She pursed her lips.

That's an environmentalist message.

Environmentalism was the new religion, true adherents capable of killing for their beliefs. Greenpeace had already admitted in court filings that they lied in their propaganda, and in essence, shouldn't be believed.

Never let what will happen over the coming days happen again.

That final line actually terrified her. *Coming days.* Not what had already happened, but what *was* to happen. The city was already in chaos, and they promised to make it even worse?

The doors to the elevator opened and she herded her kids out, suddenly wondering if they wouldn't have been safer locked alone inside the apartment, rather than out here with her. Sirens and shouting filled the air, the chaos outside merely muffled by the glass façade of the main lobby.

One of her neighbors rushed inside, her eyes wide with fright. "I wouldn't go out there. Not with those kids."

The woman rushed past, catching the elevator before it closed. Larissa stared after her, then girded for what should only take ten minutes. Ten minutes to secure their next ten days. She pushed open the door and stepped outside, the sirens ear-splitting, the flash of red and blue lights flickering off every surface around her disorienting. "Okay, kids, everybody hold hands." She gripped her two youngest and jogged toward the nearest corner store.

"Mommy, what's wrong?"

"Nothing, Michael, just in a hurry." She held up at the street corner and waited for a National Guardsmen to indicate it was safe to cross. He motioned them forward and she squeezed their hands tighter, pulling her children across, then hurrying into Mr. Moe's Mini Market, at least a dozen people already there. She grabbed three baskets, handing one to each of her children, then took two for herself. She made a beeline for the back of the store and stopped, pointing at the canned soup. "Fill your baskets with those."

"How many?"

"As much as you can lift." She continued to the coolers in the back and reached in, pulling an armload of water bottles and sport drinks from the shelf, letting them tumble into the first basket before repeating the exercise with the second. She lifted them with a grunt, wondering how they would manage getting back home. She found her kids, their baskets overflowing, their faces straining as they barely lifted them off the ground. "Okay, let's go."

She reached the cash, a few people in line obviously in the know, others wondering what was going on. No one was talking. The TV in the corner flashed, the Emergency Broadcast System message she had seen still on a loop, but with the audio muted. Thankfully. "Hi Sameh."

"Hi Mrs. Williams. You going to be able to carry all this?"

She shrugged. "We'll figure out a way."

He rang in the purchases, returning them to the baskets. He leaned forward and whispered. "You're a good customer. Take the baskets, just promise to bring them right back."

Larissa smiled gratefully then whispered a response. "I'll probably be back for more."

The door chimed and several people rushed in. Sameh frowned. "I don't think anything will be left by the time you get back."

She nodded, a steady stream now pouring in, word apparently spreading. She paid by credit card, then lifted her baskets, the kids half-dragging, half-carrying theirs toward the doors. They reached the street corner, the panic now unavoidable, people rushing in all directions as they either made their way home, or toward their favorite store to stock up.

A window shattered behind her, a newspaper box rolling back onto the sidewalk as several men kicked their way into a closed store.

We have to get home, now!

Unknown Location

Sherrie White knelt beside her patient, a patient who looked a lot better since she had begun the transfusion. Gravity seemed to be working, and perhaps blood pressure—she had stuck the needle in her left arm, and the other end in Fang's right, where she presumed pressure would be lower.

She frankly had no idea what she was doing, though Fang wasn't sweating any longer, and her breathing had stabilized. Her pulse was now steady in the mid-sixties, a level Fang had indicated was her normal. She had no way to test the woman's blood pressure, which would be the true measure of whether this was working, but she had to assume it was.

Now the question was when did she stop?

She didn't think there was much danger to Fang in giving too much blood, but there was a risk to herself. She wasn't feeling lightheaded, or much different at all, and the line she was using was pretty thin, so perhaps not much had been transfused.

You need to stay physically capable.

She was their only hope of defending themselves. Even if Fang was stabilized, she was in no condition to fight. And if Sherrie were to get dizzy from any sudden movements, she wouldn't be much use either.

She pulled the tube from Fang's IV, then the needle from her own arm. "Let's see if that's enough. We can always try more later."

"I'm feeling a lot better, thank you."

"No problem. I'm going to hook the IV back up, though, okay?"

Fang nodded, some color back in her cheeks, life once again behind her eyes. Sherrie inserted the tube from the IV into the cannula then placed the bag on Fang's chest.

"Okay, that should help keep you going." She examined the wound once again, the XStat still holding. "How's the pain?"

"Still there, but not as bad as before. The palpitations have stopped, so I think I'm going to live. Assuming we get out of here."

Sherrie frowned, staring at the door. Distracted by Fang's predicament, she had so far spent no time on figuring a way out. "I'm going to do a little exploring, okay?"

Fang gave a weak thumbs up and Sherrie rose, slowly circling the walls, searching for anything out of the ordinary, but finding nothing beyond the door and prison-style bathroom. The floor was poured concrete, probably several inches thick. She knelt down and felt it with her hand. "The floor's cold."

Fang turned her head so she could see her. "Basement?"

"Probably, which means even if we could get through it, we'd have God knows how much dirt to dig through. She started tapping the walls, the thuds dull all the way around. "I think it's some sort of insulated drywall mounted directly to the outer walls. They're probably concrete too, with dirt behind them. She pursed her lips, her hands on her hips. "It's kind of a small room to be a basement, though."

Fang agreed. "Perhaps there're other rooms like this, side-by-side. You wouldn't be able to tell if the walls were thick enough."

Sherrie nodded. "That would make sense." She motioned toward the bare door, bereft of any hardware. "This door suggests it was built to be a cell, so it makes sense there could be others. I wonder if there're any other prisoners here."

"Could be, though if that Katz woman isn't working for the Assembly, then this place is probably hers. I doubt she's going around collecting people."

"Why not? She took us, why not others?"

Fang shook her head. "I think we're leverage because of who we are, or rather, who we're dating."

Sherrie sat cross-legged beside her. "That makes sense." She smiled at Fang. "And I would hardly describe our relationships as 'dating,' would you? I think Chris is going to propose to me soon."

Fang's face clouded over and she turned away slightly.

"What's wrong? Are you and Dylan having problems?"

Fang turned back, her eyes glistening. "I don't know. He seemed distant when he came back last time. He couldn't look me in the eye."

Sherrie frowned, a thought crossing her mind, one she didn't dare voice. Kane was a spy, and spies were asked to do things ordinary people wouldn't. It had already been made clear to her she'd be expected to sleep with men if it were necessary. In fact, one of her first assignments had been to seduce Leroux and get him to spill state secrets. It had been a test, and he had passed, greenlighting the accelerated career path he now found himself on. Director Morrison now trusted him, implicitly.

It had broken her heart when Leroux had found out the truth, the betrayal doubly so as he had developed true feelings for her. The worst part was that she too had fallen for the shy, awkward geek, even requesting to be removed from the assignment. Her request had been denied, the mission too important. It was Kane that had brought the two of them back together, Leroux forgiving her, the two of them inseparable since.

Kane loved Fang, though she knew from his lifestyle he wasn't the commitment type—at least not before Fang. Kane was a changed man, and if he were feeling guilty about something, which was what it sounded like to her, then he still loved her. "What do you think is wrong?"

Fang sighed. "I think he slept with another woman."

Sherrie's teeth clamped down on her cheek for a moment. "You think he's having an affair?"

Fang shook her head, a little too vigorously, wincing and grabbing for her wound. "No, but I think he slept with someone on the job."

Sherrie decided there was no avoiding the subject, and dove in. "You know it's part of the job."

"I do, and that's not what upsets me."

Sherrie's eyes narrowed. "It isn't?" She thought of how she'd feel if Leroux slept with someone else.

I'd tear his dick off.

"Then what's wrong?"

"Well, I thought we were close enough that we could tell each other anything."

Sherrie smiled, placing a hand on Fang's shoulder. "You know he can't tell you anything about his missions. They're classified."

"I know, but he can tell me when something is bothering him. He doesn't need to give me specifics, just tell me what he had to do so I can tell him it's okay." She sighed. "I want his heart exclusively, not his, well, you know."

Sherrie grinned, patting Fang's shoulder. "Oh, I know." She drew a quick breath then sighed. "You know, I think when you see him next, you're just going to have to confront him. Make him tell you what's bothering him, and if he won't, tell him what you suspect. If it isn't that, then you'll both feel better, and if it is, and he knows you're not upset, then he can share his feelings."

Fang looked at her, a slight smile on her face. "I think that's a good idea." Her smile spread. "You're good at this. You should have your own talk show."

Sherrie laughed. "Right, 'Relationship Advice from a Spy.' I don't think so."

Fang grunted. "Well, you're better at it than some of the people I see on afternoon TV."

Sherrie laughed. "I can't remember the last time I watched a show like that. Probably not since I was a teenager."

Fang huffed. "Try being an unemployable former Chinese Special Forces soldier. You'd have lots of time on your hands to watch those ridiculous things."

Sherrie smiled at the woman, understanding the frustration. Fang was used to being a woman of action, but now she had to keep a low profile and could never hold down a job that might make use of her former skills. Not that she needed a job. Leroux had told her a generous pension had been arranged for her. She'd never have to work again.

Which was probably the worst punishment a grateful nation could bestow upon her.

Fang stared up at the lights in the ceiling. "I think the only way out of here is either through that door, or through the ceiling."

Sherrie glanced up at the camera dome. "Yeah, but she's watching us."

Fang pursed her lips, her eyes narrowing. "Is she? If she's working alone, then I doubt she's sitting on the other side of the wall watching a monitor. She's off somewhere, doing something."

Sherrie yawned, eliciting a concerned look from Fang.

"You should get some rest."

"You should too."

Fang smiled. "I'm feeling good right now. I'll take first watch. We don't know how long this will last."

Sherrie regarded Fang, not really wanting to sleep in case something happened, though the woman was right. She was exhausted, and wouldn't be of any use in a few hours regardless. And Fang might not be in any condition to watch over her by then. She nodded. "Okay, but wake me if you need me."

Fang smiled. "Don't worry, I will."

Sherrie lay down beside her and positioned several pressure bandages under her head.

And was out in seconds.

Interrogation Room 8C, CIA Headquarters
Langley, Virginia

Nadja Katz stared at Kane. "I have no idea who the Utopians are, but I guarantee you they're not behind this."

Kane leaned back in his chair and folded his arms. "And why should I believe you? You're a criminal. You lie for a living. You claim to know what's going on, yet"—he waved a hand at the television— "this would suggest everything you told me is bullshit."

Kane played the game well. He had to know she would never turn herself in without reason, yet he was right about one thing. A critical part of her story was now in question. She had been honest about her desire to take down the Assembly, yet the reason she had given for this to also be in the best interests of the CIA, was what the Assembly was now doing to the country. If they weren't responsible, then the CIA's motivation had just been eliminated.

Good thing I still have leverage.

"If you don't believe me, then we're done here. I'll deal with the Assembly myself." She uncrossed her legs and began to stand when Kane raised a finger.

"You're not going anywhere."

Katz sat back down, a smile, expected in these situations, forced onto her face. "You forget I have your women."

Kane nodded. "You do. Tell me where they are, and I'll let you go."

"Do you think me a fool? They're the only thing keeping me alive." She pointed at the screen. "I guarantee you that they are not behind what is going on."

114

"A bold statement, backed by nothing."

She leaned back, staring at the glass. "I can prove it if you'll let me."

"How?"

She continued to stare at the glass, certain whoever had the power to let her leave, was standing on the other side, Kane a mere pawn in this game. "I'll take you to their top operative within the government, and I'll make him talk."

Kane leaned over, breaking her line of sight. "And just who might that be?"

She shook her head. "No. I'll take you to him. That's the deal."

Kane drew a deep breath, letting it out slowly. "And just where is this operative?"

She smiled, this time genuinely, a perverse pleasure at work here she wasn't accustomed to. "If I know how your government works, at this moment, he's probably at the White House."

Kane laughed. "Bullshit."

She shrugged, tapping her watch. "Time is ticking. Your women die in less than twenty-two hours. Do you really want to quibble?" She leaned forward. "Listen, if I'm right, we stop what's going on. If I'm not, we still bring down the Assembly, and you save the lives of your women. Either way, you win, and I win. Everyone walks away happy."

"You're telling me that the Assembly has an operative with access to the President of the United States?" Kane shook his head. "I don't believe it."

Katz wagged a finger. "You misunderstand. I'm telling you that I will take you to *one* of their operatives with access to the President. He will confirm everything I've told you."

Kane's thumb rapped on the table as he stared at her. "I need a name."

"You wouldn't believe me if I told you." She tapped her watch again. "Tick tock."

Someone knocked on the window.

Checkmate.

Albany, New York

Joseph Medina sat across from the targets' residence, awaiting confirmation from his Assembly contact. Apparently, a former agent, Nadja Katz, had interfered with Assembly plans. He had worked with her once before. She was efficient and brutal, precisely the type of agent the Assembly went for. In fact, he considered himself efficient and brutal as well, though he never saw her take any pleasure in carrying out her missions, whereas he did.

To excess.

Nothing gave him a surge of exquisite pleasure like shooting someone, or better yet, beating the living shit out of them. There was something about hearing a victim cry out in pain, begging for their life, offering their soul to avoid any further blows or cuts or ripped flesh.

Torture was fun.

He enjoyed inflicting pain in a methodical, deliberate way. He didn't indiscriminately beat someone—he targeted specific areas repeatedly until he achieved the desired result, whether a broken bone, a collapsed lung, or a damaged kidney. Pain was what he desired, pain delivered by him.

He just hoped he would be given a chance tonight.

His phone rang and he swiped his thumb. "Yes."

"It's been confirmed. Katz has the targets. You're a go."

He turned to the others in the vehicle and smiled. "Let's go to work." He climbed out of the SUV and closed the door, walking across the street toward their target's humble home.

The home CIA Special Agent Dylan Kane had grown up in.

Rick Kane sat in his La-Z-Boy chair with his feet up. By his side, sat three fingers of Glen Breton Rare, worked down to one. His head lolled to the side as he battled to stay awake, the built in massagers indecently kneading his entire body.

It was exquisite.

"Why don't you go to bed?"

He opened his eyes and gazed at his wife, Jenn, through his ecstasy, his body melted butter, a delicious numbness coursing through his veins. "I'm too comfortable."

"I swear half our electrical bill goes to that chair. You're going to wear it out."

"Then I'll buy another."

"You already had to buy that one on layaway."

Rick grunted. "Don't harsh my mellow."

Jenn stared at him. "Excuse me?"

"Isn't that what the kids say nowadays?"

"Maybe the kids do, but a grown man old enough to be a grandfather should never say those words. You sound ridiculous."

He grunted again. "I don't think I'll ever be a grandfather, so don't worry about it."

"Why do you say that?"

"You've met our son, haven't you?"

"Rick! That's not fair!"

"Isn't it? He quit a perfectly good career in the military to become an enforcer for the big companies, gallivanting around the globe, never settling down." His chest tightened as his greatest regret resurfaced.

"That's your son you're talking about."

He frowned, downing the rest of his scotch. "Yes, it is. My son, the biggest disappointment of my life."

"I will not sit here and listen to you say such horrible things! He loves you! What would he think if he heard talk like that?"

"If he loves me, why is he never here? He knows how proud I was when he joined the Army. Hell, I even supported him dropping out of college to do it. But to work for an *insurance* company as an investigator? There's only one reason he did that—to spite me!"

"Hogwash! It's an excellent job. He makes good money, he's secured his future, and he's still young. He'll settle down eventually and give you those grandkids you want."

A burst of air erupted from his lips. "He spends most of his time outside the country, and almost never comes home for vacation. You know he's probably got a piece of ass in every port of call. A boy like that will never settle down."

"I can't believe—"

A loud banging sound from the front door ended the conversation. The echo of heavy footfalls rushing down the hallway had Rick struggling to get out of his chair as his wife leaped to her feet.

He pointed at the phone. "Call 9-1-1!"

Four men rushed into the room, guns drawn.

"I'd prefer it if you didn't."

Rick, his hands half raised, glared at the man. "What the hell do you want?"

"Take anything you want, just don't hurt us!" cried Jenn.

The man who had spoken, darkly tanned with a pansy-assed bleach blonde hairdo, sneered. "We're not here for your things, we're here for you."

Rick's eyes narrowed. "I think you've got the wrong house. We're nobody."

Blondie chuckled. "Yes, *you* are nobody. But your son isn't."

Rick's chin dropped. "Dylan? What the hell are you talking about? He's an insurance investigator for Shaws of London." Rick stopped, his head beginning to shake. "That sonofabitch! This is about one of his claims, isn't it! Did he turn you down? That's what they do, you know. They find any excuse not to pay, to stick it to the little guy while they continue to rake in the premiums." He lowered his hands. "I'm with you! Screw Shaw—"

"Your son doesn't work for Shaws of London."

Rick stared at him. "Umm, yes he does."

Blondie shook his head. "No, your son is one of the CIA's top operatives."

Rick laughed, relief sweeping over him as he realized they definitely had the wrong house, and this should soon be over. Even Jenn giggled. "Oh, our son is a lot of things, but he's no spy."

Blondie stepped closer. "Your son, Special Agent Dylan Kane, is a spy, who has killed countless people for your country. And unfortunately for you, he has become an annoyance to my employer. You will be coming with us"—he held up several zip ties—"the easy way"—he held up his gun—"or the hard way."

But Rick wasn't listening anymore.

Dylan, a spy?

It couldn't be true, yet it had to be. These men knew his name, had guns, and wouldn't be here if it weren't true. Mistakes like that weren't made. His jaw dropped as nearly ten years of his son's life were rewritten. He hadn't quit the military, he had merely changed professions, to something he couldn't tell them about. It explained so much. He could never understand why his son had left the Army, left something he had loved so much.

His chest ached. What must it have been like for the poor boy to lie about what he did for all these years? What must it have been like for his son to hear the horrible things his own father had said about his profession, a profession that was only a cover, a cover meant to protect them from the dangers his new career could expose them to.

I'm so sorry!

He turned to his wife, her eyes filled with tears of pride and confusion and fear. She smiled at him and he returned it. Then glared at their captors. "We won't cooperate. We won't let you use us against our son."

Blondie laughed. "You're operating under the mistaken impression that you have a choice." He stepped closer. "I'm going to enjoy this."

Observation Room 8C, CIA Headquarters
Langley, Virginia

Dylan Kane stared through the glass at Nadja Katz as she sat, unmoving, exhibiting none of the nervous ticks most prisoners did when they knew they were being watched. No nails were picked, no scratches itched, no teeth rubbed with the back of a tongue. Nothing. It was as if she were completely comfortable, completely relaxed. "She's a psychopath."

Director Morrison, just returned from Washington, nodded. "Close. Once we had prints, we were able to pull her file."

Kane's eyebrows rose. "We've got a file on her?"

"Not us. The Germans. She was in their foster care system when she was a kid. Other than that, we've got nothing on her beyond what we know from last year."

Leroux leaned against the glass. "What does it tell us?"

Morrison shook his head. "Not much, except for one important thing. She was in a severe car accident when she was a kid and suffered brain damage. Apparently, she can't experience emotion, or she's very limited in what she can."

Kane whistled, turning back toward Katz. "Well, that explains a few things. We're trained to suppress our emotions, but they still get in the way. If she didn't have any, she could kill efficiently, without remorse or hesitation." He pursed his lips, sucking in a deep breath. "That makes her extremely dangerous, but very predictable."

Morrison's eyes narrowed. "How's that?"

"She's dominated by logic. She'll do exactly what she thinks will allow her to achieve her goals. Human emotion won't enter into it."

Leroux sighed. "That means she won't hesitate to kill Sherrie and Fang if she thinks it will help her."

Kane nodded. "Exactly. She's not governed by what's morally right or wrong. She won't feel any last minute remorse and change her mind. If she commits to killing them, then she will. There will be no stopping her."

Morrison grunted. "But that can work to our advantage."

Kane eyed him. "How?"

"Logic. If we can reason with her, to show her how letting them live helps *her*, we just might be able to convince her. Just as remorse or morals won't get in the way, neither will arrogance or bullheadedness. If she's completely logical, we just need to figure out how to convince her it's in her best interest to let them go."

Leroux shook his head. "She's determined to bring down the Assembly, and she needs our help to do it. And if they're linked to this current crisis, letting her might work in *our* best interest."

Morrison leaned against the door and folded his arms. "Go on."

Leroux pushed off the glass. "Look, she has Sherrie and Fang. She'll never hand them over because she knows that's her only leverage over us. We should forget trying to convince her to change her mind. She won't. So, if we want them back, we need to help her achieve her goals as quickly as possible, especially if one of them is wounded."

Morrison looked at Kane. "And you? What do you think?"

"I agree with Chris. Let me go with her to Washington. What can it hurt?"

"She could escape."

"If she wanted to get away, she wouldn't have walked in here in the first place. And if she did escape, then she would no longer need leverage, so she should, logically, release Fang and Sherrie."

Morrison tapped his chin when Kane's phone vibrated in his pocket. He fished it out, the call display indicating his father was calling. His eyes narrowed.

"Something wrong?" asked Morrison.

"It's my dad."

"And that's unusual?"

Kane said nothing, instead staring at the vibrating phone.

Something must have happened to Mom.

"They almost never talk," whispered Leroux to Morrison.

Kane swept his thumb. "Dad?"

"We have your parents. Do not interfere. The Assembly is eternal."

The call ended and Kane's chest tightened as his heart pounded. He squeezed the phone hard, the reinforced case cutting into his hands, the pain snapping him out of the fog of emotions that overwhelmed him. "They've got my parents."

Leroux's hand darted out, taking him by the arm as Morrison grabbed a phone off the wall. "Who?"

"The Assembly. They said that they have my parents, not to interfere, and that the Assembly was eternal."

Morrison turned away from them, his voice low. "I want a team sent to Special Agent Dylan Kane's parents' home immediately. Notify local law enforcement of their possible abduction. And send units to Analyst Supervisor Chris Leroux's parents' house as well."

Leroux's head whipped around, and Kane watched the color drain from his face. His hand reached into his pocket and he pulled out his phone. Tears filled his eyes as he held up the phone for Kane to see.

Mom and Dad.

"Put it on speaker."

Leroux swiped his thumb, tapping the button so everyone could hear. "Hello?"

"We have your parents. Do not interfere. The Assembly is eternal."

The call ended and Leroux collapsed into a chair. He looked up at the others. "Wh-what do we do now?"

Morrison put a hand on his shoulder. "We do our jobs."

"But they'll kill them!"

Morrison nodded. "They might. But we have to assume from their track record that they'll kill them anyway." He turned to Kane, jerking his head toward Katz. "Take her. Do what you need to do."

A smile climbed up half of Kane's face. "Rules of engagement?"

"None."

Mount Baker-Snoqualmie National Forest, Washington

Garry Suzuki leaned over from his perch, staring down at the loggers gathered below as he held up his cellphone to record what was about to happen. "You're all murderers! Trees are living creatures and have rights! Every time you cut down one of these majestic beings, you mortally wound Mother Earth, you weaken Gaia even more. Once you wound her enough, she'll die, and us along with her."

"You're a nutbar you eco-Nazi piece of shit terrorist! If you don't get out of that tree, I'm going to get my shotgun and blow you off that branch myself!"

Suzuki grinned, the logger's reaction exactly what he wanted. Death threats. They made for great PR, helped further the cause, and allowed for charges to be sometimes laid, though today the few police gathered seemed to be ignoring the crime just committed. No matter, he had it on camera, and when he returned to what modern man considered civilization, he'd upload it to the web for the world to see.

He rolled back into his perch, nestled among the massive branches of the Douglas Fir, the chains holding him in place uncomfortable, though more for show. They were lightweight, in reality only looped around him once by necessity, the rest out of his commitment to the cause. It was the handcuff linking him to the end of the chain that was the true bond merging him with this beautiful tree. He had no key, and he had filled the lock with Krazy Glue. No one was getting these off him without a fight.

And it was a fight.

Modern man was destroying the planet through living in a way nature had never intended. Sprawling cities, built from concrete and steel torn from the ground, acted as massive heatsinks that warmed the planet, sucking in nature's bounty every day before regurgitating it through tons of garbage and liquid waste. The earth was never meant to sustain so many people in such a concentrated area. The proof was what would happen if the system shut down.

It would be disastrous.

Millions would die.

He had no desire to see that. He wanted people to move out of the cities and embrace a simpler lifestyle, not driven by consumerism. Simple meals prepared with ingredients from local farms, modern technology leveraged to provide clean, renewable power, and telecommuting allowing people to work among nature rather than the concrete jungle. A life centered around family, friends, and community, where nature and healthy lifestyles were the norm, rather than fast food and video games. A return to respecting the land, respecting the planet, and saving it for future generations to enjoy.

It was a dream, one that would never come true in his lifetime, but he was determined to do his part, so that when he did die, and faced the great cosmic creator, he'd be able to look Her in the eye and tell Her that he had tried his hardest, and if She agreed, She'd grant him entry to a life of eternal oneness with the living planet, Gaia.

He sighed, closing his eyes as a smile spread across his face, actually looking forward to the day when he did finally die. Part of him wanted that ignorant logger to go and get his gun, to make good on his threat, and shoot him out of this tree. He'd die for his beliefs, and his eternity would be set, a martyr for the cause.

A black SUV pulled up on the logging road, a man and woman in dark suits and sunglasses climbing out.

Feds. What the hell do they want?

The man stepped closer to the tree and stared up at him. "Are you Garry Suzuki?"

"Who wants to know?"

"I'm Special Agent LaForge, this is Agent Alfredson, FBI. I need you to come down immediately."

"That's never happening, pig! It's my human right to be here!"

"Get your ass down here now, asshole!" shouted one of the loggers.

Special Agent LaForge held up a hand, silencing the loggers, now even more riled up with the arrival of the Federal Government. "Sir, you are under arrest for acts of terrorism against the United States. A full list of charges will be provided to you when you come down."

Suzuki's eyes widened.

Terrorism?

"What the hell are you talking about? I'm sitting in a tree, saving it from *those* terrorists!" he yelled, jabbing a finger at the loggers.

"Sir, are you a member of the Utopians?"

"Proud member!"

"Sir, your organization, the Utopians, have admitted to being behind the recent attacks on our infrastructure. By order of the President, this organization has been named a terrorist organization, and all members terrorists. Do you deny you're a member of this organization?"

"Never!" His chest tightened, that perhaps not the wisest of responses. Yet none of this was making sense. What terrorist attacks was he talking about? He had been in this tree for three days. He had no idea what was going on five trees over, let alone around the country. There wasn't exactly Internet access here.

"Sir, if you don't come down, we'll have to force you down."

"Come on up and just try it!"

LaForge shook his head. "No, sir, you misunderstand. We have no intention of putting our lives at risk, and we have no time to waste." He turned to the loggers. "Who wants to cut down a tree?" Half a dozen men raced for their pickup trucks, brandishing chainsaws moments later. LaForge turned back and stared up at Suzuki. "Your choice."

Suzuki's heart sank. They were going to cut down the tree, even with him in it.

Bullshit!

It was ridiculous. Police wouldn't do something like that. It would be against the law. He was just a protester. He could see the loggers doing it, they were already murderers, but not FBI agents. It made no sense.

They think you're a terrorist.

He frowned. If he were an Islamist terrorist, sitting in a tower, they'd shoot him without hesitation. And if that's what they thought of him, if something indeed had happened, and the organization he represented was being framed—for that's what it had to be, there was no way his group would commit violent acts—then they might just kill him. "Wait! I'm coming down!" He began to extricate himself from the chains, then cursed, staring at the handcuffs. "Umm, I've got a problem."

"What?"

He held out his hand. "I can't get these off."

LaForge stepped back, pointing at the tree. "Bring him down."

The loggers stared at each other, confused. It was clear they had assumed the FBI agent was bluffing, yet now the order had been given.

"Umm, you serious?"

LaForge pointed up at Suzuki. "You know what's been happening around the country? All the people that have died because of those hacks?"

Heads bobbed.

"Well, it was his group that did it."

The one who had threatened him earlier glared up at him. "That's good enough for me." He fired up his chainsaw. "Hang on, asshole, I'll be seeing you soon!"

The Oval Office, The White House
Washington, DC

Roger Croft shook President Starling's hand with a smile, a firm handshake something his father had taught him the art of when he was young, and it had done him well throughout his years of empire building.

"Mr. Croft, a pleasure to meet you. Harry has been talking you up for some time."

Croft smiled at Vice President Vance as they all took seats in the Oval Office. "The Vice President is too kind. I just hope he hasn't shared some of our more illustrious stories from our college days."

Starling chuckled. "Oh, I've heard a few, but don't worry, he never implicated you in any. At least not by name!"

Vance laughed. "Oh, I guarantee you that Roger was around for a few of those stories. I won't embarrass him by telling you which ones. But I will say this. We go way back. Almost forty years—"

"Ugh, we're getting old!"

"We are indeed. But forty years of knowing somebody tells me whether or not they can be trusted. And Mr. President, Roger can be."

"High praise, indeed. But, forgive me, gentlemen, we're in the middle of perhaps the greatest crisis our nation has experienced since Pearl Harbor. What was so important that you needed to see me now, of all times?"

"Mr. President, our country is under attack, by a non-traditional enemy."

"Interesting choice of words. Non-traditional. Do you know something I don't?"

"I choose my words carefully, Mr. President. If a specific nation were attacking us using military power, we could retaliate. Forgive me, Mr. President, but we would bomb the living hell out of them until they stopped. But with cyber attacks, it's different. Can we justify bombing someone when all they've done is hack our computer systems? Personally, I say yes, however, who do you bomb? With the way a cyber attack can be staged, the Russians could make it appear like the Chinese were doing it, or even the Germans. There's no way to be sure, at least not quickly.

"We're only two days into the current crisis, and our nation is at a standstill. My understanding is that transportation into and out of most major cities, especially New York City, has come to a stop. Our ports are moving at a crawl, our airports are grounding most flights, and our rail system is operating at less than a quarter of its normal speed, with no way to move their goods from the terminals in the large cities."

"He's right," said Vance, his head bobbing profusely. "Our cities are being strangled to death. Already, there's looting and hoarding. The store shelves are bare. There's nothing left. Those who don't have food already, won't be getting any more."

"Exactly. Mr. President, our nation is in trouble. Serious trouble. With this new threat of contaminated water, the population is being told not to drink anything that doesn't come out of a bottle. But there isn't enough bottled water in the nation to supply the needs of just *one* city for more than a day or two. We have scores of cities that are going thirsty. People will become desperate and will drink that water and become sick. People are going to start going hungry very quickly, and hungry people will become desperate, and begin stealing from their neighbors. Mr. President, we may be beyond recovery within a few days."

Starling stared at him. "You paint a pretty bleak picture, Mr. Croft. I'm not sure I agree with your dire predictions."

Croft bowed slightly. "Of course, Mr. President, you would have better advisors than I would, however picture this. When your neighbor steals from you, when your neighbor refuses to share what they have, and your baby is crying because she's hungry, even if the crisis ends the next day, will you ever forgive your neighbor, will you ever trust that person again? We're already a nation divided over politics, we can't risk it becoming even more so over something as basic as food and water."

"We're working as hard as we can to identify the perpetrators and bring them to justice. Our systems are already being repaired, and things should be back to normal within a couple of days."

Croft raised his hands, palms up, and nodded. "Perhaps. But what if you haven't plugged all the holes?"

"Excuse me?"

"Mr. President, our systems were hacked, exploiting security holes that in some cases have been ignored for years due to budget restrictions, ignorance, or a complete lack of caring. Bringing these systems back online doesn't solve the problem—they can be hacked again."

"I would assume they'd patch them, or whatever they call it."

"Of course, I hope they would. But what if they can't? You need a system that will be able to detect this type of activity, shut it down, then tell you exactly where it came from so you know who to retaliate against."

Starling smiled slightly. "And let me guess, your company has just a system?"

Croft grinned. "As a matter of fact, we do. Our SecuraVault system will protect the backbone of our entire communications infrastructure, whether government or private sector. We're already installed on thousands of servers worldwide, and with your approval, we can begin installing *tonight* on an emergency basis."

Starling pursed his lips, staring at Croft then glancing at Vance. "What do you think?"

Vance waved his hand. "It's a no-brainer, Mr. President. I've read the briefs. Hell, I've been telling you for months after that Korean incident, we need a system like this. We went to war over what some madman did."

Starling, having been caught up in that crisis during a G20 meeting, should know all too well how close they had come to all-out war.

"Your system could have prevented that?"

Croft nodded. "Yes, Mr. President. Our system would have identified the hacks immediately. Even if it didn't, and a human identified there was a problem, the system would then have been able to track back everything to its genuine source, not the spoofed source. Within minutes, we would have known who was behind it, and you could have responded militarily before hostilities with the North Koreans had ever gotten beyond the saber-rattling stage."

Starling rose and paced as he pinched his chin between his thumb and forefinger. He leaned on the edge of his desk. "If you install this system, you'll be able to prevent any further hacks?"

"Yes, sir. And tell you exactly where they're coming from."

"How quickly can you implement it?"

"Mr. President, we have over twenty thousand employees, spread across every city in our great nation, awaiting your order. If you give me the word, they'll begin installing tonight. I can have our country secure within forty-eight hours."

Starling looked at Vance, who nodded slightly. Starling sighed then stood. "Do it."

Interrogation Room 8C, CIA Headquarters
Langley, Virginia

Dylan Kane entered the interrogation room and waved a hand at Katz. "Okay, let's go."

Katz looked up at him. "Not now."

Kane's eyes narrowed. "What the hell are you talking about?"

"Not now." She tapped her watch. "Now I must rest. Tomorrow morning we will begin."

Kane tensed, his fists clenching as he advanced on her before stopping himself. "We don't have any time to waste!"

She stared at him. "Something has changed. What?"

He sucked in a breath, debating whether he should reveal what had happened to his parents and those of Leroux. "Nothing."

She shook her head. "Not true. You've become emotional. You know I have your girlfriend, and I am here, with no ability to hurt her. You already know only time can hurt her, and if I felt there wasn't enough time for us to begin until tomorrow, we would be going now. Something else has happened. Tell me, or I let your girlfriend die."

Kane's hand darted out, grabbing Katz by the throat and shoving her out of her chair and onto the floor. He squeezed hard, her face turning red. Yet there was nothing in her eyes, no fear, no anger—nothing at all. He let go and she gasped for air, her flushed cheeks returning to normal.

"If I were a vengeful person, I'd let your girlfriend die for that."

Kane put some distance between them before replying. "You and I both know you aren't."

A slight smile appeared, something Kane initially thought shouldn't be possible, before he remembered that she apparently could experience mild emotions.

Or was she faking the emotions, a learned behavior to fit in better with others?

All he knew was that it was frustrating not being able to read her.

"You've read my file."

"What little of it there is."

"Then you're aware of what happened when I was younger."

"Yes."

"Then you know there's nothing you can do to me that will make me change my mind." She stood, straightening her clothes. "I will require a bed, facilities, dinner and breakfast, and my bag."

Kane's eyes narrowed. "Your bag?"

"My car is in the parking garage. The keys are behind the rear tire, the bag is in the trunk. Tomorrow at eleven a.m., we will depart for Washington. By then, I believe your country will be sufficiently motivated to do whatever needs to be done."

Kane glared at her. "Eleven?"

"Eleven. If anyone bothers me a minute before, our deal is off, and your girlfriends are dead."

Kane punched the wall, leaving a fist-sized divot, before storming out. He burst into the observation room, struggling to control himself. "I'm going to kill her."

"In good time," replied Morrison. He turned to Leroux. "Make the arrangements, then get some sleep. Both of you. We'll all be able to think better in the morning when either this thing begins to resolve itself, or things get a whole lot worse."

Kane glared through the two-way mirror. "Oh, trust me. This is getting worse before it gets better. Far worse."

Virginia Mason Medical Center
Seattle, Washington

Garry Suzuki cradled his broken arm, his eye swollen, his shoulder aching, and hooked up to more leads and tubes than he cared to count. He was lucky to be alive, the sonsabitches having actually cut the tree down. He had been fortunate it had fallen away from the side he was on, allowing him to ride the trunk, rather than have it fall on him. Yet here he was, lucky to be alive, but that poor tree was dead.

I hope they at least make good use of it, rather than let it go to waste.

The FBI agent responsible, Special Agent LaForge, stepped into the hospital room with his partner Alfredson. "Are you ready to talk?"

"Ready? Don't you mean 'able,' you psycho! I'm going to sue your asses, all of you. I'm suing those terrorist loggers, the company they work for, the FBI, everybody I can think of! You're not going to get away with what you did! I have rights, you know! You can't do what you did and think you'll get away with it!"

LaForge pulled out his notepad and pen. "Mr. Suzuki, I already have. I have a dozen witnesses willing to testify that when they arrived, they found you lying on the ground, some unknown person having already cut down the tree. We arrived, effected your rescue, and brought you here for treatment."

"That's bullshit and you know it!"

"Yes. And who do you think the judge is going to believe? Two decorated FBI agents, or you, a person of no fixed address with a record a mile long?"

Suzuki glared at him, the heart monitor beeping far faster than it should. He sucked in a breath and held it for a moment, before exhaling slowly, the heart rate easing. "This is the problem with today's society. The government has too much power."

"And is that why you did what you did? To try and bring down the government?"

"I sat in a goddamned tree, you psycho! How the hell is that going to bring down the government?" The beeping raced higher.

"Not you, Mr. Suzuki, your organization."

"I have no clue what you're talking about."

LaForge motioned to Alfredson, who tapped on a tablet before turning it around. Suzuki watched a recording, his eyes widening as he witnessed the death and chaos occurring, then gasped when the organization he had pledged himself to, took credit.

"Th-that's impossible! You're lying. You photoshopped that or something."

"No, Mr. Suzuki. The Emergency Broadcasting System was hacked and that played on a loop until the system could be shut down. Hundreds are already dead, perhaps thousands, and things are rapidly getting worse. Transportation within our cities is at a standstill, and at the moment, we can't get supplies in, and millions across the country are fleeing."

Tears filled Suzuki's eyes as he imagined the fear and terror those poor people must be going through. "I-I'm sorry to hear that."

LaForge frowned. "I don't give a shit if you're sorry. Your people are responsible, and you're going to help me put a stop to it."

Suzuki shook his head, jabbing a finger at the tablet. "I don't care what that thing says, there's no way the Utopians are behind this. We're peaceful. Yes, we advocate a return to a simpler way of life, where we bulldoze the cities and everyone returns to the land, but we want people to do it for themselves. We try to educate them, to show them what they're missing, to show them how city life is making them sick and miserable. Through education, they'll voluntarily leave." He flicked a wrist at the tablet. "But not this! This is chaos. Mayhem. Murder! We would never condone that. Never!"

"Well, somebody is behind it, and until we can eliminate your group, we're going to assume it's responsible. We need the names of everybody in your organization."

Suzuki laughed. "Everybody? Are you nuts? I've never met *any*one let alone *every*one."

LaForge stared at him. "What do you mean?"

Suzuki shrugged, instantly regretting it as a stabbing pain surged through his upper body. He winced. "I mean, I get a text message telling me where to go and when, and they put some money in my account to cover expenses, along with a stipend."

LaForge held up a finger. "Wait a minute, they pay you to protest?"

"Sure, that's how it's done now. Not everyone, of course, but when you're trying to bring attention to a cause that isn't necessarily popular, you need to outsource things."

"You outsource protesting?"

"Absolutely. It happens all the time. Somebody pays for the bus to take the protesters somewhere, somebody pays to feed them. Our organization and others have taken it a step further by also paying a little bit so we can at least subsist."

"And just how much are they paying you?"

"Not much. Enough to feed and clothe myself, get from point A to Point B, pay for hotels if necessary, pay for supplies. Cellphone, that type of stuff."

"So basically everything you need to survive without working."

Suzuki shook his head, holding up a finger. "Now wait, I work. I protest. I bring attention to the travesties going on around us."

LaForge grunted. "Bullshit. You go to where you're told, and protest what you're told. Do you even believe in what you're doing, or is it just a job to you?"

"I believe! A hell of a lot more than you do! What have you ever done to save the planet?"

LaForge shook his head. "Okay, we're getting off topic. You said you get text messages. Have you ever actually talked to someone?"

"Not since the day I was recruited."

LaForge exchanged a frustrated glance with his partner. "Who did you meet then?"

"Jeff Bixby. He was the founder. That was about ten years ago, I guess. Since then I haven't actually spoken to anyone. Well, that's not true. We spoke for the first few years, but then everything went completely digital. Text messages and websites. That's it."

"And were you always alone when you protested?"

Suzuki shook his head. "Not all the time, no."

"And do you have any of their names?"

"Nope. We were always instructed to use first names only. That way if we were ever arrested, we couldn't name names."

LaForge glanced at his partner. "Sounds like a terrorist cell if I ever heard one."

Alfredson agreed.

LaForge jabbed his pen into the pad. "This Jeff Bixby. Where can we find him?"

142

Suzuki caught himself before he shrugged again. "No idea." He glanced around the room. "My phone will have the text messages, though. Maybe you can trace the number."

Alfredson stepped out for a moment, returning with a plastic bag, his personal items inside. She pulled out a shattered cellphone. "Is this it?"

He nodded. "I guess that's not going to be of much help."

LaForge exhaled loudly. "Okay, do you remember the number?"

Suzuki grunted. "Who uses numbers anymore?"

LaForge shook his head then stepped toward the door.

"Umm, can I go now?"

LaForge turned. "No. You're under arrest for terrorism. You're not going anywhere for a long time."

"But I didn't do anything!"

LaForge flipped his notepad closed and left the room, shutting the door behind him, leaving Suzuki to turn his head away and sob. He had been a victim his entire life, and now, once again, karma was biting him on the ass for some cosmic reason he'd never understand.

He just hoped that one day he'd rebalance things, and save his soul.

Maggie Harris Residence, Lake in the Pines Apartments
Fayetteville, North Carolina

"Do you think things are going to get worse?"

Command Sergeant Major Burt Dawson glanced at his fiancée, Maggie Harris, as he pulled on his boots. "Definitely."

Maggie frowned. "You're supposed to say, 'No, beautiful, I'm going to fix up everything by morning.'"

He deadpanned her. "No, beautiful, I'm going to fix up everything by morning."

"Ha ha. What should I do? I'm probably not going to see you for days."

Dawson stood. "Watch the TV. If things start to get bad here, take your ID and head for the base. You're still an employee, so they'll let you on. I'll make sure the Colonel has you on the list in case they decide to restrict access to military only. You'll be safe there."

"Should I go now?"

He pursed his lips, watching the images flashing on the screen. "No, I don't think so. It looks like it's limited to the larger cities." He pointed to the closet. "You've got a two-week emergency kit in there, so there's food, water, medical supplies, batteries—everything you might need including zombie killing implements—"

"BD! I'm scared enough as it is!"

He grinned. "Remember, aim for the head. You have to scramble their brains."

She punched him in the arm. "You're an asshole!"

He grabbed her and pulled her close, giving her a hug then a kiss on the top of her head. He could see the scar from her gunshot wound through her hair, and thought of her recent stroke from which she was still recovering. He sighed. "Changed my mind. I want you on the base."

She looked up at him. "Are you sure? A minute ago you said it was safe."

"It is, but you're still weak from the stroke. I don't want to be worrying about you when I'm gone."

She frowned. "It's not really fair, though, is it? I mean, I'm taking advantage of my position."

"Damn right you are, as you should. But you know the Colonel. He needs someone organizing his life, and he hasn't taken an assistant since that last disaster personnel sent him. He'll be happy to have you there, and you'll actually be doing your country a service." He pointed at the screen. "Now's not the time to be selfish." He grinned.

"Oh, you're good. You should go into politics."

Dawson grunted. "You know what I do to people I hate, and I'd just end up hating myself."

She patted his chest. "This is true."

There was a knock and Dawson peered through the peephole before opening the door. "Hey, guys!"

Sergeants Carl "Niner" Sung and Jerry "Jimmy Olsen" Hudson stepped inside, Niner closing the door behind them. "There's some excitement in the streets, so I thought we should come on over and make sure things are good."

Jimmy jerked his thumb at his chest. "*I* thought we should, cuz' I'm a caring sort of guy."

"Thanks, *Jimmy*," said Maggie. "I'm going to get ready."

Niner stepped toward the television. "You're coming in?"

"BD insists it's my duty to help our country in its hour of need."

Niner's head bobbed as he dropped onto the couch.

"Make yourself comfortable," said Dawson.

Niner grinned. "Don't mind if I do. Got snacks?"

Dawson squeezed his junk.

"I said snack, not a meal, you gorgeous specimen of a man."

Jimmy groaned.

"Niner, behave!" called Maggie from the bedroom.

"Yes'm!" Niner went all business. "So, what do you think is going on?"

Dawson shrugged. "Dunno, but somebody's sure got a hate on for America today."

Jimmy grunted. "What else is new? The question is who? It could be a country, or a kid in his mom's basement."

"Right now I think that's more a CIA/NSA/FBI issue," replied Dawson. "When they figure it out, they'll let us know where to go, if anywhere."

Niner frowned. "Do you really think they'll do nothing?"

"Oh, they'll do something, but it might be cyber related. If China or Russia did this, do you really think we'll be sending in bombers when they've got nukes?"

Niner sighed. "I wish we had never invented the bomb. Then we could go in and blow the living shit out of them."

Dawson jabbed a finger at him. "And *that's* why countries like Iran want the bomb, so we don't do just that."

"Don't worry, we've got a treaty now, so that's unpossible!"

Jimmy laughed at Niner's Ralph Wiggum impression. "Now, now, remember, ours is not to question why…"

"Yeah, yeah. Stupid is as stupid does."

Maggie reappeared, looking fabulous yet practical. "Okay, gentlemen, is my escort ready?"

Niner leaped to his feet, bowing deeply as he extended an arm toward the door. "Your chariot awaits, madam."

Maggie grabbed her chest. "Madam? What is this, a whorehouse?"

Dawson grinned. "Some ni—"

Maggie slapped his shoulder with the back of her hand. "Careful!"

Niner smiled with delight. "Ooh, you're going to pay for that one."

Jimmy pointed at the television. "Look at this."

They all turned to read the headline on the muted television.

President orders emergency security upgrade to nation's electronic infrastructure.

·

United States Strategic Command Headquarters

Offutt Air Force Base, Nebraska

Captain Cartwright escorted the team from Croft Technologies to the primary server farm buried deep under the base. He was new, posted only a few months ago, though knew his stuff—you didn't get assigned to the United States Strategic Command if you didn't. But it also meant the night shift. Next year, when the next crop was rotated in, he'd be more senior, and would be asleep next to his wife at this hour.

But not today.

He eyed the two men, sharply dressed in suits that were beyond his paygrade, with physiques that would have them fitting into any Marine outfit with ease. "I just got the order from the Pentagon an hour ago. You guys must have already been in town."

The lead, a man introduced to him as Clarence Daniels, nodded. "Lucky break. We were installing an upgrade in Omaha yesterday. It took a little longer than expected, what with everything going on, so we booked a hotel. We were asleep when we got the call to come here."

Cartwright swiped his security pass, the panel going green, a beep and click signaling they had been cleared for entry. He pushed open the door. "After you, gentlemen."

The two entered, heading down the hall and stopping in front of another door.

Cartwright's eyes narrowed. "Have you been here before?"

Daniels shook his head. "No. Why?"

"Well, you seem to know your way around."

Daniels pointed up, a series of cable conduits overhead, most taking 90 degree turns into the room on the other side of the door they were now in front of. "Just logic."

Cartwright chuckled and shook his head. "You know, when I first got here, I noticed it too. I guess eventually you stop seeing what's right in front of your nose." He swiped his pass again then pushed open the door to the server room. "How long are you guys going to need?"

"It's going to take a while, but we should be out of your hair by tomorrow evening."

Cartwright's eyebrows rose. "That long?"

Daniels motioned at the massive room lined with rack upon rack of equipment powering the backbone of the nation's defense systems. "It's a big job, and we're only two guys. With the transportation problems, we wouldn't be able to get a team here to help until the afternoon, regardless."

Cartwright laughed. "Yeah, I guess so." He pointed toward the station where the servers could be accessed. "There you go."

The two men strode over, the second sitting in the chair as he unbuttoned his suit jacket. He turned to Cartwright. "I'll need you to log me in. Root level access."

Cartwright frowned, hating to give anyone that level of access, yet his orders were clear. Full cooperation, full access. He leaned over and entered the user id and password set up for the task, then hit Enter. "You're in."

"Thank you."

Daniels turned to him. "If you've got things to do, feel free. We'll be here for hours."

Cartwright smiled slightly, shaking his head. "Do you honestly think the Pentagon wouldn't court-martial me if I left two civilians alone in here?"

Daniels nodded. "Suit yourself." He sat in the only other chair, leaving Cartwright to wonder if he shouldn't have planned this better.

Temporary Quarters, CIA Headquarters
Langley, Virginia

Kane lay in the narrow bed, this not the first time he had spent the night at Langley, nor would it be the last. CNN was on mute with the closed captioning turned on, and he found himself staring at the small wall-mounted television, rather than getting the sleep he had no doubt Katz was getting several doors down.

She was a terrifying woman.

It wasn't that he thought he couldn't take her in a fight, though he wouldn't make the mistake of thinking it would be easy, it was that she was the type of cold, methodical killer one rarely encountered. There were psychopaths in the world, lots of them, though there were few that had managed to have a series of life events provide them with the skills to become a lethal killing machine, or the contacts to employ those skills for an ultra-secret organization hell-bent on world domination, or some other such thing.

This woman had somehow been trained to be the best at what she did, was somehow found by an organization that had no scruples or morals, and was now expecting, in her entirely logical mind, for him to forget everything she had done, and partner with her for their mutual benefit.

It was almost laughable.

Yet it made perfect sense.

They had a common enemy, and as someone far wiser once said, 'The enemy of my enemy is my friend.' Psychotic friend, perhaps. Yet she was right about one thing. It was now the middle of the night in the cities of America, and it was mayhem. There was rioting and looting, images of empty grocery stores and BestBuys, playing on a loop, CNN occasionally scrolling a count of the confirmed dead, and it was already approaching five hundred, with the unconfirmed numbers far higher. Most cities were now under curfew, and in LA there were reports of the National Guard shooting looters, the initial public reaction favorable.

That will mean open season before morning.

Which was good. He agreed with that. Looters should be shot. The danger would come when the looters started shooting back. Gun battles in the middle of overcrowded cities were never a good thing.

Initial tests of the water supplies were negative, but that apparently meant nothing, the eco-terrorists, as these Utopians were being labeled, stating it was undetectable. His personal feeling was that this was a bluff, something to further their goals of making the cities uninhabitable. Already millions were fleeing the cities, mostly on foot, refugee camps springing up in the countryside surrounding most metropolitan areas.

The problems were cities like New York, where the points of exit were few and blocked, and where the surrounding areas were simply more concrete jungles. Where do millions of people go when they're surrounded by millions of others in the same predicament? This was a disaster on an unprecedented scale. Even if it resolved quickly, he had a feeling people would be seriously reconsidering their life choices.

Cities were incredible, a marvel of modern engineering, yet they had obvious drawbacks if critical elements of that design should fail. Especially if they failed all at once. The GPS system was still screwed, the satellites not accepting the update needed to fix it, forcing the ports to handle the docking of ships manually. The nation's trains were rolling again, albeit slowly, but traffic inside the cities was barely moving. Thousands if not tens of thousands of cars were abandoned with no hope of ever moving them in a timely manner.

His eyebrows rose as he watched a large plow push across the Brooklyn Bridge into New York, car after car shoved to the side as a convoy of supply vehicles trailed behind.

That's one way to do it.

He frowned, his cover career as an insurance investigator wondering what a disaster like this did to the insurance industry. Tens of thousands of cars would be totaled over the coming days if this were the method employed to clear the streets. Would they pay the claims? And if they did, would they demand bailouts from the government after the fact? And then would they pay huge bonuses to their executives afterward?

Somebody always benefits.

He watched a Breaking News Update and shook his head, the President ordering the installation of an unnamed security system across the nation.

I wonder how many billions that will cost, and if anyone bothered to see if it worked.

Kneejerk reactions were almost always bad. The country needed to bring down whoever was behind this, which would stop further attacks. Repair the systems, get the nation moving again, and when done, analyze how it had happened and determine how to prevent it from happening again. Installing something so quickly, across so many systems, before knowing exactly what had happened, was foolish, and seemed uncharacteristic of a President he actually respected.

He must have been pressured.

There was a knock at his door and his eyebrows popped. "Come in?"

The door opened and Leroux poked his head in. "You awake?"

Kane motioned toward the television as he propped himself up. "Sort of." He indicated the lone chair in the room and Leroux sat. "Can't sleep?"

His friend shook his head. "No. I can't stop thinking about Sherrie. Katz said that they'll die within twenty-two hours, and I can't stop picturing how she'll do it. It has to be some sort of trigger device, maybe when the time is up, the room fills with water or sand or something. Or gas."

Kane smiled slightly, turning on the bedside lamp. "Or it could be as simple as they run out of air. That's the most likely."

Leroux nodded slowly, staring off into the distance. "That could be it. That would be the easiest, I guess."

"And least painful."

Leroux stared at him. "I never thought of that. But would Katz be humane?"

Kane grunted. "You're asking the wrong question. Would Katz be *in*humane, I think, is more what we're wondering. If she's logical, then the easiest, most efficient way of killing them is what she'd use. I don't think she's interested in punishing them or scaring them. They're leverage over us. We're the ones who are supposed to be scared, and it's *our* imaginations that are running wild, coming up with all kinds of horrible scenarios, all of which motivate us to work with her."

Leroux frowned. "Clever woman."

"Yes. The damned woman is practically Vulcan."

Leroux brightened at the mention of Star Trek, Kane well aware his friend was a huge fan. "So, if we think logically, then we should analyze what was said, and if we do…" Leroux's eyes widened. "We run into a problem."

"What's that?"

"What's the one detail we know?"

Kane shrugged. "Enlighten me."

"That they have twenty-two hours to live."

Kane held up his watch. "Twenty, now. Your point?"

"How could she know how much air they would use? I mean, she could make an estimate, but if she were wrong, they could last for hours longer, or…"

Kane nodded.

Or hours less.

It would be a big risk for her to take. She had to know that if the CIA held up its end of the bargain, and Katz delivered two dead bodies, they'd pursue her until the end of time. "She'd have to err on the side of caution, I guess."

Leroux brightened slightly. "So then we've got more than twenty hours."

"Only if you're talking air. You could be right in that it's something else that's triggered. It could be water or gas, or as simple as sucking the remaining air out of the room at the deadline."

Leroux's shoulders slumped.

"Listen, buddy, there's no point dwelling on it. All we can do is help her. Give her what she wants, take down the Assembly, then hope she holds up her end of the bargain."

Leroux looked up at him. "How the hell are we going to take down the Assembly in less than a day? We've been looking for them for years."

Kane wagged a finger. "Nuh-uh, you're looking at it all wrong."

Leroux's eyes narrowed. "What do you mean?"

"What I mean is that we're there to help *her* take down the Assembly, and she thinks she can do it all tomorrow, with our help. There's only one way that's possible."

Leroux's jaw dropped as his eyes widened. "She already knows where they are!"

Outside Pateros, Washington

Jeff Bixby leaned forward in his chair, flipping through different news channels, all showing his plan was succeeding brilliantly.

And it was terrifying.

Heartbreaking.

He had been raised by hippy parents to believe that Mother Earth should be placed ahead of all else, even if that meant mankind should be forced to live a more honest, meager life. He wasn't anti-technology by any means, and in fact, as the founder of the Utopians, felt it was the solution to the problem.

Birthrates were already dropping. By educating and improving the lives of those in the Third World, the entire planet could benefit when all of society embraced a birthrate below the replacement rate. Over generations, the population would drop to a more manageable level, allowing the Earth to sustain her population with ease, and the raping of her resources could slow.

But that was only one step.

The real agenda of the Utopians was to resolve the problems posed by the cities. They were a blight that had to be stopped, yet things were continually getting worse. Already half the population of the planet lived in cities, and it was going up every year. It would eventually mean that very few lived independent lives, all reliant on the hardy few who work the land. When cities could starve within days because nothing was grown there, it meant the human population as a whole was in catastrophic danger.

And that was what this was all about.

He had tried educating the public for the better part of thirty years, but his message always fell on deaf ears, few even bothering to listen, fewer still buying what he was selling.

It had been discouraging.

With the Internet, he had raised enough money to keep a few dozen eco-warriors working the cause, and they occasionally received some press from the mainstream media when they committed something truly audacious, though with today's 24-hour news cycle, it always flamed out quickly, leaving him struggling for funds once again.

But all that had changed two years ago.

Two years ago, he had been approached by a man in a parking garage. A man in the dark. A man who asked him a simple question. "If *you* had to empty the cities, how would you do it?"

And that had been it.

A single question, and the man was gone. It had got him thinking. He had always wanted people to come to the realization on their own that leaving the cities was a good thing, that moving back to the country was the future. Telecommuting meant there were millions of jobs, confined to the city, that needn't be. Yet convincing corporations of that was nearly impossible, so the employees weren't going anywhere, even if they wanted to.

But this simple question had him wondering about the problem in an entirely new light. "If *you* had to empty the cities..." So in other words, what changes could *he* make to move the population, rather than wait for the population to move itself. He was already familiar with the dangers of city living from a supply management standpoint—it had always been his argument that if anything went wrong, and the food couldn't get into the city limits, or the water was cut off for any significant amount of time, people would be literally dying of thirst within days, starving within weeks.

And simply taking the facts he already knew, then thinking of how to trigger that event, allowed him to put together a plan on how to do just that.

Disrupt the system.

And a week later, in the same parking garage, there was a note on his windshield with an email address.

"Send me your plan and I'll fund you indefinitely."

He wasn't an evil person. He didn't want people to suffer, to be killed, and frankly, it had never occurred to him that there was anything to it. A mysterious man asked a question, then later asked what answer he had come up with, offering to fund his organization's good work.

So he typed it up and sent it.

No harm done.

It was a fantasy, regardless. Nobody would act on it, certainly not him. He had no means to execute it. But a week later, the plan had been sent back to him, with modifications, and another simple question: "Will this work?"

They had expanded upon his plan, modified some of it, and included terrifying detail along with casualty expectations. It was so well thought out, that he had no doubt it would succeed with horrible efficiency. Yet there was still no way he could execute it, the tech resources and know-how required far beyond his capabilities. He had delivered a make-believe scenario where the transportation infrastructure was shutdown, preventing movement within the cities, and the movement of goods nationwide to feed the cities, was slowed.

A simple plan that in theory would work, with no real idea of how to accomplish it.

Whoever this man was, he seemed to know exactly how to do so.

Which terrified him enough to not risk ignoring the message.

So his answer to the simple question was brevity itself. "Yes."

And besides anonymous, generous donations through the Utopian website that he assumed were from the mysterious stranger, he hadn't heard from him again until two days ago. A simple text message.

"Leave the city. Now."

The fact they knew he was in Seattle scared him. Normally he practiced what he preached, he and his family owning a hobby farm outside of Seattle. But he had been in the city, meeting with a student group interested in hearing about his cause. The message, received near the end of his speech, rattled him so much, he had completely lost his train of thought, bumbling his way through his closing remarks.

Then he had rushed out, begging off any questions from the enthusiastic students. He was barely out of the city when the radio reported the 9-1-1 outages, a part of the plan added by whoever had warned him to leave.

And that was what had him so terrified tonight, one eye on the screen, the other on the door, his shotgun resting on his lap. Why had they warned him? Was it out of some sense of obligation, since he had helped them? He could see that, yet the more cynical part of him saw a darker, more sinister reason.

He was their patsy.

His organization had been named in the Emergency Broadcasting System message, and since then, he had been waiting for the police to knock down his door. In fact, he was so convinced of it, he had sent his family to stay in a local hotel until this blew over. From what he was seeing, however, it didn't appear it would blow over any time soon.

These people, whoever they were, had total control. His plan—their plan—had been executed perfectly, in ways he could never have thought of. It would never have occurred to him to mess with the GPS system to delay boat traffic, or to hack the railroad crossings to delay the trains. His plan had been simple, basic, and undetailed, and had been implemented so perfectly, so efficiently, he had to wonder how powerful a group was behind this.

And how vicious.

Surely, they weren't motivated by the same altruistic dream that drove him. He wanted Utopia, one brought on by man's own realization it had made a mistake, not through a bloodbath of orgasmic violence like he was witnessing. If the authorities thought he was behind this, he was going to prison forever. He'd never see his family again. His life was over, all because he had answered a simple question.

How?

He had been a fool. His entire life he had been trying to futilely change minds, and when asked for how to force it, his Social Justice Warrior self had leaped at the opportunity to come up with a plan.

But it had been a fantasy.

The latest death toll estimates appeared, and he closed his eyes.

This is my fault.

He opened his eyes and noticed lights flashing on the walls around him. He pulled aside the curtain and saw at least half a dozen police vehicles pulling up his long driveway. He stared at the gun.

And made a decision.

Special Agent LaForge flinched at a weapon discharging, the muzzle flash briefly illuminating the interior of the house they had ridden up on, everything black once again, only the flickering of what was probably a television, now visible.

"Surround the house!" he shouted, local police quickly executing his order, guns drawn. Yet he had a feeling it was completely unnecessary. A single shot, no evidence of a window broken, no evidence of a shot taken at his team as they arrived. It could have been a misfire, an accidental discharge triggered by a shaky finger at the sight of the flashing lights, but he doubted it.

Jeff Bixby, founder of the Utopians, had shot himself rather than be taken.

That was the act of a guilty man, the act of someone who wanted to turn himself into a martyr to his cause—that was the act of a terrorist, and exactly what he'd expect from a coward who would wreak such havoc on his fellow citizens, all for ideology.

A megaphone was handed to him, and he turned it on. "Mr. Bixby, this is the FBI. You are surrounded. Come out with your hands up. This is your only warning."

He lowered the device and everyone waited, the only sounds the idling engines and what to him, a city boy, sounded like agitated cows, sheep, and chickens, in a nearby barn.

I wonder who takes care of the animals, now.

Bixby had a wife and children. Perhaps they would stay on and work the land, though quite often in these cases, the spouse was only humoring their partner, with no real interest in living the life chosen for them. He glanced around at the barrenness, a few lights visible in the distance, probably neighbors, but little else. He couldn't live like this. Not so isolated. And what was there to do?

Where's the nearest IMAX? Starbucks?

162

Bixby would say he was part of the problem. So, tied to the life that a city provided, he knew no better. And the man would be right. But what was wrong with that? Modern society had developed enough that a few could feed the many. Modern infrastructure allowed those goods to be moved quickly and efficiently, and feed millions within the concrete jungles that the majority preferred.

Though perhaps that wasn't entirely accurate. If people preferred cities, why was suburbia so popular? If so many wanted that patch of grass to tend, perhaps there was still some intrinsic part of being human that drew us back to the land we had lived on and toiled over for countless millennia.

The Utopians were wrong to want everyone to return to the land. There simply wasn't enough land for that many people to work, though they had proven a point. City life was fragile. The reports he had heard on the way here were terrifying. Rioting. Looting. Empty store shelves. Hospitals overwhelmed. Troops in the streets.

And it had barely been two days.

They had attacked all manners of transportation, as well as sowed distrust in the water supply. Yet they had left communications untouched. People were free to spread panic and false news over the Internet, to glue themselves to their televisions and computers, and feed their fear.

It was brilliant.

The panicked mind was its own worst enemy. A panicked nation was as well.

He sighed, flicking his wrist, the SWAT team he had brought surging forward. It took only minutes for the house to be cleared, the team lead stepping outside and motioning him over. "The family isn't here. He's in the living room in front of the television. Single gunshot wound to the head." The team lead frowned. "It's messy. Shotgun."

LaForge stepped inside the living room, Bixby in his chair as described, half his face splattered on the wall behind him. "Light."

Alfredson flicked on the light switch, revealing the true gruesomeness to everyone. Somebody gagged, and LaForge pointed at him. "Get out of here before you contaminate my scene." The officer rushed outside, these townies not used to what he saw nearly every day. He envied them. He stepped closer, the shotgun in Bixby's lap, one hand still on it, leaving little doubt it was self-inflicted.

He glanced at the television, CNN reporting roving gangs in Los Angeles squaring off against National Guard units, the governor giving orders to open fire on anyone armed with anything. Zero-tolerance appeared to be the name of the game, and he had to agree—nip it in the bud quickly, and in the end, more lives would be saved.

He had no doubt the armchair quarterbacks with the benefit of hindsight would be hypercritical when it was all over, but what else was new in today's society, one so polarized between left and right, that the country was tearing itself apart.

"Sir."

He turned toward the voice, a young officer pointing at a laptop computer sitting on a desk wedged in the corner.

"Looks like a suicide note."

He stepped over and read it. And frowned.

"What's it say?" asked Alfredson.

"If we're to believe Mr. Bixby, then he's not behind this."

Alfredson grunted. "Do you believe him?"

LaForge shrugged, waving his hand at their surroundings. "Does this look like the headquarters for an operation that's taken down a nation?"

Assembly Command and Control Facility
Unknown Location

"The major news networks have picked up our stories on people getting sick from drinking the water in New York City."

Number Four turned to his senior controller, his liaison between the dozens of staff controlling the operation and himself, handing him a tablet. He took it and smiled. "In their rush to not be scooped by their competition, they're reporting first, vetting second."

"Yes, sir. It's exactly what happened on 9/11."

"Precisely, and that was before Facebook or any other modern form of social media had taken control." He shook his head, his smile spreading. "Ten years ago this wouldn't have worked. But today it's almost too easy. Everything is so integrated, and with everyone on tight budgets, known security vulnerabilities are left unpatched. And the people don't trust their media or government, so they're willing to get their information from anyone."

"Including us."

Number Four's head bobbed. "Including us." He spun on his heel, heading for the door. "Keep me informed. I'm going to bring the Council up to date."

"Yes, sir."

Number Four left the buzz of the control center filling most of this level of the complex, and headed for his office. He sent a secure email updating the council, then debated returning to monitor things. He was exhausted. Would a few minutes to himself really hurt? And who would know?

He headed for the elevator and hit the button. It chimed almost immediately, the doors opening. He hit B-3 and pressed into the corner, closing his burning eyes. Moments later, he was at his destination—the VIP residential area, the entire level reserved for him and visiting dignitaries—Council member representatives. Today, only he and domestic staff were here.

"Can I get you anything, sir?"

He nodded at the busty blonde he had chosen to serve him. In more ways than one. There were advantages to absolute power, and he indulged himself at every opportunity. He had been a member of the Assembly Council for almost two decades now, the trappings of money and inherited power something he thought he had understood before he was approached all those years ago to join this ancient organization his father had been a member of.

When his father had died, the truth had been revealed, and he had been given a choice. Replace him. There really hadn't been a choice, in fact. The option had been presented to him, the responsibilities explained, and there never really was any doubt he'd accept. Now he realized if he hadn't, he'd probably have been killed immediately, since he would have known too much.

But he hadn't hesitated.

He had grown up with wealth and power, thanks to his father. If these people were the source of all that, he wanted it. But with the shackles of modern morality and laws removed, he finally experienced *real* power. If you never worried about being arrested, never worried about being judged, you could fulfill all the desires the deepest recesses of the mind could conjure.

He had committed every manner of pleasure and depravity to every manner of person on the planet. And they had enjoyed it if that was what he had demanded, or begged for mercy, if that was his desire of the moment. He had killed, he had tortured, he had raped. He had saved lives, rescued the innocent, and made tender love to women he truly felt for. He had done it all, living at the fringes, at the extremes, little demanded over the years beyond the occasional action, such as the current operation.

Starting as Number Twelve all those years ago, with each advancement, he had learned more, though even now he wondered how much he actually knew.

They were ancient.

How ancient, he wasn't sure if even Number One knew, yet he knew it was many generations. They had been involved in countless human conflicts, manipulating things in the background, relishing in wars that were significant enough to advance mankind technologically. Under his term, they had manipulated several Middle-Eastern conflicts, and even had their fingers in the current Korean, Syrian, and South China Seas hotspots.

Though what they were doing today would overshadow anything that had come before. It would trigger the ultimate conflict, one that would eventually solve many of today's problems, and force the advancement of mankind beyond its current stagnation. Competition fueled ingenuity.

During the Cold War, the United States and Soviet Union had fought to outdo each other, whether in nuclear weapons or fighter jets, or rocketry and computers. The Space Race had spurred technological innovation that still resonated today, yet that spirit of competition was nearly dead.

Instead, it had been replaced with cooperation and profiteering. Countries no longer dreamed big, and corporations instead focused on shareholder returns, rather than innovation.

But recreate the Cold War, and the competition would return. Already, their efforts were paying off. Russia was the enemy again, modernizing their military and developing new weapons capabilities that were forcing everyone from the United States to the Chinese, Japanese, and Indians, to respond. It was an arms race that now had more than two participants, with inconsequential countries like North Korea and Pakistan now nuclear powers, the Japanese debating tossing aside decades of passivity, and the Chinese asserting control over the territorial waters of sovereign nations that had once been their allies.

It was the perfect storm, nurtured by those like him, waiting for one final match to be tossed on the kindling of decades of subtle manipulation.

A match he was responsible for.

"Sir?"

He shook his head, realizing he had been standing in the hallway, staring at the dessert he had brought with him. "Ice cold Diet Coke, glass of skim milk, and two Boston Cream donuts."

She smiled. "So your usual."

He grunted. "Yes."

She squeezed her chest together slightly. "Will you be following your dessert with…dessert?"

He stared, a stirring below, then shook his head. "Maybe later."

She almost looked disappointed. She, he treated with tenderness. There was something about her that he liked beyond the sexual. He had never hit her, never treated her with anything beyond respect—or at least the level of respect one could have for someone you could order to pleasure you at the drop of a hat.

He headed for his quarters, feeling reinvigorated, a spring returning to his step that had him checking his watch.

Perhaps a little dessert?

He smiled.

Dessert while eating dessert.

It was settled.

He swiped his pass, the door to his quarters unlocking with a beep, and he stepped inside, still marveling at what unlimited funds could buy. The windows wrapped around two sides of the living area, yet the view they provided were actually projected images that he could select depending on the mood he was in. Whether that was a lodge in the Serengeti, or the view from a hundred-story penthouse, it was hyper-realistic.

The current view, looking down upon the minions of New York City, was one of his favorites. Central Park to the right, skyscrapers dwarfed by his to the left. He sighed as he loosened his top button and stepped into the bathroom. Splashing water on his face, he stared into the mirror. He was showing his age. Just a hint. Most would look at him and guess he was in his early forties as opposed to late fifties, the hormone therapies available to the super-rich working wonders. Yet he still felt weary at times, more mentally than physically.

Never more so than now.

Thousands were dying, and millions would ultimately die before this was over. *He* might even die, though he doubted it. Not here, buried underground in the middle of nowhere. He and those lucky enough to be inside, would live through whatever horrors the world brought upon itself. And in the end, it would be people like him that would lead the brave new world, steering mankind back to the path of greatness it had let slip away over the past generation.

He sat on the leather couch, the overstuffed cushions enveloping him like a tender embrace. He smiled, closing his eyes. There was a knock. "Come."

The door opened, and his dessert entered on a tray and in high heels. "Change of plans, darling."

She smiled. "I had a feeling."

I think she really likes me.

He drew a deep breath as things were daintily removed.

She's paid to like you, and you're an old fool if you think it's anything more.

Yet did it really matter? If she were putting on a show for his benefit, then so be it. It was the illusion he was paying for, and she was living a far better life than she would have been on the streets of Prague where he had found her. They both got something out of this relationship, though to call it consensual, would be pushing it.

I wonder if she knows she can never leave alive.

She dropped to her knees in front of him, spreading his legs apart. He leaned past her and grabbed the glass of milk and one of the donuts. "Darlin', you're too good to me."

She unzipped his fly. "It's about to get even better, Mr. Croft."

He took a bite of his donut and leaned back, closing his eyes as he savored each chew. He groaned.

The Assembly is eternal.

Unknown Location

Sherrie White woke to find Fang's breathing shallow once again. She rolled onto her knees, checking the woman's pulse. Rapid and weak. "I'm going to give you another transfusion."

Fang shook her head. "No, you'll end up killing yourself."

Sherrie ignored her, instead inserting the needle once again in her arm.

"I said no."

Sherrie stared at her. "I feel fine. We both need to survive long enough for them to find us, and this is the only way."

"I'm dying. I'll be dead long before anyone gets here." Tears filled Fang's eyes and she raised a hand, taking Sherrie's and weakly squeezing it. "Tell Dylan…I love him, and I'm sorry."

Sherrie raised Fang's hand to her lips and kissed it, squeezing her burning eyes tight as she fought the tears that demanded release. "You're going to tell him that yourself." She placed Fang's hand back down. "And what the hell do you have to be sorry for?" She switched out the IV drip for the tube she had previously used for the transfusion.

"For leaving him alone."

Sherrie paused, and she thought of Leroux. What would he do if she died? He had been alone until they met, and though he had grown over the past couple of years, she feared he would revert to his former self, turning inward once again, shutting out the world around him.

Perhaps Sonya will make a move.

Her stomach flipped at the thought, already jealous of the woman for what she might become to him.

You're being ridiculous. You're not even dead yet, and you have him shacking up with his staff.

"We're both going to live, we're both going to go home to our men, and we're both going to kill that bitch that put us here." She watched the precious fluid flow through the tube toward Fang's arm. Fang reached to pull it loose, but Sherrie swatted the hand away. "Don't make me put you out."

Fang smiled slightly. "Fine. Kill yourself."

"That's the spirit." She looked about. "You know, I've been thinking. I don't think she's watching us. If she were, she'd be providing us with supplies to save your life. She has to know that if we're supposed to be some sort of security for her, then we have to be alive to be of any value."

Fang nodded. "Yeah, but she knew I was wounded."

Sherrie motioned toward the supplies they had been left. "Yes, which was why she left what she did. I can't believe IV bags and XStat were in her original plan. But I don't think she counted on the wound being as bad as it is."

"I told you, I'm dying."

"Piss off with that talk. You're depressing me." Sherrie grinned. "Now, like I was saying, there was no food left for us, so that means we aren't meant to stay here long—probably no more than a few days." She tapped her watch. "And we've been here about half a day. We just need to last long enough for whatever endgame she's after to play out, and we'll probably be set free."

Fang sighed. "You don't have enough blood in you to keep me going that long."

173

Sherrie smiled. "Don't you worry, we'll be fine." She looked away, not trusting she wouldn't reveal her true fears. For Fang was right. She might be able to do this one more time, if that. Any more and she risked her own life. She was willing to do it, and she would, yet she feared whoever did find them might find two corpses. They had to get out of here—waiting wasn't an option.

She stared at the door then up at the ceiling. "When we're done, I'm going to check out that ceiling."

Fang moved slightly and Sherrie looked at her. "You okay?"

"Yeah, just getting sore from lying in one position for so long."

"You have to stay still."

"Tell that to my bum."

Sherrie chuckled. "Yeah, I hear ya. Mine's getting a little sore too." She pointed at the door. "How do you suppose that's locked?"

Fang closed her eyes. "Could just be a simple lock. Key, tumblers. Nothing special."

"Right. But this place was prepared. There's the camera for one thing. The wires are hidden, so it wasn't just slapped in here. And a door with no lock or any hint of hardware on one side, isn't a standard order. This place was prepped long before yesterday."

"What are you getting at?"

"Well, if this was prepped, I wonder if they'd use something as simple as a key. Keys can get lost, keys have to be duplicated if you want more than one person to have access. I'm thinking they might have gone a little more hi-tech."

Fang shrugged and winced. "Well, even if they did, it's all on the other side of that door, so we can't get at it."

Sherrie's head slowly bobbed. "I wonder…" She let out a quick breath. "I wish Chris were here. He's the tech guy. He'd probably already have us out of here."

"So would Dylan."

Sherrie patted Fang's shoulder. "Well, they're not here, and it's a well-known fact that we're not only beautiful, but intelligent. I think it's time we puzzled our way out of this box, don't you?"

Fang smiled, already appearing a little better than a few minutes before. "Absolutely."

Williams Residence
Bronx, New York

Shannon stared at the news channel, no longer registering what she was seeing. It was all just too much. The kids seemed enthralled, and though their mother had said they couldn't watch it, the two times she had tried to change the channel had resulted in temper tantrums. It was just easier to let CNN babysit them.

She occasionally caught herself watching it too, what was going on simply too cool to completely ignore. School was canceled, which was awesome, but this morning she had been railroaded into babysitting the neighbor's kids, though she was getting paid double her normal rate, so that was good. She just couldn't wait for Mrs. Williams to get home so she could go and meet up with her man before her own mother got home and enforced the stupid curfew.

She stared at her phone and sighed. The Wi-Fi was down for some reason, and she had no internet access on her phone anymore. She had kept going over her bandwidth limit, and her mother had cut her off.

Bitch.

If she didn't want her going over her cap, then she should pay for a better package.

I can't afford that!

Then get a better job.

Her mother was an idiot sometimes, and she was never there. Between the three jobs she was holding down, she almost never cooked a proper meal or cleaned the apartment. Now her mother wanted her to do all the things she never had time for. It wasn't fair. She was fifteen. She wasn't some slave.

She couldn't wait to leave, to escape this prison of rules her mother had created. She wished her father was still around, but he had been shot in a drive-by three years ago. Her mother had said he was just in the wrong place at the wrong time, though she knew better. Word on the street was he was a low-level dealer that had moved onto the wrong corner.

But one day she'd get even.

She knew who was responsible, and they'd get theirs once she got her own piece. Her boyfriend, Levar, had promised to get her one if she treated him right, and she was doing everything she could to make her man happy, though with no Internet access on her phone, sending him dirty pictures was nearly impossible unless she went to McDonald's and used their free Wi-Fi.

But that took away the spontaneity of sexting.

It sucked.

Her mother would probably be happy. She kept warning her about sexting and sending nude pictures, though her mother was so out of touch with how things were today, Shannon didn't pay attention to much if anything that came out of her mouth.

Besides, Levar loved her.

There was no way he'd share those pictures with his friends. She was his baby, and he had promised to take care of her forever. When he finally made his bones, he'd be given his own corner, make mad stacks of cash, and they'd be set. She'd move out of her prison and into his crib, living large with no rules, with her daddy avenged.

"I'm thirsty."

She ignored the little whiner.

"I said, I'm thirsty."

"Then you shouldn't have drank all the water your mom left."

"But I was thirsty then, too!"

"Nobody should be that thirsty. Now leave me alone."

"There's more."

"More what?"

"Water."

She glanced up from her phone. She was thirsty too, and her mother had said not to drink anything from the tap, something she thought was bullshit until she heard it repeated on the news over and over. "Where?"

Terrence jumped to his feet. "I'll show you."

"No!" cried his older brother Michael, but Terrence was too quick, his tiny legs already propelling him down the hallway toward the bedrooms.

Shannon rolled off the couch and followed, the other kids trailing behind her, yelling at their brother to stop. Terrence opened the master bedroom door and rushed inside.

Shannon hesitated.

The one room always completely off limits when babysitting was the parents' bedroom. Terrence emerged with a bottle of water.

"See? I told you!"

"Where'd you get that?"

Terrence disappeared again, and Shannon stepped inside the forbidden room. He yanked open the closet and she gasped. Dozens upon dozens of bottles of water along with canned goods sat neatly stacked—enough to last them probably weeks. She stepped slowly toward the trove, still not believing her eyes. She reached out and ran the tips of her fingers along the supplies everyone so desperately needed.

She had heard about the looting, of course, and heard about hoarding, but had never actually witnessed it. They had so much, yet she had heard Mrs. Williams explicitly tell her mother that they had almost nothing left.

That lying bitch!

A rage built inside her.

Why should she and these runts have all this? Why do they deserve to eat while the rest of us starve?

She pulled out her phone and texted her man.

You're not going to believe what I just found!

Assembly Detention Facility

Washington, DC

Joseph Medina shoved Dylan Kane's parents into the room, the other couple, presumably Chris Leroux's parents, jumping to their feet. He yanked the hoods off his two prisoners as Mark Leroux shouted at him.

"What's the meaning of this? Why have you—" Mark's eyes narrowed and his jaw dropped as he finally took notice of the new arrivals. "Rick? Jenn? They took you, too?"

Medina pointed toward the half-height wall at the back of the room. "Bathroom. Do your business in there, get water there, nothing else." He pointed at a box in the corner. "Food." He glanced up at the camera in the center of the room. "Don't try anything stupid, we'll be watching."

Rick Kane turned toward him, blood caking the side of his face from where Medina had coldcocked him earlier. "Why are you doing this?"

Medina's stared at each of them. "Because your sons are in our way. When this is over, you'll be released." He turned to leave then stopped, raising a finger. "Assuming they don't do anything stupid." He stepped outside and pulled the door shut, the electronic lock beeping, the indicator turning red.

He peered down the long corridor, door upon door lining both sides, the underground storage facility converted in the eighties for Assembly purposes. He and his team strode toward the Watchman's office, a quick rap on the door prompting a buzzer to sound. He pushed open the door and stepped inside, the lone occupant putting down a half-eaten sandwich.

"All done?"

"Yes."

"Papers?"

Medina motioned and one of his men handed over two files. The Watchman quickly scanned the bar codes on the coversheet of each file, the computer pulling up their info.

"Anything I should be aware of?"

Medina shook his head. "No, they won't be a problem. None have any medical conditions that require active treatment, and none have any special training. Just ignore them. If anything happens, just contact me, I'll deal with it."

"You want me to Code Nine them?"

Medina thought for a moment. Code Nine meant the security monitoring would be disabled. It was used in special cases where the Assembly didn't want even the Watchman knowing what was going on inside a cell. He nodded. "Let's."

The Watchman tapped a few keys, one of the security monitors going blank, a white on red message appearing, "Code Nine."

Medina's eyes narrowed and he motioned to another display with the same message. "You've got another Code Nine?"

The Watchman glanced over at the other monitor. "Yeah, it was like that when I came in."

"Who's in there?"

He shrugged. "No idea. Once it's declared Code Nine, the monitors are off, and the files are sealed." He motioned toward his terminal. "Do you want me to set an expiry?"

Medina shook his head. An expiry entry could mean multiple things. Either the time left before you wanted the occupants killed, or the time you wanted them automatically released. This, of course, didn't mean the opening of their cage, it meant a humane gassing, then removal, where they'd be placed in some public location where they would wake and move on with their lives.

In his case, his orders were to hold until further orders were received. Nothing more. "Negative."

"Okay."

Medina gestured toward the other Code Nine. "Does that one have an expiry?"

The watchman tapped a few keys. "Yup. End of the day."

Medina nodded. "Okay, we're out of here." He turned, exiting the Watchman's office, and strode down the corridor, his men following. He eyed the cell with the Code Nine.

And shuddered.

One of these days, that could be me.

Sobbing hugs were exchanged before Rick Kane sat on one of the two beds, his wife beside him, the Lerouxes opposite.

"Do you have any idea what's going on?" asked Mark Leroux.

"It has something to do with our boys."

The Leroux's exchanged nervous glances.

"What? Do you know something?"

Mark looked at his wife who nodded. "Our son works for the CIA."

Rick batted away the offering as if it were worthless. "Bah! Everyone in town knows that. It's not exactly a State secret."

Liz Leroux appeared almost hurt. "Oh, well, we were told not to talk about it." Her eyes narrowed. "Who told you?"

Rick shrugged. "Don't remember."

"Dylan told us."

Rick nodded at his wife. "That's right, it was Dylan."

Mark's eyes narrowed. "Why would he do that?" His eyes widened. "And how would he know?"

Rick leaned against the wall, trying to get comfortable for what he feared would be a long wait. "Like I said, it's not exactly a secret."

"You mean others know?"

Mark shrugged then thought back. Had he ever actually heard anyone else mention it? Had *he* mentioned it? The Lerouxes weren't exactly a topic of conversation. They knew each other through their boys when they were friends in high school, but other than that, there hadn't been much contact beyond the occasional encounter at the grocery store or Home Depot. "I...don't know. Come to think of it, maybe I only ever heard it from Dylan." He shrugged. "Sorry, maybe you're right. But I doubt your boy has anything to do with this."

Mark stared at him. "We're here, and they told us it was because of him, so obviously he has something to do with it." Mark jabbed a finger in the air at him, pissed for some reason. "What does *your* boy have to do with any of this? He's just an insurance agent."

"He is *not* an insurance agent!" cried Jenn. "He's an insurance investigator. Big difference!"

Rick held up a hand to quieten her. "No, he's not. It turns out that was just a cover story." His chest swelled with pride. "Our boy's a spy."

The Lerouxes exchanged glances then burst out laughing. "Dylan? A spy? I think someone's been pulling your leg, Rick. Don't you think if he were, Chris would have told us?"

"If he wasn't allowed to tell *us*, why the hell would you think your son, the minor analyst, would be authorized to tell you, or even be privy to that kind of intel?"

"Privy to that kind of intel? Do you hear yourself? And I'll have you know, my son is not some minor analyst, he's an Analyst Supervisor now, with his own team of ten. He runs ops and everything for the CIA. Why, if your son *is* a spy, my son is probably ordering his narrow little ass all over the place!"

Rage flared and Rick leaped to his feet, his opponent doing the same. The wives intervened, his own shouting at him.

"Sit the hell down, Rick! We're in this together. This isn't a competition. Obviously, both our boys are important, and both are in the CIA."

"Exactly," agreed Liz, pushing her husband back onto the bed. "We need to all calm down and figure out what we're going to do. Now's the time for us to come together, not tear ourselves apart."

Mark nodded and rose, extending a hand. "I'm sorry, Rick. I'm just angry, and I took it out on you."

Rick shook the hand then pulled Mark in for a thumping hug. "Forget about it. I was an asshole."

"Yes you were, but so was I." Mark grinned. "Two assholes locked in a room together can be dangerous."

They both sat, and Rick glanced around at the plain room, his eyes settling on the door. A door with no handle. "What the hell is this place?"

Mark shook his head. "No idea. Our heads were covered when we were brought in. It sounded kind of closed in though, like a narrow hallway or something. Our footsteps echoed, you know?"

"Yeah, I noticed the same thing. We arrived in a car or something, and it was parked inside. We went through a security door—"

"How do you know it was a security door?"

"I heard a buzzer sound then the door opened."

"Oh."

"Then we walked. Somebody asked where the 'other two' were, somebody else said 'Cell Sixteen,' then we walked some more, and here we are." Rick flicked his wrist at the Lerouxes. "I guess you were the 'other two.'"

"Yeah, same thing with us, except when that same question was asked, they were told you hadn't arrived yet."

Rick closed his eyes for a moment, suddenly realizing how tired he was. They hadn't slept all night, and it had to be morning by now. He checked his watch, only to remember it had been removed. "Does anybody have a watch?"

Everyone checked, head shakes the response.

"I guess they don't want anyone knowing what time it is."

Mark grunted. "Or they think we have some sort of fancy James Bond type watches that can send secret signals to our sons."

Rick chuckled. "Something tells me it isn't like the movies." He sighed. "So what do we do now?"

"I think we sit and wait. If our sons really are involved, then they know we've been taken, otherwise, why would they take us?"

Rick looked at Mark. "What do you mean?"

"Well, we're obviously some sort of leverage or ransom play, right? That only works if the other party knows we've been taken. Didn't that guy say something like, 'because your sons are in the way?'"

Jenn nodded, and she jabbed at the air between them. "Yes, that's right. That's exactly what he said. Then he said that we'd be released, assuming they didn't do anything stupid, or something like that."

Rick pursed his lips as he drew in a breath. "Okay, that could be a problem."

Liz's eyes narrowed. "Why?"

"Because my Dylan is an idiot who is always doing something stupid."

"I always thought Dylan was a fine young man," said Liz.

"Who quit college and quit the military, who quit everything he ever started."

Rick's wife turned on him. "Rick! You know that isn't true! He left college to fight for his country! And now you know he never quit the Army, he joined the CIA to become a spy!"

Rick frowned, nodding slowly. He was still processing this new bit of history-redefining information. Everything he knew about his son for the better part of the past decade was a lie. And he had treated his son like shit because of it. He *was* an asshole, an asshole of the worst sort. He had shunned his own son.

You're a horrible father.

His wife squeezed his hand, staring up at him, as if she knew what he was thinking.

Mark broke the awkward silence. "So your son's a spy. You must be so proud!"

Rick squeezed his eyes shut, fighting the burn, allowing only a quick nod.

"Yes, we are," replied his wife for him. "Very proud. Shocked too, to be honest. I always knew something was going on. He could never really look me in the eye when I'd ask him about his job. He seemed

186

distant, almost ashamed. I had always assumed he was ashamed of what his crotchety old father felt about it, but now I guess he was ashamed of having to lie to his mother." She sighed, and Rick opened his eyes, knuckling them dry. "The poor dear."

Rick sucked in a deep breath. "So, back to the question of the hour. If we're being held because of what our sons do for a living, what do *we* do about it?"

Mark shrugged. "What *can* we do about it?" He motioned at the room. "We're locked in a room with no door knob, with a camera watching us at all times. I think we should sit tight and let our boys deal with it. If they're good enough to piss people like this off, then they're good enough to save us."

Rick felt another surge of pride at the words. Mark was right. Their boys would save them. And then they'd have a long overdue conversation.

Father and son.

Assembly Command and Control Facility

Unknown Location

Roger Croft entered the control center, a smile on his face, well-rested for the first time in too long. The operation was on near autopilot now, his team well trained, having rehearsed this operation for over a year, and performed mini-dry runs to test their abilities to penetrate government and private systems, for even longer. With Internet hacks, it was far too easy to make it appear someone else was behind it, and when those looking for someone to blame were involved, they almost always jumped at the first piece of evidence they found.

He and the others had enjoyed a good chuckle when the Americans had blamed the Russians for hacking a power plant because a remnant of code once used by the Russians was found. That was akin to blaming Japan for a car bomb because a Toyota was used.

Laughable.

Yet convenient.

Everyone was hoping it was the Russians, Chinese, or North Koreans. It wouldn't have fit the narrative if it were the Iranians, since there was a shiny new treaty with them at the time.

And when this operation was over, the proper breadcrumbs would be laid, and there would be someone to blame, someone who could never be forgiven, and Cold War 2, already underway with Russia's renewed belligerence, would coalesce into something that would last decades, every bit as fierce as it had been from the 50s to the 80s.

And in the ensuing decades, mankind would advance by leaps and bounds, peace would once again be reached, and this time the annoyance that had helped destroy it this time, would be eliminated, or at a minimum, dramatically curtailed.

He stared at the displays, the chaos continuing. "Status?"

"They're starting to organize."

"As expected. Status of the Offutt Air Force Base op?"

"Unknown. Until they're finished, our operatives have no way to communicate with us. We expect late afternoon, early evening, before we can trigger the endgame."

Croft drew in a quick breath, unable to suppress his excitement. "Things will never be the same."

His senior controller smiled broadly. "Agreed. And mankind will never know who they have to thank for their next great leap forward."

Croft put a hand on the man's shoulder, pride washing over him. "The Assembly is eternal."

Temporary Quarters, CIA Headquarters
Langley, Virginia

"Are you ready?"

Katz remained seated, trying to assess Kane's mood. His tone was curt, and the tautness of the muscles in his neck and face suggested annoyance, if not outright anger. She was leaning toward anger. After all, she had made them wait almost half a day.

But there was a method to her perceived madness, for it was never madness with her.

Madness implied emotion, something she was never driven by. To say she wasn't extremely motivated, would also be false. She was. Though death was something she didn't fear, it wasn't something she welcomed. She enjoyed her life, such as it was. There was satisfaction in doing a job well, of accomplishing something she had set out to do.

And there were the small pleasures. At times, she did find herself not driven by emotion, but driven to experience it. They were there, buried deep within, and those rare occasions they did surface, they were enjoyable, even if they were negative.

They were something, a distant memory from her childhood that part of her yearned to experience once again.

And to do that, she had to remain alive, and to ensure she did, the Assembly had to be removed from the equation so hit squads the world over would stop searching for her. And a motivated American government would be her best hope of achieving her goals.

She rose, tugging her skintight leather jacket down slightly, her man-distracting cleavage bouncing with a pop. "Yes."

Kane motioned toward the four-inch heels on her boots. "You're going to fight in those?"

She clicked one on the tile floor, the metallic sound giving away her secret. "I always train in what I'm going to wear. They're solid metal. One kick and I can crush a man's skull in." She stared at him. "Care to test them?"

He gave her a look. "Let's just keep those puppies on the floor, shall we?"

She smiled slightly. "I'll need my weapons."

"Out of the question."

She sat. "Then I guess your girlfriend dies."

He glared at her. "Why do you need a weapon?"

"Weapons." She stressed the S.

"Okay, weapons."

"Because, Special Agent, we're going to be kidnapping someone. Someone who is *very* well-guarded."

Seattle FBI Field Office
Seattle, Washington

"Any luck with that number yet?"

The FBI tech shook his head, and Special Agent LaForge frowned. "How hard can it be to trace a phone number?"

"It's VoIP, so the number can be from anywhere."

"What do you mean? It still has to link back somewhere, doesn't it?"

"Yes, but when you create an account, you can pick what area code you want to use. You can be sitting in Pittsburgh, and make it look like you're in Kansas City."

LaForge exhaled loudly, dropping into a chair. "So the number's useless?"

"I didn't say that. I'm running a trace on it now. I've got a buddy at the NSA who's running it through their system. We should know pretty soon every single call made to or from that number."

LaForge's eyebrows rose. "Is that legal?"

"Hell no. Is that a problem?"

"Not according to my orders. Apparently, the word from the top is to not worry about the courts, and worry about the country."

The tech grunted. "We're all going to lose our jobs when this is done."

"Yup. But if this doesn't stop, we'll be losing them anyway." His partner entered the room. "Anything?"

Alfredson shook her head. "No, like you suspected, there's no way Bixby was running anything from there. He's got dial-up Internet, for

Christ's sake. I ran his home phone records, and we're rounding up the people he called. Mostly just locals, a few out of state that might be related to the Utopians, but I don't think he has anything to do with this beyond what his letter said."

LaForge sighed. The letter had been detailed though brief. He claimed responsibility in that he had come up with the kernel of a plan, communicated it with some unknown person, then been told to leave Seattle. He felt responsible, couldn't live with what he had done, and wanted his wife and kids to know he loved them, and was sorry. Beyond leaving the phone number he had been communicating with, and the single Gmail address he had sent his plan to, there were no other details that were of use.

The Gmail account had been opened by Tiberius Kirk the day of the initial communication, and closed the day after the final email was sent. The address was 24-593 Federation Drive, San Francisco, the apparent address of Starfleet Headquarters, and the account's security question had a mother's maiden name of Uhura. They were clearly meant to think some über-dork had created the account, though he wasn't so sure. So much of what they had uncovered to this point was misdirection. The Utopians had been a red herring, meant to waste valuable time. The email address was a dead end, and this phone number would likely end up the same.

And half a day, if not longer, would have been wasted.

Here it was, day three of the crisis, and they were no closer to finding out who was behind this. And if they didn't, they wouldn't be able to prevent this from happening again.

The door opened and two suits entered, accompanied by an FBI staffer who pointed to a terminal in the corner. "Over there."

The tech spun in his chair. "What's up?"

"They're from Croft Technologies. Here to install the SecuraVault system."

The tech's eyes narrowed. "Umm, why wasn't I informed?"

"Check your email. Everybody was just a few minutes ago. Emergency directive from HQ. Apparently, this thing is being installed nationwide. Every system."

LaForge tensed slightly, and he looked at Alfredson. "Why do I have a bad feeling about this?"

New York Ave NW
Washington, DC

Kane sat in the passenger seat as Katz drove their Homeland provided SUV toward a destination she had refused to share. A chopper had brought them from Langley to save time, though Washington was almost untouched by the crisis, something that hadn't gone unnoticed by the populations of the cities that were devastated. People were demanding to know why the city where the "fat cats" lived hadn't been hacked, why the politicians weren't suffering, and how they could take the crisis seriously when they weren't experiencing it themselves.

He understood their rage.

He turned to Katz. "Who are we targeting?"

"You'll see when we get there."

"And he's guarded?"

"Yes."

"By?"

"Does it matter?"

"Yes, if you intend to kill them."

"Secret Service."

Kane's eyes popped wide. "Really? Who the hell—"

"You'll find out—"

"Yeah, yeah, when we get there." He sighed and reached into the back seat, pulling forward an aluminum case. He entered a code on the small security panel and it clicked open. "Okay, if they're Secret Service, we are *not* killing them."

Katz glanced at him. "You're so fickle. You wouldn't hesitate to kill Secret Service equivalents in China or Russia."

"They're not Americans."

"So it's okay to kill anyone who's not American?"

"I didn't say that."

"What if they were British? Or French?"

"They're our allies."

"So only if they're the enemy."

"Yes."

Katz's head slowly bobbed. "Interesting. So you morally justify killing by what country happens to be on the wrong side of your government's Friends-Enemies ledger."

Kane stared at her. Was she serious in her questions? Normally, he would think she was simply pushing his buttons, but with the brain injury she had suffered, was this actually a learning experience for her? He imagined that during her life, there would be few if any she could ask these questions of. Surrounded by criminals since she was recruited, any questions asked would probably have received dubious responses. He might actually be the first moral person she had ever had a conversation with. Could his answers make a difference? Could he actually influence her in some way?

He doubted he could change her mind on an emotional level, but if she were truly logical, did right and wrong come into play? And if it did, would morality and human decency determine what was right or wrong, or would it be the law of the land? If it were written down somewhere that it was wrong, would she obey that? She hadn't yet, though perhaps she had merely never been given a reason that made sense to her logical mind. "Because" wasn't an answer to someone like her. She needed a logical reason to follow a rule.

Or, his pop-psychology could be total bullshit, and it would never matter what he said to her.

"It's not that simple."

"What do you mean?"

"In a democracy like ours, we have to assume what the government is asking of us is legal, that those who they say are our enemy, are in fact that. If we don't agree, then we vote them out of power, and if our side loses, we either accept that fact and follow their guidance, or remove ourselves from positions where their guidance might conflict with our personal beliefs."

"So you'd quit the CIA if your government ordered you to do something you didn't agree with?"

"Yes, if it meant not killing someone I felt was innocent."

"So you don't just kill everyone you're told to?"

Kane frowned as he flashed back on every face of every victim. "Not everyone. Sometimes, if I can get what I need from a target, I leave them alive. Sometimes. Ninety-nine times out of a hundred, those whom I'm asked to kill are very bad people, so there's no question."

"And those other times?"

"That's when you have to make a moral judgment. Do you let them live and put your career, and perhaps your country, at risk, or do you fulfill your orders, and assume that perhaps you don't know everything, and that those above you do have a legitimate reason for killing the person. That's why following orders blindly can be dangerous. Quite often, when I hesitate and demand to know why, I'm given a reason that immediately tips the scales, and I execute my orders. In this business, we're not always told why we're tasked to kill someone."

Katz nodded as she turned left. "The same is true in my business. We're rarely told why we're killing someone. I just assume they've done something wrong with respect to my employer, so I eliminate them. I guess it's the same as with you."

Kane shook his head emphatically. "No, not at all the same."

Katz's eyes narrowed. "Why not? You're given orders to kill someone, just like I am. You don't always know why, you just need to know that those giving the orders have a good reason to do so."

"You're missing a critical point, though."

"What's that?"

"*Who's* giving the orders. In my case, I can safely assume that my government, who is issuing the orders, has a legitimate legal or moral reason for ordering someone's death. You, on the other hand, are employed by criminals, so you know they don't have any legitimate legal or moral reason. Automatically, from the get-go, your orders to kill are illegitimate."

Katz pursed her lips, as if considering his words. "Something to think about." She motioned toward the case. "What's in that?"

Kane opened it, removing a prototype weapon he was thankful he had requisitioned. "It's a semi-automatic wireless electro-shock weapon."

Her eyes widened slightly, a rare genuine reaction, if Kane was interpreting her nearly inscrutable signals. "Excuse me?"

"Think of it as a semi-automatic handgun that fires electric bullets that incapacitate your target rather than kill them."

She smiled slightly. "How does it work?"

"Each bullet, for lack of a better term, has its own capacitor, so the charge is self-contained rather than coming from the weapon and traveling over wires." He held up a magazine. "Each mag holds seven rounds. Just shoot at their torso and let the weapon do the rest." He loaded one of the weapons and handed it to her. "*No* killing."

She nodded, tucking the weapon behind her back. "I can't make any promises."

He frowned, knowing it was a statement and not a joke. "So, where are we going?"

She pointed ahead. "There."

Kane's eyes widened slightly as he realized where she was pointing—an upscale restaurant. "What? Are you hungry or something?"

Katz shook her head. "No. Our target has lunch here every Thursday at noon without exception."

"Even in the middle of a crisis?"

She pointed at a black limousine with two flags on the hood, a pair of suits guarding it. "Apparently."

Kane cursed. This was going down, and this was why she had forced him to wait overnight—she had known where and when her target would be most vulnerable. Katz drove past and turned down an alleyway a block later, guiding them to the rear delivery entrance of the restaurant. "You've been here before?"

"I've been planning this for a long time." She pulled the pulse weapon and flicked off the safety.

Kane sighed and did the same. "So this person we're here to see, he's Assembly?"

She nodded.

"Like you?"

She shook her head. "No. He *is* Assembly."

Kane's eyes widened. "You mean he's part of the leadership?"

"Yes."

Kane's pulse ticked up a few points as he realized the opportunity this presented. "How many are there?"

"At most twelve at any given time. After the CIA revealed they knew the identities of several of them, the others had them killed immediately. Replacements were then sought."

"And they've already replaced them?"

"There's always a list being vetted for just such an eventuality. And almost no one says no."

Kane pursed his lips as he eyed the unguarded rear entrance. "Why? Is life leading a massive criminal conspiracy actually that good?"

"You saw the names. Were any of them criminals?"

Kane's head bobbed slowly as he ran down the list of those they had managed to identify a year ago, and had to admit, until they had known they were Assembly members, none had been on their radar from a criminal standpoint. They were all known for their money and positions, but all had been thought to be on the up-and-up. "So what are you saying? It's not a criminal organization?"

She shrugged. "According to you it is, so I won't dispute that. But they don't see themselves that way. They see themselves as trying to better mankind. If people have to die to achieve their goals, they are merely casualties of war." She turned in her seat. "Think about it. Are your leaders criminals because people die due to their actions?"

"That depends."

"Does it? If your President orders ISIS bombed, and terrorists are killed, is he a murderer?"

"Of course not. They're enemy combatants."

"And when civilians are killed during the bombing, even if by accident?"

Kane frowned. "Well, no. They weren't killed intentionally."

"They were collateral damage."

"Right."

She stared at him. "And when you ordered that missile strike, and those kids ran into the target area, did that make you a murderer?"

His heart slammed and his ears pounded as he pushed away from her, his back pressing against the door as the nightmare of that day threatened to overwhelm him. It was his one regret, a regret he had tried to wash the pain of away with copious amounts of alcohol and women, yet had never succeeded in doing. The memory of those kids would forever be burned into his mind, their laughter, their smiles, and his desperate pleas to abort the missile he had ordered, only to be told it was too late. He had watched through his scope, and though it was an invented memory, could picture every single one of those children torn apart by the ensuing explosion, the pain on their faces, their cries of terror, their horrible, painful suffering.

"How-how did you know about that?"

"I've read your file." Her eyes narrowed. "It still troubles you."

He nodded as he calmed himself. "What kind of question is that? Of course it does."

"Interesting. You did nothing wrong. You were cleared of any wrongdoing. So why dwell on it?"

"Because innocent kids died!" he growled. "And if you had a heart to go along with that damaged brain of yours, you'd know that kind of thing tends to screw someone up!"

She shrugged. "I guess I'll never know." She checked her watch. "Let's go, it's time."

Kane shook his head as he climbed out.

Time for what?

"I assume you've got a plan?"

"Yes."

"Care to share?"

"No." Katz strode toward the rear entrance and yanked it open with confidence. Kane followed her inside and found himself in a dingy hallway, the sounds of the kitchen ahead. Katz pulled something from her jacket and palmed it, what, Kane couldn't see, but he didn't like the idea of her doing something without his knowledge.

No killing!

She entered the kitchen and walked past the serving station, scanning the tickets of the several dishes already up. She held her hand over one of the them and Kane squinted, not sure if he had seen something drop from her hand. Katz didn't stick around long enough for him to ask.

"Hey, you can't be in here!"

Katz beamed a smile at the chef, turning her impressive weapons of mass distraction at him. "I'm sorry, sweetie, but I'm lost. Where's the bathroom?"

The chef blushed then jabbed a spatula toward the door. "Through the door and to the left."

"Thanks, sweetie." Katz wiggled out, and Kane followed.

"You lookin' for the bathroom too?"

Kane smiled. "No, sweetie, I'm her bodyguard."

The chef grunted. "That's one body I'd like to guard."

Kane grinned. "You have no idea."

The chef's face slackened slightly as he muttered, "You lucky bastard."

Kane followed Katz into the hallway and found her standing by the men's washroom. She grabbed him and began kissing his neck and nibbling on his ear, her firm grip on his head controlling where and when he looked. Her breath was hot on his skin, and he found himself responding physically despite his best efforts. Two waiters walked by with trays loaded with food.

"That's going to his table," she whispered in his ear before clamping down on his earlobe. She freed it, and he was certain she had drawn blood.

"Did you put something in his food?"

"Yes, a bloodroot derivative. He'll need to throw up shortly." She pulled him tighter against her, grinding against him. "I thought I disgusted you."

She almost sounded turned on. It had to be an act. Could a woman with hardly any emotions actually experience sexual arousal? "He has a mind of his own." He kissed her neck as the waiters returned, their trays empty. She moaned.

Could she?

"Are you ready?"

His distracted mind fought the instinctual urges flowing through him, and he tried to picture Fang, tried to picture the woman he loved, and he once again felt an overwhelming sense of failure and betrayal flow through him.

Dishes crashed, and there was a commotion in the eating area. Heavy footfalls followed.

"Three seconds." Her lips pressed against his as she turned his head slightly so he could see down the hallway. And his heart nearly stopped.

Are you kidding me?

Their very recognizable target was rushing toward them, four Secret Service agents rushing after him.

"Now."

Katz let him go, spinning around as her weapon extended out in front of her. She fired, the first agent freezing in place as his entire body spasmed from the 50,000 volts paralyzing him. Kane drew, firing at the agent on the far left, Katz already moving onto her second target. Within seconds, all four were down, and Katz grabbed the target by the arm.

"No, I'm gonna be sick!"

"Plenty of time for that," said Kane as he grabbed the other arm. They half-carried, half-dragged him through the kitchen, their weapons still at the ready, the kitchen staff raising their hands high as they passed through, and moments later they were outside.

Katz opened the rear door and tossed the man into the back seat. "I'll drive," she said as she rounded the vehicle, Kane climbing in with their prisoner. Katz started the SUV and floored it, sending them hurtling down the narrow alleyway and out into city traffic.

"I'm gonna be sick."

Kane leaned over and lowered the window. Their target stuck his head out and heaved whatever lunch he had managed to eat. Kane yanked him back in. "Done?"

He nodded, though didn't seem confident. The man stared at him. "Who the hell are you? Do you have any idea what you've done?"

Kane stared back, his heart hammering as he continued to process what had just happened. He glanced toward Katz, watching in the rearview mirror. "Who I am isn't important, and as to what I've done, well, I've just kidnapped the Vice President of the United States."

Katz glanced back. "And Number Seven of the Assembly."

Grand Hyatt Hotel
Manhattan, New York

Atlas sat with his back against the wall of the hotel room they had been assigned, a suite commandeered for the emergency. The entire Bravo Team were spread about, plus enough gear to fight a small war. Their mission wasn't traffic control or even riot control. They were a rapid reaction force meant to deal with foreign governments or terrorists attempting to take advantage of the situation. He expected little if any action.

Yet he was antsy.

His sister lived about ten miles from here, and he hadn't been able to reach her. Her cellphone was going directly to voicemail, the system apparently overwhelmed despite pleas from the government to stay off the phones. She was a nurse, and all medical personnel had been asked to report to work if possible, with the vast majority doing so.

And if he knew his sister, she'd have been first in line.

"Man, I'm going shack-whacky."

Sergeant Will "Spock" Lightman's eyebrow rose at Niner's outburst. "We've only been here a few hours, and you're already complaining?"

Niner leaped to his feet, pacing in front of the window, wisps of smoke dotting the horizon as rioters and vandals took advantage, lighting fire to abandoned cars with near impunity. "We should be out there, doing something. I mean, we're twelve highly trained, handsome with some exceptions"—he eyed Jimmy who flipped him the bird—"soldiers, living the high-life in a fancy hotel, rather than getting out there and kicking some ass! This city is falling to pieces, and it's only a few people responsible for it."

Dawson grunted. "A few thousand would be more accurate."

"Yeah, but drop us in the middle of one of the hot zones, and we can clean that up before nightfall."

"It would mean killing Americans."

Niner shrugged. "So? The moment they started looting they lost their rights, as far as I'm concerned."

Dawson's head bobbed slowly. "Maybe. But how do you separate the looters from those just trying to survive?"

Spock raised a finger. "Umm, the one with the jug of milk is trying to survive, the one with the TV isn't?"

Dawson laughed. "That's one way." He motioned toward the television, CNN playing. "We might be called in regardless. This is getting out of control. They're shooting at the resupply helicopters now."

Niner stopped his pacing and spun toward the television. "Are you kidding me? Why the hell would they do that?"

"The gangs emptied the stores, now there's already a black market for food and water. If the supplies get through, then there goes their profit."

Niner cursed, throwing his hands up in the air then clasping them behind his neck. "This country has gone to hell in just days. What's it going to be like tomorrow?"

"According to the President's address this morning, 'better.'"

Niner glanced at Spock. "Riiight. And he knows that how?"

"Things are starting to move. The ships have switched back to manual methods, so are moving again. The trains are running again.

The airports are open. It's just getting things in and out of the cities that's the problem."

Niner pressed his forehead against the wall of glass and peered down at the streets below. "Have you looked outside? There're thousands of abandoned cars. And it's not just a matter of the owners coming back for them. When the National Guard bulldozed their way into the cities, they created thousands of wrecks that'll have to be hauled away. That's going to take weeks, if not months, to deal with."

Spock grunted. "Bus pass sales will go up, I guess."

Niner turned to the unusually silent Atlas. "You've got family here, don't you?"

Atlas looked up at him. "Yeah. My folks and my sister and her kids."

Niner sat in one of the chairs, leaning forward with his elbows on his knees. "Have you been able to reach them?"

Atlas frowned. "My folks are visiting family outside of New Orleans, so they're fine. I talked to my sister last night, but haven't been able to reach her since."

Dawson reached out and patted his friend's shoulder. "I wouldn't read anything into that. Most of the phone systems are jammed."

"Jesus, look at this!"

They all turned toward Spock, pointing at the television, a banner splashed across the bottom of the screen.

"Vice President Kidnapped!"

Dawson's phone rang and he answered it, speaking in hushed tones for a moment before ending the call. "They want a team in DC." He pointed at Atlas who raised his hand, cutting off what was about to come.

"BD, you know I hate to ask this, but can I stay here?"

Dawson nodded. "Done." He turned to Niner. "Niner, Spock, and Jimmy, you're with me. Red, you're in command here, don't do anything I wouldn't do."

"That leaves everything pretty much wide open."

Dawson grinned then pointed at Red's furry red lid. "While you're waiting, why don't you give that thing a shave?" He jerked a thumb at Niner. "You're scaring my boy here."

Red drew his bowie knife and ran the razor sharp blade between his thumb and forefinger. He glanced at Niner. "Tennis ball decked out for Valentine's Day, huh?"

Niner flipped over the back of his chair, putting it between him and Red. "Hey, who told you?"

The entire room replied in unison, "I did."

Niner looked about. "Hey, most of you weren't even in Mexico!"

Red stepped toward him. "News travels fast."

"Yeah, and mouths apparently run fast too." He held up his hands. "Hey, I think it looks great. It was meant as a compliment. I mean, who doesn't like Valentine's Day. And tennis? I mean, come on, tennis is awesome! And those fuzzy balls, why, they're so cool. I could spend hours playing with fuzzy balls like those."

The room groaned.

"Hey, that came out wrong!"

"So you like to play with fuzzy balls?"

Flies unzipped around the room.

Niner jabbed a finger at Atlas. "Don't you dare. We might be about to go into battle and I don't want my comrades here feeling inadequate."

Atlas gave him a look, enjoying the momentary distraction at Niner's expense. He squeezed his package. "Nobody has ever called them tennis balls."

Niner grinned. "Volleyballs?"

Atlas' head bobbed. "Once or twice."

Niner jabbed a finger at Atlas' nether region. "Keep them holstered. I don't need to be traumatized before I go into action."

"Your loss."

Niner turned his attention back to the knife-wielding Red. "Get your ass in the bathroom and put that thing to use."

Red tapped the side of his head with the dull edge of the blade. "So let me get this straight. You like to play with fuzzy balls, we've established what kind of balls those are, so essentially, what it boils down to is, you called me a dickhead."

Niner's eyes went wide for a moment, his head tilting to the side. "Umm, close one eye for me, and I'll let you know."

The room roared with laughter as Red lunged at Niner, Niner hopping back toward the door.

Red turned to Dawson. "BD, you better get him out of here, I'm liable to test my blade out on that turkey waddle he calls a set."

Niner feigned personal injury. "One harmless little comparison to a red tennis ball, and we degenerate into ball shaming."

Atlas' impossibly deep voice delivered the knockout blow. "With balls like those, shame is the only honest reaction."

Niner bit a knuckle then turned to Dawson, his voice cracking with his best Eddie Murphy Delirious impression. "Tito, get me a tissue."

Dawson rolled his eyes. "Let's go before *I* kill you." He jabbed a finger at Red. "And I'm serious, you should do something about that. Your wife's already called the Colonel asking him to order you to."

The entire room roared, Red blushing slightly as he ran his hand through the fuzzy top he had grown since his ordeal in Syria. "Is it really that bad?"

"Yes!" cried the chorus.

He frowned. "Fine. Did anybody bring some clippers?"

"Yeah." Atlas rose and grabbed his electric razor with trimmer, tossing it to Red. "You might want to rinse it out first."

Red looked at it. "Why?"

"Because the last time I used it was on my volleyballs."

United States Strategic Command Headquarters
Offutt Air Force Base, Nebraska

Captain Cartwright's head drooped and he immediately woke, a surge of adrenaline rushing through his system as he glanced around. The two contractors were still at the terminal, as they had been since last night. He had called for a chair to be brought in, and had told his day shift replacement he would stick around until the job was done—a decision he was now regretting. It was getting ridiculous, though the few times he had asked, he had been assured everything was going according to plan—they were simply triple checking everything, as USSC was too important a facility to screw up the installation.

He had to agree.

If World War Three were to start, this would be where America's response would be triggered. A common misconception was that the "football," the briefcase that always accompanied the President, actually launched the missiles. It didn't. It merely sent coded, authenticated orders that would be routed to this facility, where they were then actioned. It was this installation that would transmit to the silos and subs, the orders to launch the missiles, through the very equipment in this room.

The system was completely isolated, with no way to hack it, though there were also systems in this same room with external links, those the contractors were securing. The two systems, however, had no physical connections. The isolated systems used hard lines to the silos spread across the country, manned by crews specially chosen for the task—it took a special type of soldier to turn the key that meant the death of millions. There was a reason they had been called "steely-eyed missile men." They were the human component that ensured it was a person who actually performed the launch, the risk of an accidental technical glitch simply too nightmarish to contemplate.

It took two turned keys to launch each batch of missiles, with the orders delivered from this facility. It was essential that things be secure. Though the missile control system couldn't be hacked, disrupting the other systems could still wreak havoc across the facility, proving a distraction should there be an emergency.

He yawned and rubbed his eyes with a pair of knuckles, his head drooping once again. A snort woke him, and he forced himself to his feet. He glanced toward the terminal, only one of the contractors at it. His eyes narrowed and his heart raced. "Where's the other guy?"

There was no answer as fingers flew across the keyboard. He stepped forward, grabbing the contractor by the shoulder and spinning him around. "I said, where's the other guy?"

A shoe scraped on the floor behind him followed by something pressed over his mouth and nose, a pungent odor filling his nostrils as he instinctively gasped for breath. His world became a fog as the seated contractor rose, staring at him as his reality slowly slipped away. A shot of adrenaline pumped through his system as a stray thought caused a visceral, horror-laden reaction.

These men weren't here to install a new security system.

They were here to hack the missile control system.

They were here to launch the missiles.

"Please, don't..." His mumbled plea fell on the deaf ears of ideologues, who could do no wrong.

Minuteman III Launch Control Facility
Outside Karlsruhe, North Dakota

Captain Tony Daugherty stretched then spun in his chair. The two-person Launch Control Facility was claustrophobic, though they were tested for that. You couldn't station a soldier in a closed environment, with no possible exit for 24 hours at a time, if they had any phobias about tight spaces. Personally, it didn't bother him, though by the end of a shift he was ready to escape like a bat out of hell.

The isolation was one thing, and though he liked the guy he worked with, there was only so much you could talk about, especially this time of year. Football was finished, baseball had just started, he didn't like basketball, and his partner hated hockey. You could only debate The Walking Dead for so long, and beyond that, they didn't like the same television shows.

They kept busy doing their drills and inspections, these tasks specifically designed to keep them on their toes to pass the time, yet they only filled the void for a relatively few minutes of an otherwise extremely long day. One of the problems previous generations of crews used to suffer was complete isolation from the outside world. When inside the bunker, they used to be completely cut off, but recent upgrades had made Internet and Satellite TV available to them.

Though not today.

The systems were undergoing maintenance, a far too frequent event. No Internet, no phones, no access to the news. And today, that was particularly frustrating, especially with what was going on when they had arrived last night. "I wonder what's happening out there."

His partner, Lieutenant Jon Fraser, leaned back in his chair and turned toward him. "I think the zombies have already taken over the Eastern seaboard, and are making their way inland."

Daugherty grunted. "Seriously, enough with the zombies. You're going to slip up and tell me what happened in last week's episode, then I'm going to be pissed and have to shoot you."

Fraser raised his hands. "Okay, okay." He shrugged. "I don't know, but the way things were going when we pulled in, I'm not sure what we're going to find when we walk out of here."

"If things truly went to shit, they'd let us know though, right?"

"I doubt it. Worried about someone in particular?"

Daugherty folded his arms. "Most of my family lives in cities. My wife and kids are off base, of course, so I think they're safe, but my folks are in Chicago, and so are my sister and brother. It looked like they were getting hit pretty hard by all this."

Fraser frowned. "My mom's in Seattle, my dad's visiting his folks in Atlanta. Both weren't looking good, either. Maybe when we get out of here, they'll have figured out who's behind it, and it'll all be over."

"My money's on North Korea."

"Or the Russians. Or Chinese."

Daugherty shook his head. "No way. They're not stupid enough to do something this big. Thousands are dying, billions of dollars are being lost. When this is over, we're going to war, and whoever is behind it knows that, they're just too crazy to care."

Fraser sighed. "Then you better throw Iran into that mix. They're nuts."

"Could be. And they're Twelvers, so they're a special brand of insane."

Fraser scratched at his five o'clock shadow. "Do you think the Koreans would be that crazy, though? I mean, the Dear Leader or whatever he calls himself, has to love himself too much to risk death, right? He has to know we're going to bomb the shit out of them until we know he's dead."

Daugherty shook his head. "It can't be them. He doesn't want to die."

"Then who?"

"It could be the Iranians. They want to bring on Armageddon, and this is one way to do it."

Fraser's eyebrows shot up. "Shit, do you think we'll get a launch order?"

Daugherty shook his head. "No way, we'll just use conventional weapons on them. Bomb them into submission. Once they have the nuke, though, it'll be another story."

"Yeah, but we've got a treaty now."

Daugherty grinned at Fraser's sarcastic tone. "Don't get me started on that."

Fraser held up his hands in mock surrender. "I'm sorry! I forgot. No talking about Iran or Islam or any other bullshit like it."

Daugherty bowed slightly in his chair. "I thank you for your cooperation, and so does my doctor." He made a show of checking his pulse. "Crisis averted." He motioned at the door. "What do you plan on doing?"

"Getting my ass home, finding out what's going on, and taking action accordingly. My wife and I already hit the grocery store when I heard what was going on, and we already had a disaster kit, so we're fully stocked. I'll probably just sit tight, but if things truly go to shit, I'm thinking I might pack up the family and take them to my sister's cottage. It's about a day's drive. I could be back in time for my next shift, and they'd be safe up there."

Daugherty frowned. "I can't see it being that bad, can you?"

Fraser shook his head. "I don't know, it was getting pretty nasty before we came in here, and it had only been going on for two days."

A red light flashed on the panel for a split second, then went dark.

"Did you see that?"

"No, what?"

Daugherty leaned forward, tapping the communications failure indicator. It remained dark. "I could have sworn the comms system failed for a moment.

"Sensor glitch?"

"Must be. Let's run a diagnostic. With everything going on now, we can't be too careful."

Unknown Location

Sherrie stepped up onto the sink, praying it would hold her weight, and for the moment, it appeared it would. She tapped the ceiling, the sound as solid as every other surface surrounding them, which was a disappointment. There'd be no false ceiling that would lead to ductwork they could crawl through and make their dramatic escape.

It's only that easy in the movies.

She took a chance. There was a camera with complete coverage of the room, yet no one had come yet to tell her to stop what she was doing, further confirming their theory that Katz was not here. They were alone, unmonitored, left to their own devices. She grabbed the frame surrounding one of the four lights spread across the room, then yanked at it. It moved a couple of inches, and she gave it another tug, then another, pulling it free after a few more tries.

Revealing a solid ceiling behind it, with some wire bundles.

"What do you see?"

"Some wires. I'm guessing electrical, maybe a line to the camera. Cutting that might get someone's attention."

"What good would that do?"

"I could jump them, or demand some more supplies for you."

The sink tore loose from the wall and she dropped to the floor, grabbing one of the bundles of wires, tearing it loose from the ceiling. The entire lighting assembly crashed to the floor, wires torn loose from what appeared to be a plaster job applied over the wiring installation. Water sprayed everywhere, the wires, some of them torn, sparking.

This can't be good.

She picked herself up and stared at the wall where the sink had been mounted, the pipes inside bent, one of them broken. She spotted a cutoff valve and twisted it, stopping the water, then stepped away from the still sparking wires.

"Well, if that doesn't get her attention, nothing will."

Sherrie grinned at Fang. "I've never been known to be subtle." She strode quickly to the door and pressed her ear against it. Nothing. She waited, still hearing only the continued arcing of the torn wiring.

Yet that could mean everything or nothing.

If the door were thick enough, she wouldn't hear anything regardless, yet she had to believe if they were being monitored, what had just happened would produce a reaction. Surely Katz wouldn't let them get away with what she had just done. Though perhaps she had merely dismissed her actions as fruitless attempts at escape. They were no closer to getting out of here than they were a few minutes ago. No great secret escape tunnel had been revealed.

Her eyes narrowed. Or had it? She rushed back toward the hole in the wall and peered inside. She could see pipes running parallel to the floor, but not very far, the area behind the wall pitch black, the dead light for this corner of the room providing no help.

If only I had my cellphone.

She reached inside and felt nothing beyond the pipes in either direction. She leaned back on her haunches and eyed the hole. It appeared to be a triple layer of a hardened drywall, with insulating layers between—a club sandwich of noise-suppressing materials, all coated with a half-inch layer of plaster.

Not as impenetrable as she had thought.

Yet what was beyond, was the real question. The pipes suggested wherever they were, *if* there were anything beyond these walls, it would be to the sides, not the back. The front, where the door was, would obviously lead out, but she had to assume if any wall were reinforced, it would be that one.

"What are you thinking?"

She looked at Fang. "I'm thinking that I might be able to tear apart this wall, and maybe get into the next room."

"What would that give us?"

"Perhaps access to a room with an unlocked door."

"Or to a room with someone we might not want to meet."

Sherrie frowned. The thought had occurred to her. If this was a prison, then whoever was on the other side of these walls might not be a nice person. Yet this wouldn't be a regular prison, where only bad guys were sent. This was some sort of illegal prison for freelancers like Katz. If that were the case, those in the next cell might be as innocent as they were.

It was an interesting conundrum.

She stared at Fang, who wasn't looking good. "We have to risk it. I don't know how much longer you're going to be able to hold out."

"Go ahead. Just be careful."

Sherrie nodded then returned to work, grabbing a chunk of the wall where the sink used to be, and pulled. Three raps on the pipes had her halting her efforts.

"What the hell was that?"

Three more raps, slower this time, followed by three more quick raps. Her eyes widened. "It's an S-O-S!"

Mark held his belt buckle in the air as everyone listened for a response. There had definitely been some sound that had come from the bathroom area, the pipes carrying the vibrations of some nearby event that didn't sound controlled. He tapped out his Morse code SOS on the pipe under the sink, and waited, the others gathered around in silence.

"Are you sure—"

He held up a finger, cutting Rick off as the message was returned.

S-O-S.

He turned and smiled at the others. It had to be another prisoner. There was no way one of their captors would respond.

"Now what?" asked an exasperated Rick. "What good is tapping out S-O-S back and forth?"

"Let's just see."

He quickly tapped out another message.

Do you understand?

"You know Morse Code?"

Mark nodded. "I was a Sea Cadet when I was a kid, and Chris and I used to do Morse code for fun."

Liz frowned. "They'd do it at the dinner table if they didn't like what I had cooked."

Mark's eyes widened and he looked at his wife. "You knew that?"

"Of course I did, I'm not an idiot. The two of you tapping away with your fingers at the table? I knew what you were doing."

Mark grinned. "Sorry."

A response came back. Short, but perhaps game changing.

Yes.

"What did they say?" asked Rick.

"They said they understood me." He smiled. "We can communicate."

"Christ, what are the chances of someone else in here knowing Morse code?"

Mark shrugged. "I don't know, but I'm buying a lottery ticket as soon as we get out of here."

Liz leaned forward. "What should we say?"

"Umm, how about we find out who they are?" suggested Jenn.

"Good idea." Mark tapped at the pipe, his faded hope renewed. For how long, he had no idea.

Williams Residence

Bronx, New York

Shannon flinched then jumped from the couch as the kids bolted for the door. "Don't you dare open that!" she hissed, her heart hammering with terror at what might be on the other side. The television was constantly broadcasting warnings to stay inside and lock your doors, and the looting and rioting were replayed with gleeful abandon by the networks, making her wonder at times if it was just footage of the same riot, repeated to make it look as if it were a nationwide problem. A riot in LA would pull in only so many viewers. Riots nationwide, ongoing, would pull them all in.

She peered through the peephole and smiled. It was her man. She unlocked the door, and little Michael grabbed her hand.

"Mommy said no visitors."

"Shut up, you little runt." She pushed him aside and pulled open the door.

"Hey, baby." Levar stepped inside and grabbed her, pulling her close and laying a kiss and grind on her that had her thighs steaming and her heart hammering. "So, show me this stuff."

"Huh?"

"The stuff you texted me about."

She gasped as half a dozen of his crew appeared from either side of the door, all packing, all looking around warily, as if expecting trouble. "I-I didn't mean for you to come here, I just wanted to tell you what I saw."

"Hey, baby, am I not welcome here with you?"

Her heart palpitated. "No, that's not it, it's just I'm going to get in big trouble if Mrs. Williams finds out you were here."

"Hey, what she don't know can't hurt her or you, baby. Now, show me the stuff."

She nodded, trembling, his tone no longer gentle. The kids cowered in the corner, wisely keeping their mouths shut, their eyes wide as they stared at the hardware the crew sported. She led Levar down the hall and into the bedroom. She pointed at the closet. "In there."

He motioned toward it, and two of his boys yanked the bi-fold doors open. He whistled. "Would you look at that!" He stepped forward and tapped one of the water bottles. "These are going for ten bucks a hit, and that's up from five last night. By tomorrow, they'll be twenty at least." He lifted up one of the soup cans. "And this? Shit, this is already twenty bucks a can." He tossed it to one of his boys then smiled at her. "Baby, with this, we're set. When this is all over, you and I are livin' large."

She smiled, butterflies in her stomach, then frowned. "Y-you're going to take it?"

He pointed at the hoard then jerked a thumb over his shoulder, his crew surging forward and grabbing the supplies by the armload. "Yeah, why else would I come here?"

"I-I thought you came to see me."

He laughed. "Baby, I can see you whenever I want. This shit"—he grabbed another can, tossing it in the air then catching it with the opposite hand—"this shit is like oil, and we've got a gusher."

"But she's going to kill me! She's got kids!"

He shrugged. "Hey, everybody's got mouths to feed. Why should she have all this? What makes her so goddamned special?" He opened a can of soup and tossed the lid on the floor. He took a swig of the chunky chicken noodle then chewed. He sighed as he swallowed. "I'm hungry too. Why should *I* go hungry?" His eyes narrowed and he glared at her. "You don't want me to be hungry, do you, baby?"

She shook her head, terror filling her. This was a side of him she had never seen before. She knew he was ambitious, she knew he wouldn't take shit from no one, but right here, right now, she had no doubt he would shoot her where she stood if she were to try and stop him.

"Besides, I'm a businessman, and this is business. You tell her that if she wants to feed her kids, she can come see me. I'll give her a good price!" He laughed, and the others joined him as the closet quickly emptied, all of Mrs. Williams' hard work taken in minutes by those who hadn't planned ahead, who were looking to exploit the situation, rather than help.

And suddenly everything she had been ignoring on television made sense. This was a crisis, people had to remain calm and work together, and what was happening on the streets was wrong. What was happening in this bedroom was wrong.

She reached out and grabbed one of the boxes from his crew. "You can't do this! It's not right!"

Levar's boy glanced at him, not sure of what to do. Levar nodded, and the box was yanked away. "Don't get in my way, bitch." He raised a finger, jabbing it into her chest. "Just who the hell do you think you are? I've got a dozen bitches like you around the hood. You think you're exclusive? You think you're special? You're nothing to me, just a piece of ass for when I'm bored." He shoved her onto the bed. "Now get out of my way!"

The words stung, each a slap in the face, each a punch to the gut. He had never talked that way to her before, and it was the first she had ever heard of there being anyone else. Her heart hammered as her chest ached. Her mouth filled with bile as she wanted to die right then and there. The others were laughing at her, the entire exchange heard by people she had thought were her friends.

She was nothing.

She was just a stupid little girl who had thought she was running with the big boys, when instead, she was just another one of his hoes, another bitch to satisfy his needs. He never had any intention of living with her, of marrying her, of having kids with her. In fact, if she thought about it, they barely did anything together except have sex. They almost never talked except when he was done with her, fueling her fantasy of what was to come.

But it was all bullshit.

It was all designed to keep her on a leash, to make sure she'd be there the next time he wanted a booty call, and if she weren't available, he would just call the next girl on the list. Her heart fluttered.

How far down the list am I?

She didn't see him that often. Maybe once or twice a week. And when they did, he was almost insatiable. She had always assumed it was because he loved her, was turned on by her, and because it had been so long since the last time. But if he was like that every day, then maybe he was getting his needs satisfied elsewhere, and she'd only get the call when none of them were available.

A pit of rage formed in her stomach and her heart pounded in her ears. This was bullshit. This wasn't fair. This wasn't supposed to be her life. And now, she was the laughing stock of all her supposed friends. And with the Internet, everyone would know. Everyone at school would know. She'd be endlessly tormented, endlessly teased, trolled on Facebook and Snapchat until she'd be forced to go into hiding.

Yet even then, there'd be no hope. Her stupid mother would never understand. She'd never let her quit school. She'd never move them to another neighborhood. She'd force her to go out and face the humiliation, day in and day out.

No freakin' way!

She rolled off the bed, Levar's back to her, as if he had forgotten she was there, or was so done with her that he no longer cared. She reached out and pulled his piece from the back of his pants then aimed it at him.

"Whoa, baby, what the hell?" He stepped back, his hands raised.

"You think you can treat me like shit and get away with it? You think you can do what you did to me, then just throw me away like some hood rat?"

He stepped back a little further, the others in the room giving her space. She edged closer to him, her hands trembling as she held the gun out in front of her. "You think you can ruin my life? Humiliate me?"

"Hey, baby, I'm sorry. I didn't mean it." He motioned toward the window. "It's crazy out there, baby, and you know me, I'm just trying to keep ahead of the man, you know. You just pissed me off when you tried to stop me. I didn't mean it. You know you're the only one. I just said all those things cuz' I was mad." He held out his hands. "Come here, baby, you know you're the only one for me."

She hesitated. He was his old self again. He was her future, her one true love, he was the man who would save her from the hell of living with her mother, the man who would help her avenge the death of her father. She lowered the gun, shaking all over, and he stepped forward.

"It's okay, baby." He held out his hand. "Here, give me that. It's going to be okay."

She nodded and handed him the gun. She fell into his arms, her chest heaving with sobs, but he didn't hug her back. She looked up at him, and he shoved her away.

"You think you can hold a gun on me, bitch?" He aimed at her chest and fired three times, though she wasn't sure about the final shot. The pain was excruciating at first, then quickly faded as the pounding in her chest, the hammering in her ears, stopped almost immediately. She fell onto the bed, her arms flopping to her sides, the last sounds she heard the screams of the little boys she was responsible for, and the laughter of those she thought were her friends.

9th Street NW

Washington, DC

Kane held his weapon on Vice President Vance as Katz blended with the unusually light afternoon traffic of a Washington perhaps unaffected directly by the chaos spreading across the country, but certainly terrified by it. She pulled into another alleyway and barreled through, the mirrors nearly scraping the buildings on either side, as she raced toward a rapidly approaching dead end.

"Umm, you see that, don't you?" She said nothing, instead holding out her phone and tapping a sequence on the screen. A garage door, disguised to be part of the wall, rolled up, the gaping maw of whatever was on the other side revealed as they plunged through. Kane looked back to see the door automatically close behind them as Katz applied the brakes, tossing him forward, his aim never wavering, merely adjusting to track the Vice President, also thrown against the seat in front of him.

"Bring him."

Kane grabbed Vance by the arm and opened the door, stepping into what appeared to be a simple garage, big enough to hold perhaps four additional vehicles, a lone Ford the only other car here. He hauled Vance out and followed Katz to the lone door, where she held her phone up to a security panel. There was a buzz then she pushed the door open.

"Is this an Assembly facility?"

She nodded. "Yes."

"And your codes still work?"

She shook her head as she stepped through the door. "No. This isn't my phone. I took it off one of their operatives yesterday."

"Won't they know he's missing?"

"Only if they find the body." She strode quickly down a corridor lined with what appeared to be storage units, some with red lights over the doors, others with green, each numbered sequentially.

"What is this place?"

"An Assembly holding facility. It's where they keep..." She trailed off, as if searching for an appropriate word. "Problems."

"And that phone gives you access?"

"Yes."

"They won't recognize you?"

"They might recognize me as someone who has used the facility before, and with this phone, as someone who is currently authorized. There will be no questions of consequence asked." She pointed at the floor. "Wait here." She knocked on a door and was buzzed in, returning a few moments later. "This way."

They walked a couple of hundred more feet before Katz stopped in front of one of the doors. She looked up at the camera, and there was a beep then a click. She opened the door and stepped inside, Kane pushing Vance after her. Katz closed the door and the lights flicked on, revealing a chamber of horrors if Kane had ever seen one.

Vance gasped. "Wh-what are you going to do to me?"

Katz glanced at him. "Ask you some questions."

"Do you know who I am? You can't do this!" Vance's head pivoted between his two captors. "Who are you people?"

Kane shoved him into a chair and Katz stepped over to a wall panel. She pushed a button, wrist and ankle irons swinging into place, magnetically sealing Vance to the chair.

Nice!

"Mr. Vice President, I know exactly who you are, but if you are also Number Seven of the Assembly, like she says, then we have a problem."

"I have no idea what this Assembly is you keep referring to."

Katz walked over to a table, gleaming metal trays filled with every manner of cutting and prying tool imaginable, carefully laid out as if awaiting a surgeon's arrival. She picked up a scalpel, holding it to the light, making a show of examining its sharp edge, Vance's eyes glued to it. Katz stared at him, her eyes dead, devoid of any emotion, the cold, calculated woman making no pretenses of understanding human emotions, and by doing so, perhaps displaying her mastery of them.

For there was nothing more terrifying than dispassion in someone about to inflict unimaginable pain. "Yes, Number Seven, you do." She stepped closer, tipping his chin up with her index finger, then running the scalpel like a razor over his cheek, scraping at his skin but not breaking it. "You were recruited over ten years ago, your membership confirmed by the Council, and you have enjoyed the perks of membership since. During the last election, your cohorts concocted a scandal that forced the incumbent Vice President to step down, and you were chosen as President Starling's running mate, a decision forced upon him by the party, and its big money supporters. You have served him faithfully since. Until yesterday."

Vance's eyes were wide as he stared up at her, her finger still pressed under his chin.

Kane stared too, shocked at the revelation. He remembered the sex scandal, of course, photos of the former Vice President showing him entering a hotel room with an underage prostitute, splashed across the news for weeks, and despite his denials, he eventually tendered his resignation to end the media scrutiny. Some experts had come forward with compelling evidence showing that the photos had been doctored, but the damage had been done, his reputation forever tainted.

Harold Vance, a Senator from California, had been chosen to replace him on the ticket. Kane had never suspected anything untoward with respect to the man. The Vice President was a mostly ceremonial position, so to destroy the former VP's reputation to take over his job made little sense.

Unless you intended to assassinate the President.

Kane stepped forward. "Do you intend to kill the President? Is that why you did it?"

Vance's head turned slightly toward Kane. "I have no idea what you're talking about."

Katz's wrist flicked across his cheek, a thin line of bright crimson revealed.

Vance jerked his head away and cried out. "I'm telling the truth! I swear, I have no idea what's going on here!"

Kane pulled a chair closer and sat. He motioned toward Katz. "I'm not sure if you know who she is, but you might recognize the name. Nadja Katz."

Vance paled noticeably. Kane smiled, suppressing his shock.

Holy shit! He knows who she is!

"I see you do." It meant he was definitely Assembly. He had doubted it to this very moment, but there was only one reason you feared the mention of a name over the sight of someone wielding a scalpel near your throat—you knew *exactly* who they were, and of what they were capable.

"I-I don't."

Kane leaned back and folded his arms. "Sorry, Mr. Vice President, or Number Seven, but you clearly do." He leaned forward, making a show of staring at Vance's crotch. "It's okay to piss yourself. You can go ahead." He leaned back. "No shame in that. I've seen far braver men than you piss themselves when they realized what they were in for." He tossed his chin toward Katz. "But if you tell her what you know, I'll make sure she goes easy on you."

Katz's hand darted out again, the other cheek opened.

"Stop it! Please!"

There would be pain, though not much, not from those cuts. It was the psychological torture Vance was experiencing that would betray him long before the pain. Blood slowly trickled down his cheeks, blood he couldn't wipe away, couldn't see the volume of. He would only feel it was there, seeping from the shallow cuts, with no idea how bad it truly was.

She's good.

"Should I tell her to keep going, or will you tell us what we want to know?"

"I-I don't know anything."

Katz's hand swung deftly through the air, an earlobe sliced open.

"Oh God, no!"

Kane leaned forward, his elbows on his knees. "I've got all day. I don't know about you." He jerked a thumb at Katz. "And I know her, she's infinitely patient, as I'm sure you already know from having read her file when your organization hired her to do your dirty work. But then you decided she knew too much and tried to kill her last year. I'd say you pissed her off, but you know that's not true. She doesn't feel things like you and I do."

232

Kane tapped his chest. "Me, I hate watching this. I mean, I'm not some sadistic bastard who gets off watching a man get slowly hacked to pieces. But I have a job to do, and that job is to help her achieve her goals. Your job is to answer our questions. So unless you want to die a slow, painful death, I'd cooperate now."

Katz sliced open the other earlobe.

"I-I can't remember the question!"

"Are you a member of the Assembly?"

Vance closed his eyes, dropping his chin to his chest, but said nothing.

Katz sliced across his forehead, opening a nasty gash, the deepest yet.

"Oh God, yes, yes I'm a member!"

"And your designation is Number Seven?"

"Yes!"

"And there are twelve members?"

"Yes, twelve Council members. There are thousands more that work for the organization on a permanent or temporary basis."

"Do they all know who they work for?"

Vance shook his head, opening his eyes and staring up at Kane. "No, most—most don't."

"Are you behind what has been going on the past two days?"

Vance hesitated, his eyes turning up to stare at Katz. She raised her hand. "Yes!" he cried, recoiling from her.

"Why?"

"I-I don't know."

Kane pointed at him. "Cut this sonofabitch." Katz complied, a shoulder sliced open. Vance screamed in agony, struggling in his chair as he tried futilely to free himself. "Of course you know. You're one of the Council."

"Not everything is shared."

Katz raised her hand again, but Kane signaled for her to hold off. "Explain."

"We only know what we need to know at our level."

"What do you mean? I thought the Council knew everything."

"No, I know everything below me, but not above me."

"What do you mean?"

"We're numbered in order of how long we've been members. When a member of the Council above us dies, we move up a level. Before you killed several of us last year, I was Number Ten. Every member knows everything that those who come after him knows, but not before, unless necessary."

"So what are you saying? That someone above you is responsible for what is going on?"

Vance's eyes widened and he leaned toward Kane. "Yes! Exactly! Six or above is behind this, not me!"

Kane leaned back in his chair, tapping his chin. "Now, why don't I believe you?" He glanced at Katz. "Is any of what he says the truth?"

She nodded. "When conferencing, members can only see those below them, newer members only. They had to vote to invite them, so they know who they are. Anyone who came before is only a number to them."

Kane pushed his lips out as he regarded Vance. "So, you're innocent in all this."

"Yes!"

"So you have no useful information for me."

"No!"

"Very well." Kane rose and drew his weapon, pointing it at Vance's forehead. "Goodbye."

"Wait!" Vance's eyes were squeezed shut, his head twisting away from the barrel of Kane's Glock.

Kane raised his weapon to his shoulder. "Yes? You have something to add?"

"I-I might know something."

"What?"

"They—they had me introduce the President to someone."

"Who?"

Vance hesitated.

"Number Seven, I thought we were past this? Cut him."

"Wait!"

Kane held up a finger, Katz withdrawing. "Yes?"

"Roger Croft. CEO of Croft Technologies."

Kane's eyes narrowed. "Why?"

"To tell the President about their SecuraVault system."

"Which is?"

"It protects against hacking. I was instructed to make sure the President agreed to let Croft install it across the country."

Kane's jaw slowly dropped. "Wait a minute. That system that they've been reporting on the news is this SecuraVault system?"

"Yes."

"And Croft is Assembly?"

Vance shrugged. "I don't know. All I know is I've known him since college, and we've kept in touch. If he's a member, then he's higher than me."

"He wouldn't tell you?"

"It's strictly forbidden."

Kane sat back down. "I see." He looked at Katz. "So you were right. The Assembly *is* behind this. And this security system they're installing must be the reason." Kane's chest tightened as he realized the implications. "If this system is theirs, then it will probably allow them to access every system they install it on through some sort of backdoor. Nothing will be safe."

Katz nodded. "It makes sense. They want control of everything."

Kane shook his head. "Look around, they already have it! They've caused havoc around the country. Clearly, they're able to access pretty much everything they want already. Why would they need to install this system if they can already get in?"

Katz shrugged. "Perhaps the system they want access to can't be accessed by any current system."

Kane's head bobbed slowly. "An isolated system. Military, CIA." He shook his head. "But surely, the first time they tried to use it, we'd figure it out and yank the installation. They could only use it once."

"Perhaps once is all they need."

Kane's eyes narrowed as he thought of what they could possibly be after that would require only a single hack. "Financial? Maybe they're trying to steal a whack of money electronically?"

"They have all the money they'll ever need."

Kane gave Vance's shins a kick. "You have to know something."

Vance stared at him, his face covered in blood, his shoulder bleeding heavily. "I-I don't know," he said, exhausted. "Normally the smaller things are debated by all twelve, but in this case, they didn't involve me. You'll have to ask Number Six or higher."

"And where can I find Number Six?"

Vance shrugged. "Like I said, I have no idea who he is."

Katz reached into her pocket, pulling out a cellphone. "He has nothing else to tell us, agreed?"

Kane rose, nodding. Katz tapped at her phone then pulled a piece of paper from her pocket, keeping the contents hidden from Vance. She held up her cellphone, recording him. "Give me the names of Numbers Eight through Twelve."

Vance's eyes widened. "I-I can't."

"It's the only way you live."

Kane pressed his gun against Vance's forehead.

"I—"

Katz flicked the paper. "I know their names, so no tricks."

"If-if you know the names, then why do you need me to say them?"

"I'm asking the questions." She pressed the scalpel against his neck, a trickle of blood released. "The names. Now."

The first name came haltingly, the remaining in a rush, as if he were trying to get it over with as quickly as possible. Kane recognized three of them, shocked though not necessarily surprised they were involved.

Katz turned the phone toward her. "Those are Numbers Eight through Twelve of the Assembly. This information will be supplied to the American government in the next five minutes."

Vance's eyes widened in horror. "Oh, God no! You can't do that! They'll kill me!"

Katz stared at him. "No, they won't." She yanked her weapon from her shoulder holster and pumped three rounds into his chest. "I will." She strode toward the door and opened it, marching down the corridor toward the exit, Kane following. He wasn't shocked at the outcome— Katz had said she was going to kill the entire Assembly—but he was shocked at what they had learned.

The Assembly was indeed behind this, as suspected, but their endgame had been to force the government's hand and have them install a security system that they actually controlled. Though to what end? Katz stopped and stepped inside what must be some sort of control room, probably telling them they had a clean-up, then reappeared.

They left in silence, and once in the garage, Katz tapped away at her phone.

"Is that the video?"

She nodded. "I sent it to one of their monitoring stations."

"Why warn them? They'll just go into hiding."

She shook her head. "Something like this will be sent to the top. Numbers Eight through Twelve will be dead within the hour, by the Assembly's hand."

Kane grunted. "Smart. So six down, six to go?"

"Yes."

"Then you tell me where Fang and Sherrie are?"

"Yes."

Kane pulled out his phone. "I need to make a call first."

"To whom?"

"I need to warn Langley about the security system that's being installed."

Katz swatted the phone out of his hand and it clattered to the pavement before she put a bullet through it. "What the hell did you do that for?"

"We have a job to do. When we're done, then you can tell your government what is going on."

Kane glared at her. "If this keeps going, there might not be a government left, or a country!"

Katz stared at him. "That is of no concern to me."

"Well, it is to me, and I have to tell them." He turned to find a way out of the garage when Katz spoke, her voice deadpan.

"You have a choice to make. Your country, or your girlfriend."

Kane froze, his stomach flipping. He turned back toward Katz. "What?"

"Walk away, and you will never know where they are. They will die, and you'll never find the bodies." She pulled a key fob from her pocket and pressed it, the lights of the Ford flashing. "Finish what you started, and you'll save them both."

Kane glared at her as the debate raged inside on what to do. He had to save Fang and Sherrie, yet he also had an obligation to his country. Hundreds of millions of people versus two. The choice was clear. He had to walk away. He had to sacrifice them for the greater good.

But he'd never be able to live with himself.

You'd never be able to live with yourself if millions die.

He frowned as he continued to try and read Katz, an effort he knew was futile.

How could millions possibly die?

That would take weeks or month, hell, it could take years, and this crisis would be over in days. They just needed to plug the security holes. If he delayed telling Langley, just for an hour or so, would it make a difference?

"How long?"

Katz smiled slightly, clearly elated with his choice. "That depends on you."

Kane's eyes narrowed. "What do you mean?"

"We need to find Roger Croft."

"The head of Croft Technologies? To stop him?"

She shook her head. "To confirm if he's a member of the Assembly."

He stared at her. "You don't know?"

She shook her head. "I knew who Number Seven was. I knew that was all I needed to eliminate him and everyone that came after him."

Kane motioned toward her pocket. "But that piece of paper. I thought you knew who they were?"

She shook her head. "Just a piece of paper, nothing more."

"So you tricked him."

"Yes."

Kane frowned as he realized his and Leroux's assumption that she knew who the Assembly members were was completely wrong. She had only known the one, and that he was Number Seven. It changed everything, making their task appear almost hopeless. "How are we ever going to find them all if you only had one name?"

"Correction. We have a second name now, someone who is clearly in the know, and most likely a Council member."

"How can you be sure?"

"I'm not, but Vance said he knew Croft since college. The Assembly likes to choose members they are familiar with. This is most likely how Vance got on their radar. He is either a member of the Assembly, or someone we can trace back to another member."

Kane followed Katz toward the Ford SUV, apparently storage services not the only thing offered here. "What if Croft's contact is one of the ones you just signed the death warrant for?"

She shook her head as she climbed in. "No, if he was, then Number Seven would know. The fact he doesn't, means it has to be Number Six or higher in the organization."

"So by finding and encouraging Croft to talk, we might find a higher member?"

"Perhaps, though I'm almost certain he is a Council member, and if he's behind what's going on, he could be very high in the organization."

Kane climbed in and shut the door. "How do we find him?"

Katz handed him her phone. "That's why I needed you."

Assembly Holding Facility
Washington, DC

"Did you hear that?"

Fang shook her head slightly. "No. What was it?"

Sherrie shoved her head deeper behind the wall, listening for a repeat of what she had just heard, but there was nothing beyond the continued tapping on the pipe. She tapped out a halt request then stood. "I thought I heard gunshots."

"I didn't hear anything except that incessant tapping."

Sherrie smiled and sat beside Fang, placing the back of her hand on Fang's sweat-soaked forehead. "It was faint, but I'm pretty sure it was three shots, close together, then nothing. Perhaps an execution?"

Fang sighed. "Water."

Sherrie went and turned the shut-off valve slightly, filling the empty IV bag through a hole she had cut in the bottom. She turned the water off and returned, helping Fang drink. "Better?"

Fang nodded. "We've established that there are others here."

"Yes, Chris and Dylan's parent's, which is insane."

"Not really. They took us for leverage, then that failed, so they took the next best thing. It actually makes perfect sense."

Sherrie's head bobbed. "You're right."

"Did you tell them who we are?"

She shook her head. "No, I don't want anyone knowing we know them. It could put them in danger."

Fang's eyes narrowed slightly. "Surely they know."

Sherrie shook her head. "I'm not so sure. Think about it. The Assembly kidnapped us. Katz, a former contractor for them, rescued us, then put us here. We know the Assembly kidnapped the parents, and put them in the same facility. That makes absolutely no sense unless either Katz is lying, and actually still works for the Assembly, or whoever is running this place, thinks she is."

"So the left hand doesn't know what the right is doing?"

Sherrie smiled. "Umm, I'm not sure if that's the right expression. If Katz were working for the Assembly, and just lying about it, the Assembly would have no reason to kidnap the parents. I think she's telling the truth. I think she's working against them, but for some reason, this facility doesn't know."

Fang nodded. "That actually makes sense. The Assembly is supposed to be a large organization with lots of people working for it that have no clue who they're working for. Everything probably works with access codes, no names. She probably was able to secure a code that still works. It's brilliant, really. She uses their facilities against them, and they have no clue it's happening because their Achilles heel, in this case, is their anonymous nature. Because nobody knows each other, they just assume if you show up with a valid code, you're meant to be here."

Sherrie grunted. "Amazing. So even if we escape this room, we're still in an Assembly facility that might be heavily guarded." She sighed. "I think I liked it better when I thought we were alone in some basement somewhere."

Fang patted her hand. "Me too." She drew a shallow breath, and Sherrie stared at her, concerned.

She's not going to last much longer.

"Well, I think I'll get back to work."

"What's your plan?"

Sherrie motioned at the camera. "That's not working anymore, and no one's come to check on us, so that means I think we're free to do whatever the hell we want in here—they just don't care. That makes me think we're dead if we stick around."

"Agreed."

"So, I'm going to work at that wall, see if I can tear my way through to another room, and cross my fingers and everything else, that it's empty, with an open door."

Fang smiled weakly. "Good luck."

Harlem Hospital Center
Manhattan, New York

Larissa Williams checked the chart then retrieved the medicine from the cart, scanning the bar codes on each to make certain they matched. They did.

"How's he doing?"

Larissa smiled at the young man's mother who had sat vigil at his bedside since he had been brought in two nights ago, hit by a taxi during the initial problems. He had been lucky. He'd survive, and in time, would make a full recovery.

She glanced at the monitors, everything appearing steady and strong. "He's looking good, ma'am. He's going to be just fine, I'm sure." She injected the prescribed dosage then disposed of the needle. "The doctor should be around shortly to give you the full story."

The mother smiled. "Thank you, nurse."

"No problem." Larissa pushed the cart out of the room and didn't make it ten feet before she heard a scream.

"Help!"

She spun around and rushed back to the room to find the young man convulsing, his mother trying to hold him down.

"What did you do? What did you give him?"

His vitals were spiking, and it was clear he would be going into cardiac arrest at any moment. She slammed her hand against the Code Blue button, and an automated system announced the emergency. Within moments, nurses rushed in followed by an intern.

"What's going on?"

"I just gave him his medicine, not even a minute ago."

"What did you give him?"

She handed him the chart. "Pethidine."

"He's allergic to pethidine!"

The intern stared at the mother. "What? Did you inform the nurse when your son was brought in?"

"Yes, I did! I told *her*!"

Larissa gulped for a moment when it appeared the mother was pointing at her, but she wasn't. It was Nina, standing behind her.

"It's true, Doctor, she told me last night, and I put it in his chart."

Another Code Blue came over the PA system, another flurry of personnel racing toward a room she had just been in. Larissa's chest tightened and her mouth went dry. She rushed into the hall, following the hospital staff to the room three doors down. She entered, and the doctor shook his head, stepping back from the bed of an elderly patient here for several days.

"She's gone."

Larissa grabbed the chart and compared it to her schedule. "I just gave her dalbavancin not five minutes ago. Does anyone know if she's allergic to it?"

"Shouldn't the chart say?" asked one of the nurses.

"Forget the chart! Who did the interview?"

Another Code Blue sounded and everyone looked at each other in stunned silence.

What the hell is going on?

Larissa pointed at one of the nurses. "Check her paper form. See what she was allergic to."

"Why?"

Larissa stared at her. "I think we've been hacked and the wrong medicines are being prescribed."

The doctor cursed and jabbed a finger at one of the nurses. "Stop all medicine deliveries, now!"

She nodded and rushed out of the room when a nurse's aide entered.

"Larissa, you've got a call from home."

Larissa dismissed her with a wave, still coming to grips with what was going on. "Not now!"

"It's your son, Michael."

She paused, her eyes narrowing as she turned her attention to the messenger. "Not the babysitter?"

"No. He's crying. I think you better take it."

She looked at the doctor who waved her out the door. "Go."

She rushed to the nurses station and grabbed the phone.

"Line four."

She pressed the button. "Michael?"

"Mommy! They took all our food!"

Larissa's heart slammed hard, a single palpitation rolling up her throat. "What? Who?"

"The men who killed Shannon."

Larissa paled and dropped into a chair. "What? Slow down. Did you say Shannon is dead?"

Everyone around her stopped what they were doing, turning toward her.

"Yes! They shot her! And they took everything. Our food and all the water!" Michael was sobbing hard, and oddly sounded more upset about the loss of their supplies than the death of Shannon.

"Okay, baby, you stay calm. Where are your brothers?"

"We're all locked in the bathroom."

She sighed, the odd echo now explained. "Are they gone?"

"Yeah, they said if we told anyone, they'd come back and kill you!"

Her stomach flipped and she trembled. "Who did it?"

"Mommy! I can't tell you! They'll kill you!"

She decided this wasn't a battle to fight. Not now. "Okay, Mommy is coming home right now, okay? You tell your brothers to stay in the bathroom until I get there, okay?"

"Y-yes, Mommy."

"Okay, now stay off the phone in case I need to call you."

"Okay, Mommy."

She hung up and shot out of her chair. "I-I've gotta go!" She rushed toward the change room and pulled out her cellphone, dialing the only person she could think of that might be able to help her.

Grand Hyatt Hotel
Manhattan, New York

Atlas frowned as he stared out the window. It was approaching the end of day three of the crisis, and things didn't look like they were getting any better to him. The streets were still mostly empty, businesses across the nation shut down, almost nothing moving within the urban areas, and outside of the cities, all reports indicated people were staying home. Those lucky enough to have relatives outside the affected areas were fleeing the cities, though for a place like New York, with most of it stuck on islands, there was little hope of that.

Cities like Los Angeles and Phoenix were seeing their suburbs empty, which in itself was causing problems. Though there were fewer people to worry about, there were fewer people to police themselves. Abandoned homes were tempting to the criminal element, and reports of homes being emptied, were increasing.

Gunfire crackled outside the window, its origin impossible to determine.

"I really wish they'd just let us go out there and start cleaning up the city."

Atlas glanced at Sergeant Zack "Wings" Hauser. "Me too. I'm going bat-shit crazy sitting cooped up like this. I want to be doing *some*thing. *Any*thing! We're trained for urban combat. Let's go drop some of these bastards."

Red snapped his laptop shut and leaned back in his chair, his scalp freshly scraped clean. "We're still on standby in case something else comes up. BD and the others should be arriving at the kidnapping scene any minute now."

Wings grunted. "Lucky bastards."

"What, you don't like being stuck with me?"

Wings stared at him. "No."

Red laughed. "Well, at least you're honest."

Wings grinned then leaped to his feet. "Gotta tinkle."

Atlas was about to insult Wings' manhood when his phone vibrated. He fished it from his pocket and smiled. "It's my sister!" He swiped his thumb and took the call. "Hey, Sis, you okay?"

"No! Oh my God, Leon, I don't know what to do. Michael just called and said that the babysitter has been shot and that all our supplies were stolen. I'm at the hospital. I'm leaving now, but I don't know when I can get there. What should I do?"

Atlas rose, the concern on his face ending all frivolity in the room. "Have you called the police?"

"No, they said they'd come back and kill me if we did."

Atlas' chest tightened, and he looked at Red.

"What is it?"

"My sister says my nephews' babysitter has been killed, and the apartment looted. The kids are alone, and my sister is at the hospital. She doesn't know when she can get there. The police can't be called because they said they'd come back and kill her."

Red dialed his phone, stepping away.

"Where are the kids now?" asked Atlas, staring out the window.

"They've locked themselves in the bathroom."

He smiled slightly.

Smart boys.

"Okay, and you told them to stay there, right?"

"Yes."

Wings stepped over. "How far are we from your sister's place?"

"About ten miles as the crow flies. If we could use our Humvee, twenty minutes, maybe? Hard to say with the roads the way they are."

Red walked over. "The Colonel says we're to remain on standby until further notice. He suggested we might want to go stretch our legs for a couple of hours."

Atlas smiled. "I'm going to kiss that man when we get back."

Red grinned. "I think he'd like that."

Wings snorted. "Just make sure I'm there to see it."

Atlas returned his attention to the phone. "Listen, Sis, I'm on my way."

"How long? You're hours away."

"No, I'm in the city. I'll be there soon."

His sister's sobs of relief broke his heart. "Oh thank God, Leon. Please, hurry, save my boys, they're all I have!"

"I will, Sis, I will." He ended the call and turned to the room. "I can't ask any of you to come with me—"

Wings cleared his throat. "Bullshit. I think I speak for all of us when I say, shall we go for a walk?"

Atlas beamed at his comrades in arms, his brothers, his family. *This* was why he loved the Army, *this* was why he loved military life. Every single man in the room was willing to risk their lives for each other, and for each other's families. He could count on each and every one of them if any of his loved ones were in trouble and he couldn't be there.

That was the military.

That was the Army.

That was the Unit.

His voice cracked. "Thanks."

251

Red slapped his hands together. "Let's gear up."

Temporary Quarters, CIA Headquarters
Langley, Virginia

Leroux bolted upright in the bed, looking about in the darkness for what had woken him. A knock at the door answered his question. "Enter."

The door opened, a rapidly expanding sliver of light momentarily blinding him. He reached over and turned on the lamp on the nightstand and blinked a few times. It was Sonya Tong, appearing apologetic, and staring at his bare chest. He grabbed his pillow and hugged it. "Yes?"

"Sorry to wake you, but I thought you should know, Baltimore Port security just found four bodies that match the description of the men who kidnapped Lee Fang."

Leroux's eyebrows popped and he jumped out of the bed, grabbing his shirt before realizing all he had on were tighty whities and black dress socks. He glanced at an ogling Tong. "I'll be there in a few minutes."

Her eyes never left his lower extremities. "Umm, yes, sir." She remained frozen in place.

"Sonya?"

"Yes?"

"Look at me."

She tore her eyes away and stared at him, then blushed. "Maybe I should wait for you in the Ops Center?"

"Good idea."

She left the room, another glance stolen before the door closed. Leroux stared at himself in the mirror for a moment. He knew Tong had a crush on him, and he was flattered, but not interested.

And slightly confused by it.

He wasn't bad looking, though he never thought of himself as sexy or handsome. Why any woman, let alone two, would be interested in him, he had no idea. He was a little soft, but nothing five pounds of weight loss wouldn't take care of. He had been naturally blessed with the ability to never really gain weight, though he sometimes wondered if that was because he constantly forgot to eat, especially when he was absorbed in some project or a good game. Sherrie made sure he never missed a meal when she was home, though between both their careers, their days apart were greater than their days together. He slapped his stomach.

I think she might be responsible for a few of these.

He hated exercise, and he doubted it would ever be part of his regimen, though he did enjoy playing the Wii with Sherrie, and had his eye on a VR system that would really get them both moving.

Moving.

He smiled. His real workouts were sexual, Sherrie almost insatiable at times. She'd get turned on at the drop of a hat, horny when she was about to go out on assignment, and even more so when she returned.

And he was a willing victim of her command over his body.

He caught himself smiling in the mirror and frowned.

I hope she's okay.

He quickly dressed, having been ordered once again to get some sleep, his attempts last night having failed miserably. This time he had succeeded, at least for a few hours, and his mind was once again focused on the problem at hand. They had had no leads since the kidnapping, and what use any would be was questionable since Nadja Katz claimed to now have them.

It had occurred to him that it could be a lie, though he had no real reason to doubt her. The fact she knew they were missing meant something. If she didn't have them, then she probably knew where they were. If they accomplished *her* goal, and took down the Assembly, they could eliminate the organization once and for all, stop the current crisis, and save Sherrie and Fang along with the parents.

The problem was how to accomplish it.

He found it hard to believe that Katz knew where all twelve members were, but it would be the only way to eliminate them within the time allotted. He buckled his belt and paused.

What if she doesn't know?

He frowned.

If she doesn't, then eliminating them is impossible, and she knows it.

His eyes widened slightly.

She's going to let them die!

That had to be it. Katz had no emotional reasons for anything she did. She wanted to eliminate the Assembly purely for matters of self-preservation. Revenge didn't play into it. But, if she didn't know who they were, then why turn herself in? Surely killing them one at a time was something she could accomplish, though, if he thought about it, the Assembly could simply replace their membership and be back up and running within perhaps months. Kill them all at once, and the possibility was eliminated.

Which meant, once again, she had to know where they all were, and needed their help to accomplish her task—after all, she couldn't be in twelve places at once, but the American government could. If that were the case, however, what was with the trip to DC?

He stepped out into the hall and noticed a buzz in the air. He spotted another team lead, rushing toward him. "What's going on?"

"The Vice President has been kidnapped."

Leroux's jaw dropped as the woman rushed past him, leaving no opportunity for any follow-up questions. His brisk walk turned into a jog.

You don't think…

But he did.

The Vice President would be in DC—he knew that from the morning briefing. And Kane had arrived there a couple of hours ago with Katz, and hadn't been heard from since. Could Kane have kidnapped the Vice President? And if he did, why?

There was only one reason he would do it, and that would be because Katz forced him to. Which meant either the VP was a member of the Assembly, or was somehow involved with them.

He shuddered at the possibility.

One bullet, one clogged artery, and the man could be President. The Assembly could control the most powerful nation on the planet, with a nuclear arsenal that could accomplish any ghoulish plans they may have. They had tried to start a war before, to what end, he had no idea, but if they wanted to destroy the planet, gaining access to the Presidency was one way of doing it.

He boarded a packed elevator, still lost in his thoughts.

There were safeguards, of course. The President's order to launch the missiles could be overridden. The Secretary of Defense was the one who executed the order. He could refuse to launch, and go to Cabinet and Congress to have the President declared unfit, though the system was designed for a rapid response.

Nukes were supposed to be incoming, with only minutes to respond, otherwise the country could be destroyed with its missiles still in their silos. Yet that only applied if they were under attack. If there was none in progress, an order from the President to launch nuclear weapons with no provocation could be stopped. Controlling the nuclear football was, in theory, only symbolic power.

He growled, eliciting looks from those on the elevator. "Sorry," he muttered.

"Don't apologize. We're all on edge," said someone behind him.

A flurry of conversation erupted, the tension relief valve opened, but Leroux ignored it. He stepped off the elevator and jogged toward the Operations Center and his team, refocusing. If Fang's kidnappers had been found, then there might be footage that could lead them to where she was ultimately taken, and that could lead to Sherrie. He paused in front of the door.

If they're dead, then Katz must be telling the truth.

He placed his hand on the pad and the door unlocked. He stepped inside and the room looked up from their stations, Tong standing.

"What have we got?"

Tong motioned toward the screen. "Umm, a problem."

He checked where she was pointing and froze. "What the hell is this?"

"It, umm, looks like Dylan Kane kidnapped the Vice President."

Gino's Fine Italian Ristorante
Washington, DC

Dawson stared at the footage on the tablet, then handed it to Niner, giving his team a look that sealed their lips and neutralized any shock they might want to display. He stepped toward Secret Service Agent Mitchell, in charge of the scene. "Any luck tracking them?"

"Not yet. The traffic cameras in the area were disabled, and nobody saw what kind of vehicle they came in." He motioned toward the tablet. "We're lucky to have that. Half these restaurants have systems that are just for show."

"So there were two?"

"Yeah, a man and a woman. They came through the kitchen, then were getting hot and heavy in front of the bathrooms. The Vice President started his meal, and within minutes became ill. He ran to the bathroom and my team followed. That's when we were attacked."

Dawson held up one of the darts. "I've read about these. Never actually seen one before."

Mitchell nodded. "I thought they were still in the research stage. Clearly, whoever is behind this has access to some serious hardware."

The Assembly popped into Dawson's mind, but with Kane involved, it could be his own government supplying the hardware. "Do you think it could be linked to what's going on?"

"It has to be, right? I mean, cause all kinds of chaos, distract us, and take the Vice President. It kind of makes sense."

Dawson grunted, unable to tell him his entire theory was bullshit— Dylan Kane had kidnapped the Vice President, and he had to have a good reason. Dawson took the tablet from the others and handed it back. "Okay, Special Agent, if you need us, you know how to reach us."

Mitchell nodded. "Thanks. We'll let you know."

Dawson headed out the back of the restaurant and through the kitchen. He paused, the staff standing, huddled together, two heavily armed agents watching them. He stepped toward the cluster. "Did anyone see them go near the food?"

Heads shook, but one hand went up.

"Yes?"

"I-I saw the woman wave her hand over the food."

One of the others snorted. "I didn't see that."

The first glared at him. "That's because you were too busy staring at her tits."

The second returned the glare. "That's bullshit, and you know it. I'm gay!"

"Oh, sorry, you were looking at him, then."

There was a grin. "Okay, I might have been."

"So then shut the hell up! I saw her wave her hand over the food!" He turned back to Dawson. "I didn't think anything of it at the time, but if the Vice President got sick, then maybe she put something in his food?"

Dawson nodded, turning to one of the guards. "You better let Mitchell know."

"Yes, sir."

The guard left, and Dawson continued outside and into the empty alley behind the restaurant, his team surrounding him.

"What the hell is going on, BD?" asked Niner, his voice low. "That was Kane, wasn't it?"

"It was. And did you recognize the woman?"

"Yeah. She's that nut we ran into last year rescuing the Doc's crew. What's he doing working with her?"

Dawson shook his head. "I don't know, but the bigger question is, what the hell does he want with the Vice President?"

Assembly Command and Control Facility
Unknown Location

Roger Croft stood in the middle of the control center, watching the various news feeds and status reports coming in from agents in the field. Everything was going according to plan, and they were perhaps only minutes away from achieving their goal.

He was nervous.

And excited.

Every muscle in his body kept clenching, and he had to force himself to relax, or he risked forgetting to breathe. They were about to achieve what they had been orchestrating since the end of the Cold War, something that wouldn't have been possible even five years earlier. With society now so interconnected, with Internet-connected devices with minimal to non-existent security behind them pervading every household and business in the country, pulling off what they had over the past several days was finally possible.

And before the day was out, the world would be a different place, at war with an enemy they would have to exterminate, and a tense détente between traditional enemies reestablished for decades to come.

It will be an incredible future!

His aide entered the room and rushed up to him, whispering in his ear. "There's a priority communique from Number One."

His eyes widened slightly, his heart pounding. Priority communications from Number One were never good. "I'll take it in my office." He strode quickly toward the exit, his aide following on his heels, both in his outer office moments later. "I'm not to be disturbed."

"Of course, sir."

He entered his private office and his aide closed the door behind her. He tapped his keyboard, killing the screen saver, and entered his password. An icon flashed and he clicked on it, the silhouetted image of Number One revealed. He bowed his head slightly. "Number One."

"Number Four, we have a problem. I'm sending you the details now."

He noticed a priority message arrive in his secure inbox. He opened it, a video attachment included. "I'll let you watch that when I'm finished. We have been compromised. It would appear that Nadja Katz has kidnapped and killed Number Seven, and had him confirm the names of Numbers Eight through Twelve."

Croft fell back in his chair. "How is that even possible? How could she possibly know?"

The silhouette's head shook. "I don't know, however this is a serious breach. If she knew the identities of Numbers Seven through Twelve, she could know more."

Croft's eyes widened. "Surely she couldn't know who I am, or you! Surely not you!"

"There is no way to know. Number Four, I have ordered the immediate termination of all members of the Council with the exception of yourself. You are too vital to the current operation."

A bead of sweat trickled down Croft's spine as he became lightheaded.

Breathe!

"I-I think that's wise, Number One." He was about to ask what would become of himself when he was no longer vital, but bit his tongue. He already knew the answer.

The distorted voice ended the conversation. "The Assembly is eternal."

The screen went blank and he lost control, his entire body shaking as he realized he would soon be dead. Number One had to be absolutely secure. Nobody knew his identity. Nobody *ever* knew his identity. But the others, there was a possibility. It all depended on where the breach in security had come from. It was at best from Number Seven himself. Eight through Twelve would have no idea who he was, so they were innocent in all this, yet ironically, that fact assured their deaths were absolutely necessary. It was Two through Six that were the question marks.

And Number One was right.

To truly protect the organization, eliminating everyone was the surest way. And that had to include him, especially considering the fact he was the one who had brought Vance into the organization all those years ago, and had just met with him yesterday.

And with the President.

His heart pounded as he realized the connection between Vance and him would be made quite quickly. He rose and opened the door. His aide looked up. "Yes, sir."

"Put the facility on lockdown immediately."

Chevy Chase, Maryland

Joseph Medina climbed into the SUV, doors slamming shut all around him, their work done. Number Eleven was dead. It was a shock, that little tidbit supplied when the orders arrived on his phone.

Eliminate Number Eleven.

The real name and current location had been provided in the same message, and that would normally be all that was needed. But to include the fact he was a senior member of the Assembly was something he had never seen before. In fact, it was the first confirmation he had ever had that there was some sort of leadership, and it was limited in size.

Number Eleven.

How many were there? There had to be more. Eleven was an odd number to stop at. Yet there couldn't be too many. If there were dozens, he could hardly imagine Numbers 33 and 42 having an argument. Nobody would remember who was who. Twelve or thirteen was probably the number. That would be nice, traditional.

But why was Number Eleven ordered killed? Had he betrayed them in some way? When he had put three bullets in the man's chest, he hadn't bothered to ask him why, and the man hadn't pleaded for his life. In fact, he was only aware he was about to die when he woke from the first bullet tearing into his chest. The wife knew, though only for a few seconds more.

It was unfortunate.

His orders weren't to kill her, but they couldn't have witnesses, and couldn't have the authorities called before they had made their escape.

If she had been out with friends, instead of taking a nap with her husband, she'd be alive right now.

Thankfully, there were no children in the house.

He had no problem killing adults, though children were something entirely different. There was a line that he didn't like to cross, though with the Assembly, you never had a choice. All orders were to be obeyed, without question. Or you would be the next one on someone's target list.

He had been on a hit last year where one of his team had hesitated. They were on camera, and he received a text within moments, ordering the member eliminated immediately. He had personally delivered two bullets to the man's head.

A nice guy.

Too nice for this business.

Never hesitate. Never question.

His phone vibrated with a message as they pulled out of the long driveway of a family with *very* old money.

Return to storage facility. Dispose of contents.

He grunted, the others looking at him.

"What?" asked the driver.

He held up his phone. "They want everyone at the storage facility eliminated."

"Holy shit! Something big must be going on."

Medina gestured toward the radio, tuned to a news station, playing low in the background. "Obviously, and we're in the thick of it."

The driver's eyes widened slightly, a hint of horror there.

Better hope nobody important sees that.

"You think we're part of it?"

Medina looked away, instead checking the side view mirror to see if they were being followed. "Ours is not to reason why…"

An original ending to his refrain was delivered from the back seat. "Because if we do, then we die."

Operations Center 2, CIA Headquarters
Langley, Virginia

Leroux watched the footage from the restaurant showing Kane and Katz taking out a Secret Service team, thankfully with non-lethal force, then hauling a terrified Vice President out of camera range. Morrison charged into the Operations Center, his eyes immediately on the looping footage. He faced the room.

"The identities of those involved in the Vice President's kidnapping are classified. No one, and I mean *no one*, will speak of this outside this room until I give the okay. Understood?"

A round of affirmatives was murmured.

Morrison stood beside Leroux, lowering his voice. "What the hell is going on?"

Leroux shook his head. "No idea. He clearly participated, though she took the first shot. He requisitioned the stun weapons before they left, so I think he suspected something like this might happen."

"Thank God. There's no way I could protect him if he killed Secret Service agents just doing their job."

Leroux nodded. "Could the Vice President be a member of the Assembly?"

Morrison frowned. "I doubt it, but then, you never know. We know the former Secretary of Defense was involved, but he shot himself before we had a chance to find out the extent of it." He tapped his chin. "But he could be. It would make sense. Like they say, only a heartbeat away from the presidency." He sighed. "No matter what the reason, Dylan Kane has just made himself the most wanted man in the country."

"If they can identify him."

"I've already talked to the President, and a lid is being kept on this. The White House is going to keep this quiet for as long as they can, otherwise the panic could spread further. Hopefully, by the time it breaks, we'll have some answers. Maybe Dylan will have already released him."

Leroux nodded. "Katz must have told him that the Vice President knew something. Once they get that intel, I'm sure they'll let him go."

Tong interrupted their hushed conversation. "Sirs, I've got Special Agent Kane on the line, asking for Mr. Leroux."

Leroux adjusted his headset and Morrison held out his hand, another handed to him. Leroux nodded at Tong. "Put us both on." Tong tapped a few keys. "Dylan, it's Chris and Director Morrison."

"Umm, hello, sir. You might not want to listen to this. Deniability, and all."

Morrison glanced at the footage. "Special Agent Kane, I'm watching footage of you and Nadja Katz kidnapping the Vice President of the United States. I trust you have a *very* good explanation for your actions?"

A burst of static indicated a deep sigh from the other end. "Sir, Vice President Vance was a member of the Assembly. Number Seven, to be exact."

Leroux and Morrison exchanged stunned looks. "Are you sure?" pressed Morrison. "This isn't just something Katz told you?"

"Yes, sir. He admitted it. We have it on tape. He also named six more members of the Assembly."

"Give them to us."

"Umm, that won't be necessary, sir."

"Why?"

"Katz sent them the video. All six should be dead shortly, if they aren't already."

Leroux's heart was pounding hard. With half the Assembly dead or soon to be, they just might accomplish their goal—or rather, Katz's goal—and free Sherrie and Fang.

"Where's the Vice President?"

Leroux could hear the trepidation in Morrison's voice, and he understood it. If the Vice President were a member of the Assembly, then in order to fulfill Katz's demands, he'd have to die. And as far as Leroux was concerned, he deserved to.

"He's dead, sir."

Morrison sighed and closed his eyes. "Please tell me—"

"Katz killed him, sir. It's all on tape. I'll have it sent to you, just a second." There was a muffled conversation before Kane returned. "It's on its way now, sir. It will confirm he was a member of the Assembly, give you the other six names, and show his death by Katz's hand."

"Where's the body?"

"In a facility in DC. It's probably long gone by now. I've been told I cannot give you the exact location otherwise Fang and Sherrie will be terminated."

Leroux's eyes narrowed.

That's odd. Why would knowing where the Vice President's body is, compromise Katz's leverage?

Morrison sat in an empty chair. "Where are you heading now, Special Agent?"

"Nowhere. I need your help."

"What do you need?"

"I need you to find Roger Croft for me."

Leroux's eyes narrowed. "Croft? As in the CEO of Croft Technologies?"

"Exactly."

"Why?"

"Well, I've got a bit of a Kobayashi Maru situation here, Chris. I can't tell you that. I just need his current location, and I need it ASAP."

"Okay, can you tell—" The line went dead and Leroux spun toward Tong.

She shook her head. "Sorry, sirs, it was terminated at the other end."

"Comms failure?" asked Morrison.

"Negative. He hung up."

Leroux frowned and sat at his station. "Should we action this?"

Morrison nodded as he rubbed his eyes, the man clearly exhausted. They all were. They were running on little sleep, nobody wanting to leave their posts during this crisis, or as long as their boss' girlfriend, and one of their own agents, was missing.

Leroux spun in his chair to face the room. "Okay people, I need everything we've got on Roger Croft, CEO of Croft Technologies, and I need his current location, ASAP. Sonya, you coordinate it for me."

She beamed. "Yes, sir." A huddle quickly formed at the back of the room and he could hear Tong handing out the assignments, keyboards and phones attacked within moments.

Morrison looked at Leroux. "What did he say there? He had a kobe something?"

"Kobayashi Maru. It's a Star Trek reference."

Morrison rolled his eyes. "Okay, you better explain it to me."

"Not to get too geek on you, but it's a reference to a no-win scenario."

Morrison nodded. "And this is well-known?"

"Among sci-fi fans, yes."

"Is it a message?"

Leroux paused as he thought about it. He had never known Kane to use Star Trek references, but he knew he was at least a passing fan of the franchise, the two of them having watched the original movies on DVD when they were in high school, though Leroux was pretty certain Kane was merely indulging his friend as opposed to genuinely interested.

He was a good friend even back then.

He looked at Morrison. "It has to be. There's no reason for him to say that particular line. He could have just said 'no-win situation,' but he must not have wanted Katz to know what he was talking about."

"Risky. For all we know, she's a Star Trek fan."

Leroux shook his head. "I doubt it."

"You sound pretty sure of yourself."

"I am. Think about it, why do you watch television?"

Morrison's eyes narrowed. "Umm, escapism. Winding down at the end of a long day. Enjoyment."

"Exactly. Entertainment."

"Okay, entertainment. So?"

"So, Katz doesn't enjoy things, she's not wired that way. She's not going to watch movies and television for enjoyment, she'll only watch them as a means to an end. Research, perhaps. She might even watch comedies or dramas so she can better mimic the human condition for when she's on a job. But science fiction, set in the future? That's of absolutely no use to her. The people in Star Trek don't represent our present, so there's no benefit to her to study them."

Morrison's head bobbed slowly. "Makes sense. So it's a cultural reference obscure enough that dinosaurs like me don't get it, and emotionally stunted killers like her would have almost no chance of having heard."

"Exactly."

"Okay, then it was a definite message, directed at you, that Katz wasn't meant to understand." Morrison stared at him. "Then what the hell does it mean?"

"I'm not sure. He said it when I asked him why he wanted Croft."

Morrison jabbed the air in front of him. "That's right. He said he had a bit of a Kobayashi Maru situation, and he couldn't tell us why. So his situation must be related to the question, or more accurately, the *answer* to that question."

Leroux straightened in his chair. "Right! So it has to be related to Croft in some way."

Morrison sighed. "But how? Is he trying to tell us that he's a member of the Assembly? Or that we should find him first?"

Leroux shook his head. "No, I don't think so. Us grabbing him first would put Sherrie and Fang at risk, and he won't let her kill him unless there's a valid reason, and the only reason I can think of is that he's Assembly. Either way, Kane needs to get to him first. But he was trying to send us a message, something about Croft, something he couldn't tell us about."

"But why couldn't he tell us?"

Leroux leaned forward. "For the same reason he couldn't tell us where the Vice President's body was. Because Katz told him he couldn't."

Morrison leaned closer. *"That* makes sense. So that means it's something important to her. It's some piece of information that she doesn't want *us* to know, because if we do, it compromises her goals."

Leroux stood, pacing, his arms folded, his fingers rhythmically tapping on his arms. "What's her aim? To eliminate the Assembly. So whatever piece of intel Kane wants us to know, would jeopardize that."

Morrison turned in his chair to follow Leroux. "Doesn't that bring us back to him being a member of the Assembly, and us getting to him first, screwing up her plans?"

Leroux shook his head. "No, I don't think so." He froze as a thought dawned on him, a smile breaking out. He spun toward Morrison. "He's afraid that if we know what it is, we'll *want* to get to him first."

Morrison's eyes narrowed. "You mean if we knew what he was hiding, we'd want to pick up Croft ourselves?"

"Exactly!"

"Why?"

"Because whatever it is, is serious enough that we'd want to *arrest* him, not protect him!"

Morrison's jaw dropped slightly. "Now *that* makes sense. Kane doesn't want us interfering with Croft, but he wants us to know that Croft is important somehow, so important, we'd be tempted to arrest him, or at least pick him up to interrogate him." He stared at Leroux. "Thin."

Leroux shrugged. "Absolutely." He turned to his staff. "What do we know about Croft?"

Marc Therrien raised his hand slightly. "He's the CEO of Croft Technologies, a company he established twelve years ago. They're a major player in corporate and government security, over thirty thousand employees spread across the world, with annual profits of—"

Leroux cut him off. "Forget about the financials. He's a one percenter, we know. What's he done lately?"

Therrien's eyes scanned his screen then his jaw dropped. "There's nothing confirmed officially, but CNN and Fox are reporting that Croft Technologies has been given a contract to install their system nationwide on every government server in the country. Installations have apparently already begun!"

Morrison rose and headed for the door. "I have to call Washington and have this confirmed. If this is true, DC might have just handed our entire security apparatus over to the Assembly."

Assembly Holding Facility
Washington, DC

Sherrie stepped back, her chest heaving from the effort, her entire body dripping in sweat. She filled the IV bag with water and downed most of it before refilling it. She knelt beside Fang and gave her a sip. "How are you doing?"

Fang shook her head. "I-I don't think I have much time left." She motioned with her eyes toward the torn apart bathroom. "How-how are *you* doing?"

"Good. I've reached the corner. It's tough stuff, but I removed part of the broken pipe, so now I've got a tool to work with. I should be through to the next room soon."

"If there is a next room."

Sherrie smiled. "Positivity, please!" She took another swig of water. "Well, back at it." She returned to the bathroom and wedged herself into the corner between the toilet and the wall. She picked up the pipe and balled up blouse she was using as a glove, and attacked the wall once again, jabbing and prying at it, small chunks of the multi-layered drywall slowly breaking away. She was around the corner now, reaching her earlier failed attempts at going directly at it. It just didn't work. Prying it away from the wall seemed far more efficient, though it had taken what felt like hours to reach her goal, but in reality had been less than one.

She shoved the pipe in behind the small opening she had managed to make and yanked it back, a large chunk snapping away. She grinned. "I can see the other wall!"

Fang didn't reply, though she heard a grunt. Sherrie hammered at the opposing wall several times, then stopped to listen. Nothing. She repeated the process twice more, and still heard nothing. "I don't think there's anybody next door."

She pried away a hole big enough for her to fit through on her side, then went to work on the opposing wall, jabbing at it with renewed vigor, slowly chipping away at what didn't appear to be a bathroom wall, no pipes visible beyond those for their toilet. Her pipe suddenly punched through the wall, and she had to squeeze her hand to prevent it from flying through. "I'm through!"

She hammered away at it some more, her progress painfully slow. She stopped to reevaluate her method.

This is going to take hours, and Fang doesn't have that.

She stared at the small hole, barely the size of her fist. Her upper body was exhausted, her arms afire, her shoulders aching. She was in shape. Incredible shape—all agents were, yet this was a different type of effort, one she wasn't used to.

But your legs are good.

And they were stronger. She smiled. Leaning forward again, she used the end of the pipe to score the wall, quickly forming an X surrounding the hole, perhaps half an inch deep. She didn't know if it would be enough to weaken the area, but she had to try. She put the pipe down and lay on her back, wiggling her way into position. She lifted both feet up and placed them against the wall, on either side of the hole, then drew her knees back.

Here goes nothing.

She shoved her feet forward, slamming them against the wall.

And got nothing.

Try, try again.

She repeated the process, several times, each attempt appearing as futile as the first, when on her fifth kick, she heard something, something different. She kicked again, and again, she heard it.

Tearing?

She didn't care what the hell it was—it was different. A surge of adrenaline washed through her from the excitement, and she kicked again against the wall, over and over, when suddenly her right foot slammed into the wall then slid to the side, a shaft of light appearing. She squealed with glee and flipped around, pushing aside the broken away corner, then poking her head through.

I knew it!

It was another room, though this one had several tables in it as well as chairs. "Hello?"

No response, something she was relieved at. The last thing she wanted was to deal with some other prisoner who might not be as friendly as the Leroux and Kane parental units. And an empty room offered the possibility of an unlocked door.

She worked at the broken away flap of wall, and managed to push it completely aside, leaving enough room for her to crawl through. She scurried back to Fang. "I'm through."

"So I heard."

"I'm going through, okay? I'm going to try and either figure a way out of here, or get help. All you have to do is hang on, understood?"

Fang nodded. "Just go."

Sherrie gave the dying woman's hand a squeeze then grabbed the pipe, crawling headfirst through the hole and into the other room. She stood, looking about, and gasped. It was some sort of torture chamber, all manner of cutting and tearing and pinching tool lining the walls and stacking the tables.

She spotted the door and stepped toward it then nearly peed when she rounded a high-back chair in her path.

Someone was in it, somebody dead, several rounds in his chest.

Must have been the shots I heard.

"Holy shit!" she hissed, recognizing the Vice President.

What the hell is he doing here?

She didn't have time to figure it out. He was dead, and Fang soon would be as well. She turned her attention to the door and frowned. It was like theirs, with no way to open it, though this one had a security panel beside it, something she could at least work with.

Suddenly there was a click and the door pushed open.

Oh shit!

Williams Residence
Bronx, New York

An SUV and overwhelming firepower were about the only way to move freely in New York City at this point, and both had served them well. It had taken almost an hour, but they were finally in front of Atlas' sister's apartment building. The streets were nearly empty, the curfew starting in a few hours, though Atlas doubted that was the reason why.

Good people were in hiding.

On the way here, they had listened to the reports of markets collapsing worldwide, the American markets closed, with no indication as to when they might reopen. The panic certain to occur if they weren't shutdown, was playing out everywhere else. The estimate was that trillions would be eventually lost, and it could take years for markets to recover, if they ever did.

But those were the doomsayers, in his opinion. If he knew the free market, as soon as this crisis was over, and it would be at some point, the markets would reopen, stocks would collapse, then the buyers with money would come in and scoop up the deals. The markets would recover, and in time, this crisis would be forgotten.

Atlas stepped to the door of the building and pulled on it. It was locked.

"Umm, break the window?" suggested Sergeant Eugene "Jagger" Thomas.

Red shook his head. "No, that'll leave everyone vulnerable."

Wings stepped over to the intercom and ran his fingers down every buzzer. Within moments they were buzzed in.

Atlas yanked open the door. "Some people are absolute morons."

Red grunted. "You're not going to get an argument out of me." He pointed at Jagger and Casey. "Secure the lobby. The rest of us will go up."

They boarded the elevator and Atlas pressed the button for the twelfth floor.

"When were you last here?" asked Wings.

Atlas pursed his lips, trying to remember. "A couple of years, at least. I keep meaning to visit, but you know how it is."

"Tell me about it. When this is all over, I'm going to go visit my folks. You just never know, you know?"

"Yeah."

The doors opened and Atlas stepped out, MP5 at the ready as he broke right, Wings left, the others following.

"Clear," said Atlas, Wings confirming the same.

"Which way?" asked Red.

"My way."

Red turned to Wings. "You and Mickey secure the elevators and watch our six."

Atlas surged toward his sister's apartment, finding the door closed. He tried the knob. Locked. He pressed his ear against the door and heard nothing. He knocked.

Still nothing.

It made sense. His sister wouldn't be here yet, and the boys were probably still locked in the bathroom, terrified. He repeated his knock, three hard raps. "Boys, it's Uncle Leon! I need you to open the door!" He heard nothing when a door to their right opened slightly, someone peering out at them.

Red stepped toward the woman, pointing at her. "I'll need you to go back inside, ma'am."

"What's going on?"

"Official business. Please go back inside. Now." Red's firm tone had the door shutting. He turned to Atlas. "Break it down."

Atlas nodded. He slammed his shoulder into the door, regretting it instantly. He stepped back, rubbing his now tender arm. "Reinforced. That's not coming down."

Red frowned. "C4."

Sweets stepped forward and placed a small charge on the lock, then attached a detonator. They all stepped back. "Fire in the hole!"

That'll scare the shit out of the neighbors.

The small blast made quick work of the door and it swung open on its own, but not before Atlas' heart broke at his nephews' screams of terror. He stepped inside, the others following as they quickly cleared the apartment.

"I've got a body back here, African American female, looks like she's in her teens."

Atlas frowned as he approached the bathroom. "That'll be the babysitter." He knocked gently on the bathroom door. "Boys, it's me, Uncle Leon. You can come out now. It's safe." He heard excited murmurs on the other side, but the door remained closed. "It's okay, boys, it's me. Your mom sent me to come get you."

"Uncle Leon, is that really you?"

It was Michael. He'd recognize that voice in a crowd of thousands. "Yes, Michael, it's me. I need you to unlock the door."

There was a rattle of the knob then the door slowly pulled open. "Uncle Leon!" The door flew aside and three bundles of terrified joy assaulted his legs as they hugged him hard. He dropped to his knees and embraced the three young boys who had gone through something no child should ever have to. He squeezed them tight as he battled the tears.

"You're safe now, okay? No one's going to hurt you."

Michael pushed away, staring up at his face. "You promise?"

Atlas nodded, the tears winning. "You have my word, little man."

The Oval Office, The White House
Washington, DC

President Starling sat behind his desk, massaging his temples. His country was falling apart around him, the eerie calm outside his window, making it far too easy to forget the horrors most of the nation was living with at this very moment. The SecuraVault system was rolling out across the country, and in less than 24 hours, thousands of installations had been completed. Phoenix apparently had full control of their traffic control systems again, as did Chicago.

It gave him hope. The public was clamoring for their city to be next, too desperate to believe their public officials when they were told it was in progress.

Thank God I met Croft before Harry was kidnapped.

He leaned back in his chair and sighed as he stared at the Presidential seal in the plaster ceiling.

Why the hell did they take him? And *use non-lethal force?*

None of it made sense. It had to be related to the current crisis, but how? The only theory he and his advisors had come up with, was that whoever was behind the disaster now facing their nation, was pissed that Vance had brought Croft in. With Croft's system now being installed, it was disrupting the plans of the Utopians, or the Assembly, or whoever the hell was behind this.

From what he knew of the Assembly, they had no boundaries. They wouldn't hesitate to kidnap or kill anyone, including the Vice President, or even himself, for that matter.

It had to be the Assembly. His latest briefing from FBI Director Fitzgerald, indicated they thought the Utopians were patsies in this entire situation, the founder duped into providing a fantasy plan on how to bring the cities to their knees.

He bought that.

Morrison was right.

He had to be. It had to be the Assembly, but how the hell were they supposed to stop an organization they knew almost nothing about? He sighed. At least once SecuraVault was installed nationwide, their systems would be protected. The problem was it wouldn't bring those behind it to justice, leaving the Assembly free to manipulate the affairs of mankind with impunity. They had to be stopped, but he was at a loss at how to do so.

His phone buzzed and he pressed the intercom button. "Yes?"

"Mr. President, I have Director Leif Morrison, National Clandestine Service Chief, on the line for you. He says it's urgent."

"Put him through." His phone beeped again and he lifted the receiver. "Yes, Leif, what can I do for you?"

"Mr. President. Is it true that Croft Technologies has been given a contract to install its SecuraVault system nationwide?"

Starling's eyebrows rose slightly at the odd question asked with such urgency. "Yes. I gave the order last night."

"Mr. President, it's essential that you halt the rollout of the SecuraVault system immediately, and detain anyone involved in the installation."

Butterflies assaulted Starling's stomach. "What? Why?"

"The Assembly is behind it, Mr. President. They're behind everything. They created the crisis so that you would install *their* system. We're playing right into their hands!"

Starling gripped his prize pen, given to him by his late wife on their first anniversary. "Are you sure? Harry recommended it to me personally. He's known Roger Croft for decades. Hell, I met the man last night right here in this office."

"Mr. President, Vice President Vance was a member of the Assembly."

The pen dropped, along with his jaw. He stood, running his hand through his thinning hair. "Bullshit."

"No, sir. We have his confession on tape. He confirmed he was a member, and named six others. They're all dead or soon will be."

Starling twigged on a word that had been said.

Was.

"Do you know where the Vice President is?"

"No, sir, but he's dead. Executed by a former Assembly agent."

He dropped into his chair. "And you're certain Croft is involved."

"Yes, Mr. President. You have to stop the installation of the SecuraVault system immediately, otherwise the Assembly will have complete control of all of our systems."

Starling closed his eyes. "What have I done?"

"Mr. President, please. Minutes count."

Starling bolted to his feet. "Understood, Leif. I'll issue the order immediately."

"Thank you, Mr. President. You're doing the right thing."

"From your lips to God's ears, Leif. Because if you're wrong, I could be condemning millions of people."

Operations Center 2, CIA Headquarters
Langley, Virginia

"Sir, I might have found something!"

Leroux glanced up at Randy Child as he rushed into the operations center, waving a tablet. "What have you got?"

Child reached Leroux's station. "I was at my desk, pulling footage on those bodies we found at the Port of Baltimore, and I might have something."

Leroux's eyebrows shot up, a wave of guilt washing over him. "Shit, I forgot about that. What did you find?"

Child tapped at his tablet then handed it to Leroux.

"What am I looking at?"

"Security camera footage showing how they were killed."

Leroux watched in awe as a woman, dressed as Nadja Katz had been, swung across the dockyards on top of a shipping container, leaping to another, before blasting the doors open as she continued through the air.

His heart leaped. "Is that—?" He hesitated to say it as two women slid down a rope to the ground with Katz.

"I believe it's Agent White and Lee Fang."

Leroux gasped as he saw Fang drop hard to the ground, gripping her side. "She's been hit!"

"Yes, sir, I believe so."

The three women ran out of frame. Leroux handed the tablet back. "Were you able to track them?"

Child nodded, bringing up another video showing a box van leaving the docks. "I believe they're in this vehicle. It came from the general vicinity of where they were running toward, and…" He pulled up a frame capture of the main gate. "…Katz is clearly behind the wheel a short while before."

Leroux sucked in a quick breath, some hope returning. "Were you able to trace it?"

"I caught it on a few video cameras, and I'm pretty sure it was heading south, out of the city. They could be anywhere, but my money's on DC."

"Why?"

Child shrugged. "Hunch, I guess. If you look at the time it would take for her to get to DC, then to here, it roughly coincides with when she turned herself in."

Leroux nodded. "See what you can find."

"You got it."

Child headed for the door when Morrison rushed into the room.

"I've confirmed with the President that Croft's company was given the contract, and the system is rolling out nationwide as we speak."

Child turned toward them, one hand holding open the door. "They're here already."

Morrison froze and Leroux spun in his chair. "What?"

"Croft Technologies, right? I saw about a dozen of them in the lobby earlier."

"Why didn't you say anything?"

Child shrugged. "I didn't know you were looking. I've been at my desk." His eyes narrowed. "Why?"

Nobody answered, Leroux already grabbing his desk phone. "Get me security. It's urgent!"

287

"One moment, please." He heard the call transferred then picked up a moment later.

"Security desk."

"Hold for Director Morrison." He handed the phone to his boss.

"This is Director Morrison. Immediately arrest all Croft Technologies staff and contractors on site. Shoot them if they try to touch a computer. Understood?"

Apparently they did, Morrison handing the phone back.

Leroux hung it up. "I hope we get to them in time."

Morrison shook his head. "Who the hell knows? The President is ordering the immediate halt and detention now, but it's been nearly a full day. If they were after a specific system, they would have prioritized it so they'd install there first. We may already be too late."

Tong stepped over. "They had to know they'd be caught, right?"

Leroux nodded. "Eventually, I guess. But would they be? If it weren't for Katz, we would never have found out about Croft."

"Right, but if their system is installed, wouldn't we get suspicious when the hacks continued?"

"I'd hope so." Leroux stood, staring at the displays still showing news reports from across the nation. He spun toward Morrison. "Whatever they're going to do, it has to be soon. Very soon."

Morrison nodded. "We need to find Croft."

Tong sighed. "If only we had a starting point."

Morrison's head swiveled toward her. "We do! The President said he met with him and the Vice President in the Oval Office last night."

Tong and Leroux exchanged excited glances.

"Security protocols would have been in place because of the crisis," said Leroux.

"Which means they'd have done an IMSI capture of his phone when he arrived."

"And scanners would have been activated all over DC."

"Which means we can track him anywhere in the city!"

"Run with it!"

Tong grinned and rushed back to her terminal, leaving a lost Morrison standing in front of an excited Leroux.

"What the hell is an imzee?"

"I-M-S-I. International Mobile Subscriber Identity-catcher. They basically pretend to be a cellphone tower and scan for signals. We can pull phone numbers, text messages, intercept calls, listen in on calls, pretty much the works depending on the phone. They're illegal and can only be used with a warrant. But in times of national emergencies, they're automatically enabled so that we can track the movements of terrorists if they had their phones turned on during an attack."

Morrison nodded. "Right, I read about those, I just never heard IMSI said out loud. So you can trace him with this?"

"If we can get our hands on the White House scan, we'll know what device to look for, then see what scanners he triggered in the city, so we can see where he went, what calls he made, anything."

"Can you just trace his cellphone?"

"Yes, once we have the number, assuming it's on and has a signal."

Morrison jabbed a finger at Leroux's station. "Then get on it. I want to know the second you have him." He headed for the door. "Now, I need to see what damage those Croft bastards did. Maybe we can get one of them to talk."

"Do you really think they know what they're doing?"

Morrison paused. "I did until you asked."

Leroux stepped toward him. "That company has tens of thousands of employees. To install nationwide, they're using most of them. There's no way they're all involved in a criminal conspiracy. At least not knowingly."

Morrison frowned. "So we could be arresting patsies?"

"I'm willing to bet that the only ones that actually know what they're doing, are the ones installing on the system the Assembly actually cares about."

"And we have no idea which one that is."

Leroux shook his head. "Not a damn clue."

Seattle FBI Field Office
Seattle, Washington

Special Agent LaForge sipped on a pitiful cup of black coffee, courtesy the cafeteria at the Seattle FBI Field Office. The flavor may have been awful, but at least it contained the necessary caffeine to keep him going. His partner, though, seemed to be enjoying hers.

"Want another?" Alfredson tapped her empty glass.

LaForge eyed his still half-full one. "Nah, I'll pass. I don't think I could stand another cup of that shit."

Alfredson shook her head as she rose from her seat. "I like it."

"I've tasted that turpentine you call coffee, so no surprise there."

Alfredson shot him a look. "You've never complained."

"What would be the point?" He held up his cup. "You know, I used to think you couldn't make coffee, but now I think maybe you actually make it that way on purpose."

Alfredson's eyes narrowed. "Oh?"

LaForge tilted his cup, regarding the putrid liquid. "Yeah, I think you actually *like* turpentine."

Alfredson rolled her eyes. "You wouldn't know a good cup of coffee if it blew you." She motioned toward the vending machines. "Want anything?"

"Something sweet. Let's see if sugar can fuel the night."

The doors to the cafeteria opened, and a confused security guard entered, her head on a pivot as she searched for someone in the nearly empty room. He had a feeling it wasn't anyone in particular.

He rose and stepped toward her. "Problem?"

Her wide eyes fixated on him. "Are you an agent?"

"Special Agent LaForge."

"Oh, thank God. There's like nobody here! I just got a message." She held up a piece of paper. "It says to immediately arrest all Croft Technologies employees on site, and uninstall any modifications they've made to our systems. It came from the President!"

LaForge glanced at his partner. "Told you I had a bad feeling about this." He marched toward the doors, tossing an order over his shoulder. "Anybody armed, follow me!"

Several chairs scraped and he shoved through the swinging doors as he broke out into a sprint, footfalls hammering behind him as more joined the posse. He reached the control room where he had last seen the Croft employees, and opened the door, weapon in hand. He stepped inside and rounded the corner, the two employees still at the terminal.

"Stop what you're doing, now!"

The first glanced over his shoulder, his jaw dropping as his hands slowly rose. The second kept typing away, staring at the screen. "Just a sec, I'm almost done."

"Stop what you doing, now!"

The first rolled his chair away from his partner, his hands reaching for the sky. "Bill, he's serious."

Bill held a finger up as the other hand continued to type. "I've got like two more commands, then I'm done. Hold your horses!"

LaForge stepped closer. Whatever was going on had to be related to the national crisis. These people were here to install a security system that was supposed to protect against it, and if they were now to be arrested, they must be behind it.

And if this person were only two commands away from completing their task...

He fired two shots into Bill's back. The Croft contractor's body slumped on the keyboard, blood quickly spreading through his crisp white shirt.

LaForge motioned at the surviving contractor. "Take him into custody." He turned to the FBI staff manning the room. "Get whoever you need in here and find out what they did to the system. These guys could be behind everything that's been going on."

The second employee's eyes widened. "What the hell are you talking about? We're trying to *fix* what's going on!" He stared at his partner as he was dragged away, then glared at LaForge. "You didn't have to shoot him! He was just installing security software!"

LaForge stared at him. "That's what *you* say." He pointed at the door. "Get him out of here."

The room emptied of armed agents as Alfredson checked for a pulse. She shook her head slightly at LaForge.

No surprise there.

"Do you think he knew what he was doing?"

LaForge frowned. "No idea." He sighed. "If he had just stopped typing, he'd be alive." He dropped into a chair as a medical team entered the room, Alfredson directing them toward the body.

"Maybe the fact he didn't stop means he knew."

LaForge shook his head. "If this system is being installed across the country, I find it hard to believe they're all involved. That would be thousands of people. Tens of thousands."

Alfredson nodded. "All it takes is one."

"I have a funny feeling he wasn't the one."

The tech they had been dealing with earlier cleared his throat as he joined them. "He might not have been the one, but someone is."

LaForge looked up at him, his eyes narrowing. "What do you mean?"

"I just heard back from my NSA buddy. He traced that number for me, the one that our Utopian guy, Bixby, was communicating with."

LaForge sat up a little straighter. "And?"

"And besides messaging with him, it was also in contact with several numbers at Croft Technologies."

LaForge glanced at his partner, both smiling, a sense of relief washing over him for a moment. Croft Technologies was definitely involved. Now the question was whether the man he had shot was aware of it. He still doubted it.

And he had a feeling this one shooting, the first of his career, would haunt him for the rest of his days.

Assembly Detention Facility
Washington, DC

Sherrie fell back behind Vice President Vance's chair and crouched, still gripping the pipe. Two men stepped inside, chatting in something that sounded like Tagalog, her training giving her a taste of many common languages so she'd at least recognize them for a debrief. They appeared unarmed.

Too bad.

She surged forward, swinging the pipe, grand slamming the first on the side of the head. He went down, unmoving, probably dead. His partner gasped, dropping the body bag he had been carrying, as Sherrie raised the pipe over her head. He turned to leave when she two-handed it down on the top of his skull, a distinct indentation messing with his hairline.

He fell through the still open door.

Someone shouted.

And an alarm sounded.

Shit!

She quickly confirmed neither had weapons, then tossed the pipe aside. It wouldn't work on prepared, armed guards. She heard footfalls in the distance as she rushed to the tables filled with the tools of the torture trade. She stuffed half a dozen small knives in her belt, then picked up two good sized ones. She stepped to the door and listened, her trained ear counting four people approaching.

If this is it, it's going to be one hell of a fight.

She sucked in a deep breath as she tried to calm her nerves, her experience at combat limited. She stepped back behind the chair, not happy with the prospect of being the sucker who had brought a knife to a gunfight. She jabbed one of the large blades into the back of the chair, then drew one of the smaller knives from her belt.

A guard appeared in the door, his weapon raised. She whipped the blade at him and he groaned, his hand reaching for the projectile now embedded in his throat. A second stepped into view, opening fire. Sherrie ducked behind the chair, Vance's body shaking from the impacts as she drew a second blade. The bullets stopped as his magazine emptied and she popped up, whipping her blade at him as he reloaded. He twisted in time, the sharp implement burying itself in his forearm as she surged around the chair, pulling her second knife from the back. The guard's eyes bulged as he slapped a new mag into the well, but it was too late.

She shoved the first knife into his belly, twisting, as the second sliced across his throat. Before he had a chance to hit the floor, she released her grip on both blades and disarmed the man, dropping to a knee as she took aim at the doorway.

Two more appeared.

She fired twice, one dropping, the second opening fire, but too high. She fired two more shots.

Then there was silence.

Except for the alarm.

She grabbed a second weapon and stuffed it in her belt, along with several magazines, as she glanced down both ends of what appeared to be a terrifyingly long corridor, considering what she was seeing. Door upon door, suggesting dozens of people might be held here against their will. Yet no more guards were visible.

How long will that last?

She rushed to the next door over and put three shots into the lock, then kicked it open. She rushed inside and dropped to her knees beside Fang. "I got out."

Fang smiled. "I heard."

Sherrie pressed the spare weapon in Fang's hand and placed another magazine on her chest. "Safety's off, fully loaded. You shoot anything that comes through the door unless it's me. Got it?"

Fang nodded, her face as pale as Sherrie had ever seen it.

"I'm going to go get help, okay? I'll be back as soon as I can. You just hang in there."

Fang's head slumped to the side and Sherrie gasped. She reached for Fang's neck and felt for a pulse. It was there, but weak.

She's out of time!

Randy Child stepped over to Leroux's station. "I've got something."

"What?"

"Well, when you mentioned using IMSI scanners to track Croft, it gave me an idea. The ports already have scanners, and once the state of emergency was declared, DC's scanners went online, so I checked for any phones that were at the port and then in DC."

Leroux's eyes widened as he anticipated Child's next statement. "And?"

Child grinned. "I found her."

"Are you sure?"

Child's head bobbed furiously. "Yeah, absolutely. I pulled the phone number, and it's the same damned phone Agent Kane used to call us!"

Leroux smiled. "Good work! Were you able to track her?"

"Only roughly. I could see what scanners she was showing up on and when, but it was enough." He held up his tablet. "I found her on a traffic camera, pulling into some alleyway. I pulled satellite footage of the area. The alley goes nowhere, it's a dead end, but..." He tapped the display, showing an aerial shot. "She's not there. The vehicle disappeared." He tapped again, a traffic camera showing her pulling out of the alleyway. "That's fifteen minutes later." He smiled. "So where did she go for fifteen minutes?"

Leroux took the tablet and flipped the image back to the satellite shot of the alleyway. "There must be a garage or something in there. That's the only explanation."

Child agreed. "Exactly. She rescues Agent White and Lee Fang, takes them to DC, disappears for fifteen minutes, then from what I can tell, drove straight here."

"When she then claimed they were her prisoners." Leroux jabbed the image of the alleyway. "She must have left them there!" He handed the tablet back. "Send the Delta team to that address. Tell them to expect hostiles with two friendlies on site."

"You got it!"

Gino's Fine Italian Ristorante
Washington, DC

"Do you think he'd kill him?" asked Jimmy as the team stood around their assigned SUV, awaiting their next orders.

Niner shrugged. "If he thought he had something to do with Fang's kidnapping, I wouldn't put it past him."

Spock's eyebrow rose. "But I thought Katz had her and White?"

Dawson sat on the running board. "She does, but she rescued"—air quotes were provided—"them from the Assembly, so if Vice President Vance is involved, then he's still to blame."

"I'd kill the bastard," muttered Niner. And Dawson knew the man was serious. Niner had fallen hard for a South Korean contact last year, and when she had been killed, he had hunted down then executed the man responsible.

There had been no hesitation.

Jimmy gave his friend's shoulder a squeeze, everyone knowing what Niner was thinking of. "Do you think they know who Dylan is?"

Dawson shook his head. "I'd assume his identity would be scrubbed from the standard systems. At most, they'd get a classified hit. I'm more concerned with the footage getting out there. If it does, his cover will be blown."

Spock frowned. "That would be unfortunate. Hell of a way to end a career."

Niner grinned, his troubles buried once again. "He could come back and work with us. He was always good for a few laughs."

"One joker's enough," replied Jimmy. "The two of you together were almost unbearable."

Dawson held up a finger as his comms squawked. "Zero One, Control, do you copy?"

"Go ahead, Control."

"New orders have been sent to your secure phone. This is urgent."

Dawson spun his finger in the air, signaling for the team to roll.

"We need you to head to the provided location, determine if there are any hostiles, and possibly rescue two friendlies."

Dawson climbed in the passenger seat, handing his phone to Niner who was driving. Niner punched the address Langley had sent into the navigation system, then hammered on the gas.

"Who's on site?" asked Dawson.

"We believe Agent White and Lee Fang are both being held there."

Dawson could hear the excitement in the young voice, probably because he knew Sherrie White was his boss' girlfriend.

I wonder if they know about Fang and Kane.

If they hadn't, they probably did now.

"And be prepared to handle wounded. We believe Lee was shot, possibly a stomach wound."

Shit! Those are nasty.

"Copy that. We've got a full med kit with us."

"What's your ETA?"

He glanced at the nav display then the light traffic. And Niner's lead foot. "Less than ten minutes."

Assembly Detention Facility

Washington, DC

Sherrie surged forward, her head on a pivot as she made sure no one from behind surprised her. The corridor was long, several hundred feet, with at least several dozen doors visible, all with green or red indicators above them. She spotted a section of the wall to her right that looked different, an area jutting out, about the width of three of her cells. There was a door hidden to the side with an intercom. She fired three shots into the lock and kicked open the door, advancing quickly inside, her highly trained eye taking in everything, including the lone occupant.

She put a bullet in his leg, dropping him back into his seat, then kicked the door closed behind her. Monitors lined the front of the small room, a weapons rack stood at the back, and there appeared to be no other way out. "Where the hell are we?"

The man, gripping his leg and gasping for breath, glared at her. "I'm not saying anything."

She shot him in the other leg.

He screamed in agony, his hands switching wounds, when she aimed at his left foot. "No! Wait, please! No more!" He rattled off a Washington address that sounded completely unfamiliar.

She motioned with her chin toward one of the phones. "How do I get an outside line?"

"You don't. As soon as the alarm sounds, we go into lockdown, so any escaped prisoners can't get out or communicate."

Sherrie frowned. It made sense, shutting down all outside lines a reasonable precaution if this were indeed an illegal detention center.

She glanced at the monitors, most showing cells with one or more occupants.

What the hell is this place?

"There's got to be some sort of override. How do you stop it once you've contained the situation?"

He shook his head. "Only an outside containment team can—" A light flashed on the control panel. He leaned over in his chair and smiled at one of the monitors. "Oh, you're dead now, lady."

She glanced at the monitor showing five men exiting a vehicle, heavily armed. She aimed at his head. "Which cell are the Kanes and Lerouxes in?"

He shook his head. "No idea."

She put a bullet in his shoulder.

"Jesus Christ! Okay, okay, cell sixteen!"

She smiled. "Thank you."

"You're welcome, bitch."

"Tsk tsk, such poor manners." She put a bullet in his head and turned toward the weapons rack, more firepower definitely needed.

Joseph Medina scanned the garage area, finding it deserted. "What the hell is going on here?" he asked as he motioned one of his men toward the door they had gone through only hours before with Kane's parents.

"Dunno, but it's effin' loud." His man at the door turned and shook his head. "No response, boss."

Medina strode toward the keypad and entered his personal code, his clearance level high enough to treat them as a containment unit. The alarm silenced to allow them to communicate with each other and listen for threats. He turned to his team. "Shoot anything that moves. We'll sort it out later."

Smiles spread across the faces of his men, one even breaking out on his own. He readied his weapon.

"I have a feeling this is going to be a lot of fun."

Operations Center 2, CIA Headquarters
Langley, Virginia

"Sir, I think I've got Croft!"

Leroux leaped from his chair and rushed over to Tong's workstation. "Where?"

She pointed at the displays wrapping across the front of the operations center, a satellite image appearing, a pulsing red circle in the center. "This is the tower that last picked up his cellphone. It's outside of Lovettsville, Virginia. At this point, he either turned it off, or went out of range."

Leroux nodded, staring at the screen. "That's a huge area. Doesn't really help us."

Tong grinned. "Well, like you, I went with my gut."

Leroux chuckled, and Randy Child lived up to his reputation of never being issued a brain-mouth filter. "Ooh, suckin' up to the boss man."

Tong shot him a nasty look, eliciting raised hands from Child then a spun chair.

"What did your gut find?"

"I checked to see if he owned any property in the area."

Leroux smiled slightly. "And does he?"

"No."

The smile disappeared, and Tong raised a finger.

"But, there's a decommissioned Cold War bunker in the area. It was sold six years ago to a holding company which just happens to belong to one of Croft's senior executives at a Croft Technologies subsidiary."

Leroux smiled, his head bobbing slowly. "That can't be a coincidence." He stared at the pulsing circle, another dot showing the location of the bunker just outside of the cell tower's range. "Get me Dylan."

"Yes, sir." Tong tapped at her keyboard then nodded.

"Dylan, Chris. You still okay?"

"Yup, never better. It's a lovely evening here in DC. One could almost be forgiven for forgetting the world outside this little oasis was falling apart."

Leroux chuckled. "Well, fun's over. I might have a location on Croft."

"Good. The conversation here isn't exactly scintillating. Where is he?"

"We think he might be in a decommissioned Cold War bunker. I'm transmitting the coordinates now." He snapped his fingers and Tong sent the intel.

"Okay, I've got it. That's quite the hike, and we're on a clock. Can you arrange transport?"

Another snap and another non-verbal order actioned by his well-trained team. "On its way."

"Great. See if you can get me the layout and some live images. I'd like to know what I'm getting into."

"Will do." Leroux paused, wondering if he should inform Kane of what they had discovered.

You'd want to know.

"Dylan, I, umm, I'm not sure if I should tell you this, but I know I'd want to know."

Kane's reply was subdued. "What?"

"We caught footage of Katz's *rescue* of Fang and Sherrie, and it appears Fang was shot during the escape."

There was a sigh followed by a long pause.

"Dylan?"

"Yeah, I'm here. How bad?"

Leroux shook his head. "Impossible to tell, but it might have been the stomach."

"Okay, thanks for telling me. Just get me that intel. I've got a lot of people to kill."

Assembly Detention Facility
Washington, DC

Sherrie continued to monitor the displays as she geared up, wishing she had thought to take a vest off one of her previous kills. Her eyes ran over the controls, and she spotted how to unlock the individual cells. She could open them all, releasing those held, which would provide the new arrivals with a lot of alternative targets, which would be good for her, but her alone.

The cells could be filled with innocents like the Kanes and Lerouxes, and the team about to contain the security breach might have orders to kill anyone and everyone.

She shook her head, readying her two M4 carbine rifles. There was no way she would risk innocent lives to save her own. She'd have to use the element of surprise. She held up her two weapons.

And overwhelming firepower.

Niner killed their speed and turned into the alleyway Langley had directed them to. It was empty. No doors, no ramps, no nothing. Dawson activated his comm as he stepped out of the vehicle, the others following.

"Control, Zero-One. Are you sure this is the right place?"

"Affirmative, Zero-One. Check for hidden entrances. It has to be there."

Niner pointed at the ground. "Tire tracks."

Dawson stepped closer. The alleyway may have been empty, but it had enough mud and grime to show a distinct tread pattern periodically leading all the way to the wall at what appeared to be a dead end. He pointed at Niner. "Bring the vehicle."

Niner nodded and jogged back to their SUV as Dawson pressed quickly forward with Spock and Jimmy. At the far wall, the tire marks disappeared into the brick.

"Well, that don't look right to me," said Jimmy.

Spock's eyebrow rose. "Ya think?"

Dawson stood back, surveying the wall. He pointed at a seam running through the brick, well hidden, but obvious once he knew where to look. "It's a door all right. See if you can find a way to open it."

Niner climbed out of their SUV, the headlights illuminating the area. He held up a bag. "I say we blow it."

Medina edged forward, his weapon held high, his men forming a wedge with him at the tip. Nobody was in sight, though at the far end there was something on the ground that might be a body. The cell doors seemed secure so far, but something had set off the alarm. Why they hadn't been greeted yet by the Watchman, at least over the intercom, was concerning.

A rumbling sound had him spinning toward the door they had come through. "What the hell was that?"

"Sounded like some sort of explosion."

Another small rumble had his finger twitching on the trigger.

"That sounded like something you'd use to blast a lock."

Medina agreed as he slowly stepped back toward the door, now about a hundred feet away. "Watch our six."

Two of his men turned their attention back toward the unsecured detention block behind him. The door opened and several armed men entered, their motions deliberate, clearly trained. His team had been sent before the breach had occurred, and weren't scheduled to be here, so this might be the containment team that would have been sent when the alarm sounded.

"Could they be ours?" asked one of his men.

He couldn't be sure, but he wasn't about to shoot a team that might be like his own. "Identify yourselves!"

Something creaked behind him.

"I've got movement!"

Sherrie cursed as the door opened again, four more armed men appearing on camera. Then smiled as the first batch all spun toward the new arrivals.

This is it.

She shoved the door to the control room open, its damaged hardware creaking, causing the two men still paying attention, to swing their aims toward her.

One shouted, but it was too late.

She squeezed the triggers on both weapons, lead belching in the confined space, mowing down her two targets. The new arrivals opened fire as well, their targets the same as hers, at least for the moment, and she made a point to avoid aiming in their direction, instead hugging the wall to give her an angle.

Within moments, the original arrivals were down, the last to fall a man with shockingly blonde hair, obviously from a bottle. As she fired her last shots, her eyes were already assessing the new arrivals, and she recognized the equipment.

These were soldiers.

American soldiers.

She lowered her weapons only slightly, just in case they had paid a visit to the army surplus store.

"Agent White, CIA! Identify yourselves!"

"Agent White, what the hell is a nice lady like you doing in this type of establishment?"

Sherrie grinned, lowering her weapons as she recognized the voice. "BD, is that you?"

The Bravo Team members quickly approached, their weapons trained on the corridor behind her in case there were any more hostiles. As they neared in the dim light, she soon recognized them all, a wave of relief washing over her as her weapons clattered to the ground. "Thank God you're here."

Mark Leroux shielded his wife as best he could, the sounds of gunfire on the other side of the door terrifying. He had never heard a weapon fired in real life, and it was immeasurably more horrifying than on television.

But the silence was worse.

All four of them were huddled in the corner, the women in the toilet area, he and Rick Kane forming a fourth wall of flesh. Yet it would be useless. If someone came in here, they'd be dead. There was nowhere to hide, no way to beat them.

They were defenseless.

His wife's hand squeezed his, and he stared at her, her eyes filled with fear. And love. He gazed into her eyes, the eyes of the woman he had loved for over thirty years, the eyes of the woman he had pursued in college for months before she had finally agreed to that first coffee. The eyes of the woman he had been with for every single day since. "I love you."

She sobbed and grabbed him. "I love you too."

The door clicked and Rick stood, Mark joining him, motioning for the wives to stay hidden. "What should we do?"

Rick scowled at the door. "Look them in the eye and tell them to go to hell."

Liz Leroux rose and took her husband's hand. "If we're going to die, then I want it to be on my feet."

Jenn stood by her husband, and the four of them faced the door, side by side, hand in hand, waiting for whatever was to come, the wait almost interminable, the silence deafening.

Finally, there was a sound and the door opened, slowly, and a face appeared that Mark wouldn't have expected in a million years. "Sherrie? What the hell are you doing here?"

Sherrie White stepped inside, several armed men visible behind her. She smiled at them with that infectious smile he knew had won over his awkward Chris.

It was then he noticed she was covered in blood and armed to the teeth. "What happened to you?" cried his wife as she rushed forward and embraced the young woman. "What are you doing here?"

Sherrie extricated herself. "Long story. Just sit tight, I'll be back for you in a few minutes, okay?"

They all nodded and Sherrie stepped back outside, closing the door.

Rick stared at Mark. "Who the hell was that?"

Mark shook his head slowly, still not quite believing what he had just seen. "That's our boy's girlfriend."

Sherrie closed the door, not wanting to risk the parents roaming about in what could turn into another live fire situation. She hurried to the cell she had been held in, and found Niner and Jimmy already working on Fang. Dawson was guarding the door as Spock jogged back toward them, having left to get a signal.

"Ambulance is on its way. ETA five minutes."

Sherrie stepped inside and knelt beside her friend. "Is she going to make it?"

Niner glanced at her and shook his head slightly. "I don't know. She's lost a lot of blood. I'm pumping her full of plasma now, and I've stopped the bleeding. If she makes it to the hospital, then, well..." He looked her in the eyes. "Dylan should be here, just in case."

En route to Short Hill Mountain, Virginia

Kane stared out the window at the terrain whipping past them below, a chopper having arrived within minutes for them. He turned his head to see Katz staring at him. "What?"

"I was just trying to understand you."

His eyes widened slightly. "Excuse me?"

"We are about to try and infiltrate, just the two of us, what could be a heavily guarded bunker. We will most likely die. I do this for a purpose. If I don't eliminate the Assembly, I *will* die eventually. You, however, could live a long life. Is love really worth dying for?"

Kane grunted and shook his head. "You know, in some ways I envy you. You probably never get scared or nervous, which could be extremely useful in my business. You'll never experience sadness at the loss of a loved one or comrade, which again, could be extremely useful. But I don't think the tradeoff is worth it. You'll never experience friendship, you'll never experience love.

"The very fact you have to ask if love is worth dying for, tells me you'll never understand what motivates normal people. Love is everything. It's the best part of living. Whether that's loving someone as a friend, as family, or intimately, it's always the best part of life. Perhaps if you loved someone, were capable of loving someone, you might understand why I'm willing to walk into that bunker, with just you at my side, in the hopes of saving the woman I love, and a woman I consider a friend. And maybe, just maybe, if you understood love and friendship, you wouldn't be doing what you're doing to those two innocent women."

"Love is a weakness. It makes you do stupid things, or things you wouldn't normally do." She waved her hand at him. "Like you. Normally, you wouldn't partner with me, wouldn't kidnap the Vice President, wouldn't stand by as he was killed, and wouldn't attack a bunker with just one other person. I understand love perfectly, and it allows me to use it against those who don't understand it, who only *feel* it."

Kane shook his head. "Then you don't understand it at all." He leaned forward. "I'm willing to die to save Fang because I love her. I'm willing to die to save Sherrie, because my best friend loves her."

Katz stared at him, unmoved. "You say these things, yet they are meaningless. You're also willing to die for your country. Your willingness to die has nothing to do with love, and everything to do with duty, something that I can appreciate."

Kane shook his head. "Wrong again. A soldier is willing to die for his country because he loves his country, loves what it stands for, and more importantly, wants to protect and preserve it so that those he loves, who live in that country, are protected. He's not dying for his duty to his country, he's dying for his loved ones that rely on that country being safe. He doesn't sacrifice himself because it's his duty to protect a line drawn on a map, he does it because if that line wavers, the people he loves on his side of it might be harmed." He sat back. "If you understood love, you'd understand *that*."

"Sir, ma'am, we're coming up on the target now."

Kane stared out at the trees below, Katz joining him at the window. "How does it feel knowing you're about to die?"

Kane looked at her. "I think my words would be wasted on you."

She nodded. "Probably."

"How do *you* feel?"

She sat back in her seat. "I wonder if I die, and there is some sort of afterlife that people like you believe in, will I be fixed."

He stared at her. "Do you see yourself as broken?"

She looked away, a flash of emotion behind the eyes surprising Kane. "Don't you?"

Operations Center 2, CIA Headquarters
Langley, Virginia

"The drone's in position, sir."

Leroux motioned toward the displays at the front, and Tong punched up the feeds.

"Where is it?" asked Child, peering at the screen.

Tong shot him a look. "It's a bunker. It's not exactly supposed to be obvious."

Leroux ignored them. "Superimpose the plans we have, sync it up with the landmarks."

Tong complied, and moments later they were watching live drone footage with the outline of the bunker, buried underground, visible.

Child cursed. "That's pretty well-hidden."

"Show me infrared."

The image changed and several large heat signatures were visible, away from the main structure.

"What are those?" asked Child.

"Probably ventilation. If I were them, I'd be on lockdown. Generators, maybe?"

Tong nodded. "According to the utility company, they're not drawing any power."

Leroux frowned. "Which means their endgame has already started."

Marc Therrien spoke up. "Sir, the airwaves around that place are hot. There's an awful lot of comm traffic."

"Landlines?"

"According to the telecom database they've got a fiber optic connection, but its satellite traffic."

Tong pointed. "What's that? Lower right?"

Leroux stepped closer. "Freeze that, zoom in." The image froze, the quadrant in question enlarging to fill the screen. "Enhance." The pixelated image refocused, revealing several round objects painted with digital camouflage, keeping them well hidden from the casual overhead observer.

But not the trained eye.

"Those aren't DirecTV dishes," muttered Child.

Leroux shook his head. "Definitely not." He pointed slightly to the left. "Some large antennas there, too." He turned to the others. "This place is fully functional. It has to be their command and control center."

Tong agreed. "Just the type of place you'd take down a nation from."

Child spun in his chair. "Yeah, but what do we do? It's going to be heavily guarded, for sure. It's not like Kane can just go and knock on the front door."

Leroux turned back toward the images. "Check the plans. We need to find a way in for them." He pointed at Tong. "And get me the Director."

United States Strategic Command Headquarters
Offutt Air Force Base, Nebraska

Master Sergeant Nathan Wells stormed toward the server room, his security detail on his heels. Communications attempts with Captain Cartwright had failed, and the captain was the escort assigned to the Croft Technologies personnel Wells had just received orders to detain.

They reached the server room door and he swiped his pass to unlock it. It beeped a rejection at him, the security panel remaining red. He tried again, and again it failed. He stepped back and motioned for one of his men to try.

Airman Anders stepped up and failed as well. "They must have scrambled the lock."

Wells activated his comm. "This is Wells. We can't get in the room. It looks like they've scrambled the locking mechanism, over."

"Get in that room, Sergeant! I don't care if you have to blast it open!"

"Yes, sir!" He stepped back and took aim, firing four rounds into the lock, then booted the door open. His men surged inside and he followed, rounding the corner to find the two civilians still at one of the terminals.

And Captain Cartwright lying on the floor, unmoving.

"Step away from the keyboard." The two rose, their hands raised slightly as they complied. Wells motioned for Anders to check on the Captain. Anders knelt down and checked for a pulse. He looked up at Wells and nodded.

"He's alive."

Wells breathed a sigh of relief, then returned his attention to the two Croft contractors. "What the hell did you two do?"

The first sneered at him, lowering his hands. "You're already too late."

"What do you mean? Too late for what?"

The man smiled. "To stop us." He charged toward them, the other joining him, both shouting, "The Assembly is eternal!"

Half a dozen weapons opened up, shredding them apart.

And leaving no way to know what they had done in the hours they had been in here alone, unsupervised.

Wells stepped toward the bodies and holstered his weapon.

"What do you think they did?" asked Anders.

Wells stared at the rows upon rows of servers and shook his head. "People don't sacrifice themselves for a job, they sacrifice themselves for a dream."

Anders nodded. "And usually their dreams are our nightmares."

Operations Center 2, CIA Headquarters
Langley, Virginia

"I might have something."

Leroux glanced up from his workstation to see Tong gesture toward the displays. "What am I looking at?" Two images were displayed, both remarkably similar, though clearly different.

"On the left is the bunker area today, and on the right, is an image from when it was decommissioned and put up for sale."

Leroux searched for any differences that might mean something. He gave up. "And?"

Tong tapped her keyboard and the same area in both images, to the east of the main structure, zoomed in. "Look at the ground here. It's different."

Leroux stood and stepped toward the display, his head bobbing slightly. "Yeah. Something's been done there. Some digging, perhaps."

Child spun in his chair. "Well, if I know my super-villain movies, don't they always have an escape tunnel?"

Leroux nodded. "Makes sense. It's far enough away that if you were to come out there, you're likely to come out behind anyone surrounding the bunker. Kane's best bet is gaining access covertly. This might just be their ticket in."

Tong grunted. "It better be. There's no way they're getting in any other way, not with the equipment we sent them."

Leroux agreed. "Send it to Kane. We'll let him make the call."

Assembly Command and Control Facility
Short Hill Mountain, Virginia

Roger Croft stood at the center of the control room, watching the displays for any indication of success, so far disappointed.

"Sir!"

He spun toward one of the controllers, waving his hand.

"The system has made contact!"

A smile spread across Croft's face as the entire room came to a standstill for a brief moment, an outburst of jubilation following.

This is it.

"Acknowledge contact."

Keys were tapped and the controller smiled. "Receipt of message confirmed."

Croft removed from his pocket the biscuit provided each morning to the Vice President, this one delivered earlier today in anticipation for this moment. He snapped it in half and pulled out the folded card inside. Opening it, five sets of codes were listed. He handed it to the senior controller. "Today's line is number four."

"Yes, sir."

Croft looked about the room. "Ladies and gentlemen, today we change our future, for the betterment of all mankind. The Assembly is eternal!"

The entire room responded in unison, the energy surging through him almost as good as sex. He stared into the eyes of the senior controller, fully aware he was about to make history.

"Send the transmission."

Kane pressed the trigger, the small charge shattering the still of the lightly wooded area, mostly bushes with a few larger trees interspersed. What birdlife there was, took to the skies as Katz yanked the camouflaged hatch open, letting it drop with a bang on the ground.

"Well, if they're monitoring, they heard that."

Katz shrugged. "We're in, and we're not supposed to be." She peered down the hatch then climbed inside, quickly descending. "I doubt they're prepared for us."

Kane wasn't so sure. He followed, noting what appeared to be a sensor on the rim, no doubt a signal already sent to some monitoring station somewhere. Yet as he continued down, unimpeded, he wondered if Katz might be right. The facility could only hold so many people, even fewer for an extended period. The facility itself was meant to withstand any assault, which probably meant fewer guards.

Possibly, not probably.

They couldn't count on anything.

Katz reached the bottom and spun the wheel on the hatch, pushing it open. She stepped through, weapon at the ready, and Kane followed into what turned out to be a brightly lit, freshly painted corridor, doors lining both sides.

A corridor that was thankfully empty.

"Maybe it's past their bedtime?"

Katz looked at him, and he wondered if she even understood the concept of humor.

They advanced in silence when a door opened in front of them, a buxom blonde in a French maid's outfit appearing.

Wasn't expecting that.

He slapped a hand over the shocked woman's mouth. "Stay quiet, or you die, understood?" Her wide eyes revealed she did, but she nodded regardless. "Where's Croft?"

She shook her head and mumbled something against his hand. He removed it.

"I don't know."

"You're lying. One more lie, and she kills you."

Katz stepped forward, her dead stare enough to send shivers down his own spine.

"He-he's in the control room or his office, Five-C."

"Where?"

"Umm, two levels down."

"Thanks, now——"

Katz put a bullet in the blonde's forehead and she collapsed in a heap.

He glared at her. "Was that necessary?"

"She's Assembly."

He motioned at her outfit. "She's the hired help!"

"Not inside this facility."

He frowned. She was right. Only the most devout would be here. He grabbed the woman by the arm and pulled her inside the room she had come from, then yanked her pass from around her neck. "Let's check his office first."

Minuteman III Launch Control Facility
Outside Karlsruhe, North Dakota

Captain Tony Daugherty leaned forward in his chair, cycling through a test procedure he had done a hundred times before. Hell, maybe even a thousand times. America's nuclear deterrent may be aimed at the world's oceans now, but it still needed to be functional and ready to respond, in case its nation needed it. He wondered what it must have been like in the sixties, when so many were positive nuclear war was inevitable. The men in these silos, back then, carried a heavy burden, one not really carried by today's crews.

Yes, they could be asked to unleash weapons that could kill millions with the turn of a key, but what was the likelihood of that actually happening today?

Miniscule.

He, like many of his fellow soldiers, were bored, demoralized, and increasing felt irrelevant in today's military. Where once his assignment was sought after and coveted, now it was something most were "volunteered" for, himself included.

He, as they all did, had a healthy respect for the awesome responsibility they bore, though it was a responsibility that would never come. Like the boy told to man the church bell against predators, in a world where all predators had been wiped out.

"Hey, I forgot to tell you what happened to my dad!"

Daugherty spun in his chair. "What?"

"He won a car in one of those charity lotteries."

His eyes widened. "Holy shit! That's awesome. What kind?"

"A Jag convertible."

Daugherty whistled. "Nice!"

"Yeah, you'd think so."

His eyes narrowed. "*Think?*"

"Yeah, I guess he shocked the shit out of them when he asked for second prize instead."

His head shook in disbelief. "What was second prize?"

"A new refrigerator."

Daugherty's chin dropped. "Wait a minute. You're telling me your dad gave up a Jag for a refrigerator?"

"Yeah, he said he wanted something he could count on to actually run."

Three ear-piercing wails erupted from the speakers and Daugherty's heart leaped into his throat.

"Raven Claw this is Castle Rock with a Red dash Alpha message in two parts. Break. Break. Red dash Alpha. Red Dash Alpha."

He straightened in his chair, his heart pounding as he exchanged an anxious glance with Fraser. "Stand by to authenticate."

"Standing by."

The transmission, its robotic quality intentional, emotion not of help in these situations, continued.

"Alpha-Romeo-Sierra-Romeo-Bravo-Echo-Bravo-Tango. Authentication Two-One-One-Two-Zero-Zero-Lima-Echo."

Daugherty quickly wrote down the codes on the form reserved for this situation. "I have a valid message. Stand by to authenticate."

"I agree with authentication, sir."

He rose and opened his lockbox, as did Fraser. He removed the biscuit inside and snapped it open as he returned to his seat. Removing the card inside, he compared the code to the one he had written down.

Holy shit!

"Enter launch codes."

"Entering launch codes."

He carefully entered the sequence, Fraser's fingers working his own terminal, both of them needed in this process, each step of the way. He watched his display and his eyes widened as the coded orders were confirmed.

"Launch order confirmed." Daugherty spotted Fraser stealing a glance over his shoulder at him. "Eyes on your job, Lieutenant."

"Yes, sir, sorry, sir. Target selection, complete. Time to target sequence, complete. Yield selection, complete."

This is really happening!

Assembly Command and Control Facility
Short Hill Mountain, Virginia

"Sir, we've got a security breach."

Croft spun toward the senior controller. "What?"

"The escape tunnel hatch has been opened."

He turned toward the wall of displays. "Show me."

One of the panels switched to security camera footage showing two people, a man and a woman, climbing down the ladder. "How the hell did they find us?"

And how'd they find the hatch?

He had it installed two years ago in the unlikely event he needed to make an escape, though he never thought it would be necessary. Yet here were two people, armed, making their way into a facility that no one should know about. "Send a team. Kill them."

"Yes, sir."

"And get that off my screen."

"Yes, sir."

The image disappeared and he returned his attention to the launch. "Status on the missiles?"

A map of the United States appeared with green indicators, but too many yellows and reds.

"There has been some delays in compliance, sir. Follow up messages have been sent. We aren't at the minimum threshold yet."

Croft frowned. They had built redundancies into their plan, with enough missiles being launched to hit their targets multiple times in case some crews failed to launch, or some missiles failed. Their agenda required complete success, and without that being guaranteed, his orders were to not launch. There had been too many reports of failed tests, demoralized crews, untrained crews, and other unknowns, to leave things to chance.

"ETA?"

"We should reach minimum compliance within five minutes, sir." The controller turned toward him. "There's nothing they can do now, sir. We've already won."

Croft admired the man's confidence, but didn't share it. He pointed at the screens. "Show me the targets that have confirmed so far."

The map updated, hundreds of population centers circled. He shook his head slowly, a smile spreading.

Unbelievable.

The plan had been impossible to achieve until the last election, when the Vice President was brought into the loop. His codes were invalid unless the President was dead. That was easy to take care of, the hack they had installed at Offutt Air Force Base acknowledging their falsified message indicating the President's death, and the Vice President's succession, thus automatically updating the system to accept his codes.

Once received, their hack then had confirmed the orders as if the Secretary of Defense had acknowledged the "President's" orders. The fail-safes were bypassed, and there was nothing that could be done now to stop it.

The controller was right.

They had already won.

By linking the internal and external networks at Offutt, they had complete access, and the military had no clue. By the time they did, by the time they broke the connection, it would be too late. The crosslink gave them direct access to the silo crews, who had no way of knowing the transmissions were fake.

And with the Vice President's valid launch codes authenticated by the system, they had no reason to suspect anything was wrong. As far as the silo and sub crews knew, they had received completely authenticated launch orders with specific launch packages targeting the biggest problem area of the planet. The swath of Islam that stretched across Northern Africa, the Middle East, and southern Asia. The agenda here wasn't to eliminate the problem, merely to thin it out.

Tens of millions would die instantly, hundreds of millions more over the coming months from radiation poisoning. Their brethren would take their revenge in the streets of the Western world, and the governments would be forced to act. The war would be won, and it would be over once and for all, but America would have lost the trust of the world.

A new Cold War would ensue, with all sides in an arms race to protect themselves from each other, and in the decades that followed, technology would advance so rapidly, the populations of all sides would become even more interconnected, to the point where they would demand rapprochement once again, demand an end to the new Cold War, and would unite, perhaps having advanced hundreds of years in mere decades.

And without the threat of a religion hell bent on dragging mankind back to the dark ages, a religion they hoped would finally be forced to confront its fundamental problems and experience its own reformation, humanity could finally realize its potential once and for all, no longer held back by radical fundamentalism and political correctness run amok.

He might just live long enough to see the result of their efforts, though he was prepared should he not. His children would, and their descendants would spread humanity through the stars.

He smiled as the compliance indicator continued to tick up, nearing the threshold needed to order the launch.

Any minute now.

White House Situation Room
Washington, DC

President Starling stared at the screen in disbelief. His missiles were arming across the country, across the globe, something that was supposed to be impossible. *He* was the only one who could launch them, or so he had thought. As was explained to him only minutes before, the Vice President's codes were also valid, though only should he be named President.

Apparently, the system thought he had.

Unbelievable!

"Why weren't his codes invalidated the moment he was kidnapped?"

General Parsons looked up from his computer. "They were, sir, but the system sent a fake acknowledgment back to us. Apparently at that point, they already had at least partial control."

"How many targets are we talking about?"

"So far it looks like about three-hundred, all cities with populations over one-hundred-thousand, all in predominantly Muslim countries."

Starling shook his head, feeling sick. "How many missiles?"

"Sir, the important number is warheads. Each crew commands ten missiles, each missile has three warheads, so thirty targets per crew. At this time, we believe we're dealing with as few as ten crews that have received orders to standby for launch."

"Just ten? Why can't we just knock on the damned door and tell them to stop?"

Parsons shook his head. "I'm sorry, Mr. President, it doesn't work that way."

"Can we send abort codes?"

"We've tried, sir, but they now have complete control of the system. We have no way to send the abort codes to the silos. Our people have just taken down the team that did this at Offutt Air Force Base, but it could take hours for our techs to figure out what they've done."

Starling's chest tightened. "But we don't have hours. There has to be something we can do." He motioned toward the drone footage of the bunker. "What if we destroy that thing, will that help?"

Parsons shook his head. "It depends on how far into the process they are. The final launch order hasn't been sent yet, and we don't know why. They're waiting for something."

"Then hit the damned thing before they can send the code!"

"Yes, Mr. President."

Director Morrison cleared his throat, his image among a grid of others jacked into the meeting via teleconference. "Mr. President, I have people in there."

Starling looked at him. "Then tell them to get out."

"We can't, sir, they're out of contact."

Starling shook his head. "Then I'm sorry, Leif, there's nothing I can do. We have to hit that bunker before it's too late."

Assembly Command and Control Facility
Short Hill Mountain, Virginia

"Sir, our security team is about to engage the intruders."

Croft motioned for the camera footage to be transferred to the main screen, and watched as the team of six rushed down the corridor, the two intruders just around the corner. The man held up a fist, apparently hearing the approaching team, then stared directly at the camera. And smiled.

"Shit! Warn them—"

The other camera showing his team provided him with the unsettling view of them dropping one-by-one, in rapid succession. Moments later, the two intruders stepped over the bodies.

"Send another team."

The senior controller looked at him. "Sorry, sir, that was our only team. They were never supposed to get inside."

"Sir! We've reached minimum compliance!"

Croft spun, pointing toward the man. "Send the final sequence, now!"

"Transmitting now, sir."

Croft turned to the screen, the compliance indicator now in the green, the map showing the impact zones filling the entire target area as planned. "Is it done?"

"Yes, sir, the system in Offutt is sending the messages now. There is absolutely nothing that can stop the launch, sir."

Croft smiled, his shoulders sagging as relief swept over him. "Then we're done." He stared at the camera showing the advancing hostiles.

The facility had been discovered, and the prudent thing to do would be to kill everyone who could threaten the success of the mission. Killing the hostiles had failed, and he couldn't risk them compelling one of his people to betray the cause.

Unfortunately, the only way to prevent that, was killing them all, obviously not a practical option—he was only one man against two dozen. He needed to empty the facility, but he had no intention of dying today, even if Number One had other plans for him. He needed to get out of here, now, and competing with two dozen others for elevators and escape tunnels might prevent that.

He headed for his office, determined to get a head start. "Evacuate the facility as soon as you've received confirmation that all orders have been successfully transmitted to the silos."

Kane stepped through the door to sublevel five and checked a map on the wall, conveniently left over from the Cold War. "She said Five-C, right?"

Katz nodded.

He pointed. "Just around the corner." They advanced cautiously, weapons ready. A single door came into view, the only door visible. "This has to be it."

He twisted the knob and pushed, surprised to find it unlocked. He stepped inside and a woman behind a desk gasped. Katz shot her in the neck and Kane cursed as he swept forward, sounds coming from the inner office. He smiled as Croft froze, staring at him, or more accurately, the barrel of his gun. His hand darted for a weapon on his desk when Kane stepped closer.

"I wouldn't do that if I were you." Kane grabbed Croft's weapon and stuffed it in his belt. "Mr. Croft, I assume you know Nadja Katz?"

Croft stared at her for a moment as she entered the room, and he paled slightly. "Yes." He motioned toward the door. "You're too late."

Kane shook his head. "We're not here about that. We're here about the Assembly, and your involvement in it."

Croft's eyes narrowed, clearly puzzled by his disinterest. "I-I don't understand."

"Number Seven, Vice President Vance, is dead. He was kind enough to provide us with the names of Eight through Twelve."

Croft nodded. "I'm aware of that."

Kane's eyebrows rose. "Really?" He stepped closer. "If you know that, then you must be a member of the Council."

Croft backed away slightly. "And if I am?"

Kane flicked his weapon toward Katz. "Then she'd like to know who the rest are."

Croft stared at Katz for a moment. "Why? I wouldn't know who they are anyway."

Kane waved his gun disapprovingly. "Now, now, you know that's not true. You would at least know those who came after you." Croft said nothing. "So, what number are you?"

"Four."

Kane smiled. "So then you at least know who Five is. Tell us his name."

"Why? It doesn't matter? Thanks to you, all members of the Council have been ordered killed. I'm dead already."

Kane threw a smile at Katz, swearing he saw a tiny curl in the corner of her mouth. "You've done it! They're all dead!"

She shook her head. "He isn't. And neither is Number One."

Kane frowned. "Isn't the rest enough? I mean, if there's only one left, how much trouble can they be to you?"

Katz shook her head. "Number One will simply replace the others. Within a few years, he will have reestablished the Assembly Council, and they will be every bit the threat they are today." She stared at Kane. "We need to find Number One, or all of this was a waste of time."

Croft dropped into his chair. "You'll never find him. Nobody knows who he is. I've never seen him. Hell, I've never even heard his real voice." He stared up at Kane. "If you're going to kill me, get it over with. My job here is done, anyway."

Kane's eyes narrowed slightly. "What was your job?"

Croft smiled slightly, some color returning to his pale cheeks. "To change the world."

"Yeah, yeah, I've heard shit like that before."

Croft stared at him. "You don't understand. I've already done it."

Kane's heart ticked up a few notches as his stomach tightened. "What do you mean?"

Croft smiled, any fear he had a moment before, erased. "We've launched the missiles. You're already too late."

Kane's jaw dropped as his eyes widened. "Bullshit."

Croft waved his hand at their surroundings. "What do you think this entire exercise was for? To mess with traffic lights? It was all aimed at getting your government to panic and let us install our system. And the first place we installed it was Offutt Air Force Base."

Kane's heart slammed.

Oh my God!

"United States Strategic Command Headquarters!"

"Exactly."

"But you need the codes."

"Which Number Seven, the *Vice President*, provided us with."

337

Kane stepped back, trying to process what was being said. Then he stopped, raising his weapon and pointing it at Croft's head. "Stop it."

Croft shook his head. "The orders have been given, and the men in the silos are now in control. And no one here will send the abort command."

Kane paused. "Wait, you mean you can still stop this? You can still send an abort command?"

Croft chuckled. "This has been my life's work. I'll never stop it." Croft's computer beeped and his head spun toward the sound, his eyes widening. "It's Number One!"

Kane stepped back, away from the computer, making certain he wasn't in view of any camera. "Why is he calling?"

"He's expecting a status report."

Kane aimed his weapon at Croft's head. "Give him it, and find out where he is."

Croft stared at him. "Are you kidding me? He'll never tell me."

Kane stepped slightly closer. "Try, or I make sure she kills you slowly." Kane stepped into the outer office and grabbed the phone, getting a dial tone. He pressed Nine, hoping for an outside line, and was rewarded with a triple beep then a steady tone. He smiled then dialed Leroux.

"Hello?"

"Hey, buddy, it's me."

"Oh thank God! Where are you?"

"Croft's office in the bunker."

"You've got to get out of there! There're a few dozen missiles inbound on you right now."

Kane ignored the warning, his focus returned to saving Fang and Sherrie. "Forget that, Number One has called here. He's on with another Assembly member. I saw a whack of satellite transmitters when we arrived. Is there any way you can find out where he is?"

"I'll try." There was a pause. "Umm, Dylan?"

Kane recognized his friend's tone, and knew there was bad news about to be delivered.

Fang!

"Yes?"

"The missiles are powering up. They can't stop them."

Guilt washed over him as he experienced relief the news wasn't about Fang, only about the impending death of millions. But it also confirmed what he had doubted until this very moment. That Croft was telling the truth. "Can't they just issue new orders?"

"No, the communications system has been compromised. We can't send orders to our own crews, only they can."

Kane turned, staring at Croft as a thought occurred to him. "And they can only send it from here?"

"That's likely."

"Then Jesus Christ, abort the hit and let me try!"

White House Situation Room

Washington, DC

President Starling stared at the screen showing the target location along with dozens of inbounds. "ETA to target?"

General Parsons whispered into his phone before replying. "First impact in two minutes, sir. We've got dozens of bunker buster missiles inbound. They won't survive, Mr. President."

Starling looked at Morrison's image. "Were you able to reach your people?"

Morrison shook his head, his face somber. "No, Mr. President. But if I know my agent, he would have told you to send the missiles himself."

Starling smiled slightly, appreciating the sentiment. Morrison was forgiving him.

"Sir! ICBM launch orders have been received!"

Starling leaped from his chair. "Are you sure?"

General Parsons nodded. "Yes, sir, confirmed. Final launch orders have been received." He lowered the phone to his chest, his voice subdued. "There's nothing we can do."

The room fell silent, all eyes turning to Starling, who stood as shocked as the rest of them.

Move. Now!

He tore his eyes away from the screen. "Get me the Russian President, now! And line up the Chinese, British, French, and Israelis. And I want flash communiques sent to every capital in the world telling them that this is not an intentional launch, and that our systems have been compromised. Tell them we are doing everything we can to abort the launches, but we are not hopeful, and they should take all necessary precautions."

"Yes, Mr. President!"

He raised a hand. "And add this. Any retaliatory launch will be met with overwhelming force."

General Parsons nodded, his face grim. "Yes, Mr. President."

Operations Center 2, CIA Headquarters
Langley, Virginia

Leroux spun toward Tong. "Get me the Director!" He turned to the rest of the room. "Analyze any signals from that area. We're looking for something new in the past few minutes. I need to know where it's coming from. Now!"

His team leaped into action as Tong cleared her throat. "Sir, I've got Director Morrison."

Leroux adjusted his headset. "Sir, we have to abort the strike on the bunker, now!"

"Why?"

"I just spoke to Kane. He's inside and alive. We need to give him a chance to send the abort message."

"We can't get the message through, Chris, the system's locked us out."

Leroux shook his head, getting frustrated at not being understood. *There's no time!*

"No, sir, you don't understand. That bunker is the *only* way to get the message through. Destroy it, and we lose any chance of stopping this!"

Morrison cursed. "Okay, stand by."

Assembly Command and Control Facility
Short Hill Mountain, Virginia

Croft didn't want to die, though he knew it was inevitable. Number One would order his execution shortly, if he hadn't already. But at least he would die knowing he had fulfilled the Assembly's agenda for the coming decades.

He had to admit he was a little resentful.

He had done the work, he had accomplished the task, and now he was going to die. He had heard the conversation in the next room, the man holding him at gunpoint apparently a government agent of some sort, not a gun for hire like the terrifying Nadja Katz. Though it didn't matter. Katz was going to kill him regardless of what the agent might say.

He had minutes to live.

It was unfortunate those last few minutes would be spent talking to Number One, the orchestrator of his demise, and not in the arms of a beautiful woman. He glanced at the intimidatingly sexual Katz.

If only.

He tapped his keyboard, linking him to Number One. "Congratulations, Number Four. You have exceeded my wildest expectations."

He could almost see the silhouette smile. "Thank you, Number One. We couldn't have done it without your guidance."

"Indeed. What is your status?"

"Sir, we've been compromised, however the final launch commands have already been sent. The missiles will be launched. I don't expect to be alive in the next few minutes."

"Understood." The computer-altered voice sounded even more disinterested than usual. "Number Four, you will be remembered. Not only by those who will succeed you, but in time, by all mankind, when we reveal ourselves to them. The name Roger Croft will be forever remembered and honored as the one who propelled our species into the stars."

He felt a surge of pride at the words, though only for a moment, as resentment at this man's lone survival took over. He eyed Katz, her reputation well known to him.

She'll slice you to pieces while keeping you alive.

"Sir, I'll be dead shortly, and I'm comfortable with that, but I fear for your safety. There will be hundreds of targets hit over the coming half hour. Are you certain you're safe?"

"Don't worry about me, Number Four, the nearest target is over three-thousand-miles from here, and the prevailing winds won't touch us. I will survive. The Assembly will survive."

He closed his eyes and nodded. Though he couldn't care less if Number One himself survived, he did want the Assembly to continue, otherwise all the good it had accomplished throughout human history would cease, and there was so much more to be done.

He stared at the image. "The Assembly is eternal."

"The Assembly is eternal. Good luck, Number Four."

The signal went dead, and Katz raised her weapon. "You failed."

She fired.

White House Situation Room
Washington, DC

"Mr. President, we have to abort the attack!"

President Starling spun in his chair, staring at the screen. "What?"

Director Morrison leaned closer to the camera. "Sir, my agent inside thinks he can use their equipment to send the abort order." The room went silent.

"Explain."

Morrison shook his head. "There's no time, sir! Abort the attack, or we face World War Three."

Starling realized Morrison was right. There was no time to debate. He had to trust his people. He rose, pointing at General Parsons. "Abort the attack, now!"

"Yes, Mr. President!"

Phones were grabbed and orders given as everyone turned toward the screens, live footage from the cameras of the inbound missiles showing their rapid approach.

"There it is!" cried someone as the target became visible, the indicator showing a lock.

"Abort the attack, now!" cried General Parsons.

Suddenly the displays went dead, one by one, and Starling stared at another showing the incoming missile locations, the green triangles rapidly disappearing from the screen.

General Parsons sighed, dropping into his chair. "Attack aborted, Mr. President." Starling closed his eyes then was nearly sick when

Parsons continued. "Let's just hope we didn't give them time to send another launch order."

Starling dropped into his chair, suddenly not confident he had made the right choice.

Operations Center 2, CIA Headquarters
Langley, Virginia

"Did you get that?"

Leroux nodded at Kane's question. "Yes."

"Does it help?"

Leroux wasn't sure. "It might. I'll get back to you."

"Okay, buddy."

The call went dead and he turned toward the display. "Okay, Number One is apparently in a location at least three-thousand-miles from the nearest target, with prevailing winds that won't reach him." He pointed at a display showing all the known target locations, the information pulled from the target packages delivered to the silos. A swath across the equator was about to be eliminated, there little doubt what the aim was.

To irreparably harm countries dominated by Islam.

"Okay, show me all the locations we think that transmission was coming from."

Hundreds, if not thousands, of indicators appeared across the globe. For the moment, the only way they had to narrow the signal was to track every single one that had come into the same satellite during the indicated time window.

There were simply too many.

"Now eliminate anything within three-thousand-miles of a blast zone." The targets dwindled dramatically, almost everything in the southern hemisphere dropped, still leaving scores of targets in the north.

"Prevailing winds?"

A swath of color was superimposed, more possibilities eliminated.

"Okay, pull the satellite logs. See if any of those have communicated with that bunker in the past several months."

Child cursed. "We don't have access, it's Russian!"

White House Situation Room
Washington, DC

Starling had never liked the Russian President. The man was an arrogant asshole, and the condescension in his voice was almost enough to wish a few of the missiles about to launch would stray off target. The lecture he was receiving was wasting everyone's time, and was pointless, though pissing the man off wouldn't be wise. All he could do was assure him there appeared to be no targets on Russian soil, probably the only thing preventing an immediate retaliatory strike.

"Sir, we need access to the Russian's Meridian-7 satellite, immediately!"

Starling glanced at Morrison, muting his side of the call. "Why?"

"We need its communications logs."

He repeated the question, knowing full well the Russian President would be asking him the same.

"We might be able to identify who's behind this. He was using it to communicate with his team."

Starling unmuted the call, interrupting the lecture. "Mr. President, I'm sorry to interrupt, but my people tell me that they need access to the communications logs of your Meridian-7 satellite."

There was a pause. "Why?"

"Apparently the person behind this situation was using it to communicate with his team. Those logs will help us identify this individual and bring them to justice."

"And why should I trust you, Mr. President? You are about to condemn the peaceful people of the world to Armageddon."

Starling sighed, gripping his temples. "Mr. President, Vlad, please. This may be our only hope of stopping this before it's too late, and seconds count."

There was a pause. "Very well, you will have it."

Starling smiled, leaning back in his chair. "Thank you, Mr. President. And God save us all."

Minuteman III Launch Control Facility
Outside Karlsruhe, North Dakota

Captain Daugherty's heart pounded as the speaker blared another alert. The wait had been interminable, and unexplained, this not the way things were supposed to happen, though after this, he'd have to review the book once again. He had always assumed everything would be done in a hurry, but perhaps that was just in the movies.

"Begin countdown. T minus sixty."

He closed his eyes for a moment, realizing that hurry he had been expecting, had arrived. He removed the key from around his neck, then glanced at Fraser. "Ready?"

Fraser nodded, the fear in his eyes obvious.

"Okay, insert launch key."

Fraser inserted his key. "Launch key inserted."

"Copy. On my mark, rotate launch key to Set." He stared at the key, surrounded by three options. Safe, Set, and Launch.

Could this be a drill?

He shook his head.

Not with this long a wait.

"Three... two... one... mark!" He turned the key to the Set position, the missiles under his control now ready to receive commands. He glanced at his partner, his hand still on the key, shaking as much as his was.

Fraser nodded. "Roger, key to Set."

Daugherty closed his eyes. "Enable missiles."

"Roger, enabling missiles." Fraser reached over, flipping red covers out of the way, toggling the switches underneath, green indicators replacing red. "Number One enabled, Number Two enabled, Number Three enabled…"

Daugherty tuned his partner out as the horror of what they were about to do took full hold. This was actually happening. On the screen, cameras showed the missiles powering up, and the countdown, updated every ten seconds, continued to blare from the speaker, inexorably pushing them, willingly or not, toward nuclear war.

"Sir, all missiles are enabled."

Daugherty sighed, gripping the key again. "Copy. On my mark, rotate key to Launch."

Assembly Command and Control Facility
Short Hill Mountain, Virginia

"Why the hell did you shoot him?"

Katz glanced at Kane. "I told you, I'm here to eliminate the Assembly. Now there's only one left."

Kane threw up his hands in exasperation. "But we could have used him."

"He never would have cooperated."

Kane heard footfalls in the hallway, and he cautiously opened the door, surprised to see about a dozen people rushing past him. He grabbed one who looked important by the way he was dressed, and yanked him inside, slamming the door shut. "Where's the control room?"

The man stared at him, confused. "Who are you?"

Katz opened the door and fired two shots, screams the result." She stepped back inside. "Take us to the control room, or you're next."

The man nodded, terrified, and led them down the hallway, pushing past uniformed staff who appeared to be beating a hasty retreat, none paying them any mind.

Could it be because we're already too late?

They reached a set of security doors and their prisoner swiped his pass. The doors opened into an impressive control room rivaling anything the CIA had at its disposal. Kane stepped out, his weapon held high, but the room was empty, abandoned by those who had already fulfilled their mandate.

The launching of America's nuclear arsenal.

The abandoned equipment continued to report on the status of what clearly was a massive launch, hundreds of targets indicated on displays that wrapped around the entire front of the room.

He grabbed their prisoner, shoving him toward the workstations. "Send the abort codes."

The man shook his head. "I don't have them. Only Number Four does."

Kane glared at Katz. She seemed unaffected.

"Besides, it's too late." Their prisoner pointed at the screen, a countdown indicator showing sixty seconds to launch. "The last crew acknowledged receipt of the order. The system has just automatically transmitted the final command to launch."

"Then show me how to talk to the silo crews."

The man crossed his arms defiantly. "No."

Kane shot him in the knee and the man collapsed, screaming in agony. "I've got lots of bullets." He pointed at the nearest terminal. "Show me, now."

The man pointed at the panel, his hand shaking. Kane grabbed him and shoved him into a chair.

"Push that. You can talk to them through the headset."

Kane fit the headset in place.

"You're wasting your time. They won't listen to you, not without the proper codes."

The man was right. They wouldn't, it would be against protocol. But he had to try. If even one crew had its doubts, millions could be saved. He pressed the button, not sure what to say. "Umm, attention missile launch crews." He glanced at Katz, wincing at the made up title. "This is Special Agent Dylan Kane of the Central Intelligence Agency. The orders you have received are false. I repeat, the orders you have received are false. The same organization behind the hacking attacks across our nation are responsible. They have compromised United States Strategic Command Headquarters, and issued false orders." He looked at their prisoner, leaving the mic hot. "Can they respond?"

"They can, but they won't."

Kane sighed, the man right. He was wasting his time. *He* couldn't convince them. He snapped a finger at the prisoner. "Get me an outside line."

No reaction.

He aimed his weapon at the other knee, and the man raised his hands. "Okay, okay!" He leaned forward and started tapping buttons.

"I want the missile crews to hear my conversation." The man nodded, a final button pressed.

"You're conferenced."

Kane dialed Leroux's number, his friend picking up immediately.

"Hello?"

"Buddy, it's me. You're on with pretty much every missile crew in the country. I need to talk to the President, immediately."

"Just a second."

Kane waited, not sure whether he should fill the silence. Instinctually, he had to. "Let's hope we don't get a busy signal, hey guys?" He smiled at Katz, who remained stoic, his humor wasted on her.

"This is the President."

"Mr. President, you are now networked with the silo crews."

Minuteman III Launch Control Facility
Outside Karlsruhe, North Dakota

"Sir, should I turn my key?"

Captain Daugherty stared at the speaker, his hand still gripping his key, procedure dictating he give a three count immediately. Though once he did, there was no turning back. The orders were legitimate, of that, there was no doubt. But the abort codes just received from someone who sounded an awful lot like President Starling had also checked out.

He didn't know what to do.

Yet he did. His training told him exactly what to do.

Launch.

But his procedures were written during an era when nuclear attack was imminent. He was certain that wasn't the case here. Launching without being certain was insanity. And this new voice, this Special Agent Kane, was forcing him to question everything up to this point. Yet he had to follow his training, leaving only one clear path.

"Sir, we've gone beyond the failsafe window. We must turn our keys."

Daugherty looked at Fraser. "But the abort codes. They're valid."

"Yes, sir, but protocol says we launch. We've gone beyond the failsafe window. We *must* turn our keys."

Daugherty stared at his key then flinched when the man claiming to be the President spoke again.

"Ladies and gentlemen, General Parsons informs me that you're already past your failsafe abort window. But he also informs me you can still do the right thing. Please, think about this. It's in your hands now."

Daugherty looked at his partner. "What do we do?"

"We turn our keys."

Daugherty shook his head. "No, it can't be right. We know about the hacks, right?"

Fraser shook his head. "There's no way they could hack our system. No damned way." Fraser jabbed a finger at the speaker. "We have no clue who that is. It could be some damned computer making someone sound like the President."

Daugherty nodded slowly. Fraser was right. It could be anyone. Then a thought dawned on him. "Wait! If the system can't be hacked, then how could someone pretend to be the President?"

Fraser's eyes narrowed. "Huh?"

"Think about it! The only way to communicate with us is through the system. So if the system can't be hacked, then the launch orders are legit *and* this call from the President is as well."

Fraser paused, his head slowly bobbing. "I-I don't know." He removed his hand from his key and turned in his chair to face Daugherty. "I-I think you're right." He sucked in a deep breath then squared his shoulders. "You *must* be right." He put his hand back on his key. "Turn to Safe?"

Daugherty nodded, relief sweeping over him. "On my mark, rotate launch key to Safe. Three… two… one… mark." He turned his key and sighed as the system status immediately changed, his missiles indicating they were standing down, millions of lives just saved.

Fraser sounded jubilant. "Roger, key to Safe!"

Daugherty had to talk to the others, to tell them why they had aborted so they too could hopefully make the right decision. He activated his comms. "Mr. President, this is Captain Tony Daugherty, 740th Missile Squadron in North Dakota, can you hear me?"

"Hello, Captain Daugherty, thank you for responding."

"Sir, we are standing down. Umm, can you connect me to the other crews?"

There was a pause. "You're on, Captain."

"Thank you, Mr. President. This is a message for the crews out there who haven't made up their minds yet. Some of you probably know me and my partner here from training or serving together. I'm Captain Tony Daugherty, and I'm here with Lieutenant Jon Fraser. I want you to know we are standing down, and if you have doubts, I want you to know our reason for doing so. If the system can't be hacked, then both the initial launch orders *and* the President's message *must* be legit. And we know they both can't be. Therefore we *must* assume that the system was hacked, and if it was, there is no way the hackers would be asking us to stand down. The launch orders must be false."

Finished, he looked at his partner, the seconds feeling like hours, when suddenly his headset filled with dozens of overlapping voices, few words understandable, but the excitement of the strays he could catch had him slumping in his chair with relief. His fellow soldiers were standing down.

And hundreds of millions had just been saved.

Assembly Command and Control Facility
Short Hill Mountain, Virginia

"Mr. President, the crews are standing down!"

Kane exchanged an excited glance with Katz as he watched the display update, someone at the President's location delivering the news over the networked comms.

"All of them?" asked President Starling.

"Yes, sir, everyone!"

Kane dropped into one of the chairs, his shoulders slumping as the count of armed missiles rapidly dropped, eventually hitting zero. Starling's voice came through his headset.

"Ladies and gentlemen, I thank you for your faith. All crews have stood down, and our missiles are still in their silos. This crisis has been averted. Your commanding officers will be contacting you, I am sure, as soon as they can, though please remember the system is still compromised. Please be patient, and I promise you, we will bring those responsible to justice."

Kane sighed as the adrenaline he had been running on wore off. He glanced at Katz, resisting the urge to hug her, one look killing the idea. She simply didn't seem to care that millions, perhaps hundreds of millions of lives, had just been saved.

"We've failed."

Kane looked at the prisoner. "And you think that's a bad thing?"

The man stared at him, his eyes wide as if he couldn't believe Kane didn't see things the same way. "Of course it is! We were doing this for the betterment of mankind."

"By killing hundreds of millions of innocent people?"

"Yes! To save billions more."

Kane shook his head. "You're insane. You all are."

Katz stepped forward and put a bullet in the man's head.

Kane frowned, staring at her. "You really need to stop doing that."

Katz lowered her weapon and stared at him, her eyes narrowed. "Why? He was the enemy."

Kane batted a hand at her, unwilling to get into an argument with someone who simply didn't care. He repositioned the headset. "Buddy, you still there?"

"Yeah."

"Any luck finding Number One?"

"Not yet."

Kane checked his watch and cursed. There wasn't much time before Katz's window was up. He turned to her. "Please tell me where they are."

Katz shook her head. "You didn't deliver on your end of the bargain. Number One is still alive."

"Yes, but eleven others are dead. And once we find him, we'll kill him too."

"I have no guarantee that will happen."

Leroux's voice came through the headset. "Dylan, pretend I'm not talking, but we just received word that Sherrie and Fang have been rescued, and so have our parents. You don't need her anymore."

Kane shook his head at her then turned to face the screen. He tossed the headset casually onto the console then drew his weapon, spinning around to find Katz's already pointed at his head. He frowned. "Well, this is awkward."

Katz nodded, her eyes dropping slightly to see his gun pressed against her chest.

"So I guess now the question is who can pull the trigger the fastest?"

She smiled slightly. "There is an alternative."

"I'm listening."

"We each go our separate ways." She motioned with her chin toward the headset he had tossed aside. "The fact you are willing to kill me, tells me that your girlfriend has been rescued."

"For a woman with no emotions, you're very intuitive."

"I'm driven by logic, so of course I am."

"I could have been told she was dead."

"Then your overly emotional self wouldn't be having this perfectly rational conversation."

Kane nodded. "You've got me there."

"Then since I no longer have any leverage over you, and you no longer need me to save your women, I suggest we let each other go."

Kane couldn't argue with the logic, and even if he could, he only had a fifty-fifty chance of surviving this encounter should he try. "Agreed." He smiled. "So, who will lower their weapon first?"

The answer was delivered with Katz's usual matter-of-factness. "You will."

"Umm, I don't think so."

She stared at him. "I'm not the emotional one here. You are."

Kane sighed. She was right. "Fine." He lowered his weapon, slowly, and she mirrored his moves, both soon aimed at the floor.

"Then we have an agreement?"

"Yes."

"Good. But there is one last thing I want from you."

Kane's eyes narrowed. "What's that?"

She told him, and he chuckled. "I'm not sure if I can deliver on that, but we'll see."

Williams Residence
Bronx, New York

Larissa stood with her back against the apartment building doors, her chest heaving, tears streaking her cheeks, her eyes closed as she tried to calm herself. The food she had stolen from the hospital was gone, she had barely managed to avoid getting arrested or worse, and she had no idea what she was facing when she went upstairs.

"Ma'am, are you okay?"

She yelped, opening her eyes and pressing against the doors even harder as two heavily armed men strode toward her.

Then she caught her breath. "Do you work with Leon?"

One of them smiled. "You must be Larissa. I'm Jagger, this is Casey." His eyes narrowed. "Are you okay?"

She nodded, wiping her tears away with the back of her hand. "My boys, are they okay?"

"Yes, ma'am. Atlas is with them now."

She sighed in relief as they led her to the elevator. She looked at Jagger. "Atlas?"

He chuckled. "Just a nickname, ma'am." He took a deep breath, imitating muscles. "You know, strong enough to carry a planet on his shoulders?"

She smiled as they stepped into the elevator, Casey remaining behind. "He is a little ridiculously big, isn't he?"

Jagger grinned. "You said it, ma'am. Me? I wouldn't dare!" The doors opened on the twelfth floor and they were greeted by two other soldiers. "Gentlemen, this is Larissa, Atlas' sister."

The men smiled and gave her two-fingered salutes. "Ma'am, a pleasure," said the first, holding out his hand, directing her toward her apartment. "They're inside."

She ran down the hallway, catching her breath when she saw the destroyed door. Then she heard laughter.

My babies!

She rushed inside and found them all piled on Leon.

"Mom!" cried Michael as he extricated himself from the tangle of limbs. Suddenly she was surrounded with bundles of energy she had feared she'd never see again.

"Oh, my little darlings, are you okay? Are you hurt?"

"We're fine, Mommy." Michael pointed. "Look, Mommy, it's Uncle Leon!"

Leon came over and gave her a hug, his massive arms enveloping her in a cocoon of safety and comfort. She closed her eyes, feeling completely safe for the first time in days. "Thank you, Leon, for helping my boys."

"Anytime, Sis, anytime."

She pushed away. "Shannon?"

He shook his head. "She didn't make it."

Tears filled her eyes and her heart ached. "Oh no! Who did it?"

"Apparently, her boyfriend."

She gasped, her hand darting to her mouth. "Levar!" She frowned. "Her mother knew he was no good. She's going to be devastated." She looked down the hallway. "Where…?"

Atlas shook his head. "Don't worry. The Guard already came and took the body." He pulled out his phone and brought up a photo. "Is this him?"

She stared, not recognizing him at first, the appearance slightly off. "Oh my God, he's dead!"

"Yes. Is this the Levar you referred to?"

"Yes. What happened?"

"The Guard caught them loading up their car with your supplies out in front of the building. When they tried to arrest them, Levar here pulled a gun. The rest, shall we say, is history."

She sighed, patting Leon's chest. Her stomach grumbled and she remembered what this was all about. "Our supplies?"

"Confiscated by the Guard. They didn't know who it belonged to until we secured the location, so it was already sent for redistribution."

Her stomach flipped. "What are we going to eat?"

Leon smiled. "Haven't you heard? It's over."

Her eyes widened. "Huh?"

"It's over. It's all over the news. They've caught those responsible, and there won't be any more hacks. Once the systems are fixed, everything will be back to normal. Probably a couple of days, though it might take weeks to clear up some of the mess. No nuclear war, no more nutbars trying to take down our cities."

Larissa's eyes narrowed. "Nuclear war? What the hell has been going on since I left the hospital?"

Leon laughed, wrapping an arm around her shoulders. "I think you're a little bit behind the rest of us."

She rested her head on his chest and smiled. "You should visit more often."

He kissed the top of her head. "The next time madmen threaten New York, I'll be sure to drop by."

She slapped his chest. "Leon James, I want to see that muscled booty here this Thanksgiving. That's an order."

One of the soldiers grinned. "Muscled booty. I'll have to tell Niner that one."

Atlas slapped his forehead. "Aww, Sis, now look what you've done!"

George Washington University Hospital
Washington, DC

Kane burst into the waiting area, finding the room jam-packed, a cluster of heavily armed Delta operators in one corner. He rushed over to Dawson, Niner, Spock, and Jimmy. "Where is she?"

Dawson motioned to a set of doors. "Through there."

"Is she okay?"

Sherrie came through the doors, covered in blood and grime. His jaw dropped. "Are *you* okay?"

"Nothing a shower couldn't fix."

"And a stick of deodorant," complained Niner, pinching his nose. She nipple twisted him, nearly bringing him to his knees.

"Fang?"

She smiled. "They got to her in time. Motor-mouth and Jimmy were able to stabilize her. She's going to be fine."

He smiled at his former team, putting his hands on the nearest shoulders. "Thanks, guys. I owe you one."

Dawson shook his head. "Don't thank us. Sherrie'd pretty much killed everything in sight by the time we got there."

Niner rubbed his nipple. "Yeah, we were just there to make the news coverage look sexy."

Jimmy stared at Niner, now rubbing both nipples. "Enjoying yourself?"

Niner continued rubbing. "Yeah, I didn't realize how good this felt. You should try it."

Kane's hand darted out, twisting the other one. "Christ, they're hard. You really are enjoying yourself."

Niner did a little groin thrust. "You wanna see what else is—"

Jimmy smacked him. "Lady present."

Sherrie grinned. "Yeah, a lady who can kick your ass."

Niner shook his head. "Promises, promises."

Spock's eyebrow rose. "I think he'd actually enjoy getting his ass kicked by a woman."

Niner grinned. "Or you, big boy."

Jimmy delivered himself a facepalm. "Just when I thought we were clearing this up."

Kane chuckled and headed for the doors, Sherrie following. She pointed to a room on the right. "In there."

He gave her a hug. "You're the best."

She laughed. "Tell the Director."

He grinned and stepped inside the room, his heart breaking as he saw the woman he loved, gaunt and sallow, hooked up to monitors revealing life signs that were steady though weaker than they should be. He sat on the edge of the bed and took her hand. She turned her head toward him and smiled slightly.

He leaned in and kissed her forehead. "So how are you feeling?"

"Tired, sore, thirsty, hungry. You know, pretty standard for getting shot and almost dying. You? Where have you been?"

He shrugged. "Oh, you know, just saving the world again. Nothing out of the ordinary."

She laughed then winced. She took his hand in both hers, and brought it to her lips, kissing it, her expression serious. "We need to talk."

His stomach flipped, those four words never good. "Now?"

She nodded.

"Umm, okay. What did you want to talk about?"

"I want you to tell me what's bothering you."

He looked away, his chest aching as his pulse pounded in his ears. He let go of her hands, but she gripped him tighter.

"I know what it is."

His head spun toward her, his eyes filled with tears. "How? How could you?"

"A woman knows."

A tear spilled down his cheek and he wiped it away. "I'm so sorry."

She smiled at him. "It was for the job?"

"Of course!"

"Then you've got nothing to be sorry about."

He stared at this amazing woman, his love for her even stronger than a moment ago, something he wouldn't have thought possible. He lowered himself gently and put his head on her shoulder, hugging her as tightly as he dared. "I love you so much."

She kissed his cheek and he felt a tear roll from hers to his. "I love you too. But next time when something's bothering you, we talk, okay?"

"Absolutely."

She patted his shoulder. "Oh, by the way, I met your parents."

He bolted upright. "Huh?"

A throat cleared behind him and he glanced over his shoulder. "Mom! Dad!" He leaped from the bed and embraced them both, tears erupting from his mother, even his father appearing a little overwhelmed in the emotions department.

But it was the smile on his father's face that he couldn't get over.

Pride.

He hadn't seen that in what felt like forever.

He glanced at Fang. "So, umm, you met Fang?"

"Yes, dear, she seems like a lovely girl."

"She is."

His father squeezed his shoulder. "So, how'd you two meet? Through your *insurance* business?"

Kane stared at his father, the smile on his face revealing something was going on. "Umm, just what do you think you know?"

His father placed his hands on Kane's shoulders and stared him in the eyes. "Son, your cover is blown." His smile broadened. "And I couldn't be more proud of you." He pulled him in for a hug and Kane returned it, a wave of emotions overwhelming him as years of hostility washed away, his family whole once again.

He gently pushed away and wiped a tear from his eye. "You know that I'm going to have to kill you now, right?"

Leroux hugged Sherrie, hard, Morrison ordering him to leave Langley and see his parents and significant other. He had eagerly agreed, leaving Tong in charge of the search for Number One. He had faith in her abilities, and those of his entire team.

They were the best.

"I'm glad you're okay."

Sherrie grinned. "Me too. I hear you helped save the world once again."

He blushed, his eyes redirecting to the floor. "No, not me. Dylan was the one who did it, really."

She patted his cheek. "And he couldn't have done it without you, I'm sure." She gently pushed him toward the door and he stepped inside, his parents sitting in what appeared to be rather uncomfortable chairs. They both leaped to their feet.

"My baby!" His mother grabbed him by the cheeks and shook his head before giving him a big hug, his father waiting patiently for his turn.

He nodded toward Sherrie. "That's quite the lady you've got there."

Leroux smiled at her, and she batted the air with an "aw shucks" expression. "Yes, she is." He stared at his father then his mother. "And you can *never* talk about what she does."

His father held up his hands, palms out. "I know, I know. Mum's the word."

"I'll leave you guys alone," said Sherrie, heading for the door. "I'm going to check in on Fang."

His father held up a finger. "Are Rick and Jenn with her?"

"I think so."

"Then may we join you?"

Sherrie shrugged with a smile. "Don't see why not." She led them to Fang's room, already crowded with the Kane clan. Hugs were exchanged between the parents, Kane and Leroux receiving hugs as well.

Rick Kane beamed at the boys with pride. "These are quite the boys we've got here."

Mark agreed. "And quite the future daughter in laws too, I think!"

Leroux's jaw dropped. "Dad!"

Grins spread around the room and he looked at Sherrie, a huge smile on her face, a smile that told him that she wanted him to ask the question, and what the answer would be. He'd be lying if he said he hadn't thought about it.

But he was terrified.

It was a huge step, and what if she said no? What if he screwed it up? Things seemed perfect the way they were. Asking her might make her feel rushed, make her feel pressured, and send her running.

Girls like her didn't marry guys like him.

Her eyes glistened, the smile still in place, and all his fears were swept away. He stepped forward, beginning to lower to one knee, when Sherrie held up a finger, bringing him to a precarious halt.

"Ahh, no. This is *definitely* not the time or place. I want the whole nine yards. Dinner, dancing, flowers, chocolates, and a romantic speech. Antiseptic spray and heart monitors will *not* cut it."

Leroux wavered in place, not sure what to do, when Kane grabbed him by the arm and hauled him to a fully standing position, then slapped him on the back, jabbing a thumb over his shoulder. "Burn Ward is just down the hall. I think you need it."

Leroux flushed, and the women in the room scowled at Kane.

"What?" he asked innocently as Leroux's phone vibrated.

Saved by the bell.

He took the call. "Hello?"

"Sir, it's Sonya. We've found him!"

Leroux's embarrassment was forgotten as he spun toward Kane, excitement spreading across his face. "Where?"

"He's in Canada. Outside Halifax, Nova Scotia."

The location made perfect sense. There was almost no chance of being affected by the aftermath of what the Assembly had planned for mankind, nuclear or political. The question was, now that their plans had failed, how long would he be there. "Have you notified the Director?"

"Yes, sir."

"Good. Send the exact location to my phone."

"Yes, sir."

He ended the call and his phone vibrated with the intel's arrival. He handed it to Kane. "Number One's location, should that be of any interest to you."

Kane tapped the display a few times then returned it. "No, none at all."

Outside Halifax, Nova Scotia, Canada

Number One sat in his chair, his frustration, anger, and disappointment, threatening to overwhelm him. Years of planning had been for naught, the news reports spreading of celebrations in the streets, of once distrusting neighborhoods, embracing one another despite their cities still being in chaos.

It was over.

They had failed, and he stood alone on the Assembly Council. He tore his eyes away from the news report and returned his attention to his computer, skimming through the files on the final three candidates he had chosen for his new Number Two. They were all good choices, though there was no guarantee any or all of them would accept the offer to join, for it was a lifelong commitment, with no way to change one's mind.

He remembered when he was Number Twelve, so many decades ago. It had been exciting and terrifying, but as the years progressed, and he slowly worked his way toward his current position, the excitement had worn off, the fear had disappeared, and the overwhelming responsibility had taken over.

The future of mankind rested on his shoulders.

An awesome responsibility. A responsibility he couldn't bear alone.

The door opened behind him and he motioned to the end of his desk without looking. "Just put it there, Margaret." He continued to read the file when he finally noticed his coffee hadn't been delivered.

He glanced over his shoulder and suppressed a gasp, though he feared his eyes betrayed his true feelings. "Nadja Katz."

She bowed slightly. "Number One."

He squared himself in his chair, gripping the arms, his knuckles turning white. "I assume you're here to kill me."

Katz nodded slightly. "You assume correctly."

He sighed. He had always believed he would have been killed by one of his predecessors, but when he had made it to his current position, he had lived under the assumption he would survive until his body finally gave out, never again worrying about assassination.

Anonymity had its advantages, though as he had discovered when he finally became Number One and had been fully briefed, the truth wasn't completely what he had believed.

"May I implore you to change your mind?"

"No."

"But in killing me, you risk an organization that has been around for longer than you can imagine, bettering mankind."

Katz stared at him, unmoved. "You should know me enough to know that I don't care about mankind, or its betterment."

Number One's head slowly bobbed. "No, I suppose you don't." His shoulders slumped. "Then I suppose this is the end."

"Yes."

He raised a finger as the thunder of choppers sounded in the distance. "Ahh, I assume that is the team sent to arrest me. I wonder how they will react when they find me dead, rather than brought to justice."

She stepped closer. "They told me where to find you. And how could I have possibly got here before them?"

His eyebrows rose slightly. "Interesting. Then I was always to die."

She raised her weapon. "The Assembly is finished."

He smiled at her. "No, my dear, the Assembly is eternal."

She put three in his chest then two in his head as the computer beeped, a silhouetted image appearing.

"Number One, I must speak with you."

THE END

ACKNOWLEDGEMENTS

First, let me say that yes, liberties were necessarily taken in the missile launch scenes. With the myriad of different systems deployed, many in the middle of upgrades, I felt artistically, it was best to go with the concept most of us have in our heads of a two man crew (women are now allowed), with keys that had to be turned simultaneously. Depending on what source you read, this can be two, four, or even five people, spread over multiple locations. It is always, however, more than one, to comply with the "two-man rule." Understandably, the United States military isn't exactly forthcoming in providing all the details, so as I said, liberties were taken for dramatic purposes.

That being said, the hard lines used provide for no possibility of an outside entity gaining access. Even the cables are pressurized so that any splicing or tampering is immediately detectable. If a signal is received over these hard lines, the crews inside the Launch Control Facilities will absolutely believe they are legitimate. By having our villains actually tap into the source of those lines, they were able to circumvent the entire authentication process beyond the actual biscuit with authentication codes the crews need to validate with their own.

And a corrupt Vice President took care of that.

In the real world, one would hope our government wouldn't resort to kneejerk reactions that would allow a scenario as described in this novel to occur. I rest easy at night knowing that governments around the world never do anything stupid.

As usual, there are people to thank. My father for all the research, Brent Richards for some weapons info, Ian Kennedy for some explosives info, Fred Newton for some nautical info, Susan "Miss

Boss" Turnbull for another last minute grammatical save, those who entered the Character Naming Contests on Facebook, my proofing team, and of course, my wife, daughter, mother, family, and friends.

Finally, I'd like to give a special thanks to my good friends Rick Messina and Chris Holder, for an awesome brainstorming session where we came up with ways to mess with the Internet of Things. Everyone should be grateful we're on your side, because if we devoted ourselves to a life of crime…

To those who have not already done so, please visit my website at www.jrobertkennedy.com then sign up for the Insider's Club to be notified of new book releases. Your email address will never be shared or sold, and you'll only receive the occasional email from me, as I don't have time to spam you!

Thank you once again for reading.

ABOUT THE AUTHOR

With over 700,000 books in circulation and over 3000 five-star reviews, USA Today bestselling author J. Robert Kennedy has been ranked by Amazon as the #1 Bestselling Action Adventure novelist based upon combined sales. He is the author of over thirty international bestsellers including the smash hit James Acton Thrillers. He lives with his wife and daughter and writes full-time.

Visit Robert's website at www.jrobertkennedy.com for the latest news and contact information, and to join the Insider's Club to be notified when new books are released.

Available James Acton Thrillers

The Protocol (Book #1)

For two thousand years, the Triarii have protected us, influencing history from the crusades to the discovery of America. Descendent from the Roman Empire, they pervade every level of society, and are now in a race with our own government to retrieve an ancient artifact thought to have been lost forever.

Brass Monkey (Book #2)

A nuclear missile, lost during the Cold War, is now in play--the most public spy swap in history, with a gorgeous agent the center of international attention, triggers the end-game of a corrupt Soviet Colonel's twenty five year plan. Pursued across the globe by the Russian authorities, including a brutal Spetsnaz unit, those involved will stop at nothing to deliver their weapon, and ensure their payday, regardless of the terrifying consequences.

Broken Dove (Book #3)

With the Triarii in control of the Roman Catholic Church, an organization founded by Saint Peter himself takes action, murdering one of the new Pope's operatives. Detective Chaney, called in by the Pope to investigate, disappears, and, to the horror of the Papal staff sent to inform His Holiness, they find him missing too, the only clue a secret chest, presented to each new pope on the eve of their election, since the beginning of the Church.

The Templar's Relic (Book #4)

The Vault must be sealed, but a construction accident leads to a miraculous discovery--an ancient tomb containing four Templar Knights, long forgotten, on the grounds of the Vatican. Not knowing who they can trust, the Vatican requests Professors James Acton and Laura Palmer examine the find, but what they discover, a precious Islamic relic, lost during the Crusades, triggers a set of events that shake the entire world, pitting the two greatest religions against each other. At risk is nothing less than the Vatican itself, and the rock upon which it was built.

Flags of Sin (Book #5)

Archaeology Professor James Acton simply wants to get away from everything, and relax. A trip to China seems just the answer, and he and his fiancée, Professor Laura Palmer, are soon on a flight to Beijing. But while boarding, they bump into an old friend, Delta Force Command Sergeant Major Burt Dawson, who surreptitiously delivers a message that they must meet the next day, for Dawson knows something they don't. China is about to erupt into chaos.

The Arab Fall (Book #6)

An accidental find by a friend of Professor James Acton may lead to the greatest archaeological discovery since the tomb of King Tutankhamen, perhaps even greater. And when news of it spreads, it reaches the ears of a group hell-bent on the destruction of all idols and icons, their mere existence considered blasphemous to Islam.

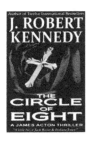

The Circle of Eight (Book #7)

The Bravo Team is targeted by a madman after one of their own intervenes in a rape. Little do they know this internationally well-respected banker is also a senior member of an organization long thought extinct, whose stated goals for a reshaped world are not only terrifying, but with today's globalization, totally achievable.

The Venice Code (Book #8)

A former President's son is kidnapped in a brazen attack on the streets of Potomac by the very ancient organization that murdered his father, convinced he knows the location of an item stolen from them by the late president. A close friend awakes from a coma with a message for archaeology Professor James Acton from the same organization, sending him on a quest to find an object only rumored to exist, while trying desperately to keep one step ahead of a foe hell-bent on possessing it.

J. ROBERT KENNEDY

Pompeii's Ghosts (Book #9)

Two thousand years ago Roman Emperor Vespasian tries to preserve an empire by hiding a massive treasure in the quiet town of Pompeii should someone challenge his throne. Unbeknownst to him nature is about to unleash its wrath upon the Empire during which the best and worst of Rome's citizens will be revealed during a time when duty and honor were more than words, they were ideals worth dying for.

Amazon Burning (Book #10)

Days from any form of modern civilization, archaeology Professor James Acton awakes to gunshots. Finding his wife missing, taken by a member of one of the uncontacted tribes, he and his friend INTERPOL Special Agent Hugh Reading try desperately to find her in the dark of the jungle, but quickly realize there is no hope without help. And with help three days away, he knows the longer they wait, the farther away she'll be.

The Riddle (Book #11)

Russia accuses the United States of assassinating their Prime Minister in Hanoi, naming Delta Force member Sergeant Carl "Niner" Sung as the assassin. Professors James Acton and Laura Palmer, witnesses to the murder, know the truth, and as the Russians and Vietnamese attempt to use the situation to their advantage on the international stage, the husband and wife duo attempt to find proof that their friend is innocent.

Blood Relics (Book #12)

A DYING MAN. A DESPERATE SON.
ONLY A MIRACLE CAN SAVE THEM BOTH.

Professor Laura Palmer is shot and kidnapped in front of her husband, archaeology Professor James Acton, as they try to prevent the theft of the world's Blood Relics, ancient artifacts thought to contain the blood of Christ, a madman determined to possess them all at any cost.

Sins of the Titanic (Book #13)

THE ASSEMBLY IS ETERNAL. AND THEY'LL STOP AT
NOTHING TO KEEP IT THAT WAY.

When Professor James Acton is contacted about a painting thought to have been lost with the sinking of the Titanic, he is inadvertently drawn into a century old conspiracy an ancient organization known as The Assembly will stop at nothing to keep secret.

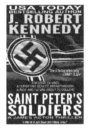

Saint Peter's Soldiers (Book #14)

A MISSING DA VINCI.
A TERRIFYING GENETIC BREAKTHROUGH.
A PAST AND FUTURE ABOUT TO COLLIDE!

In World War Two a fabled da Vinci drawing is hidden from the Nazis, those involved fearing Hitler may attempt to steal it for its purported magical powers. It isn't returned for over fifty years. And today, archaeology Professor James Acton and his wife are about to be dragged into the terrible truth of what happened so many years ago, for the truth is never what it seems, and the history we thought was fact, is all lies.

The Thirteenth Legion (Book #15)

A TWO-THOUSAND-YEAR-OLD DESTINY IS ABOUT
TO BE FULFILLED!

USA Today bestselling author J. Robert Kennedy delivers another action-packed thriller in The Thirteenth Legion. After Interpol Agent Hugh Reading spots his missing partner in Berlin, it sets off a chain of events that could lead to the death of his best friends, and if the legends are true, life as we know it.

Raging Sun (Book #16)

WILL A SEVENTY-YEAR-OLD MATTER OF HONOR
TRIGGER THE NEXT GREAT WAR?

The Imperial Regalia have been missing since the end of World War Two, and the Japanese government, along with the new—and secretly illegitimate—emperor, have been lying to the people. But the truth isn't out yet, and the Japanese will stop at nothing to secure their secret and retrieve the ancient relics confiscated by a belligerent Russian government. Including war.

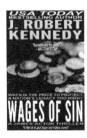

Wages of Sin (Book #17)

WHEN IS THE PRICE TO PROTECT A NATION'S
LEGACY TOO HIGH?

Jim and Laura are on safari in South Africa when a chance encounter leads to a clue that could unlock the greatest mystery remaining of the Boer War over a century ago—the location to over half a billion dollars in gold!

Wrath of the Gods (Book #18)

A THOUSAND YEARS OF HISTORY ARE ABOUT TO BE
REWRITTEN!

A strange people land on the shores of the Mayan Empire, triggering a battle for the very survival of a civilization already in upheaval. A thousand years later, Acton and Laura are invited to an incredible discovery that reveals the truth of what happened, yet before they can fully explore this amazing find, they are thrust into the middle of the Mexican drug war.

Available Special Agent Dylan Kane Thrillers

Rogue Operator (Book #1)

Three top secret research scientists are presumed dead in a boating accident, but the kidnapping of their families the same day raises questions the FBI and local police can't answer, leaving them waiting for a ransom demand that will never come. Central Intelligence Agency Analyst Chris Leroux stumbles upon the story, finding a phone conversation that was never supposed to happen, and is told to leave it to the FBI. But he can't let it go. For he knows something the FBI doesn't. One of the scientists is alive.

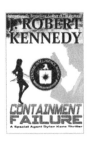

Containment Failure (Book #2)

New Orleans has been quarantined, an unknown virus sweeping the city, killing one hundred percent of those infected. The Centers for Disease Control, desperate to find a cure, is approached by BioDyne Pharma who reveal a former employee has turned a cutting edge medical treatment capable of targeting specific genetic sequences into a weapon, and released it. The stakes have never been higher as Kane battles to save not only his friends and the country he loves, but all of mankind.

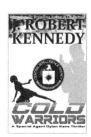

Cold Warriors (Book #3)

While in Chechnya CIA Special Agent Dylan Kane stumbles upon a meeting between a known Chechen drug lord and a retired General once responsible for the entire Soviet nuclear arsenal. Money is exchanged for a data stick and the resulting transmission begins a race across the globe to discover just what was sold, the only clue a reference to a top-secret Soviet weapon called Crimson Rush.

Death to America (Book #4)

America is in crisis. Dozens of terrorist attacks have killed or injured thousands, and worse, every single attack appears to have been committed by an American citizen in the name of Islam. A stolen experimental F-35 Lightning II is discovered by CIA Special Agent Dylan Kane in China, delivered by an American soldier reported dead years ago in exchange for a chilling promise. And Chris Leroux is forced to watch as his girlfriend, Sherrie White, is tortured on camera, under orders to not interfere, her continued suffering providing intel too valuable to sacrifice.

Black Widow (Book #5)

USA Today bestselling author J. Robert Kennedy serves up another heart-pounding thriller in Black Widow. After corrupt Russian agents sell deadly radioactive Cesium to Chechen terrorists, CIA Special Agent Dylan Kane is sent to infiltrate the ISIL terror cell suspected of purchasing it. Then all contact is lost.

The Agenda (Book #6)

THE SYSTEM HAS FAILED.
THE COUNTRY IS ON ITS KNEES.
CAN DYLAN KANE SAVE IT BEFORE IT'S TOO LATE?
With the cities starving and his girlfriend critically wounded, Kane is in a race against time to save not only the country he has sworn to protect, but the only woman he has ever loved.

Available Delta Force Unleashed Thrillers

Payback (Book #1)

The Vice President's daughter is kidnapped from an Ebola clinic, triggering an all-out effort to retrieve her by the elite Delta Force just hours after a senior government official from Sierra Leone is assassinated in a horrific terrorist attack while visiting the United States. As she battles impossible odds and struggles to prove her worth to her captors who have promised she will die, she's forced to make unthinkable decisions to not only try to save her own life, but those dying from one of the most vicious diseases known to mankind, all in the hopes an unleashed Delta Force can save her before her captors enact their horrific plan on an unsuspecting United States.

Infidels (Book #2)

When the elite Delta Force's Bravo Team is inserted into Yemen to rescue a kidnapped Saudi prince, they find more than they bargained for—a crate containing the Black Stone, stolen from Mecca the day before. Requesting instructions on how to proceed, they find themselves cut off and disavowed, left to survive with nothing but each other to rely upon.

The Lazarus Moment (Book #3)

AIR FORCE ONE IS DOWN. BUT THEIR FIGHT TO
SURVIVE HAS ONLY JUST BEGUN!

When Air Force One crashes in the jungles of Africa, it is up to America's elite Delta Force to save the survivors not only from rebels hell-bent on capturing the President, but Mother Nature herself.

Kill Chain (Book #4)

WILL A DESPERATE PRESIDENT RISK WAR
TO SAVE HIS ONLY CHILD?

In South Korea, the President's daughter disappears aboard an automated bus carrying the spouses of the world's most powerful nations, hacked by an unknown enemy with an unknown agenda. In order to save all that remains of his family, the widower president unleashes America's elite Delta Force to save his daughter, yet the more they learn, the more the mystery deepens, witness upon witness declaring with certainty they never saw any kidnappers—only drones.

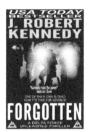

Forgotten (Book #5)

> ONE OF THEIR OWN IS DEAD.
> NOW IT'S TIME FOR REVENGE.

On a mission to rescue a young American woman held by ISIS as a sex slave, one of the Delta Force's Bravo Team is killed, betrayed by a mole within the Unit. As the team reels from the loss, the CIA presses hard to find the young woman and give the team a second chance to fulfill their mission. And seek revenge for the death of their comrade.

Available Detective Shakespeare Mysteries

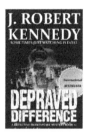

Depraved Difference (Book #1)

> SOMETIMES JUST WATCHING IS FATAL

When a young woman is brutally assaulted by two men on the subway, her cries for help fall on the deaf ears of onlookers too terrified to get involved, her misery ended with the crushing stomp of a steel-toed boot. A cellphone video of her vicious murder, callously released on the Internet, its popularity a testament to today's depraved society, serves as a trigger, pulled a year later, for a killer.

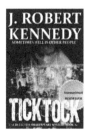

Tick Tock (Book #2)

> SOMETIMES HELL IS OTHER PEOPLE

Crime Scene tech Frank Brata digs deep and finds the courage to ask his colleague, Sarah, out for coffee after work. Their good time turns into a nightmare when Frank wakes up the next morning covered in blood, with no recollection of what happened, and Sarah's body floating in the tub.

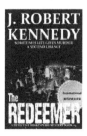

The Redeemer (Book #3)

> SOMETIMES LIFE GIVES MURDER A SECOND CHANCE

It was the case that destroyed Detective Justin Shakespeare's career, beginning a downward spiral of self-loathing and self-destruction lasting half a decade. And today things are only going to get worse. The Widow Rapist is free on a technicality, and it is up to Detective Shakespeare and his partner Amber Trace to find the evidence, five years cold, to put him back in prison before he strikes again.

Zander Varga, Vampire Detective

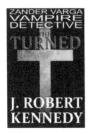

The Turned (Book #1)

Zander has relived his wife's death at the hands of vampires every day for almost three hundred years, his perfect memory a curse of becoming one of The Turned—infecting him their final heinous act after her murder. Nineteen year-old Sydney Winter knows Zander's secret, a secret preserved by the women in her family for four generations. But with her mother in a coma, she's thrust into the frontlines, ahead of her time, to fight side-by-side with Zander.

Made in the USA
Monee, IL
01 December 2022

18984172R00236